S0-GGI-593

PRAISE FOR
SUNDOWN IN SAN OJUELA

"Olivas's San Ojuela is a place between Bad City and the Twilight Zone, crumbling and gentrifying at the same time. It's full of deeply human (and not-so-human) characters, fighting to outrun the darkness outside and the darkness within. Paintings moving on the walls, the desert night whispering, long-simmering Mexica vengeance and spiritual debts, flashes of stark violence, blood on the sand, guilt, redemption, forgiveness…it's a dark, thrilling ride. And just when it's getting bleak, Olivas gives us a wise-ass talking skull or a fish that sings 80s Brit pop. With so many lush, beautiful sentences that my highlighter dried out. This book is both luminous and so, so dark."

—Cynthia Gómez, author of *The Nightmare Box and Other Stories*

"A weird, lovely book which taps your shoulder gently to get your attention. When you turn around, it snatches you immediately away into a wild ride of brujas and old Aztec gods, chupacabras and haunted houses that gets stranger, darker, and more dire with each turn of the page. There are ancient injustices to be avenged. The monsters and the heroes are equally, gorgeously terrifying. And the smell of lavender will never again comfort you the same way."

—SFWA Grand Master Nalo Hopkinson

"Bold and brutal horror from an urgent and powerful new voice."

—Sam J. Miller, author of *Boys, Beasts, & Men*

SUNDOWN IN SAN OJUELA

SUNDOWN IN SAN OJUELA

BY M. M. OLIVAS

LANTERNFISH PRESS
PHILADELPHIA

SUNDOWN IN SAN OJUELA
Copyright © 2024 by M. M. Olivas

All rights reserved. No part of this book may be reproduced in any form without permission in writing from the publisher, except for brief quotations used in critical articles or reviews.

Lanternfish Press
PO Box 34569
Philadelphia, PA 19101
lanternfishpress.com

Cover Design: Kimberly Glyder

Printed in the United States of America.
28 27 26 25 24   1 2 3 4 5

Library of Congress Control Number: 2022952089
Print ISBN: 978-1-941360-75-0
Digital ISBN: 978-1-941360-76-7

Para Mamá

PROLOGUE
The Boy in the Black-Striped Serape

THE WAY THE BOY in the black-striped serape had described Casa Coyotl on the drive over, Oliver had imagined it rotting—turreted and spiderwebbed like a haunted Victorian house in a bloated jump-scare movie. From the property's iron gates, the house looked shapeless. A dark mass hunched beneath cypress trees that dragged their fingertips against the night. And now? Standing up close, at the base of the front steps? There was something horrible about the house that no movie could have captured. Something old, and heavy, and waiting.

It wasn't Victorian at all. It was a Spanish hacienda, its stark white clay sculpted out of the land itself with the horribleness baked in. The flat, mission-style bell tower that rose from the facade pulled a memory from deep in Oliver's belly: touring the San Diego missions one hot spring day in the fourth grade, while Miss Lambertson monologued about how beautifully designed the former slave quarters were. How Oliver's skin had itched so much that he scratched his arms raw between those walls. How he couldn't stop thinking that he stood on bones. Bones. Bones.

With a skeleton key that he'd pulled from his serape, the Boy unlocked La Casa and pushed in the doors, which cackled as they swung—a dozen *hehehaha*s escaping from the house's maw.

"Was that the ghosts?" Oliver asked him. "Or a cry for some goddamn WD-40?" He stood with his hands in his pockets, trying his best to look smug or bored. Trying not to mind the damp fear pulsing down his spine or his father's voice echoing in his head, calling him *coward, coward*.

"That was funny," the Boy replied. "But you're not laughing."

The Boy stepped into the house; Oliver followed. In the foyer was a grand staircase that reminded Oliver of old Disney movies, but when he peeked inside the smaller rooms, he saw digital clocks, flat-screen TVs, computer monitors—things that told him a person had lived there recently, a real person. Not the shadow of a memory from elsewhen.

They kept the lights off, "because if we turn them on, Samuel will know someone's here," the Boy said in his thin, scratchy voice. "He's the groundskeeper. He sleeps out in the dock house across the lake, and he doesn't like trespassers. But I come here all the time when I'm not allowed, and he never finds out, because I'm okay with the dark."

"That's cool." Oliver nodded, not listening. His attention was on the hulking forms of antique furniture that clogged the halls, gleaming with the night's sickly green. Oliver wondered just how much you could make pawning antiques that no one would miss.

The Boy whistled a lazy tune into the dark. He smelled of death and desert sand, and his eyes glowed dull red with the touch of the moonlight.

A voice in Oliver's head told him, *Turn back!* But with each step deeper into La Casa, a darkness pulsed through him that left his head fuzzy, as wild and exciting as the desert wind. He'd felt the same darkness for the first time earlier that evening, when the Boy caught his eyes from across a gas station parking lot.

❀ ❀ ❀

Oliver was on the run, heading east towards the California desert and the country beyond. The night before, he'd traded verbal blows with his father again, one of those Mexican family arguments that started out of something small and grew till it rattled windows. He'd asked if he could go on a road trip, just him and his friends, but his dad said no and his mom nodded, tight-lipped. It was his dad's final comment that got him. "¿Para qué quieres gastar todo tu dinero, ah?"

As if that was all he'd done since high school: waste time and money. Still the same burnout kid with the same burnout friends, and all the family arguments since were just epilogues tacked on to the old one, which festered, terminal and ugly. Oliver's father was concerned with the chisme his church friends or Oliver's tíos and tías would speak if his son ever did anything "off." Anything not "appropriate." He was always trying fit Oliver into his machismo-choked idea of what a man was.

In the summer, Oliver could ignore it more easily. He'd spent the last days of the season with his friends, smoking in the parking lot's ocean breeze after long work shifts left his feet tender and throbbing. But summer was over now, the next one eons away. It was mid-October, and all his friends had scattered across the country to colleges he couldn't afford. Places where their parents couldn't barge in and yell, "You never turn off the lights!" or "What do you have to complain about, eh?" or "You're not depressed. You're fine."

Their argument that final night had tapered off like all the others, with mutters and scoffs and a greater gulf yawning between them than when it had begun.

Oliver slept in the next morning. Woke at twelve and ate at two. He was pulling his server's uniform out from the dryer in the garage when he stopped to look at his father's 1972 Dodge Challenger—the oldest thing his father owned and the only remaining link to the life his family had once lived, back before buying this house that, for the first time, didn't come with window bars. His father polished the car every weekend with buckets of leftover shower water that he captured in plastic bins throughout the week. Oliver was forbidden to drive it. Even to back it out of the driveway. If Oliver ever stepped too close to it, his father would mumble, "Careful, careful."

The voice in his head told him, *Go!*

So he snatched up his dad's keys, threw some shirts and packets of ramen into his backpack, and left.

An hour into the drive, his mom called. He didn't answer. She left a voicemail that began, "¿Oliver? ¿Qué hiciste—"

He shut off the phone. Stuffed it into his back pocket. He wondered if his parents would think about *why* he'd run away. If his friends would. If his father could figure it out, given enough time. Probably not.

He was somewhere along the 74, the Dodge roaring beneath him, the electric twang of Jimi Hendrix's "Voodoo Child" thrumming, when he rounded the bend where the ICE checkpoint waited. He didn't notice it at first—he was too focused on the pumpjacks jutting from the mountaintops. Skeleton horses bobbing their heads up and down, up and down, blackened in the desert sun.

The officers waved Oliver down. Singled him out from all the other drivers passing by. In the moment he almost let the music take him—almost stomped on the gas until the checkpoint was just an arc over the highway line in his rearview. But then he thought of his father: the way an ICE officer once broke his ribs when he refused to show papers, ten years back. Oliver had never seen his dad so scared, turtled up on the parking lot's asphalt. So, despite the fear and music pulsating through him, Oliver shut the radio off and pulled to the side of the road.

A man in a black uniform rapped a knuckle on the driver's side window and asked Oliver where he was going and where he'd been. Said: "Relax, kid," and "Shouldn't you be in school right now?" and

"Is this yours? Hell of a car."

When the officer asked for his license, Oliver flinched. "But I didn't do anything wrong."

That was what did it.

What caused the officer waiting in the shade to rest his hand on the black, gun-shaped bulge hanging off his belt. What caused the other officer to say, "I'm going to have to ask you to step out of the vehicle."

Oliver protested—he hadn't broken any laws; he shouldn't be detained—but the officer dragged him out and bulldozed him into the ground. Asphalt kissed his chin. The officer twisted Oliver's arms behind his back and leaned close enough that his stubble prickled Oliver's ear. His breath a hot waft of sour milk. "I'm not going to say it again. Now, hold still."

The officer slid Oliver's wallet out of his pocket, found the license, and slapped it down beside Oliver's cheek. "That wasn't so hard, was it?"

They let him go after that.

And Oliver drove slowly and steadily for the next dozen miles until he pulled off at the first exit he found, someplace deep in the Inland Empire where the dirt was red and serrated mountains carved up the sky like knives: a town whose sign read *City of San Ojuela*.

He couldn't get out of the car fast enough. Filled up his tank with shaking hands and kicked the fuel shaft half a dozen times, shouting, "Stupid—stupid—stupid," until he slipped in an oil slick and hit his elbow on the chrome bumper.

You can still go back home, he thought. It wasn't too late. His mom would forgive him, like she always did. But his dad would be waiting with a loaded diatribe for this new mess Oliver had made.

An attendant glared at Oliver from the window of the 7-Eleven. He half expected the guy to storm out and demand he head on back the way he came. Oliver ignored it, paid for his gas, and was back in his car, ready to get the fuck out of that sundown town, when the gas station's double doors split and the Boy in the black-striped serape rushed out into the neon glow. Their eyes met.

And the desert pulsed through him.

The Boy took off running across the parking lot. The doors split open again behind him and a bunch of high school kids spilled out, chortling like a hyena pack as they corralled the Boy against the streetlamp, lashing at him with words like *wetback* and *bitch* and *witch* and *prick* and *faggot*.

Oliver revved his engine. A powerful snarl. He drove right up to those assholes and stepped out in front of the headlights with his sunglasses on and arms crossed, like the badass he definitely wasn't. How quickly they scattered.

Oliver tried to help the Boy up, but he pulled his hand away.

"I didn't need you to do that," the Boy said. At least, Oliver assumed he was a boy; he could have not been. His hair hid his face, and his voice rasped. He didn't look older than seventeen.

"Okay, dude. You're welcome. Wasn't no problem anyway." Oliver flexed his hand, a faint burn pulsing where he'd touched the Boy's skin.

He would have left it at that, but the Boy said, "I'd leave town quick, if I were you."

Oliver's guts twisted. "What?"

"But not that way." The Boy pointed in the direction Oliver had come from, toward the highway. "The cops hang out there. It's the only big road that comes in and out of San Ojuela. They'll pull anyone over for anything. And nobody has your kind of car here. Someone like you, driving a car like that..." The Boy's eyes glittered at the Dodge. "Oh, yeah. They'll get you."

Oliver sighed. "Alright, then, what would you do?"

"You'll wanna take the back road. Past Tassajara. You go for a mile or two till you hit the pumpjack field. From there you find another way onto the 74 so you can keep running." He paused. "You are on the run, aren't you?"

It was the way he said it. The way those eyes seemed to know him, and how the tingling darkness warmed his hand. That same darkness seemed to cradle the Boy; it kept him safe from whatever was out here.

Oliver wanted that safety, that bravery. That was how he found himself offering the Boy a ride. Across town, past blocks of decaying, boarded-up strip malls where dead leaves tumbled on cracked roads. The Boy spoke only to tell Oliver, "Turn right here," or, "Turn left there." In the red of a stoplight, he elaborated. "A lot of people who used to live here couldn't make the rent. Now there's not many of us old ones left. You're gonna wanna take another left." Soon enough they'd made it to the gates of the hacienda, where the desert ended and lush trees grew among the cacti.

"People around here think it's haunted," the Boy said. "You can come in, if you want. If you need a place to stay, no one will bother you here."

Now, Oliver took in the interior of the house the Boy called Casa Coyotl: its cracked walls, the faint smell of lavender and rotting wood.

The bones beneath his feet.

It felt like a dream. If someone had pulled him aside to tell him it was—that he'd wake up back home tomorrow to continue waiting tables, cleaning bathrooms, getting stoned, and sleeping late, waiting for his true life to begin—he'd have believed them.

"The kids used to have a song about this house," said the Boy. "You know Spanish, yeah?" When Oliver nodded, the Boy chanted:

> Casa Coyotl, Casa Coyotl
> Dentro del pueblo con ojos
> Profundo en los desiertos
> Aullando y esperando
> Allí con los dientes agudos—
> Para comerte mejor
> El cuerpo hasta los huesos.

He flashed a crooked smile that made Oliver think of a broken heart. He had a soft face, and his skin was pale copper. The rest of him he kept hidden behind the dark patterns of his shroud.

"I mean, yeah, that's definitely a creepy-as-fuck song, I guess," Oliver said.

"When I'm here, I feel the soil and listen to the sad songs buried underneath. It's sad as hell here, don't you think? Everyone thinks the house is evil, but it's not, at all. I think it's a gentle place. Safe."

Oliver realized he knew the rhyme. He'd heard it years ago from one of his cousins around some campfire out in Joshua Tree, back when that was the thing they'd do. They'd share their stories of duendes and ghosts and chupacabras in the dark. Oliver remembered the crunch of distant footsteps, the blare of a faraway train's horn. Everything he knew of the unknown he'd learned out there.

"There's a story about the people who lived here years ago. A man moved in with his two daughters. And he was nice enough, if a little odd. But who isn't, you know? Problem was he'd grown up here, escaped, only to end up back again. They say the ghosts within these walls didn't want the man to ever escape the house again, so they drove him mad."

Something was howling outside—wailing? Some creature beyond the property's edge. That was the thing about deserts and the way their unsettling sounds carried. They could either be far away, or right outside. The desert never let you know which it was.

"No one knows what happened to the two girls. They were here one day, gone the next. Some versions say they died in gruesome ways, but that's all urban legend shit. Most people say their mom took them away and the police locked up the father. The only one who stayed behind was the aunt who owned this place, but she got old, and now the house is dying slowly."

He let the silence settle.

"That's not a scary story," Oliver finally said. "It's just sad."

The Boy blinked. "You know, I think so too."

Eventually the Boy led him to a door at the center of the house, where the weight of the place sagged above them, as if held on slender strings. The Boy took Oliver's hand; whispered, "Quick—I wanna show you something." And together they stepped into a flood of moonlight.

There was a massive cavity at the heart of the house. A courtyard with arched cloisters and a fountain that bloomed in the middle.

"What do you think?" the Boy asked.

Oliver could hear nothing, see nothing of the world beyond the walls. He walked toward the fountain at the center of it all and looked up: above him stretched a cascade of a billion beautiful stars twinkling in black velvet. Back home, there were no stars. Just brown light pollution. No open spaces like this. Tight walls. Locked doors.

He'd never seen so many stars before.

"I...I think it's amazing."

He couldn't hear distant sirens like he did in San Diego. No buildings cutting into the sky or planes roaring in. There was only the desert's hollow call. He wasn't looking up from earth to sky, he was looking down into the universe entire.

How could he go home when there was so much still out there? Oliver felt for the phone in his back pocket and clicked the home screen, but nothing happened. Right. He'd shut it off. Dozens of calls and texts from his mom must be lurking there. He just had to turn it on.

If he called her, he'd tell her he was sorry, and stupid, and she would forgive him, because unlike his father's, her love wasn't built on what kind of man he had yet to become. It would only take two hours, driving through the night, to get back to her. The thought tugged at the tendons of Oliver's heart, and maybe he did abandon course in some other, parallel life; but it was October, and his dad would be there, and the feeling was only a sadness tugging at him, the past reaching out to say goodbye.

"I'm sorry for snapping at you earlier," the Boy said, bringing him back. "When you helped me. I was still coming back into myself. But it was rude."

"Back into yourself?"

"My skin. When my *friends* get like that, it's a lot easier to just lose myself. Kind of go somewhere else, out there or deep inside, until they're gone. You know? But don't worry. I'm used to it." The Boy forced a smile. A broken heart.

"Fuck those guys, dude. People can be awful."

"They don't like the tricks I can do," he said. "They say I give them nightmares. But that's impossible, they're just paranoid assholes."

Oliver remembered what they'd called him at the gas station. *Witch*. He didn't say a thing.

"You're not afraid of me." The Boy raised an eyebrow.

"I'm not."

"Why?"

"Because I don't think I have a reason to be. It's normal people that hurt people," Oliver said. He forced a laugh.

The Boy crouched in the darkness. Oliver felt his eyes on him. Swore he saw them glowing.

"We should go." The Boy said it quickly—moved too fast for Oliver to think. He could only follow the Boy back through the house, propelled by instinct: across the courtyard and foyer and out the double doors to the roundabout where he'd parked. Only now the car sagged in the gravel. The tires hung off the rims in tatters. The trunk was ripped open—a gaping wound.

That was when he saw the shape prowling behind the car in the dark. A moaning thing—an undead thing. Its skull shaped like an animal's, exposed and raw, with the shine of half a dozen monstrous eyes jostling in each socket, battling each other for dominance.

A feather crown atop its head.

"*What the fuck?*"

The creature lunged. The Boy pulled Oliver back into the house and slammed the door. The creature pounded against it, splintering the wood and lock, but they pinned the door shut with all their body weight and held it there until the howling stopped. Oliver shut his eyes. *It's a dream*, he repeated to himself. *It's a dream*. All he had to do was open his eyes and he'd be in the bed he'd always known. When he did open his eyes, though, they met two bare feet. Attached to them was the Boy, staring down at him.

"Bro, what the fuck was that?!" His own voice sounded far away from his body. He was reduced to a hysterical, screaming thing he didn't recognize. Shouting over the Boy as he tried to calm him down. The Boy told him he had to stop it and shut up, or else—

"What's going on here?"

They stopped shouting.

A stone gargoyle shifted in the deep shadows of the house and stood upright. No: an old man, his stance strong, with a full mustache and placid eyes and a bolo tie fastened with a dark stone around his throat.

"The groundskeeper."

"Thank Christ." Oliver pushed the Boy away from him and

scrambled up. "Sir—there's something outside."

The man opened the door, looked into the emptiness outside, and closed it again. With a thick Spanish accent, he said, "You certainly did a number on that. That's an old lock. It's going to take a specialist to come in and make it right again."

The way he spoke was calming. Oliver's pulse slowed, and he wondered what it was he'd seen out there—if it was worth being so scared of. Probably just a starved and mangy coyote, made monstrous by the moonlight. And those kids from the gas station had thought it would be funny to slash his tires. "I—I can pay for it. I'm sorry."

"Don't worry," the old man laughed. "It's just another antique. But you look tired. You've had a long day. Maybe it would be good to get some rest?"

Yes, Oliver thought. *Right. Rest.* But something nudged him to stay awake. Something about bones under the dirt.

To the Boy, the groundskeeper said, "Get him comfortable and we'll see him off in the morning, okay? You don't want the police finding you out so late."

The Boy nodded. He led Oliver back to the courtyard. Oliver sank back in a cushioned chair, and the Boy made room for himself on the couch facing it. *He's right*, Oliver told himself. *You'll be alright. You'll be safe. You'll wake up tomorrow and that groaning thing, the bad dreams, the cops—they'll all be gone.* The thought of his mom lying awake crept into his head, but he told himself he'd deal with it in the morning. He promised himself he'd call her.

I'll fix us.

For a while neither the Boy nor Oliver spoke. Only when Oliver had faded into a dream haze did the Boy's voice crawl back into his ear:

I knew someone like you once. He hated this town and wanted to leave. But the boys caught us together behind the bleachers and their fists pulped his face. Then he brought a knife to school and held it to one of their throats against a bathroom stall—but you'd understand why he had to hurt them, right?

You get it, even if they didn't. They said expulsion, assault with a deadly weapon—called him terrible things that drove him to run away. Now the night calls to me. In my sleep it whispers to my blood and purrs in my bones. Samuel makes the whispers hurt less, so I can hear the coyotes howl.

Oliver woke up.

A pale lamp buzzed above him. The courtyard was gone, and interior walls boxed him in, killing any sound, any wind. He tried to stand but leather straps pulled him back into the chair. He tried to kick his feet, but those were bound too. He remembered the feeling of all the bones buried beneath the mission's dirt.

Dread plunged into him.

He thrashed in his seat, twisted against the straps until skin split and rough wood drank up the blood. Chest constricting, he gasped for sips of air.

"Relax, it's okay," a voice said at the edge of the light. It was the Boy, watching with strange curiosity from a chair across the room. The chair was turned backwards, his arms crossed over its top rail. "We're in a room deep in the house. No one will hear you if you scream, so you might as well not."

Drowning. Drowning. Oliver was drowning.

"Cut it out, dude. What the fuck is going on?" The words spilled from his mouth. "I—I have to go. I gotta go, I gotta get home. I'm sorry—I'm sorry."

The Boy blinked. "Listen, he'll be here soon, and I can't ever stand to watch." He got up, backed into the dark until only his eyes remained. Sad, amber-red eyes. "When he's here, just go inside yourself. Dig down and hide there, Oliver. I promise it won't hurt when you're far away."

Oliver was crying, pleading. *Please, please, please—*

"I'm not a bad person," the Boy said. "I want you to know that. We try to keep it with just bad people, but it doesn't always work out like that. Listen, it isn't your fault, okay? It's just bad timing is all. It's always just bad timing. On the bright side, you don't have to go home. You'll be free from all that awful shit."

Tears stung Oliver's sight, blurring the Boy until he was a shadow of a wraith watching him. He needed his inhaler. Or his phone. If he had his phone, he could call his mom, he'd tell her he was sorry.

"I think…if things were different, maybe we could have been friends," the Boy said. Oliver began to sob. The Boy nodded. "Right. Okay. It will be okay," he said. Then he walked away into the dark.

A door shut behind him. Soon it creaked open again, and a shadow crept forward. Hand wrapped tight around a dark blade.

Oliver didn't scream. Even when the shadow began to carve, and the pain was shooting whiteness. He just bit his tongue and thought of the stars.

In the morning, when the sunrise stretched mountain shadows long across the valleys and bluffs, a fire crackled in the desert, miles outside the town of San Ojuela. Flames snapped around what might once have been a Dodge Challenger. The paint curled and the seats crinkled. A spire of smoke rose from the burning wreck, reaching its black hand into the morning as the wind sighed across the desert sky.

ACT I
The Return

ONE
Dark Liz, Who Can See the Dead

ELIZABETH WAS FOURTEEN the night La Muerte dragged herself out of the mirror in the corner of the bedroom, the glass smoking then rippling like water until the ends of her toes slipped through. La Muerte smelled of hot wax and sweet marigolds, and the taste of ash kissed Elizabeth's lips.

It was after midnight. Elizabeth had been lying awake in the ocean of her new bed, trying to ignore the shouts pulsing up from the floor below. Her mother and stepfather. She caught *should have* and *could have. Goddammit, they could have fucking died!* Each bodiless voice took turns between rageful concern and regret. Cabinets slammed and Elizbeth flinched in the dark.

She didn't want to sleep. A nightmare waited behind her eyes—the shattered glass, her father's stumbling, Mary crying in the back seat, and the two cars crunched into each other on the side of the road as the horns blared. That mangled, bloody body.

For hours, Elizabeth rolled from one side of the bed to the other, the stiff new sheets rubbing wrong against her skin. She starfished her limbs to take up as much room as she could. To be big—to stop herself from sinking in further. She felt small anyway.

A constellation of glow-in-the-dark stars shone above her. Her mother had tacked them up that morning, "because I want you to feel at home here," she'd said. "And I know you're afraid of the dark."

But the darkness was too thick, too heavy for the fake stars to push away, so Elizabeth pulled herself away instead. Away from that room, that house, until she was somewhere else entirely, looking down at a movie screen where a brown, curly-haired girl tossed in a bed—but it was not her bed. Her real bed and home were miles and miles away.

Then the voices downstairs hushed. And the wind cut out, and the curtains hung slack. The sounds of sirens and street cars outside died away and left only Elizabeth's breathing. And the heartbeat of some other, nameless thing.

That was when La Muerte came.

She stood in the corner of the room, crane-thin and spavin-legged. Even in the dark Elizabeth could see the thick jewels glinting on her collar piece, her bare chest beneath it, her velvety skirts. Her arching crown with flowers and feathers erupting from it.

Elizbeth couldn't move. La Muerte hadn't yet noticed her; her attention seemed focused on a black box that hung from her throat. Elizabeth recognized the shape: a polaroid camera. Her Tía Marisol had one with all her other vintage things back home—no, not home—not anymore. Candles and terracotta tiles and vaulted ceilings and thick woolen sheets. All of that had shattered when her father finally lost himself, when the cops threw him in the back of their car. Any hope of finding its pieces had been stolen when her mother came and ripped her away and brought her here. Alone, with La Muerte before her.

La Muerte was fumbling with the camera, which had spat out a blank white square. She caught it between long, blackened fingers and shook it in the air. As soon as her back was turned to Elizabeth, Elizabeth slid from her sheets and crept towards the window—towards the curtains. Because that was what her father used to tell her to do when they'd first moved into Tía Marisol's house and she used to hear groaning in the dark. He'd said curtains were sentries powered by moonlight.

"Don't worry," he'd whisper. "Las cortinas te cuidarán. Even when I can't."

She slid behind the lacy fabric. But these were not thick curtains. She could still see through them to the photograph as it blotched into crispness: it showed her sister Mary, asleep in the bedroom down the hall. La Muerte inspected her work, tucked the photo beneath the folds of her shroud. Then she turned to Elizabeth.

Breathing stopped. Shaking stopped. All that was left was Elizabeth's heart—an animal kicking violently at her rib cage.

La Muerte swam through the air, casting a phantasmagoria of stars behind her. She stopped just before the curtains. A red cloth hung over her face. They watched each other through their veils.

Elizabeth wanted to scream for her dad. But he wouldn't come, would he? No. He was far away. Worlds away. Somewhere behind bars, like the horror he was.

"What do you want?" Elizabeth croaked to that maybe-dream woman. To Death. La Muerte.

She held the camera up to her veil and said, SMILE.

A flash stamped the shape of Death into Elizabeth's sight.

The photograph hissed from the camera. As Elizabeth blinked away spots, she saw La Muerte fanning it. When it was done, she looked at her work just as she had done before—then let out a sigh of anguish that chilled Elizabeth to her core.

La Muerte backed away.

What? What is it? Elizabeth wanted to ask. But she could not find her voice. *What's wrong with me?*

La Muerte heard anyway. YOUR SOUL, she said in her voice of a thousand sighs. OH, POBRECITA. She held up the picture and showed Elizabeth the void in the middle of the shot. The camera had been aimed straight at Elizabeth, but it showed only empty curtains hanging in the window, and an ugly shadow where Elizabeth should have been.

Elizabeth started seeing things no one else did after that night. Ghoulish things loitering in empty sports parks or superstore aisles, wearing scuffed Nikes or wrinkled button-ups. Some ghosts were crisp and distinct. Like Wet Boy, who lived at the community pool. Like Bean, named after the stain on his shirt, which was the same every day when she passed him in the crosswalk on her way to school. But others had dwindled into black wraiths, hovering just above the ground. Featureless and dark—their identities forgotten. Those were the ones that scared her.

In those early months, she grew obsessive over the ghosts. She'd study their hazy details to try and guess who they must have been when they were alive, where they came from, how long they'd been dead. There were a lot of them at her local mall, and she wondered if the mall had grown up around them or if they'd died as unlucky shoppers. None of them ever touched Elizabeth; few even noticed her. They seemed to listen if she spoke to them, though. Elizabeth thought maybe they liked the company, even if most never spoke back and the ones that did grunted one-word responses or repeated a single phrase, sometimes a command or reminder, sometimes a name. So she kept speaking to them. It was what she would have liked in their place. And if she could ease their pain, she would.

One day, she made the mistake of telling her friends Jannah and Kylie about this gift, back when she first joined the dance academy and wanted so badly to make friends. Kylie laughed. Jannah whistled and said, "That's fucking metal."

Never again, Liz decided. The dead would be something she kept to herself.

Elizabeth was nineteen now. Staring at her reflection in the *Dirus Dance Theater Company* locker room. Four years she'd been separated from her soul.

You're not me, she whispered to the naked girl in the mirror, sure of it. *You don't look right. It changed you. Something's missing.*

Behind her, the locker room was alive with the chatter of the other dancers as they stretched and bundled back their hair. Most of them thin-boned, fair-skinned, straight-haired. Every weeknight they'd gather at the dance studio and strip down to bare skins. Elizabeth would retreat, like she always did, to the very back of the locker room near the empty stalls where she could change alone.

She scrutinized her reflection. Her curly hair, indigenous nose. Her skin looked like cling-wrap over fat and bone, tight and bunchy across chest and shoulders and bulky hips. She tugged her leotard on, adjusted it, shifted her stance. But it didn't work. No matter what she did, her physicality looked soulless. Dull. A sack of flour.

"You're here," she told herself. "You're alive. You're Elizabeth Remolina."

A voice vaulted over the lockers—Miss Turner, the head choreographer. "On your marks, girls! You got two minutes!"

Shit. Elizabeth split open her bag, laced the shoes and filled the water bottle, and rushed out with all the other women.

The studio lights burned, drenching the sixteen dancers in harsh neons. Six of them took up the center stage, Elizabeth included. Men and women alike dressed in plain black leotards and clustered tightly together. They waited crouched on their marks, spines curved, faces hidden behind their hands. The drone of an organ reverberated into Elizabeth.

Remember to breathe, she told herself. *Don't be afraid.* She felt the heat of Jannah beside her. Felt Miss Turner watching them with a predator's focus, clipboard in hand. Felt her mother's gaze, too—always on her, whether half the city separated them or not. *Shut it out*, she thought, then focused on her muscles, wound up tight and ready to spring. She waited for the music to strike.

She asked herself, *Are you sure the dead can dance? Well, are you?*

She counted in her head to the explosion of movement. *One, two, three, four, five, six, seven, eight—*

A cymbal struck and the dancers sprang up—reached out a hand to clasp the one reaching back—held the pose. One hand on their face, the cymbal tapping on like a ticking clock. Then on beat their fingers split apart to flash their eyes. To quick cello cuts, Elizabeth spread out with the dancers, catlike and focused. Making a hoop with her arms and arching them up, bringing them down, contracting them in, pushing them out—moving like a marionette on a string with her eyes fixed to the darkness beyond the lights. Every move a precise calculation. The studio was alive with sharp breaths, the damp smacks of feet on floor and hands to thighs matching the symphony rhythm.

Miss Turner called the dance *Desire*, a study of possession. What do we possess? What possesses us? Like addiction, want, purpose, depression. A looking in, and a looking out. Elizabeth kept her face stern, eyes wide. She kicked back one leg and threw herself into a damn-near perfect arabesque, matching not just the beats of the cellos and quick violins but also the rockera beat forever pounding in her head.

Elizabeth gave herself to that beat—to the emotion behind each move—let the muscle memories laced through her throbbing tendons drive her quick lunges, her sharp pivots. She allowed herself to move from fluidity into distorted jerks, opening herself up raw to the music. "Dance isn't just flowy leaps and twirls, it's aggressive," Tía Marisol had once told Elizabeth, back when Marisol used to perform Baile Folklórico in a Mexican ensemble. "Dance can be ugly. Dance can be pain." When Marisol danced, there was a violence to her. A puppet ordered by precision. Her calmness just focused rage, compressed to a needle point. Elizabeth used to study her tía from the window, looking down into the central courtyard of Casa Coyotl, captivated by Marisol whirling her Jalisco dress into rippling rivers of black.

The floor sang with squeaks against waxed wood. The music rose, and Elizabeth followed. It dropped and she did too—too fast. The world crashed up against her knees. She bit her lip and locked her throat. Felt a warm gush seep between her teeth.

Again, she thought.

Get up!

She threw herself back to the trumpet in her head, the guitar possessing her down to her bones, the fall a now-distant memory. Other dancers had stumbled or slipped, and Elizabeth would too a few more times through the rehearsal of the new motions, cursing herself each time but snapping back up. She threw herself into a spin and kept at it, snapping her head back on point and gaining speed, the stage dissolving until it lost all shape and character and melted into gliding streaks of red, black, yellow, beige, green. She reduced herself to the adrenaline pulsing through her blood, making her weightless. Her shoulders flared; the arches of her feet strained beneath her weight. She welcomed it—loved it, because Marisol had told her performance meant being in the moment, in the body. And Elizabeth wanted her body to feel—wanted to occupy it and tell its truth—to be present in the rhythm and flexing and hingeing and arching and scrunching and snapping back. To feel her body alive again.

Back in the locker room again. That uncomfortable fucking feeling.

The smell of sweat and baby powder. The hiss of steam as Elizabeth's teammates peeled away their uniforms and scrubbed off two hours' exhaustion under running showerheads. She caught herself gazing into the haze of skin and steam and snapped her eyes elsewhere, warmth filling her cheeks.

But it was impossible not to look at everyone; the dance house was absolutely ancient. Its tiles were 70s teal, and the shower dividers were little 4'5" walls that made whoever stood behind them look like nude office workers.

"Hey, Dark Liz!"

It was Jannah, freshly showered, fitting on her shoes on a nearby bench. Her hair hung stringy and dark over her left shoulder. "Dark Liz," she chirped again. "I have something important to tell you."

She walked right over, peeling Elizabeth's attention away from aching feet and shoulder blades.

"Don't look so scared. I just wanted to say you were really great out there. Your intensity was fucking dope," Jannah said. A smile flickered on her lips and Elizabeth's pulse quickened, if only for a second. Jannah had one of those centered teeth—she'd spotted it the first time they met, when they were both acne-faced fourteen-year-olds, the two worst dancers on their high school's competitive team. Whenever Jannah smiled, Elizabeth noticed her centered tooth.

Elizabeth shrugged. "I fell enough times to make sure my knees will be powder by the time I'm thirty."

When Jannah laughed, she leaned her weight against the locker wall. The smell of her shampoo fluttered to Elizabeth's nose. Elizabeth shrank into herself a bit more. "Yeah, well, that'll be all of us. Maybe we should make a coven about it."

"Or we could just invest in physical therapy."

Jannah stuck out her tongue. "Just take the compliment, Liz."

To that Elizabeth did smile.

"Anyway, you got plans for Halloween? I mean, I'm sure the Queen of the Night has important things to do on Samhain, but just in case you don't…"

Elizabeth cringed at the nickname. *Queen of the Night, Dark Liz.* Those goth labels had clung to her like a tarry shadow since high school. Because she was prone to moping and wearing black, always listening to music that her mom called "hideous." She drew endless sugar skulls in the margins of her notebooks when dyslexia made the words on the whiteboard go crisscrossed and ugly. Once upon a time, all that had made her feel edgy. Now, dark things were as comfortable to her as her own skin. *Dark Liz. Queen of the Night.* Better than nothing at all.

Elizabeth had envisioned going to a cemetery with a couple friends on Halloween, reading tarot cards and sipping wine, or maybe staying home watching B-movie shlock that no one else cared for.

"I'm asking because Kylie is having a thing at her place," Jannah said. "Some of the other dancers already agreed we'd go, and—you're kind of like the spirit of Halloween, yeah? So I thought it would be cool if you came with." When Elizabeth arched an eyebrow, she added, "There'll be alcohol, and the older girls probably, definitely won't give a fuck about it if we have some."

"Oh."

"Look, it's gonna be a good time, Dark Liz, you gotta come. Just text me, k?"

Elizabeth nodded, knowing she'd made up her mind four exchanges ago. No. She would not go. Because she liked Jannah and the other performers and wanted them to keep liking her. She'd joined the dance company a few months back hoping to perform for real, to travel and put on *actual* shows that people paid to see, to be as good as the rest of them. But she never spent time with her troupe outside of rehearsals. Any closer and they'd start to bring her along to things, and she'd try to force smiles and laughter when really all that would be going through her head would be, *You idiot, you're bringing down the mood. Why can't you follow the script?*

Better to keep up the illusion that they did all fit together, those infinitely better dancers and their token goth Latina friend. She decided she would text Jannah later, once she was on the road and at a safe distance, that her mom had asked her to stay home instead.

Elizabeth showered after the last of the girls clicked the locker doors shut behind them. Just her and the empty stalls. She unwrapped the crusty gauze from her feet, peeled off her leotard, and let cold water rush over her face. Pale stretch marks striped her hips and thighs. Soreness in the muscles told her she was still alive, still anchored to the body the mirror claimed was hers.

Posters of too-prim ballet dancers watched from the walls. Elizabeth ignored them. She thought of her tía instead, and how they both preferred anything with quick slashes of hands, feet, elbows, knees. Wished once again that it could be Marisol who'd eventually watch her from the audience and not her mother. It would let her show Marisol how much her influence mattered— how her niece had never forgotten her.

But of course, Marisol would never see her perform; she hadn't seen much of anything for a long time. Her body was sixty miles away in a nursing home with thin-slit windows, while Alzheimer's eroded her mind. The last time Elizabeth had visited her, she'd asked where Elizabeth's father was, of all things.

Elizabeth shut off the water.

The air ducts hummed. Droplets slithered down her calves. The shower head dripped little Morse-code echoes through the quiet locker room. The feeling of being watched pressed heavy on her shoulder blades.

"Hello?" Elizabeth called into the dark.

No response. Just a hum. And those drops. Muffled chatter outside, worlds away. A dozen pairs of paper eyes on posters.

She was drying off when a voice called back to her.

"*Hell.*"

It came from the bench at the far end of the room. Elizabeth froze. Fogged breath curled from her mouth. She couldn't see but sensed a heavy mass in the dark. Sitting upright and rigid on mildewed wood.

"*Oh.*"

Liz stood up, slowly, quietly, without taking her eyes from the corner. "Who are you?" she asked, thinking it must be another one of her private ghosts.

"Hell," it repeated. "Ohhhh."

Not one to linger where she knew she was unwanted, Elizabeth threw on leggings and a sweater and stuffed her dance clothes back into her bag.

The showerhead drips had stopped. How long had they been quiet?

"Hell…"

She backed towards the door she knew was behind her. Just six steps away. She counted one, two, keeping her eyes on the gap where the light died.

"Oh?" the voice said again. "Hello?" A dragging noise scraped along the ground. And with it: breathing. Elizabeth fumbled for the door. The voice moaned, a low and lonely cry that swelled louder. Came closer.

Elizabeth flung the door open behind her and bolted out into the hallway. Overhead, moths danced at the edges of the flickering fluorescent lights. Beneath them the air was filled with the smell of lavender and rotting honey.

"Liz niña," the voice sighed. "Liz niña. Hello."

Elizabeth turned. A black wraith hung in the air, bare feet suspended above the floor tiles. It shifted its head, as if confused. Then it locked its hollow gaze onto Elizabeth.

"Liz, la que perdió su alma, I found you."

Elizabeth wrung her bag's shoulder strap. *It cannot hurt me. It cannot hurt me.* A shadowy mantilla draped its head. Not it—*she*. The realization kicked the air from her lungs.

The dead woman poured over Elizabeth, fast and rippling. She grabbed her by the wrists and pulled her right up against her own smoky skin. She stank of hospital disinfectant and urine and embalming fluid, and her terror was alive, crawling up Elizabeth's ribs. The wraith opened her mouth, pressing her face against Elizabeth's, smearing damp lips on Elizabeth's cheek.

"Liz child! Mi vida—ten cuidado!" Her voice was shards of ice. "El Coco me mató y te busca a ti. Vuelve a mi casa con cuidado, o no vuelvas más. Ten cuidado, mi niña, beware! Beware!"

Elizabeth screamed—

—and then Marisol was gone.

They found her curled up against the trophy display case, clutching her bag. Miss Turner kept asking if she was alright, but Elizabeth didn't understand. She nodded to all the questions, but they sounded so far away. The voice kept repeating in her head. Elizabeth felt cold around her wrists where purple fingerprints bloomed on her flesh.

They don't touch you. Ghosts never touch you. But Elizabeth knew that hand, even if she hadn't felt it in years. The grip had been burning ice. *She sounded so afraid.*

Jannah gave Elizabeth some water, then touched Elizabeth's forehead with the back of her hand. "Shit, you're freezing."

Elizabeth blinked away her tears. She fixed her eyes on the two moths still buzzing against the lights, wafting the odor of lavender, flashing the starry-eyed patterns of their wings.

A week had passed from the night when Tía Marisol visited the locker room. Elizabeth sat in bed with her knees tucked to her chest, pale in her laptop's grainy light. She'd put on a spaghetti western while she waited for her parents to go to sleep, one she'd seen a dozen times before. Clint Eastwood stood four inches tall on a pixelated screen while the Mexican man with a bandolier across his chest waited, hand hovering above his holster. By the sound of the trumpets swelling, someone was about to die. Intense closeups fired across the screen, guns and hands and the men's sunbeaten faces.

Her throat still stung from all her sobs. She was sure the ghost had been Marisol, same as she was sure of her own beating heart and her soulless, empty innards. When she'd gotten back to her mother's house that night, she'd put off going inside, wishing yet again that she could just move out. She would have by now, if she could afford more than junior college. She'd waited in the driveway while blaring synths and guitar growls washed over her, savoring those last moments of in-between. When she'd finally opened the front door, her mom had her phone to her ear. Their eyes met, and Elizabeth knew. She turned away—didn't need to hear it—shot straight for her room, but the news came anyway.

"Liz, the nursing home just called. It's your Aunt Marisol."

"I know. I already know."

That night, she'd held everything in long enough to get the bedroom door shut behind her. Then she sobbed until there was nothing left inside her but space, and she was hollow again. When her eyes dried, she'd pulled her phone to her face and slid a hand down her jeans and read the laziest smut she could tap on—trying to jolt herself alive again—and rubbed herself until her feet knotted and her spine went stiff and in a final gasping breath she shuddered back into her sheets. Back into the numbness that reverberated across her body, with her limbs unfolded, exposed to air, just like the night when La Muerte had told her she'd lost her soul.

She'd stayed in that state of unlife for days, not leaving her room even to go to class or dance rehearsal, hardly eating but watching movie after movie—letting the world pass by.

It was Friday now. The handprint Marisol's ghost had bruised into Elizabeth's wrist was still tender. She pinched it until the mark stung with a dozen pale half-moons. Each one a reminder that she was in fact alive, and feeling. And that the ghost had in fact been Marisol.

The crack of Clint Eastwood's gun shocked Elizabeth upright.

The Mexican spun—fired a shot into the air before toppling back in the dirt. Elizabeth rubbed her eyes, blinking as Clint's white hand cocked the hammer and fired again. *Crack! Crack!* until the dead Mexican's hat flopped over his face.

The music picked up; soon the credits would roll, but Elizabeth shut her laptop, killing the movie. She listened closely to the sounds of the house. Her sister Mary was still awake somewhere, shouting into a headset, arguing about kill streaks in a video game. Their mother and stepfather had taken shifts knocking on Liz's door over the past few days to make sure she was alright. She wasn't, and they knew that, so it would have been a nice sign that they cared, if they were truly just being sympathetic. They weren't, though. They were worried she'd hurt herself—they'd found some sketchbooks of hers years ago and seen admittances of wanting to not-be, to fade away or sleep for years and wake up new and fully formed. She was trying to be poetic. They were sure it was a suicide threat.

When the house was finally quiet, Liz unearthed a Ouija board from the closet. She'd bought it in high school when she was still trying to make a personality out of edginess and apathy. Dabbling with demons was, in her opinion, a white-person phenomenon that people of her own culture knew better than to fuck with, yet she was Dark Liz and had wanted to entertain her friends with some *real* brujería. She'd felt something when she used the board, a dark feeling that crawled up her arms.

Marisol had brought her a warning last week in the locker room. But she'd spoken half in Spanish, and Spanish words quickly lost their shape in Liz's brain. Marisol had tried to teach her the language, once, but since her mother had never followed up, she'd forgotten most of it. One sentence remained etched in her skull: *El Coco me mató y te busca a ti.*

She googled *El Coco* and found: *ghost-monster, boogeyman, el Cucuy.* A vague, ill-defined threat.

Marisol's ghost had wanted to warn her about *something.* That much she knew.

Elizabeth had been grieving for years already. The end of Marisol's life had been full of IV tubes and crinkly hospital gowns. Everyone had known her time was coming, a storm on the horizon getting closer and closer. Now, Elizabeth's blood rushed with more feelings than grief alone: excitement and fear and the need for answers. She lit candles in a circle around her on the floor. *I'll find out what you need to tell me about the boogeyman.*

She took a deep breath, put her hands on the planchette, and asked aloud, "Marisol? Are you there?"

Nothing.

"Marisol, what did you need to warn me about?" she said again. "What's in that house?"

Nothing. The rest of the words knotted inside her. *Who is El Coco? How did you die?* She could not speak them.

What happened to my soul?

She woke on the floor the next morning, the sun casting warm stripes across the room through the blinds. Birds were chirping; somewhere a lawn was being mowed. Mary was nudging Elizabeth's ribs with her foot.

"Bed wasn't doing it for you, huh?" Mary was already dressed, backpack slung over her shoulders, penny board tucked under her arm. The candles had been placed back on the bookshelf, the Ouija board folded up beneath them. Elizabeth didn't remember doing any of that.

Elizabeth groaned from the carpet. "Leave me to be eaten by dust bunnies."

"Mom wants us to get going or we'll miss the train," Mary said.

They were supposed to go back to the house. Back to Coyote House in San Ojuela to hold the funeral and take stock of the estate. Elizabeth could already see it, cold and empty, blacker than the charcoal sketches in her notebooks.

She didn't have to go. Her mom had said she could stay with Brian and work her feet raw rehearsing her dance routine all weekend if she wanted to. But Marisol was dead. And Elizabeth was tired of watching old movies. In that house there might be answers: parts of Marisol, maybe even parts of Elizabeth left between the walls.

"Fine," Elizabeth said. "Let's get it over with."

TWO
The Sheriff

I MEET THE VAQUERO at a quarter to eight on the roadside. It's only two hours into my shift and there's sleeplessness crumbling from my eyes. He's right off the 74, a back road along a ridge with orange groves not too far off. The tang of them perfumes the smoke-clotted air.

Seventeen new fires bloomed across the Inland Empire yesterday. Each eating brush and homes through the orange night. Now, in the morning light, I can make out a fresh plume of smoke rising miles away on the horizon, like a grey leviathan hunched over the Earth.

The vaquero points a shaky hand down the ridge, where a much smaller, much closer plume rises from a blackened wreck.

There, he tells me. And I see it's only about a quarter mile off. Close enough to walk, and it's not like I have anything better to do.

The sun beats down, relentlessly hot even for the morning, and the breeze is drying out my skin. Already there's sweat squelching in the soles of my boots. I have my mask on, but the vaquero's breathing this toxic air. His lips are dried up and wrinkled like the leathery skin below his eyes. I can't help but wonder if I'll end up as shriveled as he is one day. I go back to squinting at the wreck—

I want nothing more than a gulp of the cold water waiting in my patrol car.

Before the rest of my deputies arrive and this quiet morning is drowned with sirens and photo snaps and small talk that might compel me to lock myself back in the oven of my car, I jot down my initial thoughts on the crime scene: It's not a crash. I don't think it's an accident either. Heat waves ripple around the black, smoldering thing in the middle distance. It's hard to make out the details, but the smell of gasoline and char wafts heavy.

The vaquero says something to me and at first it's little more than a mumble scratching my ear. I'm not listening, but he keeps going, and I keep nodding because he probably thinks his voice is better than a bitter morning's silence.

It's too early for this.

Yesterday the boys up in Riverside County found another corpse baking in a field between prickly grass blades. A couple of vagabonds—VanLifers?—whatever they called themselves had been out there for whatever reason and found her, heart carved from her chest. The girl on the phone said a rattlesnake had made a home of the dead woman's ribs, all coiled up where her heart meat had been. It was not unlike some other corpses we had in the catacombs of the city, going back decades. We keep finding them, year after year, most often in shallow graves. A dozen now, all with the same tell-sings. You get used to how this is the kind of stuff you see in this line of work, if not worse. You go on, you don't be a pussy about it. You swallow it down, you deal with it.

But there's something about the autumn heat today. The howling wind.

I was bringing my girl Daisy up the pass, the vaquero says to me. You see, she got out of her pen. Daisy's always getting out. But the queer thing is, all my cows have been going crazy this season. Daisy was my sixth to run away, and we were finding the others dead. But I was driving back home from getting the groceries and saw her standing right here, grazing on the roadside. I couldn't believe it. Anyways, then I saw the smoke, so I called you. Now here we are.

Mm-hmm, thanks, I tell him, tucking my notepad away and squinting at the wreck again. And that was what? 'Bout thirty minutes ago?

Yessir.

Every time I turn to him, he flinches. I almost want to scare him a bit, but I don't, that would be wrong of me. Instead, I'm wondering why he would even call us if he was going to act so skittish. I know I wouldn't. But he's already told me how he respects the force, has friends in the force. Has thanked me for our hard work against *those types*, who don't know the sacrifices we make.

Out here, cars can burn for days or maybe weeks. You hear stories of gangs driving cars out to Lucerne Valley. They park them there and douse them with gas and set them aflame. And they'll burn for days and days, so by the time any cops show up, the evidence is black ash in the sand. Plenty of things *do* combust out here by accident too, though, on account of the dryness. Gran once said the desert took what it wanted and did what it pleased, and we were never supposed to live here. Maybe that's why I'm rambling. Thinking about Gran.

We're lucky the wind didn't pick up, I say—not really to the vaquero, more thinking out loud. If it had, the embers would have spread to the dry grass and we'd have far worse things to worry about.

The drought don't help things, he says.

No, it doesn't. Welp. Let's go have a look, yeah?

I start my descent down the hill, careful over the treacherous gravel. I stop when I'm a few feet away from the vaquero. His cow is still eating grass and paying no attention to either of us, and this far down I can't smell their musk anymore. I say, By the way, you can't be saying that. Calling things that.

He wrinkles his brow, looks at me with a sort of grimace or confusion. Huh?

Queer. The word slips off my tongue. Bothers people if we go around using that word like that, these days. So, you know, don't go around saying it.

Last week I arrested a fellow officer for beating his wife. Enough paperwork on him had piled up, so much that we'd sent him through several reform programs. I'd even instructed one. Overheard him during lunch, complaining about *bullshit waste-of-time classes*. Joking the whole way through. But he was right, they were a waste for him, in consequence of his own actions.

When I got the call, I pulled up to his home, a nice place at the end of a court. I already knew the way without GPS. I'd been there before, invited to a barbeque or something. They had a pool out back. I parked behind the other cop cars, all our lights washing the house in red and blue and red again, and even in the moment I noticed the desert hills cutting the sky beyond the fence. It made me think he lived on some kind of razor's edge. Between our world and whatever lived out there beyond the rocks.

I cut his badge off him—he'd been wearing his uniform when it all happened. Used the pocketknife I keep slung in my belt loop. Ripped the rest of his blue shirt off and left it smacked in an ugly tattered pile on the carpet. He yelped like a dog when we hauled him outside. Kept repeating, C'mon, compa. As if our shared skin tone would make me let him off easy. His wife was yelling something awful too, when we threw him in the back of my patrol car, but I didn't pay any attention to it either.

I still have his badge. Officer Ramirez. I've hated staring at it so much that the first thing I did when I came in today, before the sun even peeked up from the east, was throw it in a shoebox and lock it in my bottom desk drawer. It's sitting there now.

I replay the moment in my head, like I did on the drive here: the yelping, the stiff elbows. No matter how many times I replay it, I can't grasp *why*. Right before a shift. Crazy. Now everyone will say, *Look! More proof cops are a fucking gang.* After his arrest, I pulled over at a ravine like the one we're in now, with Ramirez still scowling in the back of my car. He'd been spitting nasty shit about Gran and Mom and calling me a *fucking gringo mutt*—like the slurs so many folks let slide easily off their tongues when I was young— and that was it. You don't need to know what I did to him on that ravine edge with clenched fists and keychain-wrapped knuckles. In the report, I wrote that he slipped. No one bothered to dig deeper. Because I'm good at my job.

I'm just trying to do my job, trying to help keep the community safe from the wolves.

Or the coyotes.

From the bottom of the ravine the vaquero's stray cow looks like one of the plastic farm animals I gifted my niece on her last birthday.

The car is a Dodge, a Challenger, an early 1970s model. The license plates have been removed, and the papers are ash. In what was once the trunk of the car, I find a backpack, or rather the shape of one, the edges still sizzling orange and smelling like burnt hair. Delicate ash wisps all around it. Remains of food baked into the smoldering pile. Whoever the car belonged to, that person had somewhere they meant to be but never got to.

You know, you don't have to be down here, I say.

For a second, I don't think the vaquero hears me, but a

heartbeat or two later, he looks up, shrugs, and says, I called it in. I want to stay and see it through.

I should order you right now to take that cow of yours and get on your way.

I probably shouldn't be talking to him, either. None of this is protocol, yet I don't send him off. I keep listening to his rambling. Maybe it's the claw marks ripped into the back of the car. The ribbons that were once tires. I ask him again to tell me what happened to his other cows.

Something keeps coming and spooking them at night, he says.

That's not unusual. Kids around here like to go cow-tipping, as if life's some old 80s movie.

But it's not that, the vaquero says. We find them afterwards, and it's never good to look at. They are eaten, torn apart, sir. Ripped to pieces but never any blood. We called you guys a dozen times about it. Then you told us to stop calling.

I nod. Yes sir, you can get fined for clogging up the lines. I'm sure we looked into it as much as we should have.

That part's true. I'm sure one of my deputies looked into it, found that it was a waste of time, and went on to do more important things. But with the claw marks in the car, and the torn-up cows, there's something I want to ask him, a feeling, gnawing at the nape of my neck. Growing up out in San Bernardino, you hear all manner of stories. The werewolves up in Big Bear Lake, skinwalkers in the desert, the Dark Watchers. Chupacabras—a dark and ugly word that makes me think of fangs. Blood. Feathers and claws and a desert storm.

The vaquero doesn't see me watching him, or if he does, he can't see my eyes behind my sunglasses. *Say the word*, I think at him. *I bet you believe in it. Then I can tell you how it's a childish, superstitious thing.*

ACT I: THE RETURN

Only the vaquero doesn't say anything. I tell him, There's a lot more coyotes out these days. We got a real problem with those bastards running around, and we get a lot of calls about it too. They're getting bolder. I wouldn't be surprised if that's what's getting your cattle.

The vaquero nods.

In the distance, the white tops of patrol cars ripple in the heat, and their sirens chase the wind. Hot air pressing on our skin, we wait, and I sigh with relief. No longer afraid. But in this moment when it's just the two of us men, I realize that I don't even know the vaquero's name, and I don't think I've told him mine. It's a small eternity as we wait for the cars to arrive.

We never exchange our names.

THREE
The Town of Eyes

METROLINK TRACKS roared beneath the train. The hum reverberated up through metal and carpet to one of Mary's feet; she swung the other lazily into the aisle. The coach smelled like old people. The morning's coastal view had changed into a dry landscape of inland hills.

Once Liz had agreed that she'd go too, their mother had decided that the girls would take the train into San Ojuela and check on the house while she went to the nursing home to handle Marisol's funeral arrangements. A devious ploy, really. Designed to keep them all from killing each other while zooming down the 215 at sixty miles an hour. Not that the train ride from Oceanside was any faster. An hour to Fullerton Station, where they'd waited another hour. Now, in the last stretch of the journey, all the novelty of Mary's first time in a thousand-ton machine shooting in a single direction had worn off. The train was now just a train, bearing ever closer to San Ojuela.

"Have you noticed that everyone here looks depressed?" Mary glanced toward her sister, who'd hardly spoken since Mary was caught skateboarding down the aisle by a white woman who told Liz to keep a closer eye on the wayward teen. Liz had simply let out a sour laugh and said, "I have no power over her." After the woman stormed off, Elizabeth had shot a glare at Mary, then pulled the strings of her hood tight around her face and rested her head against the window.

Now Liz was just a nose engulfed by a sea of red—one Mary was determined to pull a word out of. Or to flick her septum ring if that failed.

"It's Saturday, and we're on a train, and none of them seem to care. The living dead—all of 'em."

Liz peeked out of her hood and looked up and down the coach. It was less crowded than the one they'd taken to Fullerton Station: only a smattering of people with briefcases, checking their watches.

"What do you expect? No one ever goes to San Ojuela."

So she does yet speak!

Liz said something else from under her hood, too muffled for Mary to catch. *Don't bother me*, maybe?

"I beg your pardon?" Mary said.

Liz said something just as muffled but more aggressive.

"Nope. You're gonna have to lose the hood."

Liz ripped the hood off. "I said I don't wanna be here. I just wanna get this done with so I can go back home and practice and perform better by Monday."

Mary scrunched up her face, deciding the best course of action with deep concentration. "Can we get boba when we arrive? I've heard there are good ones in San Ojuela, and I'm thirsty."

"Milk tea isn't a substitute for water, Mary."

"That's just ridiculous."

"Should I dye my hair?" This question came from nowhere. Right out of the blue, but then again, Liz had been staring at her reflection in the window all morning. Liz played with a coil of hair. "Maybe red or something. Just—not *this*."

Mary sighed. "Mmkay, so you're clearly not doing well. Come on, talk to Mary. What's going on? Besides, you know, the obvious."

Liz looked at Mary with a deadly serious face. "Mary, do I look right to you?"

"You look like you always look, dude."

"No, I mean. Is there something…missing. Wrong."

"I don't think so, Liz," Mary said, realizing she was out of her depth, like she always was with her sister. The age gap between them was half a decade, and Mary was stuck in the shallows. "You look exactly like yourself. I don't know what else to tell you."

"Forget it."

Liz scrolled through her phone; Mary listened to the tracks thundering below. It was her turn to ask questions now. Time for anything but this stale silence. "What was it like back then? Living with Dad?"

Liz put her phone down. Raised her eyebrows when Mary didn't immediately follow up with an explanation.

If Mary Remolina thought really, really hard about it, she could recall glimpses of her life at Casa Coyotl. But they were scattered, hazy. A gaping courtyard, a deep forest, the smell of wood and rust. Sometimes Mary could only remember words, detached from feeling and sound, like she'd read them in a history textbook. Stories told to her later on. "Like. How was it like living there?"

Liz didn't get angry. She laughed. It was quiet, but Mary caught it, a delicate butterfly of a laugh that she didn't know what to do with as it lay in her hands.

"You should know," Liz said. "You were as much a part of the main cast as anyone."

Mary shrugged. "I can't remember the details. How Dad was *really* like." She waited, looking into her sister's sleepless eyes, sunken with dark circles and thick eyeliner. Her question teetering on the edge of an abyss.

Their mother was a second-generation who hardly spoke Spanish at all. Tía Marisol, their father, and the house in San Ojuela were the last crumbs of a culture Mary only knew secondhand. She wanted to know more before she saw the house with different eyes. To know *something*. Only now she was losing the opportunity, mile by mile, as the town crept closer.

Closer, closer.

Liz blinked. "He was just a deadbeat drunk, I guess. I don't know what to tell you. He was hardly even around by the end of it. Oh, look!" Liz pulled herself upright and looked out the window at the orange rooftops zipping past. The smell of soot and ash were already seeping into the coach. "We're here."

They tumbled out into hot, chalky air alongside the handful of stragglers whose stop was San Ojuela. The engine hissed. The wheels began to churn again, faster and faster, as the coaches slid onward. In the slivers between them Elizabeth caught the shape of a man watching her from the other side. He wore black, tattered clothes; rust-stained gauze wrapped his face. But she lost him in the blur, and by the time the train was gone, the tracks were empty. October leaves swirled where he'd stood.

Right, Elizabeth told herself. *Just another ghost.*

The apparition left her with a sad feeling, like the first one she'd met, years ago on a rocky beach. That ghost's dress had been damp, blue with yellow flowers but brown where blood stained it. It wept softy where the waves crashed against the boulders. "Are you lost?" Elizabeth asked the ghost girl. Ten yards away a dog crouched with hackles raised, growling. The seagulls kept their distance too.

"Do you need help?" Elizabeth said, a bit louder this time. "Maybe I can help you."

The girl stopped crying. "Oh?"

Elizabeth couldn't make out a clear face, but maybe that was because of the sun in her eyes. "What are you looking for?"

"I..." The girl started weeping again. "I'm sorry. I don't remember."

Now the coast was miles away. The sky bled charcoal from the northern fires. Mountains jutted up all around them. And still there were ghosts.

In the Uber, they drove through downtown blocks where the trees were adorned with fairy lights; jack-o-lanterns, cobwebs, and plastic spiders filled every shop window. Outdoor dining tables spilled onto a walk-only street, and a green sign reading *Welcome to San Ojuela* hung off a steel arch over the intersection. They passed craft breweries, freshly painted condos, and gated communities before Elizabeth recognized something familiar—the Mexican bodega their father used to take them to on Sundays for menudo and pan dulce. Abandoned now.

Mary asked, "Does Dad still live here?" A question that smelled of liquor and stirred the angry, hungry thing Elizabeth thought she'd buried at the bottom of the pit of her guts.

"Oh. No," Elizabeth said, trying to sound distracted, listening to the radio. But the woman was talking about a massive Día de los Muertos ofrenda in downtown LA, dedicated to all the undocumented lost souls.

"Oh," Mary said.

"He hasn't in a while. Marisol was the only one left."

The boba café the driver brought the girls to was a "saloon" that occupied the corner of a decaying strip mall where plywood boarded up several storefronts. It, too, looked closed from out front, but the driver said it was open.

Inside, a ceiling fan spun slowly, creaking heat and stale air across the saloon. The shades were drawn and the interior lighting dim. Elizabeth's eyes adjusted to the dimness and focused on the hollowed-out sockets of a plastic skeleton hanging in the window. She stared for so long into the blackness of the sockets that they no longer looked painted. They became real voids.

I'm not scared of you, Coco.

She jumped when her sister tugged on her sleeve. "Fuck's sake. What do you want, Mary?"

"They only take cash."

As Elizabeth fished for loose dollars in her wallet, Mary eyed her up and down, then the skeleton hanging next to her. "You gonna kiss him or what?" Mary said as she took seven dollars from Elizabeth.

Elizabeth clenched her jaw. Relaxed. "You know? Maybe. He doesn't look half bad, really. Just a little bone-headed."

Mary rolled her eyes and went back to the register. Elizabeth tapped her foot, waiting, wanting to get out of the saloon and town and be anywhere but here. She needed more time. She thought of the bookstore Marisol used to take her to—replaced with a pet spa; they'd passed it on the way. The bakery where an abuelita used to give Elizabeth and Mary conchas with crumbly seashell tops—that had been torn down too, and an *On the Border* restaurant built on its site, complete with a sign for margarita happy hours. The town of Elizabeth's memory was gutted. Bits and pieces of it ripped out and replaced, its identity distorted. And she'd grown and swelled beyond her place within it, too—a giant returning, too afraid to step and crush it under her boot.

The ceiling fan creaked.

Three men played cards silently at a back table, cross-hatched by shadows and sun peeking through the blinds. The barista served

Mary her drink. Elizabeth moved toward the door, but Mary had stopped to take pictures of the menu.

"Come on, let's go," Elizabeth said. Mary waved her off.

"If we're going to be here awhile, I need to familiarize myself with the options."

"But we're not staying long," Elizabeth snapped. "It's just one weekend. We're doing what we have to, then getting out quick."

Mary ignored her.

"I said let's go! The driver's waiting." She only meant to tug on Mary's sleeve, not yank her by the wrist and make her yelp and stagger, interrupting the quiet card game at the back table.

The men were staring. Elizabeth's face reddened. "I'm sorry!" she said. "My kid sister. A handful. El oh el!"

"I'm fourteen," Mary protested.

Silence. The fan squeaked above them.

"Right. So," Elizabeth said. "Sorry."

She had her hand on the door when the man in the middle spoke up loud enough that his voice carried across the saloon. "You girls not from around here, are ya?" His voice was thick, and he spoke with an accent that reminded her of her father.

Mary slurped boba and chewed loudly on the tapioca balls. "Get a load of this guy," she whispered.

Elizabeth flinched a smile. "Just visiting."

"It's not the safest place to be a stranger. Especially for little girls."

Goosebumps prickled up Elizabeth's arms. "We're—not strangers. My aunt lives here." Lived. *You saw her ghost.* "I used to live here. Down the road a ways."

"I've never seen you. I'd remember a face like that."

Mary interjected, "We lived here a long time ago. Before this place sucked ass."

The man shot up, his wood chair blowing back against the blinds. He might as well have grabbed for an imaginary gun at his hip, but his friends crowded around and settled him back into his seat. "Whoa, whoa there, bud." One of them turned to the girls and said, "Sorry. He's had a bit to drink."

Mary tilted her head. "It's boba, though?"

The drunk guy jabbed a finger toward Mary but kept his eyes on Liz. "You keep an eye on your sister there, yeah? People like you. Come through from LA, make their yoga gyms and vegan restaurants, ruin the place. But you know how many people like you go missing around here? Yeah. Just look at the signs. Me? I've been here all my life. I'm not going nowhere."

People like you. As if all it took to sever them from him was the Spanish they didn't know. Never mind the smells, the tastes that were so familiar: sweet mango, charred pastor, guajillo chiles. The stares they all got from the same worried eyes.

"Is that a threat?" Mary smiled wickedly, stepping forward before Elizabeth could do a thing to stop her, filling up the room with all five feet two inches of her. Elizabeth tugged her arm.

"Mary. Stop."

"It's friendly advice," the man said, staring Mary down. He was ignoring Elizabeth, expecting the real fight to come from anyone but her.

"We're not afraid of you," Elizabeth said, suddenly pissed as hell. "We're the girls who lived on Canyon Crest Street, south of Ojuela Ranch and the orange groves. You know the place." The words crackled like gunfire, *bang! bang!*—driving the men back, leaving them slack-jawed.

Had they ever been brave? They looked like beaten dogs more than anything else.

Their hands look like Dad's.

The men stared at the girls, realization in the shine of their eyes. They knew the house she meant. Pride—a glaring, raging beast—swelled up within Elizabeth.

Yes, the famous sisters from your town's stupid little urban legend. We're back. We survived.

ACT II
What Dread Hand

ONE
The Law Man Comes
(The Case of Sonora Madrigal)

I DRIVE TO THE SAME PLACE I always do when the work day has dragged on too long with its court orders and committee meetings in stiff rooms, and when my uniform has started pinching my elbows, shoulders, and knees all wrong. But today's been worse than usual. Behind every piece of thick, professional paper I've scratched my signature into, I've seen claws splitting metal, teeth ripping tires like the birds rip up a dead dog on the side of the road, leaving its guts bashed against the soundwall.

A brief ride with the windows cracked and the wind whipping my face is usually enough to steady my hands and numb the uniform pinches. But sometimes, like today, I keep on driving, an hour past the county line to Riverside where the dirt is redder and the mountains close in like gaping jaws. I always end up back here sooner or later: pulling up to the home of Sonora Madrigal.

The heat is feral, snapping at everything, and the sun casts long shadows that would make a superstitious man think of ghouls or desert wendigos. Instead, I'm thinking how Gran's house isn't too far from here.

Diana's still on the phone asking if I'll be back in time for dinner. It takes a repeat or two for the words to sink in, and for me to finally register the sound of her voice nudging my ear like a faint gear squeak. Sometimes, when I come out here, I tell her not to worry about it, or that I'm out for cigarettes. It's a cruel joke that I shouldn't find amusing but do. An effective cliché, repeated so that if I really don't come back one day, she'll learn to joke about it and tell her friends I just went out to get cigarettes. She'll never have to say I died on the job. It's what I told Mom when I moved out, after Dad got so upset about my new job aspirations that we fought in the yard. I pulled away from him, panting and covered in grass strains, because I was stronger, younger, and a bigger person than he'd ever been. What did he know? He'd told me to be a man; that's what I became.

Where are you going? Mom had called when I set off, the sum total of my belongings in the passenger seat of my car.

Out for cigarettes.

Yeah, I'll make it, I tell Diana through the phone. I'm gonna be held in for about an hour, but that's it. I'll be home soon enough. Love you.

Okay, love you too.

She hangs up.

Engine's still humming.

Back home, staying up past bedtime earned you a spanking with the belt, Dad's big one with the brass Texas buckle that would split tally dashes in your skin if it clipped you on its edge. He wanted to instill respect and obedience in his kids; we did our best, but now and again trouble came calling anyways, dressed up as late-night *Dragon Ball* reruns or mockumentary haunting shows. Javier preferred the cartoons and I the dramatic, shaky-cam reenactments of the supernatural. Sometimes we managed to compromise and would watch a show together with hushed voices and our blankets sheltering us and the TV screen. Other times we resorted to fists and elbows, and Dad would catch us, obviously. Rodrigo being the youngest meant he was quick to run and hide and beg for the forgiveness he always got. Javier would play stupid, but that never saved him. I was the oldest, the responsible one who knew better and should have led by example, and for that I tasted the belt licks first. But it was worth it, staying up to watch those paranormal shows. I'd always be up at six the next morning to walk with Gran down the block to the bakery, with questions of the supernatural prepped and ready for her to answer, which she always did. She'd have some story to answer with, or at least she'd know some guy whose prima was bedeviled by some spirit, or the devil.

I grew out of those things eventually. Belts with brass knuckles bit more than ghost stories excited me, and I learned that the real violent creatures live in your own home, down the hall in the bed where your mother sleeps.

Driving to Riverside, I thought of the vampires and chupacabras Gran would fill my head up with. All fangs and claws. Those names were also written on the stained pages of Sonora Madrigal's case file, forever pressed there in crisp black ink—shadows behind the testimony of a half-grieving, half-hysterical woman, reminders of the horror stories I'd given up when it was time to be a man. I shook them out of my head and out the windows of my car to land on the gritty roads pulling away behind me. I told myself I didn't need them; I'd outgrown the supernatural a long time ago.

Coughs and soft medical beeps echo from patient rooms as I sit in the reception area, waiting for Sonora to return from her work shift to this home-turned-hospice. Someone's muttering, *Shit! Shit!* from a cracked-open door, and I'm trying to ignore the smell of wax and cheap hand sanitizer that burns my nose like tequila. The air conditioning is crisp where the sun slapped my back.

Would you like some water?

It's Carrie asking. Sonora's aunt and the owner of this hospice. She's let Sonora live here since the incident, and I always ask how her day's been when I see her. Usually she smiles and says, "Pues, ahí va." But today she's tensed up, rocklike. The other nurses shoot scurrying glances at me as they dart down the hallways.

Because I'm still in my uniform. After hours, I change into a loose t-shirt, but for once I'm here on the clock. They're all Latina here, and none of them like cops. Give him dark skin and suddenly they don't know what to think, asking themselves, should they be less scared? Or more?

I'm sure they prefer me like this, though, compared with the type of agent I used to be when I first came around. Not that it bothers me any. Our opinions might differ but they're just that. *Opinions.* Carrie's an honest woman, doing her best to provide, and there's nothing wrong with that. I understand this, even if they don't.

No, thank you, I tell her. How much longer until Sonora gets home?

A few more minutes now.

The air conditioning kicks into a sprint from its jog, wheezing out as much cool breath as it can manage while the sun keeps beating down outside. The wind has picked up too; it's battering the windows. The beeps get louder. The sounds claw over one another: pencil scratches, shifting pants, dishes clanging, flies buzzing, dogs barking outside. A sneeze. A sigh. Phone tapping. A football game crowd cheering. The wind howling.

Howling like it did the night I found Sonora.

We'd corralled the detainees inside when the alarms first blared, before the night sky tore open and raked the earth with lightning fingernails, sand whipping with the wind and rain. The dogs were going rabid. The line between desert and sky had smeared entirely, or the desert had wrapped us in itself—its raging fury. I followed

ACT II: WHAT DREAD HAND

the facility's chain-link fence, rushing from one watchtower to the next, shouting, Anyone still out here?

Never venturing beyond the shafts of light.

Sand pellets popped against my goggles and gloves, the kind that cut up your nose and mouth and ears if you expose them. I was wrapped in my windbreaker, had a bandana pulled over my mask, and still the storm grabbed me, tugged me this way and that and wouldn't let go. Then a scream cut through the rage.

Yes? Hello? Is there anyone still outside?

The wind pulled the fence—thwacked it back against the support beams. Again, again.

Another scream. It came from beyond the fence, where the storm choked out the lights and the darkness was thick, heavy, warm. I waded towards it. Another scream.

I remember fear.

It's Sonora who nudges me awake. She's staring at me in the afternoon dimness. One eye deep brown, the other stained red around a grey pupil. She's younger than I am but stress has carved her face. She's still wearing her blue and mustard work vest and keys hang between her fingers.

Sheriff Jackson, she says. I didn't know you were coming.

Sheriff Jackson? She never calls me that. It rakes like nails over dirt to hear it from her mouth. For a moment I'm sitting there not knowing what to say until I flick the brim of that stupid hat, and I laugh.

Forgot I was wearing it, I tell her, setting it on the coffee table. She picks it up when she sits down and begins to fiddle with it. Her shirt's open just enough for the fabric to bend away and flash the ugly webbing of scars across her chest.

I don't know why they make me wear it, I say.

I think it rather suits you. She pinches the hat. Her smile always makes me think of blood splashed on pale dirt. She says: It's like you're a cowboy, you know? Tell me, do you ever imagine yourself as a lone ranger with that big iron on your hip?

I do my best to ask catching-up questions first, like the way we used to talk before my job demanded more and more of me. She tells me about a guy she's been messaging online, and about how she helps Carrie with the hospice when she's not at her other job, trying to climb her way out of the mountain of medical debt she's found herself in. I tell her how the job's been treating me: I can't complain. I tell her about the growing silence between Diana and me, and share some on-the-job stories. I mention the officer who beat his wife, and I tell her about reports of some person who wanders San Ojuela's streets at night, masked and lurking in shadows. My own guys have seen them, but they always vanish by the time we corner them. Everyone's too afraid to speak on them though.

That all sounds very hard-boiled, Sonora says, smirking. That kind of strangeness only happens in towns like that—

Her voice catches in her throat. She peeks at the envelope I've had on my lap since I came in here, and her smile drops away.

You're not here just to catch up, are you?

In the last few months of my old job, after they'd sewn her back up enough that she no longer needed to live plugged into a hospital bed, I used to spend my evenings here, piecing together the shards of her testimony from that night. She'd hiss through the medical numbness, I'm not going to tell you shit about my brother, and I'd tell her I wasn't there for work, just to make sense of it all in my own mind. But the truth was that I'd been the one who found her, and it had branded a sense of parental responsibility onto me, a need to see her safely through to the end. Eventually, my strings of questions filled out into conversations, shared stories of growing up in the kind of town where stepping through metal detectors was the ticket into school. Jokes invited belly laughs, and eventually Sonora forgave me for who I'd been the night we met. Maybe that's why I keep coming back even now. She knew me before they dressed me in beige and pinned a heavy, gold-plated badge to my chest. I sit up straight, refuse the urge to shift in my seat, and try to be the Law Man I've become.

I tell her, No. Not just to catch up.

Millimeters open between us as she pushes back against the couch, as if trying to squeeze herself between the cushions. What's changed, she asks.

More missing people.

I hand her the file, knowing full well that this is a breach of security and I could lose my job if she ever came out with any of it, but I trust her. She fans out the laminated photographs, looks at the Dodge carcass, the charred seats, the claw marks gashing open metal.

I tell her the pieces of the story that have made homes in the gutters between my thoughts. The body we found last month in Riverside with the same injuries as the ones we keep finding on others, freshly buried in unmarked graves or left out in the desert: her throat slit, heart torn out. The vaquero's story of missing cows. The car ripped to shreds by something that makes me think of the monsters Gran used to tell me about.

Then there's Sonora—what she saw in the dark that night. Her memory of the storm exists in broad strokes. Her brother had been an activist—a coyote, smuggling immigrants across the border—who disappeared one day, his truck never pulling back up to their family's driveway at dusk. Sonora drained her savings looking for him, spent weeks in this dry mouth of a desert. She was alone out there the night of the storm, the night she claims a monster tore her open.

We've been here before, me questioning her like all the investigators, lawyers, psychologists, and insurance agents. None of us ever entertained her idea that the monster she spoke of was a literal one. That's why I'm here, I realize. Why I sat through the constriction of Saturday traffic to get here, and why I cannot drain Gran's stories of ancestors and faith from my head.

I point to the photographs between us and ask, What creature would you say could do that?

What about the creature you described back then?
Didn't you say it had claws?
Do coyotes have claws like that?

You mentioned that when you were a girl one of the street dogs bit your thigh, after you said you weren't afraid and the other girls dared you to pet it, right? And you've been scared of them ever since?

Sonora digs fingernails into the couch leather, which groans. I tell her that I'm right here, that she doesn't have to be afraid. I tell her, Nobody is going to hurt you, you just have to tell me about that animal.

But she shakes her head and insists, I don't want to think about it.

I stab my fingers on the photographs. That's why I'm here, I say. I'm trying to help people.

Help people, she snaps with a laugh or a sob—I'm not sure which. She keeps going: You patrolled those walls so many nights. Did you ever keep count of how many people came through, or were you too busy applying to city after city in the hopes that any department would pick you up and push you through the academy and hand you a cop badge?

Sonora—

Lucas, you already know everything! I've told you!

But the other part. About—the chupacabra.

I say it aloud. Let the word breathe between us, undoing all the years of therapy she's had to remind her that there is no such thing. That monsters aren't real, it's only evil people who are real.

Chupacabra.

Sonora's red eye holds me now, bloodshot, never fully healed. It makes her look twisted, like something she's not. Like whatever she says isn't her words, but the Mal de Ojo's. I've told her about Dad, and belts, and spiteful rebellion that manifested as shoplifting. I admitted to her long ago that my high-school years were full of nights spent in county jails, and she forgave me. She understood why law enforcement was the only job my blunt and clumsy hands could ever have been good at.

Patients are looking toward us now, peeking through their yawning doors. Carrie's watching from the kitchen. The wind is spanking shutters.

My uniform's strangling my chest, and I'm struggling to breathe, but I sit here, take it, and eventually Sonora shuts her eyes to concentrate.

I remember he promised me things, she finally mumbles. If I could get what he needed, he'd help me too. He was kind—he said all the right things, that he believed in my brother's cause. He wanted to help, and all it would cost was a rag of my brother's favorite shirt, and the locks of hair I took from his bed. Some snake's venom and coyote blood. Then, he would find him.

My heart's clawing at my ribs; I'm forgetting to breathe. It's all new, this information spilling word by word into a shadow man between us, staring me down with a smudged-up face.

Sonora's quivering. She says: He showed me how the night rippled to the push and pull of the moon. He fixed my asthma, he wiped away the pain in my knees. But he did it with this awful rotting hand, and—and—fuck! She smacks palms to her head. I can't remember the rest.

Remember what? I ask too quickly, leering like an idiot.

He's a vampire!

She says it the same way she did the night I found her—after we'd corralled the migrants to shield them from the storm, shuffled them inside the cellar where they'd stay for sixteen hours with rationed water and no food and nowhere to sit, just standing in the stink, chests to shoulders and elbows to stomachs, while we made sure the storm didn't rip the whole facility out of the dirt. The dogs were howling, the wind barking at my ears. I found Sonora in the crimson light of a watchtower beam, fingers wrapped around the chain links, the wind slapping the fence repeatedly against the beams.

I ran and touched those hands—freezing through my gloves. I tried to pry her away but those fingers were locked. I called for help, but no one could hear over the ragged wind. All the while she whispered verse after bloody verse in Spanish, her heart thumping in the scraping air, exposed and raw and bloody and beating through the tear in her ribcage.

Ayudame, ayudame.

Now she's wiping tears from her eyes.

He sucks the life out of you, she says—emotions, memories, until you can't feel anymore, or can't remember, because he's siphoned it all up. I remember that, but I can't anymore, Lucas. I can't. I don't want to talk about this anymore.

She's rocking in her seat now. Carrie is rubbing her back, easing her toward the land of the present and inland heat. She says: Things still look for me at night. Snakes and dead owls. After work I hear coyotes chittering, and I hold mace all the way to my car in parking lots.

I want my mom, she begs, even though we both know she is gone, has been gone, and there's nothing anyone can do to bring back the dead.

Sonora, all I need is a name, I tell her. This man, is he still alive? A name, a face, anything I can use to find him. Was he a coyote too?

She looks at me cold, her face gone slack, and she laughs, one *Ha*. Full of scorn.

ACT II: WHAT DREAD HAND

You were there too, Lucas. The only reason you've kept coming back *years* later is because you don't want to believe your own memory. You want *me* to change what *you* saw.

Then she waits.

Lucas, what did you see out there? That made you quit ICE. What monster finally scared you?

I leave her after that. Hiding under the brim of my sheriff's hat, I thank Carrie for the water and head to the door. Something chirps in the parking lot and I flinch like an idiot. My left hand already on my hip. For a heartbeat I'm back in the howling storm, holding Sonora as my vest sponges up her blood, sticky and heavy, and I'm shining my flashlight out into the darkness and rage because there is something else screaming out there, I can hear it. I'm sweeping my light to flash the shape of its jaws, its feathery mane, before it backs away and sheds its edges, becoming one with the shadows twisting in the storm.

Something groans and I jolt around, hand on my hip and waiting. It's two nurses leaving the hospice at the end of their shifts. They're both watching me with horrified eyes and I tell them with a laugh, My bad, before I take my hand off my belt and the weapon hanging heavy from it.

I stand here in the parking lot, looking at the hospice. It occurs to me that people can live their whole lives and die in the same rut they're born in. How sad.

In my car I wait, tapping my fingers on the wheel. Waiting for what?

A call, maybe.

My phone rests in my hand. The screen's dark. Mom doesn't live that far from here, just twenty more minutes down the freeway, right before the mountains and high desert on the other side. Gran will be there. With her sweet voice, and her way of speaking that always eases me. Hush, child, she used to say when Dad's yells startled me tight. It's alright, it's alright.

Javier will be there, and Rodrigo too. Not Dad; he's dead. His heart gave out in the living room late one night after he watched some boxing match on TV, and Mom found him in the morning with cheap infomercials flashing off him. It happened before I could transfer out of ICE and into the Sheriff's Department, before I could tell him, Look, I'm standing here, and you're all the way down there. He denied me that. Had to get one last lash in.

I often think about going back to see Mom and reintroducing my new self to the family, answering their questions while sitting on those plastic covers Mom's fitted over every couch we've ever owned. But the truth is, outside of Christmas, I hardly ever go.

TWO
Inventory

"ALRIGHT, LAST ONE." Elizabeth's father had sat at the foot of her bed, his weight denting the mattress, bending her world into his orbit. His smell of pine and wood chips eased her—as much a part of her father as the calluses on his rough hands. "So listen carefully, or you'll miss its point. This one's a favorite of mine."

I won't miss it, Elizabeth had thought. *I'll remember.*

A dark sea of wool separated the two of them. Candlelight licked both the rough and gentle creases of her father's grin. His brow and left cheek were bathed in pale moonlight. He flipped through his slim book of poems, moth-chewed at the edges, with white creases striping the spine. He'd read Elizabeth two stories already, one about a fatherless prince coming back to reclaim his throne and the other about a mischievous god who'd coerced a mortal into putting his body back together again—she hadn't liked them. Not as much as she used to. Elizabeth was nearing ten, and a life of double digits was staring down at her, getting closer. Ten-year-olds weren't supposed to enjoy their fathers' bedtime stories.

And yet she'd asked for one more. To keep him from going back into the hallway and leaving her alone again. She didn't want another epic fantasy, though—her favorite characters always died—

nor did she want ghost stories like La Llorona or El Coco, either. Tiresome.

"I just want a story where everyone lives," she told him.

"That's not up to me."

Poetry was their middle ground. He'd always loved it, and she'd always loved the familiar rasp of his voice after weeks where she'd heard it only over fleeting phone calls. But tonight, he was there: flesh and bone, speaking gently.

> *Tyger Tyger, burning bright,*
> *In the forests of the night;*
> *What immortal hand or eye,*
> *Could frame thy fearful symmetry?*
>
> *In what distant deeps or skies,*
> *Burnt the fire of thine eyes?*
> *On what wings dare he aspire?*
> *What the hand, dare seize the fire?*

Her father's accent crept in as he spoke in that storytelling voice of his. It was always there—Spanish coiled under his tongue no matter how hard he tried to rid himself of it. But it always peeked out just a bit more when he returned from his long work trips, and when he lost himself in verse.

The clock shone a neon twelve from the bedside table. Mary was already fast asleep beside Elizabeth; her hand had gone limp in Elizabeth's grip. Her warm breaths brushed the nape of Elizabeth's neck. Elizabeth should have been asleep too; Tía Marisol never let them stay up past ten. But sleepiness only tugged on her eyelids; her mind was as awake as the full moon outside. Beyond the open window, the night sighed, the candles flickered. Candles, because Elizabeth had asked for them. Not because she preferred them over nightlights or the blue glow from a cell phone, which she also used to fight away the darkness that crept and the shadows that groaned whenever she was the only living thing awake throughout the house. She'd asked for the candles because it took time to light them. Gentleness was required to kindle the flame. When her father did it, well, that meant he had nowhere else to be but here.

The poem ended almost the same way it began.

> *Tyger, Tyger burning bright,*
> *In the forests of the night:*
> *What immortal hand or eye,*
> *Dare frame thy fearful symmetry?*

When he finished, he let silence fill the room for effect. Breathed in the summer's cool night air. He shut the book. Outside the wind stirred and Mary shivered. Cold stiffened Elizabeth's spine.

"It's just the wind," her father said.

Elizabeth turned away, feeling the warm rush in her face. She'd thought he wouldn't notice that time. She tried her best to hide her flinches at the moaning of the wind and the bat chirps, because ten-year-olds should not be afraid of such things. Her father had seen through her anyway.

He said, "I can check again, you know. If you'd like?"

She nodded. He got up and checked in the closet, under the bed, out in the hallway. "No monsters, no ghosts."

But there had been something. She'd heard it scratching between the walls. Muffled. Constant. Right above her head. Mary had heard it too, but neither of the girls could do a thing about it except call for their father, who'd just returned home and was downstairs with Tía Marisol, who never cared about the sounds in the walls—she'd joke about spirits, even though the girls never found it funny.

"Even if they're real, they won't hurt you," she'd say. "You just have to get along with them. Casa Coyotl is their home too. And they're mostly just sad, anyways."

When Elizabeth's father reached the window where the curtains rippled with moonlight, the coyotes were howling again. "No ghosts out there either. Just animals."

They always howled, their high shrieks scraping the night—why locals called the property *Coyote House*. In Spanish mixed with Nahuatl, *Casa Coyotl*. But no one knew its original name anymore. That was something only the soil remembered.

He tugged on the curtains, on both sides of the window. "Still solid," he said.

During the first months at their new home, when Elizabeth had caught sight of anguished faces in the dark corners of long hallways or high, vaulted ceilings, her father had invented the story that curtains were sentries invented to tangle up ghosts. "To stop them from ever getting in," he'd say.

Now, Elizabeth raised an eyebrow at him. She was older. The trick had gone stale. "They're just curtains."

"Well, let's pretend otherwise," he said.

"Okay." Elizabeth smiled. Mary shivered against her. "She's cold."

The girls' father slid the window shut, muffling the sighs of the wind and the howls of the coyotes. The curtains went limp. Mary yawned in the stillness.

"You're right, it feels much better," he sighed. Exhaustion seeped from him. It sagged the lids of his eyes and darkened the skin beneath them. He hadn't slept in days. For once Elizabeth almost asked him where he'd gone off to this time and what new job he was planning to disappear to next. Another welding gig? More carpet laying? The words bubbled up and she almost let them out, hoping that it would be different this time and he wouldn't brush off the question. Wouldn't ruin their moment.

But that would break their unspoken agreement: she trusted

that he'd come home, eventually. Always. As long as she was there waiting, he'd return.

When he'd come home earlier that evening, he'd stumbled and Tía Marisol had pounced on him, slashing with her sharp and nasty words. That was Marisol: full of quiet fires that only blazed out in controlled bursts. Still, it was enough to scare Elizabeth out of ever intervening.

Tía Marisol should have been with them. When their father read, she usually lingered in the doorway with her hands clasped around a tazita of champurrado. But tonight the doorway was shut. Tía Marisol was somewhere else within the quiet corridors of the house, talking to herself the way she always did. Sometimes Tía Marisol spoke so naturally to herself that Elizabeth would think someone was actually there, and not just the dark and empty space, but no one ever was.

Her father came back to the side of the bed, the old floor groaning with each heavy step. "I forget you two haven't developed your insulation yet," he said, making sure to keep his voice low so as to not disturb Mary. He patted his gut. "Would you believe me, if I told you I used to be thinner?"

"Mom said you were very handsome."

"Huh." He smiled. "She said that? When?"

"Last time we visited her."

"Huh."

He was a block of a man, with mountainous shoulders and baseball-mitt hands too thick for intricacies or arts, hands that thrived as tools. Behind him, the moon shone high and the wind was a hum muted by the glass. He slipped the poetry book back into its spot on the shelf.

"Why is it a cemetery?" Elizabeth blurted.

He paused, turned. "What do you mean?"

"I don't get it. I like it—just don't get it. Why is the tiger in a cemetery? And why is the cemetery afraid? It's not a person...I mean, I can forgive that. But it shouldn't be scared, it's got all the ghosts there."

"Maybe it's scared of the tiger," he muttered to himself. Then he laughed. "Pinche niña, it's not a cemetery. It's *symmetry*."

"Symmetry?"

"Like symmetrical, when both halves look the same." He showed her with his hands. He talked with his hands a lot, those giant hands.

"Oh," she said.

"Yeah," he smiled.

He leaned in to plant a kiss on Elizabeth's cheek and tucked her in the bed, then took the candles from the nightstand and went to the door. The shadows moved with him.

"But why is it *symmetry*, then?" Elizabeth asked. "That makes even less sense." She wondered about the tiger, too: whether it was meant to be scary. She did not find it scary; she thought tigers were rather cute. Animal Planet said that, aside from the fangs and half ton of lean muscle, they were just like normal cats. Like Tía Marisol's cat, Angel Eyes—and Angel Eyes didn't do much of anything but sneak food when she wasn't supposed to. Elizabeth would have chosen a snake for the poem, because those had fangs too, but also deep-slit eyes and no legs. Snakes were horrifying.

Her father moved his tongue behind his cheek. "Well. It's a bit abstract. The tiger is nature. Like it's symmetrical, as in the stripes, and that shows God's power? Because he made the stripes symmetrical. I think."

Elizabeth scrunched up her face. She didn't get it.

Her father pinched his brow. "You know what, that's not it at all. The truth is more sinister—a fire in the forest can no longer be stopped, or controlled, even if God created it. The fire is nature like the tiger, and if it was God against a tiger, I think this tells us the tiger would win."

Silence.

He laughed. "But what do I know—it's too late for this, and my brain's gone dumb. Who cares if it means anything at all, as long as it sounds good, right?"

"I guess," Elizabeth said. "But—" She searched for a way to make him stay just a little longer. "Say it *was* a cemetery. What could make a cemetery afraid of a tiger?"

He cracked open the door to let in a sliver of electric light from the hall. He pinched out the candle flame and his face disappeared into shadow; a faint smell of smoke lingered in the air. "Maybe the tiger keeps bringing *people* there. Good night, my love!"

"Good night."

He shut the door and there was only moonlight. Elizabeth crawled under the covers and drifted to sleep, knowing he'd be there in the morning.

Birds chirped. The autumn heat was vicious and heavy, and the smoke from the fires up north had yawned in, chalking Elizabeth's throat and sheeting the air grainy like cheap slaughterhouse horror films. The girls, one grown up now and the other nearly so, were climbing the front steps of Casa Coyotl, their had-been home.

The double doors were splintered open, the lock bent inwards, like something sharp had bit into the metal. Cool air escaped between them. Mary reached for the copper handle but Elizabeth tugged her arm back. "Hold on, don't be stupid," she said. "Whoever did this might still be inside."

"Nonsense," Mary said. "Whoever's burgled us isn't burgling in broad daylight. It's *been* broken."

Seeing no flaws in that observation, Elizabeth nodded but glanced back at the road. One last chance to run. Dozens of windows watched them from high up, glossy and black. The bell tower still stood. The cacti and flowers that padded the edges of the house where its walls met the dirt still stood, not even quivering in the breeze but stuck. Stiff. Waiting. The walls were still white, the roof still red. The house was the same as she'd left it, but even from outside she could feel that it was empty. All life had been drained out and now it was old; all its weight sagged into the earth. An admission to Mary that it was the dead things waiting on the other side of the door she feared, not the living ones, caught between Elizabeth's teeth.

Mary nudged her. "Don't be shy, open her up."

Elizabeth swallowed. A gentle tap was all it took, and the doors yawned wide. If Elizabeth had ever planned to heed her dead tía's words, that opportunity was gone. There they were, standing in the maw.

They started their list in that entryway—the task their mother had assigned to them when she dropped them off at a sea-breeze-filled terminal back home. Make the list, separate the things into what needs to be fixed and what can stay as it is and what can be thrown to the curb for the garbage crew.

First there was the splintered door, where Marisol had leaned against the frame the day Elizabeth and Mary and their father first arrived, her arms crossed, a worried smile on her face. Then there was the grandfather clock, whose chime used to reach Elizabeth's room in the dead of night, when she couldn't sleep and the world was still. Its pendulum didn't move. Elizabeth jotted this down on her phone and took pictures of the cracks spiderwebbing the walls and the places where the paint was curling away.

She lingered in the foyer before moving on and checked it again—not for broken things, but for ghosts—compelled to find out if the house was supernaturally haunted or just another place where terrible things had happened. As she'd learned through her years of researching haunted houses and ghost-sighting testimonies online, places could be haunted with more than just ghosts: arguments, violence, empty bourbon bottles, slurs that trapped bodies between their letters.

Sometimes it was the place itself that died and haunted you.

And if the house was a dead thing—the foyer its head—then the drawing room was its liver, the kitchen its belly, the hallways its arms, its legs the side cottages and the catering kitchen, its feet the dark husk that was once stables, the hands the gardens, and at the center of it all the heart, the courtyard of the house, giant and empty like the hole inside Elizabeth. If she'd left her soul here in Casa Coyotl, maybe the ghosts could tell her where she'd left it. Because it had to still be here, right? Trapped in a locket or lantern like in the movies, as a flame or maybe a shadow—she didn't know which it would be, or how it worked. Only that Marisol used to tell her, "A soul isn't just a part of your body; it sticks to places and things too." If she could find it here, then she would no longer be two separate things, her body way out there, her mind within, sunken and numb, somewhere deep and cold and damp and always sinking in just a little more, every day. Her soul would fill that void—bind her back into arms and legs—and she wouldn't ever have to drag a razor's edge across her thighs to pull her back, stop her from sinking any further.

Elizabeth only needed to know what kind of shape she was looking for. How to recognize it if she came across it. The ghosts were meant to help her—why else had La Muerte given her the sight?

In the nautically themed powder room off the foyer, she found that one of the twin sinks didn't work. Several doorknobs jiggled loosely in their sockets when Elizabeth twisted them, but no ghosts.

In the courtyard she found rot in wood trimmings and gashes of bare concrete where floor tiles had crumbled away. No ghosts.

In smoky guest-room windows, she looked outside past the cacti and flower gardens to the fourteen-acre woods within the property walls—the remains of a once-was forest full of pines and willows and cypress trees, kept alive by the lake after the dams were built and the rest of the landscape crackled and dried. Elizabeth scanned the shadows beneath the trees, hoping for that movie moment where she'd glimpse a phantom figure watching or catch a clue at the corner of her eye—anything that could lead her. She wasn't picky. But all she saw were disappointing October leaves. If this was a horror movie, the house was not playing its part. Did it even care that she was back?

She listened to the air, thought she heard talking, and followed that sound to the dining room, where years ago her father had begged Tía Marisol to let them stay.

Their argument had been soft scissor snips. Elizabeth's father sat at the dining table—he had his moustache then, and combed his dark hair back neat—and Tía Marisol stood over him, her dress a wall of black. She held a mug of champurrado, the hot drink of thick atole that she always had with her because her bones were always cold.

"I don't see how that falls on *my* shoulders, George," Marisol was saying. "This is no place for a *literal toddler*." She pointed to Mary, who was sitting by the window with Elizabeth, too preoccupied with the stiff dolls Marisol had given the girls to notice she was being talked about. "There are loose nails everywhere—and the railings are shit. Neither of us could keep our eyes on both of them at all times—half the things here are rusted, for tetanus's sake. And what kind of mother just gives her kids up? I didn't ask for this—I don't want this. I don't."

Elizabeth had been trying so hard to figure out what the words meant, growing frustrated at the tones, the snips, the sharp words. It was all bubbling up in her chest and now it seemed she was going to cry.

Mary tapped her on the arm. "Do you hear that?"

A crawling sound in the walls, a scurrying.

"A squirrel!" Mary laughed.

Elizabeth nodded. "Maybe."

"What do you want me to do?" their father continued. "Send her back like an Amazon package?"

"Yes! For the love of god, *yes!* It might be the most sane idea you've had all day. What do I know about raising kids?"

That made him laugh. It was, at first, a single sudden *ha*, but that built up until he fought to hold in the laughter that still slipped out enough for both girls to look his way. Elizabeth laughed, then Mary too and eventually even Marisol. That was their father's power, always getting everyone laughing.

When the laughing died down, Elizabeth's father shook his head. "I'm not going to split them up. This is just for a little while, only until Kat can get her business going."

Marisol pinched her brow. "I know, her *consulting* business. It's set you guys back a lot, hasn't it?"

"And it's long hours," he added. "And expensive flights, and weeks gone from home. I'm going to help with what I can, you know? Do some welding, contracting, send the money back her way and she'll still see the girls on weekends. If she gets the business going and starts making some *real* money, then it will be worth it for the girls in the long run. We just—need a helping hand."

"And you?" Marisol asked. "Will it be worth it for you?"

"I'm the sacrifice I'm willing to make." He shrugged, smiled even as he said it. He was always making sure the girls never saw anything but confidence in his grin. "I'll be fine, don't worry about me."

Marisol would worry about him, though; she never hid her worry from him or the girls. All Elizabeth knew from Marisol was worry. About where they'd gone off to, where they were going. Her sadness was a mold that had long since seeped beneath her skin.

Marisol sighed, said, "Alright." She hugged him, then walked over to the girls with outstretched arms. "Come on," she said, smiling. "Your Tía Marisol will show you around. There's a maze *and* a reservoir lake that will be yours to play in. We'll get through this together. Remember, mi casa es su casa."

Elizabeth made a note about the dining table. Bare wood. Unbalanced, leaning where the floor sagged.

Next was Marisol's room. The door had always been shut—locked. It guarded Marisol's place of solitude, which the girls weren't allowed to enter. Elizabeth stopped before that old wooden door and asked the house, *Will you let me in?* Then she turned the knob, and it opened without a fight.

A stiff-tucked bed. Sweaters folded on the nightstand. Somewhere, a clock was ticking.

She crept into the room, tiptoeing on light ballerina feet to the nightstand. She tugged open a drawer. Found a gold pocket watch inside. She weighed it in her palm, found it heavy for its size, then clicked the latch and let it snap open to a grainy picture of two girls and their father, held under glass opposite the watch face. The father stood behind the girls, tall and smiling, with the confidence he'd worn so bravely in those early months.

Elizabeth shut the watch. Peeked over her shoulder before stuffing it into her sweater's front pocket and moving on. Next, she passed under the archway into the kitchen. She noted the stove burners that wouldn't work and the microwave that stayed dark when she pressed its buttons. When she brushed her fingers along the tiled countertop, her tongue tickled with the sweetness of mangoes.

"Marisol?" Elizabeth had said, sitting on the kitchen counter, swinging her legs in the crisp air. It must have been a Saturday, if Marisol was cutting mangos for a snack. It must have been spring, too, because the flowers outside were potent and the pollen smothered her eyes and nose and ears. Marisol didn't hear Elizabeth; she kept cutting the thick rubbery skin of the mango in slow knife-drags, stripping off green and red flays and handing them to Elizabeth so she could suck on the undersides. It was warm out—not as hot as it usually got there—and the windows were open to let the fresh air in.

Marisol squeezed lemon over the golden wedges she'd already seasoned with salt and tajín. When Elizabeth put down her piece of rind, she asked again—louder this time, blurting out the word that had invaded her mind. "Marisol, what's a *wetback*?"

Marisol stopped. Lemon juice ran down her hands.

"Liz, child?" she said in the tone she reserved only for adults. Calm and maybe treacherous. "Who called you that?"

Already she'd dissected the question with scalpel precision, split it open and laid it out flat. She knew it: some*one* had called *Elizabeth* that terrible word.

Elizabeth tried explaining that it was just her friend Conner who'd said it yesterday at the lunch table—he'd only said that she "technically" was one. "Because," he'd said, "wetbacks are people who speak Spanish. Like you and your dad. And work the jobs your dad does, and get sweaty as hell." It had made the kids giggle, except for Elizabeth, who'd had a sinking gut feeling she wasn't supposed to laugh.

Marisol chopped the mango knife down into the cutting board. Elizabeth flinched. The knife stayed there wobbling as Marisol demanded names. "The teacher's, the father's, the mother's, the boy who said that *bullshit*!"

Marisol swore and shouted point-blank across the counter, demanding that Elizabeth tell her *everything*. Each consonant rattling the windows. Elizabeth believed that Marisol's anger would split the whole house in two and send it crashing down around them, but that never happened. Instead, when Elizabeth would not give the names, Marisol simply stopped what she was doing and dialed the school, and Elizabeth cried out, "No, don't! Please. I'm sorry, I'm sorry!"

It would be years before she wondered: What was it, exactly, that she was sorry about? Sorry for ruining the day? For reminding Marisol that these things still existed outside her sacred walls? Sorry she hadn't been able to handle it on her own.

Through sobs, Elizabeth begged Marisol to hang up without saying anything, because if she did, her mother would find out and take Elizabeth and Mary away from San Ojuela, and Elizabeth didn't want to go—couldn't go—dug her fingernails into the black denim of Marisol's jeans so hard that when Marisol hung up the phone and pried the weeping girl off her, tears leaked from her eyes too.

"I'm sorry, I'm sorry," Elizabeth choked, thinking she never would have said anything if she'd known what would happen. She should have bottled this up inside, kept it there and never let it out. But the fire in Marisol's eyes had gone, flicked away with something softer, duller.

"It's okay, Liz child," Marisol said. Her fingers flexed tight around Elizabeth's shoulders. "Just...let me think, love. Go play with your sister." She kissed Liz on her forehead and told her she was wonderful. "If this happens again, you tell me though, okay? Okay?"

Elizabeth nodded. Marisol wiped the tears from her niece's eyes. Passed the mango bowl into her trembling hands. "Por ti puedo mover montañas, okay? I will literally move this awful earth to make sure you're okay. Because you are beautiful, and you are wonderful, and don't you forget that. Ever. You're wonderful."

She took off after that, hugging the bowl tight to her chest, reinforcing the warmth and beating of her heart. She left Marisol in the kitchen to mumble bitterly to herself. When Elizabeth looked back, Marisol's shadow seemed larger, darker, as if it had grown from her anger and oxidized, sucking up the kitchen's light. If Liz didn't know any better, she would have guessed that the shadow wasn't her tía's at all but that of some other person who stood behind her, whispering to Marisol, who whispered back.

Now Elizabeth stood in that same kitchen again.

If you're going to remember something, remember that you're wonderful.

Ten years separated her from that moment. She was no longer the child they'd torn from these walls kicking and screaming, her arms reaching back as if to rip the whole house off its stone roots. They'd thrown that girl in the back of a car, and she'd watched the house and her father shrink away through tears and dusty glass. Yards had grown between them, and yards became miles, and miles became so much more distance and time between.

"God, what am I doing here?" Elizabeth rubbed her hands over her face. *Looking for ghosts. Right.*

Maybe they were elsewhere—the second floor.

She circled back to the grand staircase. Whenever their father would stumble in after another dusk-to-dawn shift, Elizabeth and Mary would thunder down those steps—never mind that Elizabeth would catch the tang of liquor on his stubble—and cheer, *We missed you! We missed you!* before he engulfed them in a hug. She could still hear those bodiless cheers somewhere deep in the walls.

Or was it just the stairs that made the sounds? Creaking now under Elizabeth's boots as she walked up.

With each creak, the weight of her feet felt heavier, as if a hand was pulling her down. *El Coco,* her dead tía's voice echoed in her head. *It dwells there. El Coco. He's real.* And yet, feeling the polished wood of the railing, Elizabeth was warm, and home, and everything she'd lived through since melted away. *I know this place.* The hallways, her arms; those windows, her eyes. The walls radiated protection, like her old ghost-catcher curtains. *You are safe*, she told herself.

Safe safe safe.

She checked her old bedroom first. The wallpaper with the cyan vines had been ripped down to hide the bloody handprints she'd left forever ago; Marisol had replaced it with off-white paint. She thought she heard a bump in the nursery down the hall, so she checked there too. Nothing.

Every day she saw ghosts. So why, here, not a single one? They never hid. They just waited in their loneliness, indifferent to the comings and goings of the living.

She reached her father's room at the end of the hall. Also empty. He'd never filled it up anyway, save for a single crooked bookshelf and a desk and a narrow bed. How many times had she waited up for him, perched on that bed? When he was supposed to be there to read her stories of fearful cemeteries and tigers, because she was so timid and afraid of every little thing in that massive house? He'd promised to keep her safe.

Safe. Safe. Safe.

All of it, of course, leading to the inevitable long night when he'd picked the girls up from a movie Elizabeth did not remember, and stubbornly, selfishly, with liquor on his breath, ignored Elizabeth's advice to call an Uber. Instead he'd driven the girls home, right into the truck speeding in the opposite lane.

Tires screeched.

The hood of their car crunched up—glass shredded Elizabeth's palms. Everything after that was redness and noise. Their father rushed them across the last stretch of road to the house to call 911, and Marisol talked him down until morning came.

It occurred to Elizabeth, standing in his old doorway, that sometimes you leave a place never realizing it's the last time you'll ever be there. That her soul had been dying long before that final night, and now it was dead, and she couldn't ever truly go back to the old house, not the one that was. *Whatever I'm looking for, it's not here.*

Her phone blared, shattering the silence. "What do you want, Mary?"

"I'm in the living room. Come down here, you're not gonna believe this shit."

Elizabeth rushed down the steps and across the courtyard, not sure what her sister had found but hoping it was something supernatural—something real. She almost bumped into Mary when she swung around the archway.

"Hey!"

"Oh. Sorry," she said. Mary shushed her. "What? I'm just—"

Mary pointed across the room. It stood against the window, between the bookshelf and TV, gleaming in the soft afternoon pastels. The light slid off its shoulder pauldrons. Its gauntlets cradled a sword.

"That's a knight's suit of armor, right?" Mary asked.

"Yeah," Elizabeth said. "Cool."

Only it wasn't from a medieval knight, no. Elizabeth recognized the round pauldrons and barreled breastplate from grainy oil paintings printed in her history textbooks. Its helmet was brimmed, and the pants were puffy and striped.

"A *conquistador.*" Elizabeth knew it before the word slipped from her lips. *How the hell did you end up here?*

He wasn't alone. The whole living room had been filled with things that were not Marisol's: crates that stank of preservative oils and dust. Antiques like pottery, little clay warriors, obsidian stones, and skull busts had festered from the boxes to invade Marisol's bookshelves. None of them belonged there. Mary asked what the other objects were, but Elizabeth told her that she didn't know. She approached the suit of armor, never looking away from it. She reached for the sword and almost touched it—maybe she did, just barely—but then a plate crashed to the floor behind her. Elizabeth spun in time to see the thousand little shards explode across the floor and a dark blur bolt from the shelf and into the hall.

Mary was already chasing after it. "A cat!" she cheered. "Hell yeah, a fucking cat!"

Her footsteps echoed down the hallways along with her *pspspspsps*es. As quickly as the noise had erupted, it vanished, and Elizabeth was left alone again, breathing the dust hanging in the air.

Elizabeth sat on the washing machine on the back patio, the one that had never worked, not even when she was a girl. She flicked her tía's pocket watch open and shut, open and shut. Waiting for Mary to come back from the woods.

ACT II: WHAT DREAD HAND

Elizabeth had stopped studying the grainy faces within the watch. Couldn't bear to look. Every time she did, all she saw was the fear hiding behind the man's smile. He was like a scared little kid. He hadn't helped her then, he couldn't now.

There were no ghosts in Casa Coyotl. She knew that now. The house was empty, the relic of some faceless ancestor of her father's father's father's father who'd split away from the rest of the Spanish Church and made a home among the hills. He'd had the wood cut, the stones laid, and the lake dredged out by indigenous people the conquistadors had either captured or dragged up the California coast with them. Elizabeth felt stupid. Of course there were no ghosts there; it had been a slaver's house. What slaves stuck around near their chains once they were free to go?

Like cemeteries. There were never any ghosts at cemeteries. But that had always made sense to her—no one ever died in cemeteries.

Tyger, Tyger.

She stood up, clamped the watch in her hand, and with all her strength chucked it across the yard and into the trees, watching it disappear forever.

She decided not to go searching for Mary—the woods were creepy as hell, and if Mary wanted to skulk around out there, it was her problem. She turned back towards the house instead and yelped at the sight of a ghost in a black shroud blocking the doorway.

It spoke.

"What the hell are you doing here?" the Boy said, standing corpse-still on bare feet.

THREE
The Tiger

"Mary?" Elizabeth had called with the squeak of her child's voice, so many years ago. "Angel Eyes?"

She was still cradling the bowl of mangoes in her small hands. Tía Marisol had cast her out from the kitchen; her tears had dried on her cheeks. She called again for her sister and her tía's cat, but the house stretched the words and threw them back at her.

She was about to go look outside when a voice calling her own name tickled the back of her ear. Mary's voice, maybe? She turned to where it had come from: a supply closet at the edge of the hall. Empty—only a broom resting against a coat rack. Had she even heard a voice at all?

When she shut the closet door, something scratched and raked at the other side, like fingernails. She reached for the knob again. The sound exploded into wild banging, pounding on the wood. It shouted: "*STAY AWAY!*"

Elizabeth jumped. She squeezed the bowl in tight to her chest and ran from the house as quick as she could.

Outside, she wandered between pines and eucalyptus trees, her heart still thumping, looking for her sister. She was near the south gate of the property, the deepest part of the backyard woods, when she finally stopped to itch the pollen from her eyes. She set her bowl of mangoes down on a tree stump and looked for moving shapes between the trees. Pollen drifted lazily like golden snow; she remembered when her father had told her giants lived in woods like these. With a mouth full of mango mush, she called for Mary again, but a boy's voice replied instead.

She couldn't make out the words, but he was real, shouting just beyond the gate.

She took up the bowl and followed the stone wall to the south gate, which led into a mini-labyrinth. Marisol had said this gate was once the servants' entrance to the property, but along the way some great-grandfather of hers had stretched a snake's coil beyond it, with branching paths and dead ends to entertain those who chose to wander but also a clear path through its center to the other side. This ancestor had marked the entrance with the face of some Aztec god twisted into the iron bars. Marisol always tried to treat the labyrinth as something pleasant to look at, something nice, and had turned it into a garden for a while when she was young. But now it was just heaps of stones and empty pots. "I can't keep things alive," Marisol had told Elizabeth. "Plants *or* animals, really."

Elizabeth took the direct path through the labyrinth. Let the stones spit her out into a beige field of grass on the other side, where blades rustled in the wind like golden waves. The grass tickled her knees; crows took flight at the sound of footsteps.

"Hello?" she said.

"Who goes there?" the voice shouted back. A white shape peeked up from the sea of grass.

She furrowed her brow.

"I can see you," Elizabeth said.

The white thing shot up, a bedsheet ghost with cut-out eyeholes. "Who dares trespass on my desert kingdom?" the ghost said.

"I dare." She stepped forward. "I'm Elizabeth Remolina. I live right on the other side of the wall."

"I be the ghost lord of the desert!" the ghost said, his appendages rippling waves of white above his head. He made a moaning noise, then pulled the sheet off to show messy hair and a soft face, and lips that pinched up with a smile when he said, "Hey. I'm Julian."

She would come to know that smile well: the crooked teeth peeking through it; the dimple that revealed itself on his left cheek whenever he'd watch some asshole get what was coming to them; the way his hair spilled into his eyes and he'd itch it into knots in a fury; his chalky laugh and how he was quick to spot lizards and rabbits and catch them for Elizabeth to pet. But their friendship began with Marisol's mango bowl. She asked if he wanted one, and they picked at the slices together, spice and sticky juices puddling in their palms as they walked back through the south gate—the "portal," Julian called it.

"Portal to what?" she asked.

"The underworld." He gave no explanation, other than he had a feeling. And Elizabeth nodded knowingly. When Elizabeth asked him what he was doing alone out there, he told her his mom was working. "She doesn't have time to watch me, but she trusts me, so I like to explore. Do you know there's a family of coyotes out there? I saw the babies last week." The whole time Elizabeth was thinking he looked familiar, but she couldn't quite place him. San Ojuela was a small town, and she'd been enrolled in the school system for two years already. She thought she knew everyone. It wasn't until the portal released them back into the woods that she remembered.

"Wait—you're Mrs. Zavala's son!"

"You know my mom?"

She knew many people, because her father knew many people. Her dad had grown up in Coyote House, so he'd arrived knowing most of San Ojuela's residents, and being a handyman had introduced him to the rest. Mr. Remolina became known by the sawdust and wood chips that clung to his jackets. Between bigger gigs, he would pick up odd jobs around town. It was on one of those small jobs that Elizabeth, tagging along, had watched him install new gutters on Mrs. Zavala's house.

Elizabeth said as much to Julian. "He still goes over there sometimes. Helps with plumbing and stuff. He's always wanting to help, because—" *Because Mrs. Zavala's husband got very, very sick. And passed away earlier this year.* By the look of Julian, the flash behind his rust-stained eyes, he knew what she'd meant to say. "I'm so sorry."

He said it was fine, but guilt still pecked at her guts. She'd spoken too quickly. Her mother always said she needed to think first before making a fool of herself. She couldn't fathom the idea of losing something like that. A parent—so alive and real and touchable, then not. Not ever again. The pollen wasn't the only thing making her eyes water.

"Shoot—hey! It's okay, really!" Julian said, now trying to console a weepy Elizabeth—which in fact only made her feel worse. In desperation, he went on, "You're in Mrs. Sheaff's class, right? I'm in Miss Carpenter's. I heard what happened today with Conner—he's an asshole, and you shouldn't listen to anything he says. And if you want, I'll give him a *scare* to put him in his place." So sincere. That made her laugh. "Does your mom let you cuss in Spanish?"

"My mom doesn't speak it," Elizabeth said. Julian insisted that he'd heard her mother speak it when picking Elizabeth up from school. Elizabeth explained that that wasn't her mother, it was Tía Marisol. At the time, Elizabeth didn't know why the distinction rubbed her the wrong way. Why did it seem to shrink Marisol down to a substitute person? "But yeah, Marisol cusses a shit ton, she just won't teach me Spanish swears." Julian lit up at that, stars twinkling in dark eyes. He really did have gorgeous eyes.

"Well, just call Conner *un pedazo de mierda* next time. And he'll feel even more hick-stupid for not knowing what you said."

"Piece of what?" Elizabeth asked, resculpting the clay word shapes from Spanish to English.

"Piece of shit!" And the two of them laughed amid a circle of trees, rays of light beaming all around them. Julian declared them friends in that moment, when the mangoes were gone and the sun stretched the tree shadows long and dark. "I don't get many friends. And our people have to stick together."

Elizabeth smiled. "Totally."

And they did become best friends. The afternoons when Mrs. Zavala worked late became an escape-pod excuse for Julian to go home with Elizabeth, Marisol always reassuring Mrs. Zavala later that it was okay, really, and no problem at all. During those warm afternoons, the two would race back and forth through the south gate's labyrinth, watch VHS tapes of poorly dubbed Godzilla movies that Julian would steal from the video store, or film their own with Marisol's old camera, acting out Elizabeth's scripts in shaky footage. Some days it was an exchange: Julian would visit Coyote House, and Mr. Remolina would go to help with whatever had broken that day at the dilapidated Zavala house. Elizabeth hardly ever went there—Julian rarely let her visit. The few times she did, she saw the peeling paint, would try ignoring the skunk stink seeped into the fabrics, the unwashed dishes piled in the sink, the stacks of papers on every surface, the laundry abandoned on a living room seat. Meanwhile, that backyard forest, the portal, and the hedge fence of Coyote House became their secret haven where they played and whispered secrets. A safe place, where Elizabeth could always find him, Julian, the brown boy who'd sit on the top of the wall with his skin warmed by the desert's kisses, feet kicking through air, dreaming about never going home. *Whatever happened to him?*

❃ ❃ ❃

Now he stood in the doorway, breathing.

His eyes were rusty red, and his black-striped serape swayed in the breeze—the rest of him hidden beneath it, his feet coiled springs waiting for Elizabeth to make the first move. Up close, the black stripes weren't solid but laced with geometric patterns of red and green. Elizabeth almost didn't recognize him—the long, wispy hair; the oval face. The color of his skin was drained, and sleeplessness shadowed his eyes. But those were *his* eyes.

"You're trespassing," he started to say, but whatever came next Elizabeth didn't hear—she hugged him without a second thought. Engulfed him in her squeeze as if to push away all the years apart, never mind the lack of him underneath the serape, his rib bones pressing against her stomach, his spine notches between her fingers—it was him, it was Julian; Elizabeth had found her ghost.

He wrenched himself free as soon as she let up on the hug and for a second Elizabeth thought she had it wrong, that he wasn't Julian at all, that Julian was gone along with everyone else. There was shock in his eyes—but she was sure it was him. He had the same sadness.

He doesn't recognize you, she reprimanded herself. How could he? She was hardly even living; even she couldn't recognize her own face.

"Is this a trick?" he said with a scratchy voice, stepping away further, receding into the shadow of the house. "You're not her. You shouldn't even know about her—how *fucking* dare you!" He bared his teeth as if they were fangs, just a flex away from shooting out longer and sharper from bleeding gums. "They abandoned this place and left it to die out here all alone. How dare you put them on like a fucking costume."

"But it is me!" Elizabeth pleaded. "Dad did the terrible thing he did, and we moved and couldn't visit, but we're back now." She felt her face warming, the beads of sweat on her lip and brow; it was so hot that day. Her body was a clenched and bracing fist, holding in all the words that wanted to run rampant off her tongue: she was Elizabeth, she remembered him; he had to remember her, because he was the last person who'd known Elizabeth when she was recognizably herself. Before she lost her soul. Why couldn't he see it?

I'm right here! she wanted to scream—but kept holding it in. She stood there blinking, like all the other times when it was obvious no one really cared about what she had to say.

Finally Julian said, "You know, you always talked like that—telling stories." Then: "If you don't get the hell out of here, I'll have Samuel do it for you." By his tone, that sounded like something worse than calling the cops. "This is Señora Marisol's property."

"Yeah, no shit. And as of yesterday, my Tía Marisol is dead."

He stopped. "Oh."

The house yawned. Then, in a voice so much smaller than the vitriolic one he'd just wielded, Julian said, "Then do whatever it is you came here to do and *leave*." He picked up a broom that was leaning against the doorway and cut through the house and into the courtyard. Elizabeth followed, rage now searing her chest.

"'Oh?' Julian, that's all you have to say? Marisol practically raised you!" Just as she had Elizabeth and Mary, and anyone else who came to her broken and scared. Elizabeth stepped up to him. She was bigger and stronger, and he was standing where Marisol had once danced full and alive, and he wore an apathetic face in need of a fist.

He ignored her, went back to sweeping up the brown flakes of dead leaves. Were his eyes red? Or was that just the glare of sunset? The smell of him too—off. The slightest tinge of dried blood, maybe.

"What do you expect to find here?" he asked.

A simple question. And yet it socked her off her feet, and Elizabeth was afraid again. "I...Julian, we came to check for repairs." *I checked the closets and cellars and rooms and halls and found no ghosts. No monsters.*

"You're calling me that again. Stop it." He said it with such disdain. "We can handle the repairs; I can give you a fuckin' laminated list with the damn repairs if that's what you want, so what's keeping you? Huh? You don't know me, and I don't know you, and we're not friends. There's nothing for you here—nothing lives here—we're just weeds and empty rooms, so go back to San Diego or whatever white-picket fucking neighborhood you live in now."

She didn't know what to say. She wanted to cower and cry but she wouldn't let him have that. She asked, "Is this some kind of punishment?"

What he said next raked down her spine.

"That depends. Do you believe in El Coco?"

FOUR
Abandon All Hope

Leaves whipped Mary's face as she ran through the woods, vaulting over roots and dodging ferns. She swatted them away, never taking her eyes off the blur of black and white weaving through the undergrowth just ahead of her. She ducked under a grabby oak branch, following a mossy garden wall until the wall gasped open and the cat leapt up and perched at the apex of a gate.

Mary slowed in the clearing, catching her breath and tugging her shirt to drain out the musk, fill it up with fresh and shady air. Between breaths she told the cat, "Alright, now, just come on down, sweet little baby. I'm not gonna hurt you. There's nothing to be scared of."

She reached for him, but the cat's body arched like a horseshoe and he darted out of reach. The gate looked on as she struggled for the cat, its black iron bars twisted into a face—a monster's face. Smiling. Two wrought-iron snakes in profile, kissing snout to snout to form a single fanged smile and a pair of thinslit eyes. She thought, *How metal*, and laughed at her pun. Again she asked the cat if it would get down, please, *pspspspsps*; the cat just watched her, unblinking.

Something rustled behind her. Mary spun—nothing. Just dark tree trunks caging her in. Dead leaves crunched underfoot. Soot speckled the light that squeezed between the branches. Had she imagined the sound? Was a squirrel, or a fox, or one of the peacocks she'd seen pecking the cacti near the shed? Or maybe some*one*. She scanned for landmarks, and when she couldn't make out anything she recognized, she calculated how far exactly she had come from the house and how long it would take to make it back if she had to run.

Her sister had told her to not go into the woods alone, but Liz was full of arbitrary rules she parroted from their mother. Always so stiff, so timid—it made Mary want to pull her sister's hair or knock off people's hats. She'd explored the rest of the grounds already: the lake, the side cottage, the vacant stables. She hadn't thought twice about losing herself in the woods. But now the trees were thicker, crowding her in. She turned back to the gate; it must be the southern one. The ugly face sculpted from the bars shot her a look that pricked her spine, shocking muscle tight to bone—a Stay Away feeling—so, naturally, she approached.

The bars were rusted and the paint flaky. Sheeted with dust and dirt and tangled spiderwebs. Nearby along the wall, in a patch where the vines had been ripped away, was graffiti in sloppy red paint: HELLMOUTH GATE. She reached for the latch—stopped when she heard more rustling behind her. Sure of it this time. "Oi, who's—"

It leaped at her—quick-legged and spider-like, scurrying out from the underbrush and clamping to her wrist. She shrieked, batted at it, whatever *it* was, but it constricted tight, then pinched and clawed and scraped. It was up to her elbow and then her bicep, scurrying towards her face, hissing, when the cat pounced on it—knocked it from her shoulder—the both of them crashing to the forest floor in a tangle of limbs until the cat sank his teeth into the creature. It flailed and rolled, then it tore itself free and darted silently back into the underbrush, leaving Mary shaking, wide-eyed, grabbing her wrist. Blood budded where fingernails had carved half-moons into her skin, and then she was sure of what she'd seen: a severed hand. Small, gaunt, brown-skinned.

Elizabeth was standing with Julian in the courtyard when she heard Mary's screams. She was running through the house, trying to get free of its endless halls and arches and find Mary, when Coyote House came alive in a howling, pounding fury. *Crack! Crack! Crack! Crack! Crack!*—a sound like something beating against the walls. The windows shuddered. When Elizabeth wheeled into the kitchen, the window above her head exploded into a thousand razor fangs. The brick that had shattered it crashed against the tiles and Elizabeth jumped—her chest a caged animal beating at the bars— never mind that thin burning across her cheek, the warmth welling up. She cupped her hand over the cut and burst onto the back patio just as a couple of kids in black-and-white skeleton costumes launched the last of their eggs, then tossed away the carton and vanished between the trees.

She found Mary in the wood soon afterwards, pressed against the stone wall, crying and vomiting words between gasps for air, that something was out there, that it came alive and came from the bushes and clawed up her arm. That it was a hand, no body. That it was dead—undead—alive. It was alive!

Elizabeth shook her quiet. "I told you not to go into the woods. Those assholes could have hurt you!"

"You're not listening!" Mary snapped. "It was—"

"What—what, Mary? They were *costumes!* I saw them. Probably just idiot high-schoolers with nothing better to do." Elizabeth let

ACT II: WHAT DREAD HAND

Mary go, only then seeing the blood from her hands—her own blood—blotching Mary's shirt.

It's out there.
    Mary was looking through the kitchen window where the brick had shattered it, letting in a finger of the night's cold. She looked beyond the grass to the woods where leaves quivered and willows hunched haglike in the dark, branch arms hanging over their heads. To whatever was out there, she and Liz must look like a warm little picture, alight within the window, framed by a dark and sleeping house.
    Liz hadn't believed her, but Mary was sure of what she'd seen. A severed hand. Squelching and marionetting its finger legs. But Liz had told her it was a pair of skeleton kids who'd egged the house in some stupid prank. They'd left the walls spotted and runny with gold.
    The Boy who was following Liz had said he saw them too. The skeletons. They were gone already, but he knew who they were—would deal with them later. Then he'd followed Mary's gaze into the forest where the hand had vanished. "I wouldn't go snooping in places you don't belong either, if I were you," he said. "Or you'll find things that would rather be left alone."
    Thinking of that made the scratches under her sleeve burn. She didn't trust Julian. He'd kept to the shadows and glared at her, showing teeth like some wild, feral thing. She didn't care if Liz said he was a friend. That boy wasn't Liz's friend; she didn't know what the hell he was.

Just block it out.
    She took a deep breath and began fiddling with the knob for the front right burner of the stove.

"Leave it alone," Liz said from across the kitchen table, focused on her reflection in the mirror as she peeled away the Band-Aid from her cheek. A raw scab now dashed across it where the glass shard had cut her. "Huh. It's not so bad." Liz studied her reflection. "Might get a cool scar out of it. Does that seem like something I'd have?"

Mary ignored her and kept trying to get the stove to work. Liz had deemed it one more broken, useless thing to add to their growing list of broken, useless things. The Boy had showed them all the other things that needed fixing. "Well, the front door's broke, but you probably noticed that coming in. The stairs in the courtyard are crumbling off the wall. There was a fire a few years ago, so now the stables outside are too unstable to keep anything in, and I wouldn't go in there if I was you. We boarded up some windows that don't lock because kids keep wanting to sneak in, especially on Halloween." He knew all this because he worked for Samuel de Hory, who was the groundskeeper here.

"Is that who brought all the artifacts?" Liz had asked. "Marisol never owned anything like that."

He told them the antiquities did belong to Samuel. Marisol had allowed him to store them in the main house after fire devoured half of the lakeside house and stables.

Mary smelt sour gas and knew the stove would work. She twisted the knob and listened to its *snap-snap-snap*. She blew into the cavity below, releasing the rattle of a thousand crumbs, and turned the knob one last time. Another *snap-snap-snap*. A hiss.

Then firelight.

The flame *whooshed* up, singeing Mary's cheeks as she jumped back. Liz was already on her, twisting the knob off and fanning the air. "Jesus Christ," she shouted. "You're gonna immolate us both!"

"My eyebrows! Tell me I still have my eyebrows!" Mary checked her reflection. Still there, still strong and bushy, thank god.

"Are you listening?" Liz was still lecturing. "I don't particularly want us pulling a Joan of Arc in the middle of this shithole."

Mary waved her off. "A what? I was right—the stove works fine."

"It's a fucking fire hazard is what it is. We really should throw it out. If we're not careful, this whole place could burn down."

"Would that be a bad thing?"

Elizabeth ignored her. Angel Eyes had hopped onto the table between them and was licking himself clean. Folds of skin draped loose around Marisol's once-round tuxedo cat, and his left ear had been bitten off almost entirely. Liz said he used to disappear for days on end only to return mangled and sticky; Mary, cleaning gunk from the cat's eyes, wondered what he'd seen out there all on his own.

"Careful, he's an elderly gentleman," Liz said.

"I'm careful," Mary muttered. Angel Eyes had been all fangs and hisses at the sight of the Boy. Liz was sure her old friend was a safe person, but nothing seemed safe here. Nothing seemed *normal* here. Mary wondered how insane her father must have been to bring children to a place like this.

The girls' mother pulled up to the house not long after. Liz went out to help with her bags, but Mary took Angel Eyes into the bedroom Liz had said they used to share. She tossed the cat inside and told him, "You're gonna have to Bertha it, Jane Eyre–style for a while." Before she closed the door she added, "Don't worry, I won't let her get rid of you."

Then Mary rushed downstairs, heart pounding, to tell her mom about the two skeleton kids and ask how soon they could leave. She made a sharp turn sliding into the kitchen—and almost smacked face-first into the bolo tie of a man standing needle-straight in the archway.

FIVE
The Groundskeeper

"Marichica," the man in the archway said. He had kind eyes and a smile that stretched his mustache. "Díos mio, look at you."

She backed away. "Do I know you?"

Those blue eyes drank her up, and for a moment Mary was lost at sea, tossed on the waves.

"Don't be rude," Liz said, walking in. "He's an old friend. He's—"

"Samuel," Mary finished.

He held out his hand, old but strong and webbed with veins. Mary didn't want to take it, but Liz and Mom were watching, so she let his fingers wrap around hers, engulfing her small hand. "Niña, don't you remember me? You were about this big." He showed with his other hand. "Ni modo. I get it, I'm always forgetting so much all the time these days. Faces, names, and places. But not you or your sister, you two I've always kept in my heart."

"Uh-huh."

"Anyhow," he said, "it's nice to see you again."

The girls' mother asked to speak with Samuel alone, and when Mary passed him again on the way out, she held her breath to avoid another mouthful of sticky cologne. He patted her shoulder with that liver-splotched hand.

Mary and Liz lurked outside the kitchen, Liz sitting on the ground with her back against the wall, knees tucked to her chest, Mary standing with her arms crossed. They took turns peeking into the room.

"Do you know what's going on?" Mary whispered.

"No, you?"

"Nope."

"Well then."

"Yep."

They listened closely.

Samuel was speaking. "I beg your pardon, Mrs. Remolina—if you still go by that—but what is so pressing that this could not have waited until tomorrow?"

"The lock on the front of the house is broken," their mother said with a cup of water between her hands. "It needs to be fixed."

"Some kid tried to break in a few days back. Marisol always wanted to keep the house as authentic as possible, so it took a few days to find the right smith for the lock. He'll be coming to take care of it soon."

"A kid? Like the vandals who came by earlier today? Your employee told my daughter there's been a lot of that this month. What's the story there?" She looked at Samuel with heavy, sunken eyes. Mary didn't want to imagine what her day must have been like, clogged with business calls and mortuary calls, the estate's attorney, the hospice—she was exhausted thinking of it. Mom must have had to go see the body too. And that was really why she didn't want her girls with her, Mary knew. Why she'd sent them here on their own instead—so they wouldn't see Marisol cold. Mouth wired shut. Guts scooped by the mortician. Draped in a thin blanket.

"His name is Julian," Samuel said. "He's not an employee, not really. He's not on any payroll, but his mom's on hard times, and he's a kind boy who comes to help since I can't do as much as I used to—I'm old now, heh, clearly, and getting older. He does what he wants, and in return I help his family out as much as I can."

Mary's mother sipped her water. "I'm glad to know you're helping out families in the community, that's very altruistic of you." The switch in her tone was a subtle one, a gear shift to a sterner, higher pitch. Her business voice. "That's always important, and a good way to look at things too, given this new situation."

"Yeah, Marisol's...it was unexpected. I'm very sorry. She was a friend to me. I visited her sometimes, you know, once she couldn't stay here. She was lonely."

Mary sneered. *Of course he did.*

"Anyway," her mother said, wincing as if something Samuel had said prickled her skin. "Speaking of the new situation, I can't help but notice all this...clutter. The girls are under the impression that all of it belongs to you?"

"Yes!" he smiled. "Marisol was very kind. There was a fire about three years back; you may have heard about it. And while not much of this house was burned, part of my cabin was. Marisol said it was no problem moving my stuff here. I am—was—an archeologist, you know, and I still sometimes go on excavations with old colleagues, so those rocks have scientific and sentimental value both, you could say."

She sipped again. "See, the problem is, to me, they're just rocks."

"I'm sorry?"

Mary knew her mother, was very much like her mother, and knew by the set of the jaw that Katharine Remolina was trying not to smirk. "The fire, if I'm not mistaken..." She pulled out a legal pad and flipped through pages of notes. "Ah—here. The attorney told me about it. A brush fire that got so out of hand it burned the stables down. Can you explain to me how that would happen on a property that's being supervised by a full-time groundskeeper? I know it's California, but a well-maintained garden shouldn't be dry enough to burn *that much*. Should it, Mr. de Hory? Or was keeping it watered another job you gave to that teenager?

He blinked. "No, but when Marisol's health declined, I was occupied with helping her move, and—"

"Three years. Three years she's been in that facility. How is it that not a single one of these repairs have been made?" She pushed the list at him.

"It's been a difficult time for us. The city hasn't survived the housing crash, not really—"

"—looked fine to me when I came in—"

"—and Marisol's budget made us prioritize what we could and could not fix." His jaw clenched.

Katharine sighed. "What I'm getting at is the fire happened because someone cut corners, and you, sir, were the one holding the scissors. Marisol was not of sound mind in her last years, yet I was made aware by the nurses and lawyer that you pestered her with phone calls about how best to maintain the property, even suggested signing over power of attorney to you—a proposal she rejected repeatedly. Then there was this business with the will… she was *not* of sound mind, that's clear to everyone. I'm assured the changes are invalid and the sole beneficiary to my sister-in-law's estate remains my eldest daughter, Elizabeth. Until Liz turns twenty-one, I suppose *I'm* the steward."

He wasn't smiling anymore, that once-kindly man. Samuel's blue eyes were deep and calculating. Whatever lurked beneath the surface of those oceans, far down in the murk, was digging upward. Mary thought of great white sharks exploding at their prey, a thousand teeth glittering in their jaws.

"So this house belongs to me for the time being," Kat continued. "And while Marisol was fond of you, I barely know you, and you've admitted that you're no longer able to keep up the property. I'm sorry, but I don't think we can keep this relationship going."

"Keep this—"

"Mr. de Hory, I would like you to clean your stuff out of this house immediately. You have till the end of this week to find a new home. It's short notice, I know, but given all that we've just discussed, I think I'm being generous. The long and short of it is that you are no longer employed here."

Liz and Mary were fully in the doorway now, never mind having wanted to stay hidden. Samuel saw them and blinked, again and again as if to flicker this new reality away, but then he cracked.

"Señora, please, I—" He stuttered, couldn't stop the words spilling out of him now. "This is all a misunderstanding, I only had Señora Marisol's interests in mind." And: "The antique store doesn't bring in enough to cover my medical bills." And: "My father worked for your family, and his father's father too." And: "Please—this is my home. This house is all I know."

But their mother escorted Samuel to the foyer, with Liz and Mary trailing after, their loud silence willing her to reconsider. When they reached the double doors he pointed to the girls. "I knew their father, and he—"

Their mother cut him off. "Mr. de Hory, please." She lowered her voice to a whisper. "You're lucky I don't call the police."

They ate quietly after that, Mary, Liz, and their mother, once the last of Samuel's sobs was swallowed by the trees.

Mary couldn't remember the last time she'd eaten with her family at a table. Mom was always in her office taking calls. Liz would come home late after dance, fix her own plate, and retreat to her room. Now their mother sat at the head of the dining table, and Liz an ocean of lacquered wood away opposite to her. Mary had foolishly placed herself right in the middle of that heavy quiet, unable to retreat to the TV room with a plate of food like she could back home. The burger her mom had picked up for her had gone cold and soggy.

"Tell me again, what happened to your face?" Their mother broke the silence.

"I slipped," Liz said, absolutely waterboarding the hell out of a spongy fry in a cup of ketchup. She kept her gaze down, focused on her POW. She kept what she said about the Boy to a minimum, just that he'd been there, not that they knew each other and had been arguing and that was why no one noticed the skeleton kids come.

"Into shattered glass?" Kat raised an eyebrow.

"Well, the kids started throwing stuff so fast, I wasn't looking where I was going and I slipped. I'm sorry."

"Don't apologize."

"Sorry."

Their mother could do that—strip you down with a look until you were the barest twig underneath muscle and fat. She'd peck at your sides with comments on your weight or what you were wearing. She kept the girls in an almost all-white school because it had a "better reputation." She hated the rockera music that Marisol had introduced to Liz and the chola slang the girls picked up god knows where. She'd say it was their own fault if they made her get defensive over some comment she'd made about Other Latinos—that it was wrong of her daughters to correct her, that they didn't yet know the value of hard work. She'd remind them of everything she'd sacrificed to afford them decent lives. And then she'd ask what they wanted to eat for dinner as if she hadn't just vivisected them with razor words. Elizabeth had gotten her septum piercing the day she tuned eighteen, a spiteful *fuck you* to such a mother.

Kat suddenly sprang up and marched to the window, shoved open the curtains, and shouted, "Go away or we'll call the police!" at the latest group of teens who'd come prowling for the chance to spend their Halloweekend in an old and haunted place. They took off into the bushes. One of them even shouted sorry before scuttling away.

When Kat came back to her seat, she said, "If we catch any more vandals, we'll press charges. Okay?"

"Get cops involved?" Liz had to laugh.

Kat's eyes met the fresh Band-Aid on Liz's cheek. "Next time they might hurt more than just your face."

"Yes, ma'am," the girls both said.

But then Liz scoffed and narrowed her eyes. "I'm picking up foul vibes," she said. "You *are* mad, right?"

Mary almost gasped. She'd never known Liz to instigate—that was her bit.

Their mother gestured at the dust on the countertops, the chipped paint, the cracks on the walls. "Aren't you? This is unacceptable. This house—*your* house, Elizabeth—was supposed to be in great shape, but look how Samuel's left it."

"Don't you think you're being a bit hard on him?" Liz snapped. "Like, shit, you didn't have to fire him. Where the hell else is he going to live? No one's renting at the rate Marisol was giving him. And he's like a million years old."

"I think I let him off easy. You'll understand when you're older," Kat said.

Liz scrunched her nose. "I'm nineteen—what's that even mean? And he was like family."

"A rotting branch," their mother said. "Doing the right thing sometimes isn't easy. You'll want to be a charity and cut off parts of yourself to help every person you can, till you learn that everyone's responsible for their own decisions. Good ones *and* stupid ones.

Keep helping people like him, eventually all you have left are shredded bits."

Liz muttered with arms crossed, defiant to the end, that Samuel was old and did his best with what he had.

Their mom shrugged. "I can find someone who does better work, cheaper."

"Mom!"

"What?" she snapped. "Do you know how much we're going to have to do here? How much I'm going to have to take out of my own pocket to cover expenses? I don't want to talk about this anymore. Mary. I called the school already. They know you'll be out for a week. Liz, Brian can take you back Monday for dance, if you're ready to go back. But tomorrow is the funeral."

"Why do you care so much?" Liz was up now, her palms nailed to the table. "You never gave a shit about Marisol, you never spoke to her—now you're the one planning the funeral and choosing what to do with her shit?"

"No, you're right," her mother said. There wasn't any fight in that tone, that's what scared Mary. Shouting was common for them, normal even. Healthy. But it was the calm, formal tone that bit like ice when their mother said, "If it was up to *me*, I'd sell every damn thing in this house and strip it down. And once it was nothing, I'd renovate it and make something actually worth looking at, and *then* I'd rent it. Or sell it. Or whatever made us *money*. But it's not my house, it's yours. And until you're twenty-one, all I have to do is make sure it doesn't fall to pieces."

ACT III
Brujería

ONE
Sinnerman

"The wicked flee when no man pursueth."
—Proverbs 28:1

THE NIGHT YOU KILL OLIVER, you sit crouched on the floor with your knees kissing your chest, your back against the door as sounds of struggle leak through: shoes yelping streaks against the floor (you'll have to scrub them out later); the chair gasping with twists. Even if it isn't really you doing the cutting, holding the dagger, you brought him here all the same. You can't take it—the soft pounding that finds you no matter where you hide in Casa Coyotl; the rhythmic tune the night strums into your head—so you take Oliver's keys and drive his Dodge out into desert until your town is nothing more than the lights of the ICE facility twinkling on the jagged horizon. To vastness and emptiness, where coyote howls stretch out the sky and your blood itches with the songs of long-dead gods.

The night's pull is stronger here, the music louder, thundering in your ears. *Not now*, you tell the darkness. You just have to stiff-arm it away a little while longer. Maybe you could have put this errand off until morning, when the pull is fainter—but then you'd be spending the night trapped behind those walls with Samuel, and with all the things you know he's doing to Oliver.

You drove here with the lights off, the whole car rattling beneath you as its freshly slashed tires ground metal against concrete. You used your animal eyes to see the way, your eyes that glowed amber in the rearview mirror, just like they do now as you throw the last of Oliver's things in the trunk—backpack, car registration, cans of food—and drench the car with gasoline, its metallic stink stinging your nose. With bare hands, you tear off the license plates and hide them in your shroud, and then a flick of your lighter is all it takes to set the proof of Oliver ablaze.

Heat licks your cheeks. Only now do you invite the night under your skin, let it grip your bones. *Not all the way*, you tell it, and the night leaves you some slack. Yet it takes you—pumps you full of the kinetic energy of the dead—and pulls you this way then that, sending you jake-legged on all fours, starved and feral and running the bluffs with a coyote pack, chasing owls through the dark. The smell of sand, its reverberations against the soles of your feet—all of it feeding you power. You're drunk for hours, until the sun comes up again. Then the tune that pounded within you fades and the night slips out of you in ribbons, leaving you as it found you: dazed and empty. Hiding in the shroud of your shame.

There are only a few places you like to return to after the gods have their way with your body at night—Casa Coyotl; the abandoned San Ojuela Mall; and this sun-dried graveyard you're approaching, which sits at the edge of town. A place where you feel safe.

You passed one like it sometime during the night, but that one was old, a stone parliament ringing a central plaza where people must have once picnicked and played music. There were no flowers there, just old bones six feet deep who stirred when you passed, their quivers a polite request: *Please stay.*

ACT III: BRUJERÍA

Here, there are no whispers. These graves are newer—from this century, at least. The surrounding neighborhood is still waking up; morning fog coats the streets.

Somewhere a windmill creaks. Two crows watch as you climb the graveyard fence. To the gardeners who spot you dropping to the other side, you wave hello. When security men patrol among the headstones, you lurk just out of sight. Your father is buried here. On your way across the field, you pass his headstone. In a few days the fog will make room for those who come to remember their dead. They'll bring bouquets of marigolds and home-cooked foods wrapped in warm tinfoil, and you'll be among them. Alone, because Mom works long hours, and because you know it hurts like hot coals on her chest to stay here too long. She doesn't believe in the gods of the dead, but you've felt their whispers in your blood, seen skinned faces in your sleep. You'll return with arroz con plátano and a mug of hot coffee to leave atop your papá's grave.

The grave you stop at today almost touches the old train tracks that mark the end of this cemetery. You squat on your haunches and softly say to the grave with *Riley Torres* carved into its pale marble, "Hey, dude."

There's not much more to say; nothing new ever happens in San Ojuela. You tell him about the movie you and your mom watched a few weeks ago, which you know he would have loved too, because you used to sneak into Sunday matinees together. You tell him about the book you picked up from the library on your walk home from class on Monday, because he also loved dense books that smelt like grass and hid secrets amid blunt prose. You catch Oliver's name almost slipping off your tongue.

I met this boy, too, you don't say. *He reminded me of you.*

Oliver's face is still imprinted on your eyelids. You see it when you press palms to your eyes to scrub away exhaustion: brown-haired with wire-rimmed glasses, the face of someone who might have been your friend. He should have been easy, like the others. You lured him in because you smelled the sour, slick desperation on him and his need for excitement, no matter the cost. How little he cared for the house or you. And yet he'd helped you at the gas station. When he looked at you, he wasn't looking through you, and his eyes shone with an understanding of what it is to be trapped. He knew what it was like to want to run away. You changed your mind, tried to lead him back to his car and send him off so at least one of you could get out—maybe he'd invite you to go with him, and you could both leave all this behind in the dust—but it was too late. Samuel had sensed prey and sent his pet in. You killed Oliver. Saying aloud those six letters won't unslit his throat.

"Oh, but check this out," you tell the headstone. You fish out the bones you keep in your back pocket. "I've gotten better."

Femurs and teeth and rat ribs and beaks—you drop them between the railroad ties and weave your hands through the air, gathering the bones the way the moon push-pulls the sea, just as you've practiced for years. More little bones rattle across the gravel and into the dancing circle. You puppet them, your fingertips noosed to them with invisible wire. You raise your hand, and the bones jump and dive-bomb your palm; they jolt, duck, bounce—your little tricks.

You're so focused on your show that you don't notice the snake until it's too late. It rattles its tail and your bones drop dead in the dirt. You turn in time to see it, a juvenile, broomstick-thin with scales a deep rust, as if this were a creature that grew out of the tracks themselves to reach you. It snaps forward and plunges fangs deep into your ankle flesh, pushing its venom in. You yelp. The crows flap away at the sound of crunching bone.

❉ ❉ ❉

ACT III: BRUJERÍA

The snake lies there, dead. Its neck bent back, bone stretching scales. Twin punctures mark your ankle where it bit. The pain is acid and agony as venom pulses up your leg, ripping into your muscles. You grit your teeth so hard you think they might shatter to rubble, but the night's whispers return and nudge your arms with nahualli secrets. Following its instructions, you puppeteer your shadow strings and cram the shadows deep into your wounds, where they reach through your veins. When you tug them back, the venom worms out with them. You flick it into the earth and the soil drinks it up. Ants, spiders, and other desert bugs scurry up your foot to suture the wounds shut, and you're left there breathing, shaking, unsure of what you've done.

It was just a baby, too young to know how much venom was enough. Like all scared little snakes, it simply plunged as much of it as its body could produce right into you, hoping it would be enough. You can't bring yourself to leave it dead in the dirt, so you find a discarded plastic bag and take it home. In your room you put it in a shoebox, then walk out to Mom's garden in the backyard, where beds bloom despite the dryness. You're careful not to crush any vegetables. Tomatoes, jalapeños, squash. You bury the snake beside the nopales, and only then do you want to cry.

When you finish shoveling dirt over the shoebox, you feel eyes on your back. You turn and catch a single pupil watching you through a hole in the fence. You freeze for a moment, and it blinks—vanishes. When you reach the fence and peek over to the other side, nothing is there, just dead grass.

Days pass, and you fold the memory of Oliver in a different, thinner kind of box in your head and bury it there. The Remolina girls return, and you forget all about the snake until Saturday night, when you wait in the alleys of the decayed and rotted-out center of town, where storefronts gape empty and glass chips sparkle behind boarded-up windows. Here the night's already weaving into you, humming songs of how it missed the warmth of you. Your heart pulses with its raw power, coursing through you from tarsal bones to fingertips. The snakebite scars tingle, then itch, then burn.

You ignore the burn, focused on the skeleton boy and skeleton girl walking down the sidewalk across from you. Their masks hang like hoods from their throats and the boy has removed the top half of his costume and tied it around his waist. You follow them gently, crawling down from your perch on a chain-link fence where you've waited buzzard-like with knees folded up to your chest. You hardly make a sound.

Distant trumpets echo from where the school's marching band practices fall routines. This Saturday night has stirred to life late. It waited till dusk to release a gentle wind that erased the heat and rustled the October leaves, luring out those who'd be too busy with school or work on Monday to celebrate Halloween. Now, with the last of the sun swallowed behind the hills, the children of strict parents race from house to house in a premature search for candy. The air is laced with the smells of oil and candy corn and the sounds of cheers and frightful screams from the carnival downtown. Teens rush to the parties you've heard about in the school halls. Their cars blast Kendrick Lamar while all the white girls sing along to each and every lyric. The drive-thrus are clogged with more rowdy cars, and Spirit stores continue to churn out last-minute shoppers with bags full of latex masks and fake blood.

That world is so far away. Here, these are your streets—the streets the cops are afraid to slow down in. You prowl them, wrapped in your father's father's rancher serape, its quills itching the sides of your neck, and wearing your plain lacquer mask to bedevil whatever unlucky prick walks home alone at night.

ACT III: BRUJERÍA

And there have been many.

The sleazebag who used to trail women from the bar down this very block, salivating all kinds of horrible words at them even when they told him to please leave them alone. The frat bros, the kids who wandered too far from their parents after being warned. The cop who'd stomp down the tent of any homeless person unlucky enough to be caught in his headlights. But these two are different, these dime-store skeletons you've followed from Casa Coyotl. Alison and Kevin. They haven't noticed you trailing a block behind them, watching through the eyeholes of your mask.

You cross the street and a truck rips past, inches from your face. It billows your serape and whips your hair but doesn't halt or swerve, just rushes on, leaving the stink of diesel on the air. And just like that the street is empty again. As it always is.

"He should be here by now," Alison says to Kevin as they walk. Skeleton ribs peek beneath her denim jacket.

Kevin checks his phone. "He said he was picking up food first. Just hold on, he'll be here soon."

"But this place creeps me the fuck out." Alison's voice echoes up and down the empty block. His does too. Two voices bouncing back and forth.

"We'll go up a block or two and wait by the street corner, okay?"

"But did you share your location?"

"Been shared."

"You sure?"

"Yeah, I am. It even shows he read the text."

"Okay."

"Okay."

"It's dark."

"It's only nine, babe."

"This place gives me the creeps."

"You said that already."

They stop under the pale green halo of a buzzing streetlamp and share not a word.

Kevin, who grew up two blocks from your house: you two used to play with vinyl dinosaur toys in his driveway before he grew up into the athletic, light-skinned young man he is now. No one ever assumes he's from the same neighborhood as you. And Alison—a rich girl who moved in like the others a few years ago, when the land developers crowded the hills with McMansion monstrosities.

You want to hurt them. With even more spite than you felt a few nights ago, when Alison cornered you in the aisle of the 7-Eleven and begged you to please, please, please take her and Kevin and Heather to Coyote House on Saturday. She bargained with snacks and beer and said you'd totally be among friends for the price of their admittance into your space. "A totally good time," she said.

But you laughed at the way she said beer, like a toddler trying the word on for size, and you said, "Gross." Because you've put up with these kinds of people all your life. They announce their presence with *oooos* and *ahhhs* whenever they wander into Samuel's antique store but never buy anything, only ignore you behind the cash register and talk loudly about how clever they are. Brazen ignorance on full display. Alison wanted to fit your house around her like the vintage dresses she thrifts just to sell later online. To pretend she had no hand in Riley's fate.

Then, because you'd disrespected her, they chased you out into the lot, where you spotted Oliver behind his windshield. When you told them to fuck off, Kevin said some shit about your mom and you hardly had the time to spit out *"Hijo de la chingada!"* before they shoved you down. Shoulders and arms pinning you. You swallowed the urge to rip them apart as the night's power hummed viciously within you.

ACT III: BRUJERÍA

You tell yourself you would have liked it, too. Like when you snapped your words at Elizabeth in Casa Coyotl. She blinked all big-eyed like a deer in the headlights, with no idea how the walls of the house were closing in around her. How the branches reached out for her. You watched the gears turn behind her eyes as she realized that you two would not—could not—be whatever it was she remembered you two being. But you saw her face. The tears sparkling at the edges of her eyes as she strained to hold them in, even when the glass cut her cheek and blood streamed down instead. She didn't break, she stood tall, while you were so, so small, and your guilt became a kitchen knife carving a canyon through your chest. It's still bloody and raw, but you won't let it bother you now. You let the sting pulse through you.

Alison breaks the silence to tell Kevin, or no one, or just herself, "I didn't know there were people in the house. It was so stupid to egg it."

As if that changes anything. As if they'd ever give you a second chance. No, it's too late for you, and it's too late for them too.

You give yourself to the moon's quiet tunes, playing in your head. Nighttime ribbons flow out of your blood and lace your fingertips as you feel the quivers of all the bones resting mere yards away, in the dirt and in dumpsters and under stones: roadkill and butcher scraps and long-dead prey. You inch through the shadows, closing the space between you and the imitation skeletons, closer, closer.

A tumbleweed bounces between you and them, and it's Alison who clocks you from the corner of her eye.

She says your name in a questioning tone but before she can utter anything more, the night grabs her by the ankles and her words shatter to screams. Your shadows throw her down among the undead splinters you've dragged here with you, and they swarm her. Grab at her with writhing tendons and viscera and cartilage and clacking bones. Kevin screams the color out of his cheeks. He runs from her, the bones, and you, but when he turns the corner, the night's already carried you there and he stumbles back. He swings his fist and you feel the air compress, the dust and sand pulse. You swerve—he misses. It's easy to push him down when his back faces you.

Then you—black-cloaked monster that you are—bend around to look him in the eye while the vertebrae and ribs of long-dead rats lock his arms to the dirt, and you tell him though fanged teeth, "Leave that house alone. Leave the girls alone."

You're gone before he opens his eyes.

Back around the corner, Alison's pressed against the streetlamp, kicking away the bones that won't stop coming. But they pull away for you, they feel your presence and recede beyond the light's edge. Looking at Alison, you remember all the other kids she torments—how she used to corner you and ask question after question about things she knew you liked, pretending to be interested with her *Oh, wows* and *Really, huhs*, the whole time sharing glances with her friends that reminded you how she didn't care, how you were a performing animal, a seal calling at her commands while the audience clapped. The way she said she'd always known you were a fuckin' fruit when they caught you and Riley with your limbs tangled behind the bleachers all those years ago. You get your mask close enough to taste the rose perfume on her skin. You tell her, "I'll hurt you next time. Got it?"

She nods.

When a car pulls up to wash out a trembling Alison with its headlights, you're already gone, slinking through the alleys, the night alive with the song of your laughter.

❖ ❖ ❖

Behind a row of long-abandoned shops you laugh, leaning against a brick wall. You start to catch your breath and slide down against it, waiting, pulse slowing, and soon enough you're just panting. The joke's gone stale. You're staring at the pale stars beyond the bluffs, thinking maybe you went too far this time. No one needed blood tonight.

You get back up, make it halfway down the alley before it all catches up to you and the itching in your ankle turns to scorching pain. You hit the concrete with a hunger that explodes shrieking whiteness behind your eyes and blotches your sight. It's greater than the cravings you've gotten used to having after you use your powers, twisting blood and bile out of your stomach and up your throat. You vomit, limbs shaking; you hold on enough to drag yourself to a dumpster where a dozen feral cats scatter, except for the one that's too slow to break away from your desperate claws. You yank it by its tail and try not to listen to its yelps as you rip off your mask and pop open its pink stomach flesh like fruit. Warm meat slides down your throat in gulps. The clapping, pounding, drumming recedes back into the marrow of your bones. It should be enough for you to make it back out to the living world again, to the antique store five blocks from here. You just have to endure a little more pain.

TWO
Only the Living Hurt

Samuel's sitting behind the counter when you reach the antique shop. The bell chimes as you stagger in. Blood has dried across your lips. The fever's burning through you. You cough up a *Help me* before collapsing to the floor.

"Pain," Samuel once told you, when your gifts first began to bloom and straddle your guts demanding blood, "is part of the process. Part of life. Life is change, after all." Back then his steady hand, incense laced between the fingers, was all it took to quiet your terrors and dull the night's ceaseless roar.

You used to think Samuel had lived a thousand lifetimes to get all the wisdom he had bottled up inside him, revealed only in the calm and even tone of his voice. Unlike you: young, with bruised pride and fragile confidence, too quick to grit your teeth and strike back. (You don't feel as guilty lacerating people with words as when you use your actual fangs, your actual claws, though both can scar.)

You. A rabid, spiteful thing.

You try to remember when it was you first began bringing bodies to Samuel. You find blurred memories of afternoons playing Galaga

ACT III: BRUJERÍA

or Pac-Man in the back of the antique store, behind the maze of curio cabinets and bookshelves, escaping the summer heat. You'd stay till your eyes were glazed and Samuel announced it was closing time, and then the emptiness of Riley's absence would return to you, even though the rest of town had long since stopped caring about some dead, gay Mexican boy. When Samuel de Hory offered you a job, you took it quick. You liked the prickling pulses that radiated off the old things in the shop, like steam from hot rocks. Your mom opposed it. She cited the strange and awkward things people murmured about Samuel—that he was a communist. A pedophile. A grifter. A recluse, whose father never let him out as a child. But your mom was coming undone working her two jobs, trying to pay off the remnants of your father's medical bills, and Samuel offered better pay than you could hope to get anywhere else without a degree. You and your mom needed to eat.

The antique store consumed your days. When your grades plummeted, you were moved into a different kind of hell—continuation school, populated by exhausted teachers and other low-income kids who couldn't keep afloat—and Samuel sheltered you. You'd study the travelers who stopped by his shop on weekends, always on their way to somewhere else. San Ojuela was never their destination. You didn't blame them; it's an in-between place that your mom often thought about leaving too, but Zavalas stay put, rooting into the soil and sand. Your parents moved here to find work; you're here because there's nowhere else.

And yet dead gods whisper to you of the lands your blood is from. A land that you do not know and will never get to see.

The travelers never suspected they might be prey for Samuel. Most weren't, but every once in a while, one without family or friends would stay too long. After the sun went down and the townies went home.

You've always known it's wrong. But Samuel needs the blood; you both do.

He helped when you came to him broken and bitter, so far gone inside yourself that you hardly felt the reverberations of your own voice. When the cops wouldn't help you anymore. You came to him weeping, after weeks of dwindling search parties for Riley, who'd run into the desert with a gun, never to be seen again.

"I remember you," he said. "I think I can help you. Can't you see? I came here to hide, too."

The smell of burnt mushrooms pulls you back. You wake cold and shivering in a tub of ice that crackles when you shift upright. By the smell of book dust and chalky stones, you know you're in the back room of the antique store, the one Samuel never lets you into. You usually wait at the door for him to exit with this stench clinging to his clothes.

"You're in a lot of pain," Samuel says to you from the end of the tub. He's sitting craned forward on a stool, face etched by candlelight. Eyes blue as venomous frogs. Those eyes steal a glance at your ankle. "It was a rattler, wasn't it?"

"How did you—"

He leans in closer, cups your cheek the way you think a father would. "Did you kill anyone?" His breath is tar and mint gum. You're confused at first, but he wipes the blood dribble off your lip and says it again, louder. "Answer me."

"It was a fucking alley cat," you tell him. "Not a *person*."

"Ha. A feral cat suits you." He sits back and rolls up his sleeves. "What were you thinking? Playing with your gifts like a child, without the slightest consideration."

You shrug.

"You're dying. Did you know?"

You do know: the fever was jump-started by the snake's venom, but it was always there, festering inside you. Waiting. "I'm fine," you say.

"You're not at all fine," he snaps. "This wasn't *any* snake. The wound is radiating tōnalli—his tōnalli. This was Quetzal."

"It was just a stupid rattlesnake."

"Your ancestor sees through the eyes of every snake and nudges them along. He leaves his tōnalli essence in each of them. This one he sent to make your gifts blossom. These gods, they want to fill you with their power until you're no longer you and they can use your body. They say it's a gift—it's not. It's a curse. But fighting their power will kill you all the same."

You think of your mom. A widow, a single parent. If you die, there will be fewer bills to pay, and she won't have to ever deal with your bullshit again. But she'll be alone, and that fact breaks your heart.

With a molcajete Samuel grinds flower petals and spices into a potion. He salts it, spits in it too, then whispers nahualli incantations to the dead.

"What are you going to do?" you ask.

"Whatever I can to delay the process. I thought we'd have more time." There's a faultline crack in his voice. "There are so few of us left. The Remolina girls' mother…she wants me gone, Julian. I won't be able to stay here with you."

You can't leave! The words clot in your throat. *Not you too.* You didn't even notice when the candles went out in the room, but they have. The light's coming from something else now—his eyes? That's when he tells you.

"I can pull the curse out of you. Separate it from your bones and lock it into a vessel. But I need a sacrifice. I need a person whose body can be the vessel."

There is always something with this brujería. Always a give and take, and pain, and change. A price. But the thought of rotting out here all on your own scares you more than anything else you've ever endured, so you say it. "I'll do whatever you need me to do."

The sacrifices have been increasing with each year and every month. You've noticed how a fresh corpse's blood no longer refreshes Samuel like it used to, how you've needed to search for more prey more often. He's had the tōnalli energy locked within Casa Coyotl to feed on, but even the house hasn't been enough to stop his hunger from growing. Oliver should never have been another sacrifice. But Samuel needed to eat.

"We don't have much time," he says. "You are willing to do this final thing for me?"

All change is pain. You tell him yes.

He tells you he has a vessel in mind. "*Sangre sentimental.* I know you've felt the one."

Already, you know who he's speaking of. You interrupt him. "No. Not her."

"I need her if I'm going to save your soul. Her tōnalli is strong. She'll hold your power long enough for me to feed, then I won't need more for a good long while."

Tōnalli—you've always liked that word, the crispness of Nahuatl clicking on your tongue. Samuel says tōnalli is made from the sentimiento that lives in your blood—*sentimiento*, the Spanish word halfway between sentiment and sentience—but it's more. You feel it in all things, that warmness. It's your life force, your own small piece of the Tēteoh—divine essences; *gods* is too inadequate a word to describe them. It's planted in the crown of your skull; it's the part of your soul that travels when you sleep, that lingers on what you touch, what you love. Casa Coyotl is home to so much tōnaltin, left behind by all those who've lived and died there. And so much of Elizabeth's tōnalli has stuck to those walls. She's come

ACT III: BRUJERÍA

back for it, but that's not how it works. You can't pull it back inside once you've left your touch.

She was in your life until she wasn't one day, like all other dead things. You went to knock on the door to play, looking for your friend who hadn't shown up to school, and instead found Miss Marisol sitting on the steps, hair a mess and eyes empty. The handle of a shattered coffee mug dangling from her fingers. You knew before you asked that Elizabeth was gone.

And yet she appeared today, sitting in the backyard as if she'd never left and it was just another day, and you hadn't yet loved a boy, lost him, and had darkness take root inside your bones. *The living dead*, you thought. You didn't recognize Elizabeth at first, but she said your name. *Julian*. That person you're not anymore. When she hugged you, you smelled her skin. Like sweet nopales. Her. Your hunger returned too—its brightness burning out of you. You snapped away but her grip left faint imprints on your arms, phantom touches from someone who shouldn't have been there, who was once your only friend besides Riley. You bound your body wire-tight and rigid, and told yourself to ignore her, she didn't matter, she was just another girl, but then in the kitchen you almost made her cry—you almost said sorry—and then the house went mad and brick came exploding through the window and glass sliced her cheek.

It doesn't matter. Like Oliver, like the snake you killed, you have to block her out. The dead cannot come back to hurt you. Only the living hurt each other.

Samuel waits to know if you're willing to give him Elizabeth for your own salvation. It's just one more life. You don't say the words but you nod, and that's enough.

"Now then," Samuel says with an exhale.

He rolls up your jeans to find the twin scars, black streaks webbing up your leg from them. He hands you the molcajete and tells you to drink. You do, and the pain of the night burning out of you locks you in. It floods your eyes; you see nothing beyond a shrieking explosion of violet.

By the time you get home, the lights are off. Your mom's car is parked in the driveway and the sour stink of weed leaks from the front door. She's probably in the living room, lulled to sleep on the couch by the substances that she uses to push away the migraines that grind her teeth. She won't speak tonight. That hits like empty metal, leaving you clanging.

You two used to sit together at the small dinner table with its dozen little half-moons scorched into the wood by past coffee mugs. She'd ask you about your day, and you'd tell her it was fine, and she'd serve you fresh chisme from her work as a hostess for a Mexican restaurant with bottomless margaritas. You used to love the names she'd assign to the cast of her stories and the gutter swears she'd paint her boss with. "El Nariz" was an especially nosy coworker, "La Maseca" the white-washed assistant manager; you'd belly laugh along with her. Later, you two would sit in the grainy TV light deciding what show to ridicule together, and only after the screen went dark and your mom fell asleep would you escape into the night.

To avoid waking your mom, you take the long way around the house, down the arroyo, between the reeds, and up the ravine to your backyard fence. You slide open your bedroom window and slink inside. You flick on the lights and a dead boy sits waiting on your bed. He's pale, not breathing, sitting crisscross with his hands folded in his lap. His hair is brown, his glasses cracked.

"Are you really going to do it?" Oliver asks. There's a grin carved across his throat; raw tendons within stretch when he speaks.

You don't move. "Are you a ghost?"

"No, I'm not even that," he says with a sad smile. "I'm just what you remember me as."

"Then I want you to go away."

"Well, I'm dead, so…" He shrugs. His eyes are hollow sockets behind the glasses.

You look away. You turn to the mirror instead to see yourself still red-eyed and fanged. You guide your tongue over the fangs crowding your mouth. Your breath is warm and pungent—smelling still of fatty meat. There was a time when you'd vomit up guts and stomach acid for hours after a binge in a series of cramping heaves until your body shivered with emptiness. Not anymore. With a single thought, your fangs slide back up slowly into your skull, leaving just your normal, crooked bite. It takes a moment, but you blink your eyes back to white and brown, too.

When you turn back around, Oliver is studying the movie posters and your father's old darkwave records tacked to your walls. "Funny," he says. "I never thought a monster's lair would look like this."

"Cut it out," you tell him. You remind yourself he's not really there.

"Maybe I'm just a lucid dream. You've not been sleeping particularly well." He laughs. Points to the gash in his throat. "Gotta admit, Samuel has a flair for theatrics. So tell me, are you going to kill Elizabeth too?"

There's always a take; brujería is a hungry, wild thing. All the blood you've sucked, the meat you eat, the tōnalli you've absorbed into the darkness under your cloak—all this is the price. Elizabeth's blood is rich with loss and webbed memories of *has-beens* and *maybe-could-bes*.

She shouldn't have come back. That's her fault.

"But she did," the dead boy tells you. Things that should be dead seem to keep coming back.

"I didn't kill you," you tell Oliver.

He shrugs again. "Guilty by association, then. Like when Riley shot himself—"

"How about you shut the fuck up?!" You throw one of your father's vinyl records at him and it passes through like mist—shatters against your chalky drywall.

"Semantics, then," Oliver says. You just stare at him until he perks up his head and says, "Someone's coming." You hear it too—footsteps barreling down the hall.

Your mom pounds on the door. *"Julian?* Is that you? ¡Abre la puerta!" You don't get the chance to. She swings the door open with tears running down her cheeks, screaming, *What did you do? What did you do?* over and over, waving a dirty shoebox in your face. When you snap back to Oliver, he's gone. Your Mom yells at you to look at her, but you don't register anything until she shoves a shoebox into your hands, a snake's coffin caked with dirt.

"My garden," your mom pleads through tears and frustration. "Julian, what did you do?"

The stink of death wafts from the dead snake within the box. You drop it on your bed like your hands are running from blame, look out the window and across the yard to figure out what the hell she's talking about, and you see it, even in the dark. The dark, wilting shapes of the garden, which you somehow missed on your way in. All those plants, now dead and rotting over sour soil.

No.

You back up, push your mom back, but she's still shouting, not letting you go—because, she says, she's worried for you—you need help, you're sick. What can you do but tear away from that? You have to leave—out—out—out! You flick your wrist and something twists and your mom yelps, but you're already gone—escaping down the hallway and out the front door into the hands of night.

ACT III: BRUJERÍA

Aimlessly you run, not knowing where to go, until you do. To the lakeside cabin, back to Samuel. When you get there, panting, hunger and exhaustion stabbing your ribs, you stagger onto the porch and call for him, but he doesn't answer. You force the door open with all your weight and fumble into the dark. The house is empty; moonlight streams through the windows. You've been calling him the whole way over, but he hasn't picked up.

"Samuel," you yell into the dark. "We need to talk—I changed my mind. I can't do it."

Silence.

With your coyote sight, you hunt room to room for him, even in the wreck that is the north side of the house, but you only find ruined stone. The narrow living room and kitchenette you find in shambles, books and portraits strewn across the floor. Your foot crunches on an old-timey photograph of a man who must be Samuel's father. The frame is snapped, the glass in shards. Samuel's never spoken about his father.

Finally, you're desperate enough to check the basement.

You creak down the sagging wooden steps. You comb the shadows on the way down, looking for more than spiderwebs. A wet smacking echoes from the corner of the room. At the final step you see it, pale and hunched over, its skin stretched over ribs and spine and shoulder blades. Chewing something you cannot see. There's movement behind it. You spot the ancient severed hand of the bruja crawling spider-like up the pale monster's spine, then climbing to its shoulder, where it perches to whisper in the pale thing's ear: a gargling, clicking sound. The pale thing snaps its head towards you, dropping Oliver's corpse to the ground with a *thunk*—then shadows pull away from the twisted shape of Samuel's face, the severed hand perched on his shoulder. Strings of coagulated blood and meat hang from his peg teeth and his milk-glass eyes hold a look of terror.

"Julian?" Samuel's eyes blink back to blue. No matter, you're already halfway up the steps, running through cobwebs, as he calls out, "Julian, come back!"

You're out of the house—fleeing back into the waiting desert night, trying to outrun the echoes of his voice.

Run, Julian, run all you want. Xolotl will bring her to me himself, and there will be nowhere left for you to go.

THREE
Xolotl

It was two in the morning when Elizabeth woke. The LA fires stained the night sky, even all the way out here: a bleeding red that dyed the curtains, the bedroom walls, the wood floor, and the two girls' skin. Out in the hall the grandfather clock chimed. For a moment Elizabeth was fourteen again, lying awake on the too-big bed in her room with the door locked, ignoring the blood on the walls, listening instead to the echo of her father calling: "Liz? Mary? Where are you? We need to go. You can come on out now, it's all right. I'm all right."

But this time it was Angel Eyes who'd nudged Elizabeth awake. Mary was asleep, bundled in a blanket with her back to Elizabeth.

Silently, Angel Eyes leaped off the bed and began to paw at the door.

"Fuck. There's no litter box for you in here, is there?" Elizabeth got up, pulled on her red sweater, and made her way through the house in shadow and crimson moonlight. Her fuzzy socks pushed away the chill of the tiles as she searched room to room for anything the cat could do her business in.

When she checked her phone, she had three messages from Jannah:

> **Jannah (Dance), 12:05**
> How's everything with your aunt? You're at the spook-house, right?
>
> **Jannah (Dance), 12:07**
> Your aunts house that is. Was calling it spooky in bad taste??? I feel like it was sorry ;-;
>
> **Jannah (Dance), 12:22**
> Dude are you dead? I know damn well you dont sleep this early

But Elizabeth had in fact fallen asleep that early. She'd tried watching another Western on Netflix, but she hadn't slept at all the night before, and exhaustion had cradled her. She replied.

> **Dark Liz, 2:13**
> I'm awake. Thanks for checking. Everything's fine, everyone's just at each other's throats. Its like Lord of the Flies with my sister. Funeral's tomorrow, we found a cat but no ghosts, sorry to disappoint :(

She muted her phone when she was done. No need to text more than she had to; that was how people got too close, opened the way for mistakes. Jannah's texts made Elizabeth's guts flicker butterflies whenever her phone lit up. She didn't want to kill the tiny chance that hers did the same to Jannah.

A breeze flowed rhythmic and steady through the hallway. The house was breathing, restless. Julian had told her she didn't belong here, had looked at her with hate seeping from his eyes, destroying any pieces of their friendship that still survived. He'd asked if she knew what *El Coco* meant. *Tell me*, she'd thought, hoped, begged.

"You. *You're* the boogeyman here," he'd said. He was right, Elizabeth decided. Nothing here wanted her to stay. She would bury her aunt, then go.

Coyotes howled outside. No, not a pack. Just one.

You should be used to this, she reminded herself. There'd been so many nights when those howls were her only company. But even back then, she'd wondered if the sounds were truly just animals and not other skin-changing things that walked beyond where the lights shone.

Downstairs, she found Marisol's office door cracked open, a dim glow spilling into the hall. Elizabeth's mother had fallen asleep with her head on the desk, like she did at home when she worked long into the night. Even out here, she couldn't take a break. Elizabeth thought about finding her a blanket but decided it was best not to risk waking her.

At this point Elizabeth considered just letting the cat shit somewhere in the house and cleaning it in the morning, but she'd almost reached the living room, where she swore she'd seen a litter box earlier that day. She twisted between the rows of boxes and the crates full of Samuel's rocks and found it in the corner near the TV. She plopped Angel Eyes onto the sand and waited with patient hope for the cat to do her thing.

Something creaked. Or groaned, or yawned, down the hall. Elizabeth froze, but the sound didn't repeat.

"It's the wind," she told herself. Or coyotes. Or skinwalkers. Or both.

Angel Eyes was watching her with a big blank face instead of focusing on her task. Elizabeth rolled her eyes. "Fine, I won't look." She turned away and began blowing long ghosts of breath into the cold air. She followed one swirl upward to a toothy grin. The skull was carved from lava rock. Its gruesome smile was wide, with too many teeth. A crown of jagged stone feathers sprouted from its head, and she glimpsed her own reflection in the teal gems bugging from its sockets.

The noises of *living* things in the dark got under her skin. The dead and their totems did not. She giggled softly. "Oh, you're a cutie. Wif your widdle teef."

Under the skull a plaque read *Mictlāntēcuhtli: The Lord of Mictlān*. She mouthed the name, squinting to read it in the dim light.

"Mick-t-lan-tech-coo-tly...does anyone remember your name?" she asked the Lord of Mictlān with mocking pride. Because there were no real gods, not like that, not anymore. Her mother had never taught the girls about their grandmothers' culture, had replaced it instead with classic Americana to shield them from the abuse she'd faced growing up Latina in the magma of East LA in the nineties. No Día de Los Muertos, only Halloween. No quinceañeras, though Elizabeth didn't get a sweet sixteen either. Too expensive.

The stories about Mesoamerican gods were just stories to her, foreign and disconnected from times and places. Like El Coco or the chupacabra—monsters that only existed in the antique words her father spoke, which his mother had given him, and her mother before her. All that talk about tigers and cemeteries was the same. Just different kinds of make-believe.

She reached into her pocket and pulled out her phone, typed the Lord of Mictlān's name into Google, and said, "You're a sad old god, aren't you? You probably had a soul once too, huh. Did you lose it? Or did it fade away when people forgot who you were?"

If that skull rock had ever been scary, it had lost its power long ago. She wondered how lonely the Lord of Mictlān must have been for all these years, pushed to the side of a bookshelf, only the lord of dust.

"Maybe you and I are both stuck," she said. "In places where we shouldn't be."

She smiled at it. It grinned back at her. She looked back to check if Angel Eyes was done but the cat was gone. After a quick search around the room, she found her waiting on the sill of yet another broken window.

"Come on, get down from there," she whispered to Angel Eyes, who apparently interpreted the command as more of a suggestion before leaping out into the night. When Elizabeth stepped onto the back porch, she spotted Angel Eyes crossing the grass. The cat stopped and waited at the edge of the woods, where black shadows of autumn trees clawed at a bleeding sky.

"No, no, no," she called to the cat in a raspy whisper. "Get back here! Now! Don't—I swear to god, don't you—"

Angel Eyes disappeared into the bushes.

Elizabeth gasped. "Oh, you little shit."

She paced back and forth in the cold, choosing, then changing her mind again. Should she let Angel Eyes be, return back inside to her bed and warmth, and look for the cat in the morning? Or go in after her? She was set on the former, but there was that howling. And she wouldn't be able to stomach it if Angel Eyes didn't come home because of her. Elizabeth swallowed her fear, turned on her cell phone light, and started slowly into the woods.

Her socks squelched on damp leaves. The wind was frigid, biting into the marrow of Elizabeth's bones. She followed the garden wall with her hands tucked under her armpits, juggling her phone's light and grumbling to herself until she reached the south gate, where Angel Eyes balanced atop the ancient bars.

"I swear to god, if you run, I'll euthanize your ass," she told the cat in a gentle tone.

The cold had really set in out there in the woods. Her breath curled white into the trees.

Elizabeth was reaching for Angel Eyes, to snatch him up and book it back to the warmth of Casa Coyotl, when a blur flapped past her face. Elizabeth jumped—lost hold of the cat; traced thin, kidney-shaped wings fluttering amber in the moonlight, towards the iron gate. There the creature settled: a moth. Trailing the scent of lavender. When it took off again, a woman stood behind the bars, within the labyrinth, a single black shadow with no mouth, no eyes, no nose. The shadow groaned, "Lizzz, child."

Grief swelled up inside Elizabeth at the sound of that voice. It settled in her chest and she almost ran forward to the bars but stopped. *No. There's nothing here. She's dead, Liz. She's dead.* She half-laughed. Smiled. Croaked out a gentle, "I knew I'd find you, if I came." *I didn't get to say goodbye.*

Marisol groaned. "¿Por qué estás aquí, niña?"

Elizabeth scrunched up her face. "What?" Spanish again. She didn't know the words—she'd forgotten them forever ago.

"I said don't come!" Marisol cried out. "To come carefully, or not at all." Elizabeth was backing up, scared now, fighting back the *Sorry! Sorry!* bubbling inside her. "El Coco! Se viene por ti, Liz child—mi niña."

"But there is no Coco!" Elizabeth shouted, trembling with the shame, grief, and frustration that were wringing her tight. "I looked and looked—what's the point of seeing ghosts, if it doesn't help me?! If it doesn't make me whole again? I—"

"But you see *me*," Marisol said. Then she flowed right up—against the gate—feet gliding over the cobblestones, stiff, hanging. She curled bony fingers around the bars. Elizabeth dropped her phone and staggered. Frost budded on the bars. "He's coming now. Se viene por ti, Liz child. Vete! Vete!"

"What?"

That distant moaning had started up again, louder this time. Closer. How long had it been coming?

ACT III: BRUJERÍA

"*Run!*"

Then the night gasped open and a shape ripped violently through the woods to the clearing and howled—a human cry. The moon a bloody spotlight behind it, carving out black feathers that cut the night like daggers. Fangs glistening in a red maw, flesh hanging off bone exposed in ribbons. The face a coyote skull with eyes bubbling in its sockets, all of them aiming down at her.

El Coco.

Elizabeth spun to the gate and shook the chains but they caught against each other.

"Let me in!"

The gates wouldn't budge. Her dead aunt said again, "¡Vete!"

The beast launched towards her. Angel Eyes darted down the fence and Elizabeth followed, narrowly dodging the hot breath of the monster behind her. She rushed past cacti and chest-whipping branches, never minding the splinters that pegged her underfoot. She ran as fast as she could toward where she thought the house was, but she couldn't see it. It was still too far. The shape was rushing closer, the air compressing between it and her.

¡Vete!

Farther down, Angel Eyes stopped at a gash in the wall where the bricks had tumbled away.

¡Vete!

She scraped through the foliage-draped hole and into a field of boulders and wheat grass; a neighborhood twinkled down the hill beyond a narrow road.

¡Vete!

She ran for it, shredding her voice screaming, "Help! Help!" But the rocks were treacherous and skidded out beneath her feet. She fell—hit a boulder twice her size, gasped as the breath escaped her chest. The shape approached slowly then, on backwards-bent legs. Flesh hung off its face in strands; saliva dripped from its fangs and the gaps in its cheeks. It lifted a single, ragged paw and pressed it into her chest, pinning her against the rock. Its feather crown spread wide, billowing. It didn't seem real. She was going to die, and all she could think of was how vast the stars embedded within those feathers were. She closed her eyes.

The weight of the paw lifted. When she opened her eyes again, the moon had bled out its red and shone sickly white again between the clouds, and a wraith in a dark serape stood above her, hands outstretched towards the shape thrashing in the dirt. His fingers jerked, broke, and snapped back straight again while the shape's bones churned beneath its flesh. The Boy glared at Elizabeth. "Well?" he shouted with burning eyes. "Get up and do something!"

But her legs were stones. Her heart hammered her against the boulder.

"There's a lighter in my pocket, get it for me!" the Boy shouted, but the words were so far away and took so long to reach Elizabeth that they couldn't move her. "Forget it!" the Boy groaned. One broad stroke of Julian's hand across the sky, and the night tore off the shape's arm and flung it away into the dirt, where black tendrils sprouted from the stump and whipped in the grass. Julian released the monster from its flailing and took out the lighter himself. He tore off his poncho and balled it in his hands—one flick of the lighter and the wool blazed. He lobbed it at the shape, and it roared in a gust of flames.

He grabbed Elizabeth by the wrist, his eyes boring into her, red and rageful. "Come on."

They ran down the hillside, towards the road, where Julian stopped and held Elizabeth at the lip of the asphalt. The shape was catching up, screaming through blazing jaws.

"Julian, this is not the time for looking both ways!" Elizabeth shouted.

"Oh, shut up!"

The shape was almost on them. Howling—howling. Yellow headlights beamed into focus up the road.

"Almost here," Julian muttered.

Elizabeth could feel the shape's heat on her back.

"Hold on," Julian said. The semi-truck and all its tons of weight sped forwards. "Now!" Julian shoved her into its headlights, and together they raced across the road. The flaming, raging monster pounced—and the truck bashed it into a thousand blazing bits.

They climbed back through the hole in the garden wall together, Elizabeth who could see the dead and Julian who could, apparently, puppet them. Back to the woods and home, like they used to when they were friends. Elizabeth thought, *How funny*. For both of them to have been touched by the supernatural. But why them? It had to have been the influence of the house, which seemed to suck everyone into its orbit and swallow them up.

Her feet ached. She followed Julian's footfalls. He didn't have shoes on either, and his toes left shallow bean-shaped divots in the dirt. She followed him all the way to the lake, where the trees pulled away to reveal the stars above. The clouds had wandered elsewhere and taken with them the redness. Now the night was crystalline, same as the dark water reflecting it. The lake smelled of moss and mildew—Elizabeth had known they were approaching it long before she saw the water's gleam. It was an old friend. Julian sat down at the edge of the dock and dipped his feet into the water, rippling the reflection of the moon. Elizabeth sat crisscross on the sand and waited. The cool lake air kissed her skin.

"That was my grandfather's serape," he said softly but sternly. Bitterness between his teeth. "Now it's gone." Julian fidgeted, crossing his arms and then holding them at his sides, clearly unsure of what to do with them now.

Elizabeth tried being sincere. "I'm sorry."

"That was Xolotl you just met," Julian said. "Samuel's not going to like that." He looked toward the cabin across the lake. Lights off.

"Why not?" Elizabeth asked.

"Well." He shrugged. "We just killed his pet, didn't we? Sort of, anyway. It's probably temporary."

Elizabeth nodded, though she didn't get it yet. "Look, you're going to have to tell me a little more about what the fuck just happened or I'm going to lose my mind."

"Why are you here?" he snapped. Without his poncho, she saw how he really was, twig-thin in a black-and-red striped t-shirt. Sleeplessness made shadows beneath his eyes. "If you'd listened and left when I told you to, I'd still have my serape. I could have let Xolotl eat you whole, you know that? I could have let him tear out your heart; I'd warned you enough."

"Sorry."

He gritted his teeth. "Is that all you can say?"

"I *apologize*."

He turned away. Back to looking at the ripples in the water. After a moment, dark shapes began bobbing at the surface. One by one, the skulls of dead fish and birds popped their heads out around his toes. Living, glistening things swam among the dead ones. They chirped with the bones, some airy tune that the lake carried across it and back again. Scooching closer, she got a better look at the creatures, like salamanders but charcoal-colored and with little black bristles on the sides of their heads.

"They're axolotls, yeah?" Elizabeth scrounged for faint memories of them from when she was young. They never liked people or noise and would flee when the girls came to splash in the lake.

"They don't belong here." Julian stirred the water around the little creatures, their tadpole tails, their black-pebble eyes.

"They aren't supposed to survive outside the lakes in Mexico City. Anywhere else it's too hot or too cold, or the water doesn't have the minerals they need. But for whatever reason, they do just fine here. I bet there used to be thousands of them too, before the reservoir was built. But then the lake dried up and now this *puddle* is all the axolotls have left."

Anger set in inside of her. Because Julian knew more about the axolotls than she did, because he knew the lake better and the house too, as if she was the guest and none of this was for her.

"When it was Xolotl's turn to throw himself into the sun to help begin its movement," Julian said, "he refused and ran. First, he hid in the corn fields, but the other gods found him. Next, he hid among the magueys, but they found him again. Then he hid by tearing off his legs and twisting himself into the form of an axolotl. This time the other gods found his legs and burned them instead. Without his legs he was stuck as a beast—any beast, really, shifting from animal to animal because he could no longer stand upright like a man. All axolotls come from him. At least, that's the story I've been told."

Elizabeth watched the axolotls and the bones dance and traced their movement to Julian's flowing fingertips. Elizabeth thought of the Lord of Mictlān. The ragged boy with his singing bones and axolotls—for this moment, he was the lord of the lake.

"Could you bring someone back? If they're dead?" she asked.

He shook his head. "No one can do that."

"What if they're only half dead? Like not gone fully, just—in between? Maybe they're awake and walking but sort of—missing something." Julian gave her a look. Embarrassment rushed through her. She searched for an out and shifted gears. "What happened to us?" The words fell from her lips as soon as she thought them. "What happened to you?"

He gave her an even more awful look, and her face reddened. She shouldn't have asked. "Nothing happened at all," he said. "You left and never called. I stayed here."

I'm still me, she wanted to say, but she knew that wasn't true.

"After the accident, Mom gave Dad a restraining order," she said. "He went into rehab up in San Jose, and we just...well, we weren't allowed to come back here," Elizabeth said.

The first weeks back home with her mother had been waves of family and doctors and police officers. The police would sit her and Mary down in the living room that was not her living room—it was Mom's—and give her too-cold water that stung her teeth and ask mundane questions about her father. *Where did he work? Do you know where he went on the days he didn't come home? How long would he leave you in that house? How often did he drink too much? Did he ever hit you?* All questions she'd answered a thousand times before, that she repeated the answers to mechanically until the words lost all meaning and were just sounds gurgling in her throat. *He worked as a welder and handyman. No, I don't. Sometimes for two weeks. At least twice a week. No, never.*

They had visited Aunt Marisol in the nursing home a few times but only after the dementia had gnawed away most of her memories. Most of the time she didn't even recognize the woman Elizabeth had become. When she did, she would ask Elizabeth where her father was. Sometimes Elizabeth almost told her, almost opened that wound back up, but instead she'd say he was out, working again.

"Marisol gave me your new number when you left," Julian said. "I called, but you never bothered picking up, not after that one time where you said you didn't want to talk to Marisol or your dad or me or anyone from San Ojuela ever again."

Elizabeth didn't have any memory of saying that, but it might well be true. She remembered so very little of what had happened in the wake of losing her soul. Her life had been tossed into a blender of counseling appointments and a new school and trying to make friends and meeting with lawyers and everything else a fourteen-year-old shouldn't have to deal with. It wasn't her fault some things had fallen through the cracks.

"I'm sorry," Elizabeth said. "I didn't think you would miss me, not really. You had your other friends, right?"

"One. Just the one. And then he left too, and I decided I'd had enough of friends." He smiled bitterly.

"I'm sorry," Elizabeth said again.

"Stop it—don't be. It's not like you could have fixed it, you were already gone. It's okay. It doesn't bother me anymore."

He's lying. All these years later, and Elizabeth still saw it in the twitch of his nose. "What was his name?"

He told her about his boyfriend Riley while the axolotls bobbed in the starry water. How they'd kept their relationship a secret because of the comments Riley's father would make about *homosexuals.* Calling them sissies, degenerates. Riley and Julian were each other's secret for six months—until the boys at school caught them together behind the bleachers. Then Riley's father found out, threated to kick him to the streets or send him somewhere far away to fix him. He broke Riley's phone and chased Julian away.

Julian told her how the dark things in his dreams had leaked into Riley's head, until one day he went to school with a knife to end the pushing, leering, and cackling the rich boys tormented him with. He ended up plunging the metal deep into Michael Ritter's thigh meat. Then the cops got involved, and shit got serious. Even with the town in a frenzy about the chisme of it, no one noticed Riley slipping away into the desert, where he shot himself with the rifle his father had kept in the closet for them to one day go hunting like men.

Sorry was too weak a word for Elizabeth when Julian finished telling her the story. She watched his eyes fill with tears and wondered why she'd been so afraid of something so bruised. "When I asked about half-dead people," she said, awkwardly, "I...meant me. The night I left, La Muerte came to me, and ever since I've felt *wrong*. I see things no one else does, and I'm always cold, and sometimes when I'm harmed, or when people touch me, I don't even feel it, like I'm not in my body at all. Sometimes hours or days pass and I don't even notice, don't even have memories of it. Sometimes people tell me about things I did and I think, *Is that really something I would do?* But I did do those things, didn't I? I'm—" She felt the claws tightening around her throat, that same fear that always stared back at her from mirrors, and her voice broke. "I'm afraid I won't ever find my way back from that place. What if I just end up empty? Like a ghost?"

He nodded solemnly. She almost hit him, thinking he was making fun of her, like Mary.

"I'm serious!" she hissed. No one understood how terrified she was of death—of oblivion. Once she'd asked her mom what would happen to people who died if they didn't have a soul. Her mom had given the Catholic answer. Things without souls don't go to heaven. Or hell. But that's an absurd question, Liz; all *people* have souls.

"I believe you," Julian said with an earnest look. Even with his face whittled away to skin and bone, he had soft features, each dimple and nose crinkle and eyebrow crease alive with emotion.

"I came back to find my soul," she said. "But it's not here. I don't know what I thought would happen—Jesus Christ, I sound like a kid saying it—I guess I wanted to find a picture, or memory, or *something* to make it all click into place. To explain the things I see. To explain Dad. But it was just—there wasn't anything. And there aren't any ghosts here, either. Except Marisol?" As she said it, she remembered. "I saw her. At the southern gate, and—I think she was trying to tell me that she was murdered." The words reeked of certainty as they spilled out of her. "I think El Coco did it." El Coco—Xolotl? No. Julian had said, *We killed his pet.* Samuel? The name bled through her head like ink. "Fuck, man. What the hell am I supposed to do, Julian?"

"I can't help you," he said.

She looked him in the eyes. "What do you mean? We just slayed a fucking *chupacabra* together."

He shot up; the bones sank into the murk. "No, *we* didn't do anything. *I* risked my life—*my* life. Because you went prying where you shouldn't have. I'm sorry, I can't help you find your soul. Just leave, yeah? That's the best thing for you." He laughed sourly and started back towards the woods.

Elizabeth called to him, "Wait!"

He stopped for only a second. "Go on back to your real home, all right?"

Elizabeth started to follow but stopped inches from the tree line. A whisper came through the leaves. *Lizzzzzz child.*

Marisol was right. It was too dark in the woods.

She checked her pocket, but her phone wasn't there. She'd dropped it when Xolotl attacked her.

Shit.

She went back to the lake and ran her finger through the pebbles; at least the water was warm. She sank onto the sand, turning her back to the water and the axolotls that she knew wouldn't harm her, facing the true darkness of the woods. She resolved to sit there, locked up stiff and shivering, for however many hours it would take for morning to come.

Elizabeth had never liked the dark.

FOUR
The Field of Bones

I'D BE LYING if I said I went home last night once I left Sonora's. Instead, I followed the 215 for about seven miles in the opposite direction. Fifteen minutes later, I found myself pacing the front porch of Gran's house.

I kept my hat on and head down to avoid stares from neighbors I'd known growing up, but the street was mostly vacant, shuttered houses now. My boots squeezed yelps from the porch planks. My hands shook. I was re-tucking in my uniform when Gran answered the door.

Lucas, she said. Take off that hat and get inside. It's hot at hell.

Old pictures of Dad and Mom hung on the walls. They were sun-faded. In one, Dad wore a tux and grinned like a fool with Mom hanging on his arm, her skin glowing copper against his pasty whiteness. The banner behind them read *San Bernardino High School Homecoming!* in bold typeface. 1984.

Mom in denim overalls, playing in a yard with more dirt than grass. Mom and Dad's wedding day. A year or two later down the timeline wall, pictures of me. Curly-haired, dark-skinned baby boy, also wearing overalls and looking all wrong in my father's pale arms. Me, a little older, holding a red freight truck. Staring at the

ACT III: BRUJERÍA

picture, my fingers twitched with the muscle memory of converting the toy from truck to robot and back.

I took my seat at Gran's table, folded my hands over the plastic protecting the white doilies, and asked, When was the last time you visited Dad?

She said, Probably the last time you did, mijo. He's buried far away, and you know his family never really spoke to me.

Gran didn't sound sad when she said it. She kissed her teeth at the sight of Dad's last name on my badge—an awkward piece that's just as much a part of me as all the other awkward pieces I try to redeem in this line of work—and added, You know, your mom asks about you all the time. We could walk over there and talk? She knows you call me sometimes. We like to share stories about you on Sundays.

The idea of all the wrong and subjective words they would use to describe me was an animal that gnawed. Gran caught me looking away at the pictures again. You always were a quiet one, she said. She pointed to a snapshot of me and Rodrigo and Javier in matching onesies. Said, Rodrigo cried all the time for everything—Javier, too, when he was small—but you were just an easy kid. Much easier than your mother, or anyone I know, really. You're not a fussy person.

I try not to be.

¡Que serio! she laughed. It wasn't until I'd finished the lentil soup that Gran asked why exactly I'd come.

Do you remember all those stories you used to tell us, like those urban legends about things around the Inland Empire?

She laughed again. What happened, did you catch a wendigo?

Not quite.

She looked me over, probably noticed the way I tensed up. She was always able to see when something was wrong, even if no one else could. She pursed her lips. Said, I thought you outgrew those kinds of stories. It all ends up being people once the curtain's gone, you know that. Our imaginations go wild because people are awful, and monsters make more sense.

I said, I don't know. People keep talking about chupacabras and shit.

Then I looked at her, really looked at her—her eyes. Even as her hair whitened over the years and her skin wrinkled, her eyes stayed the same.

I said, I think I'm outmatched. Or—I've stumbled upon something I have no business looking into.

And you want me to tell you what to do about it?

I didn't speak out loud. Not a word, but she heard me. *I want permission.*

That doesn't sound like you at all, Lucas. You never listen to people's advice anyway, not when you feel like you gotta do something. Trust yourself. It got you this far.

Afterwards, when I finished washing the dishes, I told her thank you and kissed her cheek. Diana had probably eaten without me by then, but while she'd be upset, I knew she'd get over it. I put my hat back on. When I reached the door, Gran asked if I really came by just to talk about monsters.

I said, Not just that. I missed you.

A sea of picket signs block the road to the precinct. Black and rainbow umbrellas with peeling superhero prints break up the cluster of them. About two dozen protesters or so. They've been here for weeks now; I even know the organizers' names. They're a docile group compared to some—they mostly sit on lawn chairs or at foldout tables with water bottles and sandwiches. Their picket signs shout: ABOLISH ICE.

The ICE facility is across the lot from the precinct, accessed through the same gate, on the same side of a dusty mountain. At

ACT III: BRUJERÍA

best, to the protesters, we're just in the way. At worst, they think it's our fault the law is what it is, or that we can't just step aside and watch them sack government property.

It's six in the morning by the time I pull up to the gate. Some of the protesters are crawling out of their tents and stretching in the sunrise. They meerkat-flinch at the sight of my headlights, and then the shouting begins. I pay them no mind, drown them out with my radio. Ignore the hands pounding on my hood, the spit sprinkling my windows, the accusations:

pig;
fascist;
bastard;
bootlicker.

I drive to the top of the hill and park in my designated spot. I have a better spot with a better office downtown, but I prefer the protesters to shaking every white hand that sticks out of a tailored suit walking into city hall. The protesters' chants reach up here, although faint. I'm told not to take it personally. For the most part I don't.

My ass isn't even in my seat when Nancy pokes her head into my office. The chair's too new, stiff and not broken in, and my knees ache on the days I sit here too long. She says, Mornin', Sheriff. How you doing?

I'm doing.

She hands me a yellow folder from her binder.

You'll like this. We did a scan for all Dodges in the area that fit the year and paint job of the one y'all found yesterday. We came up with about seventy-eight of them.

Hm. I don't think I do like this, actually, I say with a frown.

She rolls her eyes and says, I'm getting there. She reaches across the desk and pokes a black and white photograph of a kid gripping the front wheel of a Dodge, glasses almost fogged up—the face of someone pulled over for the first time in his peaceful life. Nancy says the kid was pulled over at a checkpoint last Thursday.

Look at the tires, she adds. Those are sports tires. Like, expensive. They look nice, only you can't buy them anymore. The manufacturer stopped producing those back in, oh, I don't know, 2009?

A pause.

I'm pinching my brow. And?

She smiles, says, Right! I didn't notice this, so I can't take credit—that would be forensics. But those are the very same tires as on your Dodge you found. The shreds you picked up match the brand.

I lean in. All right. Not the cartels, then what? You run—

The plates? Yessir. His name is Oliver Ruvalcaba, and from what we know, he was a nineteen-year-old living with his undocumented parents. Nancy shrugs, catches her voice at the hiss of a truck coming to a stop. Sliced by the blinds, I make out ICE agents unloading another batch of detainees, leading them through the double doors. Rifles hanging off their shoulders reach for the sky.

I hate seeing that, Nancy says.

What can you do, though? I think. It is what it is. By the smell, there must be hundreds inside now. Maybe a thousand, all baking in that tin box, in the same crusty clothes they were marched in with. More and more trucks have been coming these days.

I'd rather not talk about it, I say. I ask instead about the boy.

Nancy continues: His mother filed a missing persons report on Friday with San Diego. Says he ran away and took his father's car. What are you thinking?

That I've dug up four people this month alone. And stood on a mountain of corpses in Riverside, and the people those bodies belonged to were dead for decades, their identities rotted away. I've traced gashes in metal made by the claws of some feral monster.

You okay, Sheriff? Nancy asks, staring because I haven't said anything.

Yes. Yeah. Just—

Gunshots crack outside and protesters scream. Goddammit! I shoot out of my chair and shout, Nancy, get someone out there to question the family, and follow up those leads. Put out a BOLO while you're at it.

The guards, along with my chief deputy Nick Raymond, are pushing back the crowd with clear shields by the time I reach the bottom of the hill. Some young and hot-blooded ICE guard fired off a rubber bullet. Oh, how they've crucified him. I have to shove past a sea of angry fists just to reach him, snatch away his gun before he does something really stupid, and push him back to the gate where I'll give him a verbal lashing.

A water bottle shoots through the air and bites me square on the bridge of my nose.

Crack!

All my life I've had shit thrown at my face, from baseballs to batteries, and water bottles are pillows compared to unopened soda cans. But this one fills my skull with noise and tastes like metal. It sends the protesters into an eruption of gawking and laughing, laughing, laughing. Inching closer to me.

I grab the closest picket sign I can reach and snap it across my knee, regardless of whether the owner of it is innocent or not—he's guilty enough by association—I push the fucker into the dirt and wait until we're back inside the precinct to throttle the guard. He complains that it was just a mistake and that he was mad and tired and hot, but my own shouting snuffs him into submission. I dismiss him then, hope that this lesson is one he won't forget, that it creeps up on him when he relaxes at night. He'll thank me someday. I should know after all, I used to be one of them.

I'm halfway out the door, ready to head back down and calm the crowd when Nancy starts trailing behind, her heels clacking on the tiles.

Wait, she calls. There's something I forgot to tell you, and this is the weird one!

I don't have time for this. What?

She hands me the file. Says, Trucker hit an animal last night.

I stop to face her one last time before I'm out the door.

A really big animal, she says. We can't identify it. He claimed it was on fire.

We stand staggered on the field just after sunrise, Deputy Raymond, Sergeant Manning, and I, while the fire crew drowns the last of the scattered, straggling flames. Most of the excitement is already over, Manning being the only officer who waited for us while we finished cleaning up the shitshow at the precinct. When the fire is just black plumes reaching up and sideways, Raymond heads north, and Manning east. I move southwest, following a trail of animal bones resting in damp scorch marks that pock the earth where earlier fires bloomed.

Manning briefed me when I got here. About the truck driver, half-asleep at the wheel, driving on autopilot through the night. The jolt of fear he got when a blazing creature leapt in front of the truck. The creature's bones had burst from it in all directions, starting smaller fires. It only takes one ember for the whole county to go up in flames. Miracle isn't a strong enough word to describe the disaster our firemen just prevented. They put the fires out before they truly got the chance to come alive.

Animals run into cars all the time out here. Roadkill stinks up the roads, and we always send someone to scrape the meat off the pavement. It's not out of the ordinary. *Burning* animals, however...

ACT III: BRUJERÍA

The driver said he'd spotted shadows nearby. One person, maybe two. Gone by the time he staggered from the cab.

The scorched cacti that remain stand crooked like the living dead. They smell of damp soil and char, and the stink of meat is inescapable. I keep my bandana across my face, but the smell seeps in. Pumpjacks line the horizon, past the bluffs and rolling hills. They look like skeletons, dead horses bobbing their skulls up and down, day and night sucking oil from deep within the earth. Up and down.

Up and down.

They're not too far off. I reckon, knowing the way the desert casts sound across miles and miles, that if the wind stopped, or the bugs quieted—if Raymond and Manning stopped muttering about how hot it is—then maybe I'd hear the hum of them. The rusted iron churning faintly, forever.

I wipe the crusts from my eyes, drink more coffee from my thermos.

I didn't get much sleep last night. When I closed my eyes and tried forcing sleep to come, I woke in a storm alone in the desert. Sand gurgling with blood, boots sinking in muck. I was running from something, weaving between dark and skeletal horses with their heads bobbing up and down, looking for a way to the watchtowers glowing in the distance. To safety. I had to move quickly. *There's something behind you.* It tapped my shoulder; it hooked my shirt collar. As it pulled me back I reached for the gun on my hip. *I only need my gun. Nothing can hurt me as long as I have my gun!*

But my fingers fumbled in the cavity of an empty holster, and the thing behind me pulled me deeper into the sand, its weight squeezing the life out my screaming mouth.

I grab for my gun now in the field of burnt bones. It's there. The weight hangs off my belt, the iron cool on my fingertips.

The pumpjacks are still churning.

Raymond's voice crackles through the radio. He says he's found something. I squeeze past a cluster of man-sized stones. He's resting his foot on a rock, wiping the sweat off his chin. He gestures to the scab on the top of my nose.

You all right? he asks.

I tell him, I'm fine. Really, I am. I've taken worse and given worse.

I know Raymond must think it over the top to block off the road with caution tape and detour the traffic and have a sheriff come out here, all to deal with some burning roadkill. But it's almost Halloween.

Right there, he says when I reach him, nodding at a wall up on the hillside. It's made of chipped stone and crumbling red brick. Weeds have split whole sections, but where Raymond is nodding there's a fresh, gaping hole with twigs scattered around its mouth.

He says, That's the Coyote House, isn't it?

I already know the answer. For a long time I intended to stop by and introduce myself to Miss Remolina. Her family were once major benefactors in the development of the city—at least, that's what's written in block letters at the historic center. But then she became ill, and I never got the chance.

That's not the actual name of the house, Raymond says. But I don't know a better one. Do you?

No one knows its real name, I say. Miss Remolina wouldn't happen to have kept any large felines around here, would she?

You think that thing was a cat? Raymond jokes.

What the animal hit by the trucker actually was remains a subject of debate. Bird bones—bits of talons and wings—lay charred in the damp soil. But there are also claws, rib bones, and strips of fur that scream coyote, or maybe mountain lion. Neither is uncommon here; these are their hills.

Whatever it was, it was big, I tell him. That's all I know.

Heading back to the patrol car across the field of bones, I spot it—steam rising off a dark thing halfway down the mountain, a trail of blood leading toward it. I don't want to look, but it reels me in, a fish on a hook. The closer I get, the more I'm sure that the limb I see is still alive, dragging itself through the weeds, infinitesimally slow but alive. I'm reaching for my gun. I'm crunching twigs beneath my boots, no longer walking but running, faster—faster—trying to keep sight of the crawling thing amid the grass. But when I reach it, it's still.

Always has been. It must have been the light or the steam that made me think it was moving. It's still intact. The meat stink is strongest here, rising off mangled flesh that seems to sizzle in the sunlight. The name of a creature it shouldn't belong to shoots though me and I tap the pistol still hanging off my belt.

I've found its arm, I radio in. Its razor claws are dug in deep, clutching the earth.

FIVE
Breathing Under Water

ETHANOL, OIL, CHEAP PLASTIC CHAIRS. Those were the smells Elena could not swat away as she sat in the exam room under a white light that stung her eyes while Dr. Mendes finished wrapping her wrist in a stiff, Velcro brace. They were smells she'd learned to stomach during the long years when tumors webbed their way through her husband's lungs. She'd spent so many nights in hospitals that smelled like this, while Julian waited a world away.

When Elena picked up the pain medication for her sprain at the pharmacy downstairs, she didn't look at the number on the cash register, just handed the woman her credit card and told herself, *Deal with it later.*

As soon as she stepped out into the parking lot, shielding her eyes from the morning sun, last night's headache returned. A soft throb tightened into a cramped fist striking her temples. It would only get worse, the blows harder, the sunlight more blinding, as the fist tenderized her scalp into slop.

The headaches had started when she was young—when, for the first time, blood leaked down her legs while she showered in the girls' locker room. At first she'd thought it was embarrassment that gripped her skull, took her balance away, and left her lightheaded.

The pain kept on coming, though, every day after that, never relenting. Sometimes it was too much and padlocked Elena's bones, left her stone-still and helpless in bed as the world pounded around her. Her mother, dead now for twenty years, used to treat the migraines with incense and dried flower petals.

Bruja. Bruja. Bruja.

The word echoed across the decades and settled into the car with her as she drove. Her home pueblito hadn't been able to sustain a doctor's office; most times there was only her mother. The sick or injured would fill the living room and wait for their turn with the herbs and incense. Elena would pass by on her way to the kitchen and offer them water or food, if there was any to spare. She'd smile when they said, "Gracias, niña."

But Elena's mother was dead, and she had moved so far away. Without the herbs, light became too bright and flared through her blood. She would pray for the pain to pass quickly. It rarely did; it would only be gone once she woke up from hours-long sleep. A rude guest.

As Elena turned the corner of her street, squinting in the stabs of sunlight, a car sped past going the other way, swerving inches from her bumper. She braked and shouted, "¡Hijos de la chingada!" But they'd already gone. It wasn't until she pulled into the driveway that she found out why they'd left in such a hurry. It was splattered in red paint across her driveway:

WITCH!

A bullet of pain bit her skull.

It was agony staggering out of the car and over the letters and into the living room to find the half-smoked roll she swore she'd left right there on the coffee table. No, on the side table—she lit it—one suck of smoke and already the pounding in her temples receded. The blows softened. She smoked. Soon enough, the pain was just endurable. She'd always been good at enduring.

Elena sank into the couch and let the cushions grip her shoulders. She could take her time. Julian wasn't home, and she knew he wouldn't return until sundown. From where she sat, she had a direct line of sight over the breakfast bar and through the kitchen window to the backyard, where her garden should've been. Only dark vines remained, like wizened fingers. She imagined them awakening, quivering, becoming something unnatural. Like Julian, her son, the young man who played with bones in the dirt.

Elena remembered her own sweaty days as a farm kid, chasing chickens on her father's ranch and herding cattle with switch in hand. She'd handled plenty of dead animals: her mother had taught her how to boil a rabbit, strip off its skin. She would hand Elena and her sisters the legs and they'd all take turns pulling on the slick tendons to make the feet thump. A morbid game. But only a game.

"¡Hija de bruja!"

Elena had endured that taunt each day, from city boys on the bus who refused to acknowledge her mother's local title, *curandera*. Once, one of the boys had even cracked a battery against her forehead after shouting the insult, and when she got home, her mother cleaned the cut and told her in Spanish: "Our people have a broken past, always eating at itself. Half is in the soil and temples and traditions of our ancestors. The other came from across the sea to wash that out. We are both sides of the pain. Many ignore the side that lost, claim the victor's blood over the other, and they are afraid of the power that lives in the soil. But we cannot exist without understanding both. You have to know who you are and where you come from, Elena."

Bruja.

Now they called her son that too. But his *brujería* seemed so different. So much darker. Angrier.

ACT III: BRUJERÍA

When Julian was a child, Elena had taken him to specialists, tried to get him tested, but the doctors never listened. The only treatments they had to suggest cost money she and her husband didn't have, even then. At the hospital today, she'd told Dr. Mendes that she slipped in the dark and that was how she sprained her wrist—not that her son had thrown her backward with hardly a swipe of his hand. She'd said nothing about the faint shadows that bent with him, making the lights overhead flicker. She couldn't stand to make his world any harder.

Elena knew that her son was gay, just like she knew he had the essence of a true curandero hidden somewhere under the anger and the darkness. She'd sat him down long ago and let him know that she didn't care, that she loved him no matter what, but that his world was going to be so much harder because of it. To be queer, and a brujo, in a place that rejected both. It hurt like nails and acid to admit that the world would hurt him so much, her beautiful, terrifying child.

Soon Elena's eyes were too heavy to keep open, and the cushions too nice. And the world too bright. She sank into the murk of dreams and a hot, syrupy summer when she'd swum far down the shore of a lake back home in Michoacán, to where the trees shot up straight from the water and their roots lurked in knots below the surface.

The boys had dared her, told her she was not brave enough, even though the lake's curse did not concern itself with women, only boys and men. The native girl who'd been chased into the water by conquistadors a long time ago, who'd gotten her foot tangled in the roots beneath the surface of the black water and thrashed until the violent ripples stilled—her spirit haunted those waters. Several boys through the years had gone missing there. But Elena wanted to prove she was brave. Once she was far enough, she plunged into the dark water, hoping to spot any corpses still trapped between the roots. When she was down there, the noise of the world muffled, Elena swore she heard sobs.

She found nothing and kicked back toward the surface—only the roots had wrapped around her foot, holding her under. She tugged and twisted but nothing budged, not even when her skin tore and red wisped around her. Up above the surface of the water, the sun sparkled and she reached for it, but her fingers didn't touch air.

Black stars filled her sight, the last thing she remembered before waking up vomiting gouts of water on the shore.

Elena woke with sweat on her face, gasping. She felt the warm gold of the afternoon sun and realized the dampness wasn't lake water. And she wasn't a girl anymore; she was thirty years older, slick with sweat. She cursed and went outside to splash a bucket of soapy water over the red paint and concrete.

The suds sizzled down the driveway. She squatted to scrub out the bleeding letters with her one good hand. The other she kept tucked against her ribs. If she was fast enough, she could finish before her shift at Cocina Orozco, where she would serve crunchy tacos and cheap tequila to people who wouldn't even tip unless she spoke without an accent and smiled wide.

Elena leaned back to wipe her face. The sun had reached the top of the sky. The first three letters were faint, leaving a bright *CH!*, when a car rolled to a stop against the sidewalk. The engine cut and Samuel de Hory stepped out.

"Afternoon!" he said.

Elena got up, rabbit-weary, ready to bolt. "Can I help you?"

"It's a little bright out here. Might I come inside?"

Elena led him up the steps to the door. He followed close behind. When she turned he was blocking the doorway, the shape of him a black hole in the world.

"You wouldn't by chance have seen your son as of late?"

When she didn't reply, Samuel wiped his feet and stepped inside, shutting the door behind him. The lock clicked shut and she noticed the force behind the action.

Samuel sat down on the recliner closest to him, let the shadows of blinds jigsaw his features. Elena took the couch and had to crook her neck back to see the eyes at the top of him. Even sitting, the man was a watchtower.

"He was home last night," she said. "He left this morning before I woke up. I assumed he was at the property."

Samuel sniffed the air, coyote-like. "Well, that's improbable. You see, he and I are no longer employed by Miss Remolina on account of her passing. And the new owners want to do away with the old."

He's been fired! "I'm sorry to hear that."

"As am I. It will affect all of us, I'm afraid. But that's beside the point. Doesn't it concern you that you don't know where your son is?" He placed his hands on the armrests, corpse-still yet smiling. "To be perfectly candid, because of this new development, I need his help moving some of my inventory from the house to the shop. You know how it is. A bit taxing on the body at my age."

She nodded, thinking that at the drop of a pencil he'd spring across the coffee table and strangle her with those marble hands. Would she even have time to scream?

"Looks like you'll have to resort to storage pods like the rest of us," she said. *Candid.* Who spoke like that?

Samuel leaned in, hunching down so that, finally, Elena saw him eye to eye. Eyes blue as frost. "I hope you understand the position I'm now in." He glanced at the cast wrapped around her wrist. "And I imagine *that* won't pay for itself. Tell me, how did you come by it?"

"I fell." She said it too quickly.

His tongue slithered behind his cheeks. "Mhmm. Hope Julian hasn't been causing you any trouble lately. He's a sweet boy. Just… under a lot of stress. You should really look into getting him some help; I worry. He's not been the same since Riley passed. He tells me these things. Well." Samuel rose from the chair, stretching to his full height. "Please let him know I'm looking for him. I'll pay overtime, considering the short notice. You have a lovely day, now."

He let himself out.

It wasn't until the car engine revved outside that Elena gasped for air. She wanted to take her driveway sponge and her soap and purge the spot where Samuel had sat, the upholstery still compressed with the shape of him. Then all that would need to be washed was Samuel, from her son's life.

Elena scrambled to the window, prying apart the blinds to watch his car pull away. In the back seat she noticed a crate much too big for a man like him to carry alone—an almost human-sized crate. She would think about that crate for the rest of the day, and long into the night.

SIX
The Boy and the Skull

POLICE IN DARK HATS cut across the sky. They walk high on the hilltop as you watch from the scrub at the bottom, between bars of light that pierce through bare branches; you keep to the shadows. Your serape's gone—burned—the whole of you exposed now, and shivering. Dew still slicks the stones and grass tips. The chirps of police radios chase away the peace of solitude. They're looking for bones. They'll find plenty, but not the skull; Xolotl is elsewhere.

You quicken your search between branches and logs and roots and rocks. You find vertebrae hiding under leaves near the creek bed. You follow ribs that have made their way into the shade, and you keep on following them—mud between your toes—farther from the crash site where Xolotl burst into a thousand scattered embers.

At a cluster of stones, you squat animal-like and rummage, searching for any indication of where the skull has gone. A stone rolls into the creek and you catch the reflection of dark eyes watching you from the ripples. You turn to see Oliver sitting casually on a high tree branch, staring down through the morning's freshness, eyeless gaze damning you. He salutes, two lazy fingers kissing his forehead.

"I don't want to deal with you right now," you tell him, turning back to the creek and the bones.

"You act like I chose this." He fingers the exposed tendons of his throat. "Dead, remember? What I'm wondering is, what good will collecting Xolotl's bones do you?"

"I'm still figuring it out." You hop between rocks, balancing catlike on each one as you check the crevices between them.

"So you have a plan?" the dead boy says—now sitting in the tree in front of you, not the one behind. You lift another stone high above your head and sploosh it into the creek. The ripples wash dark axolotls against the shore and they scurry back to their hiding places.

You say, "Yes—well, not quite yet, but I'm working on one." Because you have to. You're dying, and you can't go back to Samuel and the house of corpses you once filled for him and would have continued to fill, had you not witnessed the horror in the basement last night. The way he sucked the tōnalli out of Oliver's cornhusk body, so gaunt and desperate.

But you've always known the horror was there, haven't you? Ever since the first time he told you he needed blood and you crouched behind a bush after school along the path Alex Wittenberg took to get home, your fingers tight around a tire iron. Alex, who used to call you "faggot bitch" and who pounded Riley in the locker room until his face was pulp because he claimed Riley masturbated to the other boys when they showered—you remembered all that when you cracked metal against Alex's skull. You brought him to Samuel, telling yourself that Samuel needed the blood and that the world was better without Alex Wittenberg. You told yourself the same thing with each of them, and while he did his work you would slink away in your shroud because you could not stomach the screams. You never asked what Samuel did with the bodies afterwards. It sloshes your guts when you think of it, leaves you disgusted with yourself.

"You could have stayed." Oliver's voice is birdsong as he says this. "With Liz, I mean."

You left her at the lakeside but didn't make it far before the night whispers came back and the pain tore through you, leaving you raw and throbbing in the night. You passed out and woke up here to the smell of bark and damp soil, curled in a nest of twigs and leaves. The hunger woke with you, but you found a squirrel and it'll hold you over long enough. The only remaining trace of it is the blood staining your sleeves.

"You could have helped her," Oliver says. "She didn't do anything wrong. Your rage is yours to own, yeah? You know it. But helping her meant she'd see you, huh? The real, pathetic, wilting you. Can't have that, nope. That's why you let me die too, isn't it?"

"What do you want me to say?" you bark at him, the anger in your blood getting hooks in.

"I just want you to admit it. But you won't. And I feel sorry for you. It's funny, from up here you seem so small." He half-sighs, half-laughs. Forcing jokes the way Elizabeth likes to. "Who am I to point fingers, though? I'm worm food now." He vulture-crooks his neck, glaring with viscous twin smiles. "You want my advice? If you can't make up your mind, then you'd better just kill yourself. You'll be free from all of this, a perfect little dead-boy Pontius Pilate. And I'll be free from this *boring* haunting."

"If you're not going to help, then fuck off!"

Oliver shrugs. "Whatever. Try under that bridge over there. Looks promising." He points up the creek. When you look back, the branch is empty. Leaves flutter to the ground.

The bridge is small, only ten yards end to end with rusted scaffolding along the rails. Beneath it, the charred end of a serpent tail slithers down the slope on its way to the stream. Grass and flowers wilt along its thin and darkened trail. The tail has slithered all night, itching to get here. You flick it away and crouch at a small split in the earth where water trickles, and where a skull rests. Coyote-shaped. White but blackened where strips of flesh have burned off. Razor teeth run up and down the jaws in a wicked smile, but the dozens of eyes that once nestled in the sockets have melted away. You bounce a pebble off the skull.

You flick another after a moment. It makes a hollow peck.

You flick a third one. You're rolling another pebble between your fingers, ready for a fourth throw, when a thundering voice emanates from between the teeth.

WHAT THE HELL DO YOU WANT?

The jaws do not move. They're still just bones.

"Funny," you say. "I didn't think your lot believed in hell." When Xolotl doesn't reply to the joke, you say—firmly, to hide the fear coiled within your guts—"I came to request a boon."

A BOON? DON'T MAKE ME LAUGH.

You nod. The jaws snap open, bear-trap wide, and a laugh like raking stones fills the air until they clamp shut again. Stars burn in the depths of the empty eye sockets.

BURNED MY BODY TO SPITE YOUR FACE, AND YOU WANT A BOON. TELL ME, DID YOU DO IT FOR THE GIRL?

You stay silent, choke down your fear and your guilt, because you know that deep down you're a monster like him. Each of you has played your part in Samuel's game.

RIGHT, Xolotl says. THINGS ARE RARELY SO SIMPLE, HMM? OKAY. WHAT, PRAY TELL, CAN I OFFER YOU?

You pick him up and hold the skull gently in both hands, close enough to smell cooked meat and seared hair. "I'll get you your body back," you say, knowing how much an upright body would mean to Xolotl. He'd be tethered to Samuel's will no longer, free to be the god of deformity once more. The psychopomp that travels between this world and the one below. "In return, I need you to fix me. Get rid of my power before it kills me. I don't want Samuel's help."

A growl rattles the teeth. YOU'RE A MURDERER, BOY. THERE IS NOTHING I CAN DO ABOUT THAT. I'M SURE THE HUMANS WOULDN'T MIND ANOTHER DEAD MURDERER. ANOTHER DEAD, BROWN BODY.

"You have to help me," you demand of Xolotl. "What choice do you have? I can keep your bones scattered as long as I want."

YOU'RE DYING. THAT MARK ON YOUR LEG STILL FESTERS. IT'S UP TO YOUR KNEE NOW, MY SIBLING'S GIFT EATING ITS WAY THROUGH YOU LIKE THE FIRE ATE MY BONES. JUST HOW MUCH LONGER CAN YOU HOLD IT OFF? I SUPPOSE THERE'S ONE WAY TO STOP THE SPREAD. I COULD GET RID OF THAT LEG FOR YOU.

You refuse to bargain with a god. You tell him, "Help me, or I crack your skull in two and send each half down a different river, and then just try to put yourself together again."

A hollow threat. It could take a hundred years—longer than your own lifetime, with change—but gods are slow, careful, and above all patient. Even if it takes Xolotl a thousand years to clump himself together again, it will be done. A thousand years is nothing to a creature like him.

The stars within his eyes shine. Finally, Xolotl speaks: I'LL TEACH YOU WHAT I CAN. BUT REMEMBER, IT WILL NOT SAVE YOUR SOUL. KNOW THIS, JULIAN, BETWEEN FRIENDS: WHATEVER YOU PLAN TO DO, YOU'RE ALREADY DAMNED.

SEVEN
An Ocean of Faceless Names

Blood budded on Marisol's thumb where she'd pricked herself with a sewing needle. "Life is paid in blood," she said theatrically. Elizabeth was eleven years old then, wide-eyed and watching with urgent care the makeshift operating table that was the drawing room's coffee table. Marisol sucked on her thumb, then planted a kiss on white stuffing where the teddy bear's head should have been, leaving the faintest pink stain in the fluff.

Angel Eyes had caught her claws on the bear, and once there was an incision in the faux fur, Elizabeth couldn't help wanting to peek inside. She'd thought it would be fine—she was too old for stuffed toys now anyway—but guilt overcame her once the deed was done, and the stuffing poured out like guts, and the head hung from threads.

Marisol carefully stuffed disobedient cotton back inside and finished stitching the head onto the limp body.

"He'll live," she said with a sigh. "Couldn't your father take you to a damn Build-A-Bear or something? For scientific purposes?" She tied off the thread, severed it with her teeth, and tossed the bear into the air before handing it back to Elizabeth. "There you go."

Marisol leaned against the kitchen counter while Elizabeth inspected the seams. She was ten years older than Elizabeth's father and eight older than their middle sister Araceli, but she looked as young as either. Silver hairs were rare amid raven black, her crow's feet faint and kind, and her lips always so full. She'd been a surrogate mother to both her siblings. An extra mom to help their overworked and distant one while their father was far away on business.

"You always say you hate kids. I don't believe you," Elizabeth said. Her voice seemed to snap Marisol back from whatever sea she was adrift on.

"Oh? Why not?"

"You're too good at taking care of us."

Marisol smiled. "I've been doing it all my life."

"But you never married." A bit intrusive, Elizabeth knew, but it was too late now; she'd spoken the words.

Marisol thought for a moment. "Never really appealed to me. I tried hard to fit into that life—I even carved off parts of myself for the shape, chopped off my heels and toes for glass shoes that wouldn't ever fit!" She laughed. "Wasn't worth it. I'm quite happy now, just being me, with my stuff. And this house; I understand it."

"You're not lonely?" Elizabeth asked.

Marisol shook her head. "Not because of that." Silence. Then, "I have friends, and that's all I really need. Still, I can't remember a time when I wasn't at least a little bit sad." She smiled again, her teeth shining—the saddest smile Elizabeth had ever seen.

Elizabeth found Angel Eyes atop the south gate again, unharmed, her tail twitching with mild annoyance as if nothing really wrong had happened last night. But claw marks etched the trees in the morning mist, evidence that the shape—Chupacabra? Xolotl?—had been real. She shouldn't feel so surprised, she thought. The supernatural was a familiar presence, something she'd always known.

"Some help you were, last night." She glared at Marisol's cat. Her muscles ached—she'd waited by the lake till the light of morning leaked over the hills. She twisted her waist to crack her spine, yawned, and spotted the black shape of her phone lying in the dirt between monstrous pawprints.

There wasn't much battery left, just ten percent, but at least the phone wasn't gone forever.

She opened her contacts list. She had never wanted to be lonely like Marisol. She kept so many numbers: friends she no longer spoke to, family members she meant to keep in touch with but didn't, random classmates from group projects—she never dared to delete a single one. She always thought, *I might need them again someday.* And so they flooded her contacts folder, an ocean of faceless names. *There!* Her index finger found Julian's name.

Call him. He'd saved her, he'd killed that monster for her. *And all I could do was sit there, afraid.*

She didn't even know if he still had the same number. Besides, he'd left her on the lakeside; she took the hint.

In the morning glow, the labyrinth gate wasn't so intimidating, so forlorn. Just bricks and stone and rusting metal. No ghost beckoned from the other side, and the chains came off easily, once she unfastened them. She swung the gate open and stepped through, walked down a path written in muscle memory.

"Hello? Marisol?"

Nothing. Just cobwebs, weeds, dots of white flowers nestled in damp corners, and leaves the color of fire that crunched beneath her feet. When she reached the far side—the whole thing was only twenty yards across—and looked down at the rest of San Ojuela waking in the October sun, her suspicions were confirmed. The garden held no portals. It was just a maze, same as when she and Julian used to laugh through it in the summer heat, back when they were young.

EIGHT
You, Me, and Our Tía Muerta

SHOUTING ERUPTED FROM DOWNSTAIRS. It was seven thirty in the morning and Mary had hardly begun to scrub the sourness off her teeth. Her night had been restless, smothered in nightmares—muzzling hands and dead fingers that forced themselves down her throat or into her eyes; the house's walls squeezing her tight. Chewing her up. But she'd survived, she'd woken up—alone.

She caught the tail end of the shouts when she made it to the stairs: Liz was shouting at their mother that it wasn't any of her business, that she was an adult, that she'd done just fine without her for years and didn't need her now either.

"You want to be treated like an adult? Then act like one!" their mother shouted.

"I'm trying, but listen—"

"Why do you keep making everything so damn hard for me?" She stormed out, heels clicking on the tiles.

Mary had heard this same argument a thousand times before. She shrugged and went to get dressed in her black jeans and black button-up shirt for the funeral. She was adjusting her tie in the girls' bedroom mirror when Liz appeared in the doorway, her reflection corpse-pale, hair knotted, pajama pants frayed. Her red sweater hung off her shoulders, crusted with mud, and in her arms she cradled Angel Eyes.

"Aren't you a sore for sight eyes," Mary said into the mirror.

Liz dropped the cat and threw herself onto the bed. "Don't be annoying," she said.

Mary wanted to ask if Liz was okay but stopped, unsure what words wouldn't sound cliché or autofilled like a text message. They never spoke their feelings; they let silences erode the edges of arguments. Mary tried a different approach. "Man, you don't look so great."

"It's nothing," Liz mumbled. "You wouldn't believe me if I told you."

Outside the windows, mist curled around spindly branches. Somewhere out there was the "Hellmouth Gate" and the hand that had clawed her arm, now scabbed over beneath her sleeve. She was about to say, *Try me*, but Liz sat up and shushed her.

"What?"

Liz shushed her again. She got up and brushed past Mary to the bookshelf, where she hunched and scanned the spines until she stopped at one not coated with dust. "What are you doing up here?" she said. "You should be downstairs in the library with the other botany books." She slid it out and flipped page after page, looking for something. She stopped near the end, at a page break that read *Toxic Flora of North America*.

"Huh."

A few pages over, Liz found a photograph of petals the color of snow, budding at the ends of needle-thin stems. *Cicuta maculata: North American Water Hemlock*.

"Thinking of poisoning someone?" said Mary.

Liz ripped out the page and shut the book, which she stuffed back into its place on the shelf. She folded the page and hid it in her

ACT III: BRUJERÍA

pocket before heel-turning out of the room and marching down the stairs.

Mary caught up with her in the courtyard. "Yo, wait—wait! Hold on, what is this? What's going on?"

Liz had that look in her eyes, the one she had when she drilled ballet routines in the living room back home. The look she had when she played with Ouija boards and fucked with witchcraft books—the Dark Liz stare. It tickled Mary's spine! No, wait—that was just having moved too fast. She was lightheaded, out of breath.

"Stop following me," Liz said, but that had never stopped Mary before. Eventually Liz rolled her eyes. "Fine, then—just keep quiet."

Mary and Liz jogged across the field and through the woods to the wall at the south end of the property. Mary dug her heels into the dirt.

"I'm not going in there."

Liz already stood in the jaws. The lock and chains rested in the dirt. "It's just a maze," she said with a confused look.

But Mary wouldn't move. Her eyes were bees darting from corner to corner, scanning the spaces between the trees, the scurryings in the leaves. "It's not a maze. It's something else."

Liz shifted. Her eyes narrowed. "What are you talking about?"

Mary took a deep breath. "There's monsters here."

"Did...did you see it too?" Liz whispered. "The chupacabra?"

"The what?"

"What?"

Liz blinked. They waited a moment in the morning stillness, Mary with an eyebrow raised, Liz with her lips pursed. A classic Mexican standoff. Then Liz began to giggle, little by little erupting into belly laughs. Mary didn't know how anyone could laugh like that and not suffocate. "Jesus Christ, I'm going insane," Liz wheezed.

Mary wanted to laugh with her sister, but she couldn't find anything funny. She said, "No, dude, I mean it. I saw a dead hand. It came from those bushes."

An eye for an eye, a tooth for a tooth, the girls agreed. A truth for a truth. Mary told Liz about the thing that had attacked her, pulling up her sleeve to show the cuts in her skin. And Liz told her about the wild night of ghosts and chupacabras and the Boy. "I'm telling the truth, no bullshit," she kept adding. And Mary kept reassuring her that she believed every word—so long as Elizabeth believed hers, too.

"Well, obviously, I believe you," her suddenly grown-up sister said, with sincerity in her voice. "You have no idea. I'm probably the only person who can't help believing you."

Mary remembered how, when they were younger and their mother's house was still new and foreign to them, Liz would whisper about seeing ghosts or ask if there was someone in the back alley when there was no one there at all. By the time they were done corroborating each other's information of the supernatural and how it orbited Casa Coyotl, Mary had her fingers gun-shaped against her lips.

"So let me get this straight," she said. "Marisol's ghost visited you, and now you suspect *foul play*?"

"Pretty much." Liz pushed the iron gate open. Its hinges groaned. "I'm about to make sure."

All Mary's bones and muscles told her *Don't!* but she nodded, then followed Liz into the narrow passages of the maze. They chose among forking paths and dodged dead ends until they reached the center, where Liz unfolded the page from the botany book. She held the picture up to where its double crawled along the walls and read the page aloud: "Water Hemlock can be found all over the North American continent. When ingested in large amounts, Water Hemlock will cause death within minutes. In smaller doses, the plant can still cause long-term brain damage, including retrograde amnesia and memory loss similar to that of dementia." She let the words hang. "Huh," she said finally. "Samuel always used to prepare her champurrado. For the years we were here, and probably the years after we left. The whole time, and we didn't even notice. No need for brujería when you've got this."

Mary asked what she meant.

Liz said, matter-of-factly, "I think Samuel poisoned Marisol."

Poisoned.

The word floated between them with the October leaves, tapping the maze's walls. Sounding deformed and monstrous. Chills shot up Mary's spine again. She stared at the hemlock flowers as if they were about to bite.

"So we calling the cops, or what?" Mary asked.

"We're brown, Mary," Liz said. "Next thing you know, they'll call us squatters and we'll end up with twin warning shots in our backs. Also, I don't have proof—hardly even an educated guess, and that only works on Judge Judy. This shit is *real*. I'm just not sure anyone out there can help us."

It was the way her sister said "us" that made Mary's lungs swell—they had never been an us before, not even when they faced a *them* together. Not even when they both survived the car crash and ran that long stretch of night home with their father, who was sweating out booze and shouting swears at himself and at them and at the "piece-of-shit driver." They never acknowledged that they were tied by matching scars. Mary should have been afraid in the maze. She did want to cry. But she also wanted herself and Liz to never leave that maze and split back into two.

"What I don't understand is why he did it," Liz said. "Marisol was always kind to him."

Mary recalled Samuel's fight with their mother, about Marisol's will and Liz's inheritance. "He wants the house," she gasped.

"This place?" said Liz. "Fuck. I can't imagine why."

Mary shrugged. "Well, let's figure it out—all his shit's inside, he's obviously hiding *something*."

They searched. They spent the rest of the morning poring over Samuel's trinkets and Marisol's antiques, wondering if together certain items amalgamated into something supernatural. Liz googled the artifacts and the girls began piecing together the history not only of the house's relics and their indigenous or Spanish sources but also of their family. Their father's mother had raised three kids, mostly alone: fathers, the girls found, were often absent in their family's past. Their great-aunt had dropped out of her degree program at UNAM in the summer of '68 to stow away between hot metal slabs under a charter bus out of La Ciudad into the San Diego hills, because the Mexico City police had begun popping bullets into protesters, letting their blood bake on city streets. Their great-grandfather was a cruel man who had hammered the gentleness out of his children and tried to burn all the indigenous echoes out of Casa Coyotl. (Marisol had hated him.) Then there was the cousin who shot herself upstairs forty years ago—so many pieces of their family's history that no one ever spoke about, as if silence could undo the past. Etched into this house. Mary wondered if maybe it was the history Samuel wanted. If it was something he could eat. Consume. Devour.

By the end of their search, the girls found themselves at the far end of the upstairs hallway, standing in front of the door the Boy had said to keep away from. It seemed too obvious now. With her skeleton key, Liz unlocked the door, and they stepped inside.

Mary hadn't been sure what they would find. She'd imagined bones, or white sheets draped over forgotten possessions. Maybe cobwebs or corpses to match the crispness of October air, but there wasn't even any furniture. Their footsteps echoed.

The air was thick, leaking past them bit by bit, a heartbeat breeze. It smelt of wood chips and construction paint. There was a small ashtray on the floor in the center of the room.

Liz went to sit crisscross in front of the ashtray, then picked it up. She exhaled. "Just an ashtray. God, what are we doing?"

"Looking for clues?"

"Look at us. We're—*I'm* in over my head. Out of my depth. And you're just a kid. What can we do?"

"Maybe we don't have to do anything."

"He killed Marisol."

"Maybe we can just go home once the funeral is done. No one's ever going to believe us." Mary was touching her sister, petting her arm.

"No, Mary, listen…"

Mary was pulling Liz's arm now, trying to get her up and moving. "We're in a literal horror movie right now, so cut yourself some slack. Let's take our losses and make it out alive. Look on the bright side, we haven't spent time together like this in ages. That counts for something, right?"

Right?

But Liz shoved her off and she stumbled back, gasping.

"Shut up, Mary, I'm trying to think!" Liz was so much taller, so much stronger. She was glaring now, eyes burning hot. Whenever Mary would push things too far, Liz would snap and swat her away or push her against the wall—fighting, the way all sisters fought, right? The TV shows with always-caring, always-happy sisters, Mary knew, were fiction. Not reality. "Don't you get that this is serious?" Liz said. "This is really happening."

Mary hurried to wipe away tears before Liz noticed them, but when she looked up, Liz's face had softened. "Mary, I—"

"No, it's fine. You're right. I can be serious."

Liz was quiet.

"What happened?" Mary asked, wanting to haul words out of her sister like a fat rope that would fall into bundles at her feet. "Like, what happened with us?"

Liz sighed. "I don't know. Maybe I grew up…a little too fast. I'm…sorry."

"Did we always used to argue as much as we do now?"

"Not always," Liz admitted.

"Do you think we could ever go back to how it was before? Or is it too late?"

Liz shifted through the ash in the tray, shaking her head. "I don't know."

Their mother called out from the courtyard below. Time to go.

Liz stayed where she was, focused on the ashtray's stone. Obsidian, maybe.

"Liz?"

"Yeah. I'm coming."

Together they stood at the funeral, the Remolina sisters side by side, their fingers laced together as they said goodbye to Marisol. Her eyes were clamped shut in the coffin and her hands posed just above her heart. Her hair was stiff, her smile sanded over, smooth and indistinct. Thick perfumes masked the chemicals.

The viewing room was desolate—just the girls, their mother (Brian would join them later), Tía Araceli, and cousins Will and Blake. Occasionally, others would straggle in and say they were either friend or family and give their condolences. Then they would leave, shoes clicking away beyond the open doors.

ACT III: BRUJERÍA

Mary waited among the sniffles and whispers, hoping another figure would step through the doors: her father, moving quickly to compress the time he'd spent away, to finally say he was sorry. That one absence was a gaping pit between all the bouquets of cempasúchil, sucking the life out of conversations as everyone skirted around saying his name.

Before they knew it, it was time for the eulogies. For Liz's turn, she stood at the podium in a black dress with a white collar. Even with smudged makeup and a cut across her cheek, she looked beautiful. Her eulogy was short, only two poems. First was the one about tigers, then the other one about the dead.

> *Be near me when my light is low,*
> > *When the blood creeps, and the nerves prick*
> > *And tingle; and the heart is sick,*
> *And all the wheels of Being slow.*
>
> *Be near me when I fade away,*
> > *To point the term of human strife,*
> > *And on the low dark verge of life*
> *The twilight of eternal day.*

The few relatives who had gathered clapped, and Liz said, with disdain in her eyes, "Thank you. George Remolina taught me these poems. My father, and Marisol's brother. I'm sure he would have read them for her himself if he were here."

Mary was next, and she read a story of the time when Tía Marisol had taken the girls to the lake behind the house and taught them how to swim by throwing them off the dock and throwing a rescue ring after them. It was a memory she could hardly picture in her mind's eye anymore; the blank spots had been filled in by Liz's retelling. When Mary was done reading, she wished she'd picked something she could have described in her own words. But she behaved herself, and continued to behave during the burial and the reception back at Casa Coyotl, which lasted into the night.

For once, she didn't ruin a thing.

NINE
Tongue Brought Me (Oscuro)

ELIZABETH SAT IN SILENCE, listening to the other adults swap chisme—critiques of cousins' diets, funeralgoers' wardrobe choices, anti-police protests—all of it a freight train plowing through her skull. They sat in Marisol's courtyard around a fireplace whose flames pulled the moisture out of Elizabeth's skin. She was on the couch next to her mother. Across the hearth was Aunt Araceli and Araceli's husband, flanked by some strangers whom Elizabeth's mother and Araceli said they knew but Elizabeth didn't recognize, who all claimed they knew Marisol from work or college or high school. "She was always so sweet," they said. "I always meant to visit her."

They kept bending conversations back around from Marisol to themselves—how they had to go on without saying goodbye, how they'd always told her to appreciate life instead of staying locked up in Casa Coyotl. Saying lots of words while ultimately saying nothing. Olympic athletes at this sport, all of them. None asked what Elizabeth remembered about Marisol, just *How's college?* and *What are you studying again?* and *A dance company? I couldn't imagine pursuing such a risky career.*

The train in her head roared.

The fire snapped. Elizabeth held a now-warm wine glass in her lap, the contents of which had left her thoughts prickly and sluggish. Her mother's arm rested on Elizabeth's shoulders as if they hadn't been animals tearing at each other's throats just twelve hours ago. This was a message that told her: *Don't try anything.* Because that was what mattered to her mother: maintaining civility above all else.

Elizabeth had long internalized the message: *Just sit there. Just take it. It doesn't matter if they're acting ugly, they're your elders. We can't afford to push away family.*

So she did. The sun sank low and the fire crackled and the wine in her glass dwindled to a pink dot at the bottom of empty space while people spoke about the dead woman as if they'd been her friends in life. But Marisol had no friends. A woman said Marisol was always so compassionate with others at work. Elizabeth thought, *That's not true; everyone called her a stuck-up bitch behind her back.* Aunt Araceli said that, growing up, Marisol was practically a second mother, that she'd loved filling that role. *She hated every second of it. She did it because if she ever saw a struggling creature, she felt like she had no choice but to help it.* Elizabeth's mother added that she could never have done what she did with her business if it hadn't been for Marisol's help with the girls.

Then the freight train rushed out of its tunnel screaming, lights burning; Elizabeth stood up and shouted, "*Get her name out of your fucking mouth!*"

Or she would have, if she hadn't been drilled from childhood to be polite and respectable, to bite on her tongue until it popped. Instead, she told everyone that she needed to use the restroom and let her rage carry her up to her room, leaving their tipsy laughter behind, pellets bouncing off the courtyard walls. They were all having too good a time to notice that she wouldn't be coming back.

ACT III: BRUJERÍA

In the dark, Elizabeth threw her sweater back on and pressed in her earbuds. She filled her backpack: flashlight, matches, the obsidian ashtray. A knife, in case more monsters waited in the woods. Then she went outside and around to the back of the house with Siouxsie and the Banshees screaming in her ears until she reached the forest's edge, where the night's shadows grew solid.

We don't have to do anything. Mary's voice echoed. *We can just go home once this is done. No one's going to believe us.* Elizabeth considered that she could turn back and settle into the couch with Mary and their cousins, maybe start pretending even to herself that everything was fine. Just fine. And go home tomorrow for ballet, and that would be the end of her sad story here.

And her soul? Her gift to see the dead, which came in its place? What would that be for?

If I go, I'll never be able to fix myself.

She pushed onwards, up by the garden wall and through the weeds, not stopping until the graffiti that read HELLMOUTH GATE crept into her phone's halo of light. There, she waited for the shape of Marisol to emerge from the night.

Leaves drifted.

Wind sighed.

Maybe the sounds of night were speaking to her. So Elizabeth sat on the earth and listened. Hoping someone, or something, would speak.

"I saw you find the hemlock," Marisol said.

Finally. Elizabeth dug into her bag and tossed the obsidian ashtray into the labyrinth. Listened to its insignificant clunk. "I found this, too. It doesn't smell like cigarettes." It smelt damp and chalky, like burnt paper and burnt ink. And blood.

The shape of the dead woman bent down. Her fingers broke up like smoke on the first two swipes before they grew solid enough to grab the ashtray and lift it. She whispered sharp Spanish words to it, but these were lost to Elizabeth. She caught *sentimental*, and *sangre*, and *Samuel*.

"Marisol, English, please. I need to know, what do I do?"

Even with Marisol's face a shadow, Elizabeth felt the hesitation in her words. "It's, it's—es complicado. *They* keep on pulling me back, Liz child. Pero, estoy aquí, I'm still here—just. Words. Words. Words! Estas chingaderas—they are so loose. So far, so…oscuro. They don't want me here much longer. I keep fighting to stay. I need to guard my home, the way my home guarded me. I never wanted to leave. I never wanted you to come here. Mis palabras malditas, bringing you here anyway."

"I know it's about the house," Elizabeth pressed. "It's always about the damn house, and that's why I'm not *me* anymore, isn't it?" Her words were such small sounds. "That's all I'm here for, Marisol. I need you to help me find my soul."

"No sé—I don't know what is or isn't, and was or wasn't, anymore. It's still all new—too much here. I'm talking with you now, also reaching for you so far away in a locker room, and you look so afraid. I'm trying hard to see you standing there, Liz. But it's getting harder. I cannot stay much longer here."

"But you're a ghost." Elizabeth was sure of it. A ghost, like all the others.

Marisol's shadow simply said, "No soy un fantasma. Soy yo. I cannot stay here with you. I have to move on."

No, not now, not yet! Elizabeth ran her hand through her hair and groaned. "Then tell me, what the fuck do I do?!" Her frustration boiled over—rage at her father for fucking everything up. At her mother, for robbing Elizabeth of the chance to confront her father herself, and for ripping the girls away from their home and pretending they'd never had a life without her. Even rage at Marisol. Marisol most of all, because she'd never come to the city to get

Elizabeth and bring her back home. Pain splintered Elizabeth's voice when she asked, "Where's *my* place in all this?"

"Listen, Liz child. I am not the only person Samuel de Hory has killed," Marisol said, softly. "Too many have died."

Elizabeth stepped back. Fear iced her skin.

"Will you come and see?" Marisol asked, backing into the labyrinth.

The shadows closed in around Elizabeth, long and tendriled, rising up to cradle her. She flinched at the pressure of them wrapping around her limbs, wanting to throw them off and flee, but it was too late. The shadows pulled her in.

ACT IV
Power Forged in Blood

ONE
He Who Claimed the Sun

GRASS CRUNCHED BENEATH LEATHER BOOTS. The echoes of footfalls stretched thin and faint across the desert mountains—the only sound for leagues.

The sun was setting by the time the party reached the mountaintop, where the hanging tree waited for them, four brujas swaying from its branches just as the men had left them that morning. Bodies stiffening, now.

Sweat beads slid down the conquistador's neck. With each breath he sucked in a gulp of the desert's own hot breath.

Cicadas buzzed; crows cawed.

Nine shadows stretched across the mountaintop; dusk shrouded the men's faces as the sky faded to bruised blue and amber. They inched closer to the bodies. Had to cut them down. Bury them deep. Before nightfall.

They were confident that if they could accomplish this, they'd have nothing to fear but the Lord's will. As if the conquistador's feet weren't dragging when the grass brushed at his calves; as if the earth itself weren't trying to grab him and say, *Turn back*. He pressed on, leading the horse on which the magistrate rode.

At the sight of the bodies, the horse balked. "¡Tranquila!" the magistrate called from his saddle. "Está bien, Niña, está bien." He patted her mane until she steadied, then pointed the other men toward the corpses. "¡Apúraos! ¡Cortad pronto los cuerpos que queda poco tiempo!"

At the base of the tree the conquistador wrapped his fingers tight around the metal cross hanging from his neck. Reminded himself that if he passed this test, the magistrate had promised to pardon him, leaving his sin a matter between him and God. He tried to suck out whatever energy the rosary beads might hold. He even tried to whisper a prayer—a small one he'd been raised never to forget, yet he found it hard to recall the words. So he gritted his teeth and pushed down whatever grief had clawed its way up from his chest to his throat. There was no need for it; sentiment had no power here. He drew his sword and lopped the ropes one at a time. Each corpse hit the dirt with a heavy *thump. Thump. Thump.*

The stink of defecation and sun-rotted meat wafted up with the dust, but the men descended quickly to pluck away jewels and gold. Such finery these tribal brujas had.

The other men were soldiers like the conquistador, all Spaniards who'd come up from farm dirt and market streets and sailed to tame this wild and violent land—but they were not *conquistadors*. Not like him. They had arrived later. They hadn't seen Tenochtitlán the way the conquistador had, a shining fortress floating on the belly of a great lake, clad in gold and teal and crimson and jade, in the time before Cortés blasted it to rubble along with everything else. They had arrived afterwards in the company of the magistrate, to govern the land and fill in the open wounds Cortés had left behind. But the conquistador, he had witnessed it all.

It was the woman who'd been hanged first and now lay crumpled with once-gentle hands twisted against the tree roots; it was her that the conquistador refused to look in the face. The soldiers

ACT IV: POWER FORGED IN BLOOD

stripped her of falcon helmet and feathered crown, skirt of wings and talon boots—all of it fuel for a raging fire. They left her corpse bare save for some dirty rags that did little to hide her swollen stomach.

Her name was Xoco.

The men skirted around Xoco like beetles, making sure to not touch her arms or hands—conduits of blood magic, the servants had told them, limbs writhing with raw brujería powered by the tōnalli of the unborn child within her. The men signed crosses if they so much as glanced at her. They still feared her, even now that she was dead. Why wouldn't they? They'd heard her growl in a thousand monstrous tongues when they'd captured her, when the magistrate came with his men to the conquistador's ranch, to break down the door and demand he hand over the bruja dog he harbored. They'd borne witness to the nighttime horrors she'd commanded with spit and the spill of her blood. A dozen more men would have stood on the mountaintop had she not split them that morning like cornhusks, unraveled their muscles like yarn and slipped bones from their sockets. She'd been rage and passion and power. She'd woven strips of the night sky like ribbons between her fingertips, as beautiful and confident as the primordial spirits who graced her.

All of them—even the magistrate—took up shovels to bite into the dirt, save for the padre who lingered in the back, saying nothing. He wouldn't soil his holy hands, at least not like that. Instead, as the knights scooped out chunks of the earth, the padre fumbled through pages of scripture with trembling fingers, searching for the perfect verse to cleanse the brujas of the devil and make it safe to ride back home.

How ironic, the conquistador thought. It wasn't the will of the padre's God that had killed these brujas, nor God's power that might cause the baby festering in Xoco's womb to wake—to make her lurch back up onto rattling, blood-stiffened feet, a puppeteered corpse hungry for human blood.

If your God is so powerful, Padre, why are we here, so desperate to bury them before nightfall?

After the hanging that morning, they'd ridden back into town. Only then had one of their serving women told them about the danger of the cursed fetus within Xoco's womb, the reason why they had to return. To follow the ritual the native priests had taught them, purifying the graves with incense and drops of their own blood. How useful was a Spanish padre in a desert like this? With gods like those?

A jaguar's eyes caught the conquistador's from across the clearing. Dots of molten gold, watching from the trees. They hadn't seen any other animals on the hike up. Most of them—jaguars, coyotes, other creatures that belonged to the forest of the night—would not emerge before the sun was down. But he'd felt in his chest that the animals were somewhere nearby, knowing why the men were there and choosing to stay away. Now the torches were burning, and the eyes drew near.

The conquistador wondered how they must look to the jaguar, with their white skin and hooved animals unlike any from this world.

At dusk and dawn—in the in-between of worlds—the earth fell silent. *Because the sun travels every night through the underworld*, Xoco had told him once as they traced warriors out of stars in the sky, in a time before Tenochtitlán was rubble. By the order of Moctezuma, she should have gutted him, but he'd launched an arrow into her thigh meat. By order of Hernán Cortés, he then should have executed her but didn't. He'd pulled the arrow from her leg and dressed the wound with honey instead. The hate in her eyes faded, and he picked up bits of her Nahautl when she said, "Don't be afraid. The magic is just tricks."

ACT IV: POWER FORGED IN BLOOD

The sun is guarded by Xolotl, the sunset god.

God of deformities. God of sickness. God of monsters and misfortune too. The animals of the earth hide when Xolotl drags himself from the underworld and comes for the sun.

He wondered what grotesque god would be the one to come and claim her soul, if any did come.

Or what gods would come for him at the end of his life. Would his honor matter then?

They dropped Xoco into her grave. Began tossing clump after clump of dirt over her eyes, chest, belly, mouth. The conquistador ripped a shovel out of the closest soldier's hand and told the men to hurry on to the other three corpses.

"Puedo hacerlo solo."

He gripped the shovel so tightly that splinters dug into his palms. He drank up one last view of Xoco in the stillness of that sunset—her sloped nose and thick eyebrows—the features other Spaniards said made the native women look beastly and mannish, nothing like the bird-boned, thin-lipped women from back home across the sea. Her hair was pulled back into a dark braid that reached from her crooked neck to the base of her spine—where he used to trace his fingers on the nights she couldn't sleep. Skin that once radiated warmth like sun-baked clay; lips that grinned when he stumbled over his clumsy tongue trying to tell her "Nimitztlazohtla."

I love you.

Everything was still there, as if she were just sleeping. The conquistador set down the shovel and reached down into the grave to brush her face, ignoring what the others might say, hoping to feel her familiar warmth and see dimples pinch up with her smile.

Wake up! he thought, hoping that her magic was not just tricks, and not spent up, and that he could witness another of her miracles one last time. *Get up right now, and I promise this time it will be me who goes with you.*

But her cheek was cold. It was his fault. He'd made her stay with him on the land Cortés had gifted him, the land Cortés had stolen from her people. Because he thought it would give meaning to his name.

"No te olvidaré," he said. To Xoco, and the child he'd never know.

Then he pelted her with dirt, until the earth claimed her. Eventually the sun slithered away too. In a quiet and uninhabited part of the world where ruins had lain still in the jungle for hundreds of years already, and where dark roots dug cracks in the stones, the nine men circled around four fresh graves, bathed in torchlight. The padre read proudly from his holy book, but the conquistador looked past him to the darkening mountains and deserts of their New World.

Somewhere out there, Xolotl had just claimed the sun.

TWO
Myths

YOU FOLLOW A DIRT TRAIL behind the shops and breweries and clean, pastel-colored condos. The highway noise is a murmur out here, the loudest sound the gravel crunching beneath the soles of your feet. It's on this lonely mountain trail that Xolotl, the coyote skull—whom you've strung to your hip with headphone wires through your belt loop—tells you a story. The story of when his kind first found this world, a long, long time ago.

THEY CROSSED AEONS OF EMPTY SPACE AND TIME AND FOUND YOUR LIQUID WORLD IN THE FOURTH ITERATION OF THIS UNIVERSE, ALL ALONE, SURROUNDED BY BLACKNESS, WITH ONLY A SINGLE, UNMOVING STAR TO WARM ITS CRUST.

He bounces off your hip with each step you take but the words leak from his mouth without shaking.

IT WAS BEFORE YOUR WORLD WAS EVEN A WORLD. JUST FIRE AND INFINITY UP AND OUT AND ALL AROUND, AND WE WERE STILL ENERGIES, BUBBLING AND COSMIC. WE TOOK SOLID FORM. WE TAMED YOUR BEASTS, WE RODE LEVIATHANS. LABORED TO SHAPE A SECTION OF THIS WORLD FOR US AND ANOTHER FOR YOU, JUST AS MY TWIN QUETZALCŌĀTL, WHO IS THE FEATHERED SERPENT AND THE WIND ITSELF, COMMANDED.

After four failures, my twin wanted to try yet again to create a heaven out of your sour soil. I followed his plan, never realizing how it would pervert us.

I alone joined him on his descent to the underworld. To the temple on the other side of Mictlān, where we stood before the Lord and Lady of the Dead and robbed them of the bones of the past. The spirits of the Underworld chased us back to the surface, and in his haste, my twin dropped those bones upon your dirt. They lay there, scattered and splintered. It was I who said, "Let them be, Precious Serpent. Let's see what new things will sprout from our mess."

We did not see our mistake then; we were too close. But it's so glaring now.

Xolotl led you to a mountaintop earlier today. You placed him on a stone adorned with graffiti and he told you to hold out your hands, to feel the tōnalli in the desert's minerals and in all living things. He told you how to move your fingers in rhythm with them, how to grab them with your thoughts and drag them, push them around. It took you many headache-inducing hours, till your fingers were swollen and their tips blackened, and the weeds were nooses about your toes, but finally you did as Xolotl instructed and sucked the tōnalli out of the grass and weeds and cacti—they formed a burning flower in the palm of your hand.

Xolol commanded you to eat it, and its fire cleansed you from the inside out. You left that hilltop a black and rotting stain.

Now he tells you of his mother's fall. A goddess with a skirt of snakes and a face of vipers. She was the mother of them all, and the strength of her arm could lop off mountaintops. One day she swept away the top of the mountain Coatepec. The feathered Thing of anguish and sighs that dwelt there seethed in anger. In its lust for vengeance, it violated her.

ACT IV: POWER FORGED IN BLOOD

And within her womb she conceived—a growing burden.

She birthed her son alone, wept and held the warrior who'd sprung from her fully formed, armed with a snake that had also slithered from her womb.

My sister Coyolxauhqui gathered four hundred of our siblings and sought to end our corrupted mother. She was too late. My newest brother could clash snake against obsidian, rattle the earth, and split the sky. From a mountain he tossed down my sister's screaming head. Those of us who lived cried out, *Huitzilopochtli!*

Our brother of war.

When he finishes, the skull laughs—if a skull can laugh. *Hahaha*s dripping off his teeth.

It's a sad story, and goes on much longer, but no one really gets it. Not anymore.

He tells you other stories of other gods. Tlāloc, Xipe Totec, Tezcatlipoca—all of them dead now. But not dead in the way you think, Xolotl says. We aren't gods in the way your kind thinks of us. *God.* Xolotl scoffs. Such a simple word. There never existed such a word. We are ideas made life. A life-force energy—*Teōtl*. When we Tēteoh die, we lose our bodies in the mortal world, but we exist onwards, as all ideas do. We touch without sensation, eat without hunger, and remember without pain.

We are Essences. We are stories, Julian. Of the wind, and death, and water, and soil. We persist as long as we are told.

"Why you, then?" you ask the skull. "Why are you still physical while the others aren't? And you serve a human at that."

If a skull could suck its teeth, Xolotl did so. Most of us are dead, but *he* kept me alive, Xolotl growled. Your master, and

MINE. I'D GOTTEN CARLESS AND LAZY THE NIGHT I DUG UP THE WITCH'S CORPSE WITH MY CLAWS. I WAS AFTER WHAT LAY WITHIN HER, YOU SEE. THE CHILD. I HAD GOOD INTENTIONS, OF COURSE. TO SHEPHERD IT ACROSS THE RIVER OF SOULS AND INTO MICTLĀN.

ONLY SOMEONE ELSE HAD DUG HER UP FIRST. HAD CHOPPED OFF HER HAND AND REBURIED HER. HE WAS THERE WAITING FOR ME IN THE DARK, ALL THAT BRUJERÍA SMOKING IN HIS MUDDY PALMS.

IT WAS MY ARROGANCE THAT ALLOWED MY CAPTURE. WATCH YOURSELF, JULIAN, LEST IT BE YOUR UNDOING TOO.

You return home to an empty driveway. Pink blotches of what must have been words stain the concrete. You know that Kevin wrote them, or Alison, and that your mom was the one who scrubbed them out.

There's no sign of her inside, apart from the smell of weed saturating the curtains. There's fresh ash in a tray on the counter and you know it hasn't been long since she left. Your room is how you left it a night and lifetime ago: unmade bed, laundry piles. The box with the dead snake still rests on your mattress, wafting the smell of decay through the house. On your desk you find a note: an apology from your mom, asking you to be there when she gets home.

You promise yourself you'll tell her you're sorry when she comes back. Sorry for her wrist, and the garden, and the snake. You promise yourself you'll be better.

But you won't wait for her. There are things you must do, miles to go. Promises to keep. She'll have to wait a bit longer. But you'll return at the end of your day, like both of you always do.

SAMUEL WILL LEAVE HIS SHOP WITHIN THE HOUR, Xolotl says as you set him on the nightstand. HE'LL COME HERE FIRST, YOU KNOW. HURRY, OR WE'LL MISS OUR CHANCE.

"Do you ever stop talking?" you ask.

He looks at you the way any dead coyote skull would.

You've eaten enough today. Convenience store snacks, bought with the last of your pocket change. Tacos from the mercado, bought with crumpled dollars you found on the ground. You ate these things stiffly, within sight of a police officer across the park, who watched you with slits for eyes just waiting to see if you'd try anything—kid like you with no money, sitting there like that.

You're not sure of it, but think you've seen more cops than usual today, more eyes watching. Waiting, waiting. For any excuse to make their move.

Still, you ate your snacks and your tacos and that was enough. You're on your feet, the drumbeat rising. You have the strength for what you want to try.

You drop the snake from its coffin, lay it flat along the desk.

Elizabeth asked if you could bring back the dead. You'd tried it before with birds and roadkill, but it never worked. The bones would lurch and wobble, nothing more. But that was then. When you'd never extracted venom from blood with a flick of your hand. Never puppeteered bones until they danced.

Xolotl laughs, a grating rumble. YOU'RE A SWEET THING. IT WON'T WORK. NOT EVEN A TEŌTL CAN BRING BACK THE DEAD.

He's probably right; you try anyway.

You stretch out your fingers, wrap them around smooth scales, feel bones. You don't try to make them dance. You find the heart nestled amid meat and ribs and flex to make it beat, pump blood. Squeeze the lungs empty and then inflate them. You get the snake's body moving, pulsing. And yet, when you let go, she flops over dead.

It's not enough. No matter what you do, you can't spark life back into the brain or refill it with memories that have leaked out.

Xolotl laughs with his jaws wide open and fangs to the ceiling, HEHEHAHA.

The jaws clamp back shut and he says, Who do you think you are?

Oliver's voice echoes within your head, telling you you're crazy—hearing voices and drums and talking to the skull of a Mexica god.

You stand in your room, surrounded by posters on the walls and old action figures of superheroes. How badly, when you learned you were gifted with powers off a comic book page, did you want to be like those heroes, brave and stupidly good? Riley even made you a little mask with eye holes and a leather band to go around your head. You'd shown him how you rolled shadows into bullwhips, and he'd said, "You're incredible. *Fucking incredible.*"

That pain aches in your chest. It pushes sobs you've buried beneath your ribs up into your throat, but you don't have time to cry. You don't. You have to go—there's no time left.

You get your backpack, stuff the skull within it. Take your mask and tie it on. The window is your exit, the ravine your shortcut through town, toward the antique store where Xolotl says tools wait for you. You hope you can be home in time to greet your mother. You're going to fix everything, you tell yourself.

Now, you will be a hero.

Creeping through the window, the Boy is small—a lithe figure that ripples in the heat as he makes his way down the creek bed. In two minutes, the last of him has faded into the ferns and cattails and the house is left alone. Cicadas buzz, a lawnmower tears up a lawn, and the dead snake, still lying on the desk, inhales.

THREE
Tasks

IT'S NOON, the day before Halloween, and I've stopped by my office in City Hall. San Ojuela's vice mayor Sharon Anderson knocks but doesn't wait for me to say, Come in. She busts open the door and wags her phone at my nose.

We're getting more news crews, Lucas, she says. Fucking news crews! CNN, talking like we're some hick-town in the middle of ass-fuck nowhere. What were you thinking? We can't have our sheriff throwing tantrums on live-fucking-TV! Are you even listening, Lucas?

I'm looking over her shoulder, out my office doorway and down the hall, trying to name the shape that's watching this happen from the other end.

She punches a stack of papers against my chest and says with disdain thinning her lips, Try to be a professional. Not Clint fucking Eastwood.

Before I came to work today, everything was quiet. I woke up at five in the morning, early enough to beat the alarm and preserve the stillness of our home. I'd gotten home late, and Diana had stayed up for me. Said she'd waited up all evening for me, that she *wanted* me. Craved me. Her vaquero, her strong conquistador.

And when we made it to the bedroom, our clothes spilled into a puddle at the foot of our bed, Diana lying down, the heat of her rising to my chest, I tried to shake away the monsters that crowded my head, but every time I shut my eyes they were there—waiting—full of bloody claws and bloody teeth. Again and again I had to stop. The third time, Diana asked, What is it?

It's nothing, I said, remembering what my sergeants had told me years ago. Never bring the darkness home.

Diana said, You're keeping secrets.

I told her, It's the nature of my job.

It wasn't until we were lying between damp sheets, my dark arms wrapped around her pale body, that I told her I'd gone back to the old neighborhood to see Gran. And the shape of her laughed. Ugh, she said. Better you than me.

I stopped rubbing her. I'd called my home so many things during the years we'd been together: shithole, nowhere, barrio, slum. It had never bothered me in high school that Diana and her friends used to call it *the ghetto*, too. But now? Something about how I couldn't see her face, just heard the contemptuous chuckle.

I stayed up thinking about it, long after she'd drifted off to sleep.

I ate breakfast alone—two tamales with two over-easy eggs slid on top, their yolks warm and runny. I waited, considering whether to wake her like I always did, until time ran out. Then I left without a word. When I shut the house door, I could've sworn I heard feet running within.

After Sharon's chewed me out, I decide to go back to the precinct and work on the stack of paperwork she left for me, the one that's code for *Shit I Gotta Do if I Want Any of My Proposals to Move Off the Leaning Stack on Sharon's Desk*. But things get in the way, like they always do.

"You have to find him!" Mrs. Ruvalcaba howls through the phone. "Please—he doesn't do well on his own. He likes to act tough with his friends but he's so—so sweet and gentle, really. Being in the desert all alone is no place for him, he's going to get hurt. You have to find him, please! ¡AY, MI HIJO!"

I tell her that we have a few leads on her missing son Oliver and we're doing the best we can. That it's still early in the investigation. I don't have the heart to tell her that after seventy-two hours have gone by, we mostly expect to find a body. Mostly.

Still, a noise out in the office reminds me we have a witness in that case coming by. A girl named Alison Carlson, one of the last people to see Ruvalcaba. She talks a lot about the Boy she and her two friends saw him with.

Julian's got a pattern, Alison says. His friend Riley went missing a couple years ago, and the school said it was a suicide. We were all packed into the gym for an assembly about it. It was musty and hot as shit in there—hot as heck, sorry, sir. But we always questioned why Riley did it—that whole thing with a knife and all. He was cool before, you know? It wasn't until he got close to Julian that things *changed*. And Julian doesn't have friends. He spends all his time with Samuel de Hory who runs the antique store downtown.

New World Antiques and Oddities?

She nods.

She's cut of the same cloth as every rich white high school kid across this county, heavy vocal fry, thrifted clothes she didn't need to save money on. She's just started talking about how the Boy, Julian, *assaulted* her last night when I think I see something watching me from outside my office window. I blink and it's gone.

It again, the thing that itches at the corners of my eyes. I stop listening to Alison and glance past her strawberry-blonde hair, watching shadows that just might be moving. The phone at the front desk rings. Keyboards clack. Boots squeak near the jail cells.

Alison's voice rises, snapping me back. Most people know to stay away from Mr. de Hory, she says. But Julian's not right, Sheriff.

I say, How so? Please be specific.

Like, he's fucking crazy. Like, a future school shooter or something. You can ask anyone. We all know it.

Later some detectives bring in security footage from the gas station Oliver was last seen at, grainy black-and-white frames that show the shape of them indisputably: Oliver, Julian, and the Dodge Challenger. I think about the clawed arm I found where the Challenger burned. Paola in forensics took it to Riverside County to identify the animal but said that if she had to guess, it was a coyote. The word sounded like wind scraping across the desert beyond the ICE facility fences.

paranoid sheriff paranoid sheriff paranoid paranoid paranoid

I can't give any more attention to the missing persons case today. There's another job the city's been on my back about, and I've promised to follow up in person: dispersing the panhandlers in the sports park.

I pull up to the park and cut the engine. The air conditioning dies, the heat settles in. Raymond's staring at me from the cracked-leather passenger seat with one of those looks that pull goosebumps along my arms, a look of *brotherly* concern. Unlike the looks I used to get from my actual brothers.

What?

We don't have to do this right now, he says. Give it another week.

I click open the car door, but Raymond stays put, staring. He calls me Sheriff for once. Maybe it's the lack of sleep or the dehydration or that fact that (as I only now realize) I haven't eaten since five in the morning, but I cock my head and tell him, Look. Who was sheriff before me?

He responds with, McCormick.

And how long was he sheriff? Thirty? Thirty-five years? Excuse the assumption, but I don't think he was Chicano. Nor the sheriff before him, or the one before that, either. So what does that make me?

I wait for a response. He's got none.

I use my hands for emphasis. It means I'm their *experiment*.

There were men more qualified than me who the party could've put up for sheriff. Men more experienced, with impressive records and a stomach for mouth-breathing local politicians. But they were struggling with an image problem. And I was starving for any chance to put miles between me and that barrio I was born in. San Ojuela was a quiet town where rounding up panhandlers and issuing traffic violations made up the bulk of the work, so when I made the papers after stopping a gunman at a local community college, they came to me with funds and a plan. Before I even had time to clean my gun, I was running for sheriff.

The homeless camp is across the park, past the dugouts and soccer field, right where the mountain starts its crawl up to the smog and the boulders loom higher than the trees. The smell of urine stings my eyes and I breathe as little as possible. A cluster of sun-bleached tents quilt the ground between the rocks, and I count seven bums among them. More might be sleeping in the tents and under sheets; I keep one hand on my belt buckle, the other on my leather holster. An old man hunched over a lawn chair notices us first. He waves at me. Hey, Sheriff! How ya doin?

Not so bad, Ernie, I say, squinting at him. What brings you guys back out here?

He pushes himself up and stands, cracking his spine. I know, I know, he says. Promised we wouldn't be back, but there hasn't been anyone here in days. It's been hot as hell, so we saw no harm in finding a cool place to rest. You get that, right?

I do. But they lower property values. So every city pays them to take the bus somewhere else, promising job opportunities and lower rent. I have to remind myself that we're not the ones that put them here. Their decisions are their own.

Look, I say, adjusting the brim of my hat to get a better look at Ernie. Others are now peeking out from around the boulders. I got a lot of stuff going on, so please don't make this difficult. Just gather your things and I'll help you on your way.

Well, Ernie says, looking back and forth. Eight of them now, two of us. Until sundown, the park's open to everyone, yeah?

To taxpayers, I tell him.

We pay taxes, another man shouts down at me.

I'm not arguing this, I tell them. They got a center in the next city over, with beds and hot dinners.

They don't let us keep our things! Ernie barks.

They turned me away, another adds.

Raymond nudges me, saying we gotta hurry up.

I tell the men, I'm not playing, you have till the count of five.

As if they were children.

Ernie points again towards the field. There's teens fucking in those bushes, and old men watching! Go get 'em first, Sheriff.

They erupt into laughter, all of them. Hollering and coughing and spitting.

I've had enough.

I head up the slope, shoving past Raymond who's already trying to talk me down. The first tent I can reach, I rip off its stakes and toss away. The bums jump away like rats, still laughing, backing into the boulders and bramble. Ernie asks about the alley behind the strip mall. Are they allowed to sleep there? I shout, No. He asks, What about the flash-flood drains? They're big enough for seven men to lie in. They run like webs for miles beneath the city.

No—they can't go there, either.

He asks about all the empty buildings downtown.

I tell him those are private property and he cannot trespass.

Ernie throws a rock at me. *Then where the hell are we supposed to go?*

I grab him by the tatters of his jeans. I pull him down to the ground, where we wrestle in the dirt and rocks and stink and sweat. I fumble for my handcuffs but he breaks free and lurches up, laughing and kicking dirt that crunches between my teeth.

I lunge to sprint after him, but rocks slide away beneath my boots. The mountainside fights back. And I'm falling. I throw out an arm to catch myself. My shoulder crunches.

FOUR
Some Devil Like Me

THE ALLEYS lead you to the antique shop's back door, squeezed between stacked pallets and a bloated dumpster—you've taken so many breaks back here, smoking or playing games on your phone. These alleys have shielded you. Between dark rooftops the sky is a fading bruise, and soon will come the stars. In the door's black glass, your mask stares back at you. You are faceless except for those eyeholes.

WHAT ARE YOU WAITING FOR? Xolotl says from within the backpack slung over your shoulder. HURRY UP. HE WON'T BE GONE FOR LONG.

You jiggle the back door handle, just in case, even though you know it's locked. Peering through the glass, you make out the glints of streetlights on the other side, casting long and twisted shadows inside the shop. No one's home. You take a step back, grab a plank of discarded wood that's leaning against the dumpster, and swing it through the air to feel its weight. It's heavy, like the past. Like when you waited behind a bush for Alex to jog past, the hot metal of a tire iron squeezed in your grip. When Riley said he loved you, and the words made you brave enough to say it back. When you unlocked the doors for Oliver and let Coyote House eat him. When

ACT IV: POWER FORGED IN BLOOD

you saw Elizabeth screaming and Xolotl hounding her, compelled by Samuel's will the same way Samuel compels you, with his sweet sounds and shadow pull. When you chose to save Elizabeth's life.

When you ran away and cried in the desert, on the soft morning when Mom told you it was time, that the cancer had worked its will and your father was holding on, waiting for you to say goodbye.

You have choices in the gulf separating What-has-been from What-could-be, deep in the gory What-is. Like now. You're waiting on the blade's edge.

You smash the window in.

You don't have much time. You swerve around the shelves with Xolotl in your hands, letting his words pull you around the aisles, past arcade games and dolls and rows of eighties comic books. You seek the tools to strip the night from your blood; the tools to bring Xolotl's body back. You find them in Samuel's back room, the one lined with stone skulls of Mexica deities that smells of copal and fresh burnt leather.

It's not like anyone's ever even bought any of the stone artifacts Samuel displays in glass cases out front; they're just rocks to the tourists. Yet he still has these ones he keeps back, so that no one sees them, no one even thinks of buying them. They belong to him—which you've always thought was better than being in some museum or private collection, miles away from their soil and the rest of their kind. Their jade eyes watch you scan the jars along the shelves, looking for what you'll need for the potion. Then you give up on choosing, unzip your backpack, and slide as many ingredients as you can in with Xolotl—owl scat, spider legs, vials of blood from people you've helped kill. When you're done, you shut the door to the room without looking back. You'll never see those skulls again.

HURRY, HE'S RETURNING, Xolotl tells you. I FEEL HIS FEET AGAINST THE EARTH.

"Going as fast as I can," you snip.

Back in the maze of tchotchkes and knickknacks and bones, muscle memory pivots your feet, keeping you low. Hidden. Is that the little bell above the front door you hear? You know its delicate ring from all the times tourists have wandered in to gawk at vintage Disney cups. You freeze. Feel the *tha-thump, tha-thump* of a heartbeat through the floor planks. You back up, bump something fleshy and warm. You whirl around but your shoulders unknot at the sight of it: one of those rubber fish on a wall plaque. And you can breathe again. Then the fish head jerks and stares at you eye to eye before its lips open and it blares a distorted cover of an eighties pop dinner bell.

You've dropped to a crouch by the time the fish reaches the chorus, and when footsteps reach the spot where you stood, you're gone—deeper into the shadows and narrow aisles, the beats of "Hungry like the Wolf" pounding with your heart. You're ready to make a break for the back door when Samuel shouts, "They're looking for you, Julian."

And any thought of leaving is gone. Beaten away by the familiarity, the comfort and reassurance of his voice. You're just standing there.

"The police came asking for me, mijo. Asking about you. They…they think you killed someone." It means they're looking for both of you, that you got sloppy and they're catching on, but then again how long did you really think this could last?

Sounds like something Xolotl would say.

You're going to disappear once this is over, whatever that means. Even while every tendon in your chest yanks tight at the sound of his voice, begging not to let him go, you think of your mom, tired and loving, and remember that it's not a choice at all.

You have to leave him.

You're fighting the words boiling in your mouth—your need to say something, anything, to him. Because he's the only one you've mattered to. It was always Samuel who said you were special, who showed you his gifts like yours and taught you to make bones dance. He said the power was in both you and him, preserved from your ancestors who survived the siege of Tenochtitlán, but you never believed him—because why the hell would *you*, the angry boy with no dad or friends to your name, be anything more than a future burnout on the side of the road?

But the magic was real. You chose to believe that.

Samuel's words saved you.

"There's not much time left," he says, closer now. The vibration of his footsteps ripples through the floor and up your legs. "I can't stay here. I'll lose all the power that house provides us, all its protection. I'm already getting weaker, Julian, despite the sacrifices. It's my mind—I'm still losing it. My powers leech at me. Without the house, my mind will fade, and I'll be left grabbing memories like handfuls of water.

"And you, pobrecito niño. It's not just me in danger. The police think you killed Oliver. They're coming, right now. Survive them, and then what? That snake bite on your leg is spreading. Soon the Tēteoh will rip you apart. It's just you and me against the world."

He'll forgive you. He always does.

Even when you lash out or bite, he forgives you.

"Remember," he says, "I never asked you to kill at first. You told me about the boys who caught you and Riley. Alex, was it? The one who spread those rumors, terrible and cancerous? And it was you, Julian, who dragged Alex to me, weeping and gagged with blood dripping off his hair. I told you, 'Not him.' Do you remember? Yet you took him out to the bluffs, and with your claws and your fangs, *you* ripped him apart."

He's right.

And each word cuts away at your being. You told him all of that, once upon a time, and he said he understood. He helped you hide the body. The whole of you is tense and shivering. You want to cry but you bite your tongue.

"I'm here to help you," Samuel says quietly. "Just come with me, and together we can go find someplace better."

You think of Oliver, who escaped his own kind of trap only to die in the desert, and of his car set ablaze—your fault. How afraid he was, when you locked eyes with him in that 7-Eleven parking lot. You think of the stars the two of you watched on that night. You say nothing at all.

"Fine, then," Samuel says with a crack in his voice. "Do what you want. But know that I tried to save you."

The bell above the door jingles again, and the catch clicks shut behind him. His footsteps fade into the vast emptiness outside.

You walk to the back door. The hole you smashed gapes into blackness now, the sun long gone. Carefully, you sneak into the alley. At first you see nothing. Then floodlights flash your world to white.

Sirens blare behind the wave of white light. The silhouettes of a dozen cops and more flicker red, blue, red, blue. Gun barrels point towards you from the rooftops. A man steps into the middle of the alley in front of all of them with his right arm in a sling across his chest. His cowboy hat shields you from the lights.

"Julian Zavala," he announces with a megaphone. "You are wanted for murder, and we have a warrant for your arrest. Come quietly or there will be trouble."

No.

no no no no no no no no

FUCK!

You pivot to run back inside, but there are already men in dark suits and black masks charging through the store. You run into the deeper shadows farther down the alley, away from the lights, but the shadows betray you. Men hidden within them spring out—tackle you down.

No—no—no—no!

Glass shatters in your bag. They strip it off you, dark wetness leaking from its fabric. You elbow, bite, and claw, but gloved hands pull your hair and rip off your mask, shred your cheek against the concrete. Knees dig into your back.

No—no, please God, no! Fuck.

You call out, "Help!"

Someone tells you, "Shut the fuck up."

A kick to your ribs accomplishes this; you spit blood. Something bites beneath your ribs and electric shocks lock you rigid, pain flashing through you. You think that the light inside you will glow—glow! Until it tears all your skin away. They twist your wrists back behind you. Slap metal against bone and lock you in tight. The last thing you see, before they hoist you up and drag you away, is Samuel watching from behind the wall of them, the stars alive in his eyes.

FIVE
Escape

Elena rushed back and forth across the house, from the closet at the end of the hallway to the dresser in Julian's room, snatching up passports and sweaters and whatever else might be useful. Two half-full suitcases waited on the bed, coughing loose shirts and hastily folded jeans. It wasn't a lot, but then again, she only needed what she could carry; the rest could stay behind with the house, their lives here. Where they were going, they wouldn't need it.

Elena had called her cousin Ivette in Nevada an hour ago, asking if she and Julian could stay with them. It would just be a six-hour drive through the night, across the San Bernardino mountains and over wide stretches of high desert. Not unlike the drives she used to take to and from Mexico City all the time, when she was young and craved adventure. Coffee and Red Bull were all she'd need to reach the air mattress already being prepped in Ivette's living room. Just one more quick drive.

The police had called her as she was leaving work. She was still in her hostess uniform, the smell of onions wafting off the fabric. Her feet ached and her eyelids fought the weight of themselves when she answered the phone. The *Hello, this is Deputy Raymond* was all she needed to hear. It meant that they were looking for Julian, that it was serious, and that she would not offer them any information they could use.

"Is he okay?" Elena had asked.

"We're trying to figure that out, but he might be dangerous and could hurt those around him. So if you find him, let us know, and we'll try to help as best we can."

Bullshit. She called Julian half a dozen times on the drive home, and stopped amid packing to try yet again, but her calls went to voicemail every time. His phone must be dead. Or they'd gotten him already. The latter possibility was a cold fist at the bottom of her stomach.

Between the living room and kitchen, Elena stopped to make one final call. Voicemail—an outdated recording of her son's voice, from when he was fifteen and she'd finally managed to buy him his first smartphone. "Hi, it's Julian Zavala's phone." A teen's cracking voice. "Leave a message and I'll try to call you back or something." Elena spoke after the insufferable beep and begged him to please—*please!*—come straight home.

There wasn't much in the suitcase she'd decided was Julian's. Clothes and records and the notebooks he drew in were all he'd want to take. Her own took more time. She had to gather her clothes but also things like her citizenship papers and Julian's birth certificate, which she tucked in an orange folder and stored in a pocket at the bottom of the suitcase.

All she needed to do now was pick what piece of her husband to bring. His pajamas? His wallet? The vinyl Godzilla toy she'd bought for him at a flea market? She settled on the picture she kept in the hallway: him, and her, and Julian between them. The house she could lose; it had been too big for years. Pots and pans she could rebuy, and the furniture had never suited her taste. But that picture…

I'm not a bad parent, she thought, then redacted, reworded, and said it aloud: "I'm trying not to be."

In the photo there wasn't any darkness in her son. That had crept in later, after his father's death, in the blind spots of Elena's memory where she was busy teaching herself English and learning to file taxes—all the pieces she had to pick up mid-stride and keep running. For months after the funeral, she'd kept up that speed, determined not to sink into the mud. She would not drown.

And in the meantime Julian grew up. He met a boy, and Elena had to cut ties with certain family members who might have helped with their financial struggles were they not busy whispering bigotry disguised as Catholic concern. Then, half a year later, Riley committed suicide and Samuel dug his claws into Julian. *I let it happen, and for what? Pride? Money?*

No, the truth was, she'd let it go on because deep down she was afraid of her son. Afraid of the bones he'd tinkered with even as a toddler in the yard, of his dreams of flayed women, of the coyotes that howled in the distance when he'd cry. She'd pawned him off to Samuel de Hory hoping he would understand the alien brightness growing brighter inside him.

Elena packed the photograph. Zipped up the suitcase. She jogged to the front door to go start the car but yelped when she swung it open.

There stood Samuel de Hory.

Elena stumbled backward and slipped—collapsed against the floor on her heels and hands. Samuel stepped inside.

"Hola," he said.

"¿Qué hace aquí?" Elena gasped.

He stepped closer, looking down at her. In flat, dispassionate English now, he said, "They've taken him."

"¡Salte de mi casa!"

"Escúchame," he spat through clenched teeth. He grabbed her biceps and with impossible strength hoisted her up and set her back on two trembling feet. "Se han dado cuenta de lo que es. De lo que ha hecho. ¿Entiendes lo que—" He stopped. His eyes flicked to the keys clutched in Elena's fist. "¿Adónde vas?" He grabbed her wrist. The wall rattled when he pinned her against it. "You would take him away from me?"

Elena dropped the keys. Samuel lunged for them—as she'd hoped he would—and as he caught them in his palm, she'd already yanked the lamp off the side table next to her and exploded it against the back of his skull. He dropped without a scream, and she hit him again with the lamp's metal skeleton. Once. Twice. Dropped what was left of it in the spatters of blood beside Samuel's body.

She heaved for air, hand against the wall for balance. Samuel twitched in the sticky puddle growing around his head. In his open hand waited the keys. Elena snatched them up and ran to the kitchen landline to begin punching 911, but her fingers cramped after the nine as she heard a gurgle from the hall.

A gurgle, and then spitting, and then Samuel's labored laughter. Elena fought the stiff tendons in her fingers, tried to flex her hand but it would not move. Her whole arm was stiff. Her feet stapled to the floor. She turned her head so she could see him, pushing himself up to sitting, slumping against the wall.

"You...you stupid bitch," Samuel choked. "You just had to make this so *fucking* hard, didn't you? Stubborn bitch." He winced in pain—the whole house shuddered with him. "You have it too, don't you? The gift. The Tēteoh chose you, but you fought it. And won. You didn't even know what you had, what you let go unclaimed. Then they found him instead. But I—*I* wasn't *chosen*. It was a power I had to take—and one that cost me. Your son helped me manage its toll."

He stopped to groan and roll his grotesque head. He chuckled. "I believe you've—fractured my skull. I can feel my very self leaking out. But fear not, the darkness will press it back in. Fucking bitch."

Elena wasn't listening. Her heart thrashed in her chest. Her headache was back, burning a a hole through her skull.

"You're deranged!" she spat. It was all she could do. "Pathetic old piece of shit. You're going to die if you don't get help right now. ¡Suélteme!"

That was when Elena spotted it: the spindly creature inching around his shoulder, crawling down to his hand, lacing its fingers with his. The hand was decayed, stinking of pus and rot, and from its stump black tendrils sprouted. The tendrils slithered up his forearm and pressed against the hinge of his elbow until the meat gave way. They injected themselves into his veins, started sucking the color from his cheeks and into the hand's now-rosy fingertips.

Samuel held the hand in his own tenderly, as though it were a lover's. Elena tried to scream, but at a swipe of those interlocked hands her jaw snapped shut.

"No. We're not having that," he said. There was a dead, hungry look to him that paled his eyes.

Tears stung her eyes and blurred away the horror until he was just a shape staggering up, arm outstretched. "This is my last chance to actually get what I need. You can't ruin it. I can't have that."

Elena tried one last time to cry out for help, but all she could manage was a strangled scream with her mouth shut. Then her elbows snapped backwards. Next, her wrists; then more bones cracking, no longer at the joints. The pain was loud, searing, enveloping. Elena screwed her eyes shut, and as the pain flooded her, she prayed—for the first time since her husband had died.

Dios, por favor ayuda a mi hijo.

SIX
A Fist Full of Justice

WE SPEED PAST OPEN FIELDS and orange groves, the streetlamps chopping by, the zest of citrus seeping through the window seams. I feel the blue medical tape around my shoulder blade and bicep pulling but I don't wince; it's barely a scratch. I'm weaving down backroads in the dark, the fastest way to the precinct. Behind us, the Boy squirms in the backseat, shoulders thrashing. He's shouting all the unoriginal ways in which we're pigs and bastards, and to just wait and see what he'll do once he's free. I catch a glimpse of him in the rearview mirror through the gaps in the grate: sitting upright, arms taut behind his back, black-eyed and split-lipped, with red speckling his cheek where we used his face to scrub the sidewalk.

You assholes really think he's just some old man with a little antique store?! the Boy shouts. How the hell would he have known I'd be in there, huh? Do you really buy the sweet old man game? How pathetic. Real fucking good detective work there, Sherlock. You're supposed to be helping people, yeah? So *listen* to me!

He sounds like my brother Rodrigo on the day I announced I was going to pursue a career in the force. He arrogantly asked if I wanted to help people or to bully them; a stupid question. Either way, it would get me out, make me matter.

Without looking away from the road ahead of us, what little of it the headlights sift from the sea of black, I tell the Boy that threatening a police officer is a felony.

You're full of shit, you know that?

He kicks the grate—nothing we haven't seen before. His kind always act like this once they're caught, like the whole world is against them, and we're the problem. Always the tired I-ain't-done-nothing gag that's gotten stale. Knowing how he bit and thrashed after I read off his Miranda rights, I tell him he's lucky he didn't end up in worse shape.

Your mama, he snips.

Shut up, I mutter. I tune him out, continue down the empty road. In the passenger seat, Raymond chirps into his radio, telling the dispatchers that we're on our way back with suspect in custody. ETA fifteen minutes.

There are no streetlights here, no houses for miles, just the hulking shapes of agricultural machines looming in the dark and the far-off outlines of those skeletal pumpjacks, always bobbing. Already my officers have dispersed back across the county. Some stayed behind to gather what evidence they could at the antique shop, while some are at the station with the Boy's possessions. In his pack we found real horror movie shit. Jars of blood and livers, and a coyote skull larger than any I've ever seen before.

He's like a son to me, was what Samuel de Hory had said when I took him to the back room and sat him down with a white table between us. He told me how Julian had been disappearing at night, more and more frequently, only for Samuel to find him in the morning, shivering, with blood on his clothes. He said it had happened the other week, the same night Oliver was last seen, and the same night forensics determined the Dodge had burned.

I tried to help him, Samuel said with his face in his hands. Really, I did. He'd tell me they were only animals, but...he mentioned that boy too. And I just...want to make sure he gets the help he needs.

I almost feel sorry for the kid, knowing how he lives and who he's lost. I walked his neighborhood block. I stood on his porch and looked at rows of dead-lawned houses and leaning fences and thought how I'd still be living on a block like that had I not picked myself up. Bootstraps, right? Rodrigo would say it's a dumb metaphor. "Because it's impossible." But that's the point—doing the impossible.

You guys are fucking morons, the Boy shouts from the back. Seriously. He's got you all wound up like little toys and you're all dancing for *him*. He's playing all of us, and you guys seriously can't see that right in front of you?

I tell him to be quiet. I'm trying to think of all those loose ends, like the corpses dating back a decade, the kindly man Sonora mentioned. The chupacabra. In my head I hear Sharon and Diana chanting with clicking teeth. *Paranoid! Paranoid! Paranoid!*

The Boy shouts, LET ME GO! He hacks up a shining red glob and spits it through the grate, where it slaps the back of my neck.

That's it. The car halts. The dead speed of it yanking us forwards, slamming us back. I unbuckle my seat belt and, ignoring Raymond's questions, step into that sea of night. I leave the engine running, knowing this will be quick; the car is an island here. The rest is black. The Boy's still shouting when I swing open the back door. He says, You don't know me, or all the shit I've had to do to survive, but I bet we all look the same to you people, huh? You're all so pathetic. It would be funny if you didn't just shoot whoever hurt your widdle fucking feewings.

Raymond's catching on now. He's stuttering out shy requests for me to maybe calm down a little, this isn't a good idea, but I crack my knuckles—never mind the pain in my right shoulder screaming—and the Boy finally shuts up.

He blinks with wide, disbelieving eyes. What are you doing?

I say, You murdered Oliver Ruvalcaba. You burned his car out in the desert.

He thinks I don't know the pinch of steel cuffs against wrists, or the cold bite of a prison cell bench. I make sure he knows that I do. As he backs into the corner, I bend over him, holding him by a handful of hair. I tell him the only difference between us is that, unlike him, I crawled out of the shithole I was born in.

It wasn't me, he mutters, probably in disbelief that I'd stoop to his level. He says, It was *him*. Him, and the chupa—

Enough of that. I grab a bundle of his shirt, and finally he shuts up. The car shakes on that empty roadside. The night is empty and wide, and the boy yelps. The pounding fists, cracking bones, Raymond's pleas for me to stop—small sounds in the vast fields, which no one hears. By the time I'm done my fists are slick and wet. Skin from my knuckles is caught in his teeth. The same red that shines on my hands stains my uniform. I might have sprained something in my right hand, but who cares. I stagger out of the back seat, breathing heavy, and wipe sweat off my forehead before slamming the door on the crumpled-up kid.

The rest of the drive is quiet. There's only the chirping radio, the boy's scrappy breaths. But a word screams through my skull—the one I know I heard the boy start to say before I cut him off.

Chupacabra.

We uncuff the boy and throw him into an empty cell, where he slumps to the floor, a bloody pulp. Raymond asks if we should take him to the hospital, but I tell him it can wait, there's something I have to do.

Julian's not our serial killer. He's not the monster that tore Sonora's chest open. He's too small, too weak. And I feel stupid for not seeing it sooner.

I leave Raymond to watch over the boy. Soon I'm back in my patrol car, pulling out of the lot into the desert night, towards Samuel and Casa Coyotl.

SEVEN
Lose Your Soul

It first comes to you quietly. A clapping sound, a distant beat. A ringing in the back of your skull.

You're lying on the cold tiles of the jail cell they threw you in, your own blood soaking your clothes. Behind you, keys jingle. The cell door swings open with a metallic groan, and two black boots rush towards the pulp of you. They try to hoist you up, but every movement is a stab between your ribs. You're a yelping animal, and he drops you there.

The officer, whose shining name tag reads *Nicholas Raymond*, tells you help is on the way, that you'll be okay. He reaches around you, tries once more to lift you up despite your groans, your searing pain—blazing out of bone through meat and skin; you can't even scream. Just bite down on your tongue to let one pain burn out the other. The taste of iron in your mouth again.

Pain rips up your leg to your hip bone and venom surges through you, while all the sounds of the outside world are muffled; vision narrows; all you can see are the white lights buzzing above your head.

That gurgling noise is you. A wheezing for air, getting fainter. You're dying; you feel in your bones that this is true. You are going to die here.

As the world fades, the beat you tried to bury deep inside returns to you, a whisper at first, then a thumping, a clap—the night reaching out to take your hand one last time. And you give yourself to it.

The night wastes no time. It pours itself into you, scrubbing away everything you are, the moppy-haired, slouch-postured, brown-skinned body you've always known. The night tucks what's left of that boy into a corner and expands to fill the space. This body is now not only your body—it's shared with the night. And the night is the Tēteoh, not just bones and dead things but the desert, and stars, and owls, and snakes, and—

Coyotes.

This body stands up. Bones fuse back together where they've snapped. Tendons reach across chasms to pull wounds shut. Insects suture skin. The officer, now staring wild-eyed from across the room, calls to you as you stagger out of your cell. His gun is drawn in trembling, clumsy hands. But that's not new.

"Get back in the cell right now!" he shouts. Adds that you have till the count of three.

One.

Two.

The night puppets your arm, twists your fingers, contracts them into a fist—and Officer Raymond's guts do the same. You can see the knots writhing beneath his shirt all the way over there. He'd opened his mouth to utter "three," but pain stopped the word in his throat—where now a pale, shining thing blooms out his mouth instead. It slithers further, longer. He drops his gun. You reel back horrified, but you don't run; the night makes sure you watch what it—you—achieved, together. A long, white snake, thick enough to stretch his lips thin, slips from his mouth and flops to the floor. He screams, but another one burrows up, slithers over tongue and teeth. Snake after fat snake slides from his mouth until he collapses against the wall, his belly deflated. The space where his stomach once was becomes a cavity of wrinkled uniform. You watch in horror as the snakes consume his eyes.

You snap back into yourself, grab onto a portion of yourself that's still in your body and command yourself, *Run!* And you do. Swaying drunkenly to the night's rhythm, lost in it, but fast. You grab a shotgun mounted on the wall as you leave the room. There's no time to think, only react. You must keep moving. Before the night's beat consumes you entirely.

"All things have power," Marisol's voice boomed as Elizabeth stepped into the center of the labyrinth behind Casa Coyotl. An ocean of time separated them from the funeral reception Elizabeth had only just snuck away from. "There is value in all objects, and in all objects, we leave a part of ourselves."

Marisol wasn't in the shape of a phantom anymore. Within the labyrinth, she had shed her human outlines, laced hair and hands with shadows until she became the maze entire, her lavender scent overwhelming Elizabeth with every breath.

Now her voice was in the shadows too, and the shadows cradled Elizabeth.

Along the stone walls, the shadows had stretched and flattened themselves into lines of vivid red, black, green, gold, white—all bent into geometric hieroglyphs and stamped against the stones. Ridged figures with large heads, each intricately detailed with boxy or swirling patterns in their hair, their arms, their clothes. Elizabeth knew this style: it was replicated all across southern California on everything from activist street murals to taqueria menus. Aztec art, dancing to life on the labyrinth walls. When the paintings opened their mouths, scrolls of speech swirled out like smoke.

Caravans of armored men rode on horseback across mountains and plains, their banners billowing against a tezontle sky. With them, they dragged indigenous men, women, children—people they had conquered with their steel, whom they'd sacked and stripped, and who now locked tales of their gods safe beneath their tongues.

The invaders met smaller, more scattered tribes along their trek northwards. Like the southerly tribes, these people were crowned in feathers and traded maize and pelts for the booze and guns that, the invaders knew, corrupted all people. The figures on the walls showed Elizabeth how the invaders laid their hands upon the desert waste; pulled great missions from the earth; plowed fields for their slaves to reap; and bound their slaves with holy doctrine, cracking whips at their backs when they did not reap fast enough.

Watching the bloody mural reshape itself, Elizabeth almost didn't notice the hacienda that had appeared, tucked between desert mountains at the far end of the canvas: open courtyard gaping in the center, high walls, long hallways. A dozen smaller houses surrounding it, most of which no longer stood.

Elizabeth chewed on Marisol's words as she watched. She said, when she couldn't come up with anything else, "But I already know all this. About the power that seeps into things."

She'd grown up hearing the story of her family's roots told over and over. By her mother, her father, and Marisol. The cleaned-up versions and the ugly, scabby ones. She knew she had indigenous roots, and Catholic ones shipped to Mexico from overseas. They'd interwoven and made themselves inextricable from one another. A violent merger that had birthed something new.

"Te sabes," said Marisol, "all the parts of souls they left here when they forged this land, this stolen land."

"But all these people have been dead for a long time," Elizabeth said. Yet she felt an ache in her bones: the bones buried under the house, calling to her own.

"I never wanted us to lose the house," Marisol said. The shape of her hand stretched out from the shadows and placed itself on Elizabeth's shoulder. The other hand manifested too, pointing to the lines that bloomed from Casa Coyotl's portrait on the wall—a webbed city. "We all leave behind parts of our soul into things," she said. "Like pocket watches. Or stitched-up teddy bears. We leave them into our homes too."

Elizabeth rubbed her hands together, where coarse, phantom teddy bear stuffing itched her fingertips. Marisol had stained the bear with the blood of her pricked finger.

Elizabeth understood now, found a name for it, called it Sentiment. *Power forged in blood.*

Sentiment.

"And those parts go into the town too," she said, fitting the pieces together.

"This blood pumped *life* into the town," Marisol said. "It still does. There's so much power here. And people want it, always more of it. Even if they don't know what makes the city they want so special. Se traen con sus suitcases y offers of dinero. Always smiling, making deals too good to refuse, so they can strip down the land and build something grand and terrible on top. I could never let that happen, mija. That's why I never abandoned the house. I had to be its steward. There is so much of so many souls poured into these foundations, and they need care, protection, someone who understands. I cannot give it up. The vultures will rip into the soil and plunge in new foundations. They'll use up the power and *destroy* it."

That's when Elizabeth finally got it—like a neon sign sparking in her head. She shook her head at the labyrinth walls—her walls. This house was hers now; its land was hers. She was its keeper.

"I can't," she said in an almost-whisper. Then, louder, "I can't *inherit this*. I'm—I'm not *like* you." She couldn't imagine that future for herself, trapped like Marisol, another steward of the house.

The shadows curled around her. She was adrift in the night's sea, the labyrinth walls pulling back further into space.

"But this house needs someone who loves it back," said Marisol's voice.

Elizabeth could have closed her eyes and melted into sleep right there in the warmth of the shadows.

"Is my soul here then?" she asked suddenly. "Will I find it, if I stay?"

The shadows deposited her back on her own two feet, stumbling in bulky platform boots on solid ground. There was a smell of dampness between tight-running walls. A nearly full moon shining above. Marisol stood next to Elizabeth, shaking her head, with sadness at the corners of her blurred-out lips. "I'm so sorry, mija, but your soul isn't here. The pieces of it that are—they belong to the house now."

My siren screams. The lights flash red, blue, red, blue, as I swerve between the few cars scattered along these backroads. I'm pounding the steering wheel, shouting, Stupid! Stupid! Stupid. For not seeing it earlier. Because it was always there, wasn't it? Hiding in the old man's unassuming smile. I jotted down notes on crinkled yellow paper while he spoke with sincerity dripping from his teeth, that light shining behind his frosty eyes. *Kindly man.*

Sonora's voice nips the back of my neck. *Fucking vampire.*

The chupacabra.

He'll be at Casa Coyotl, in the shack near the lake or wherever the Remolinas sweep away the help these days. He's lived there all his life. His grandfather was groundskeeper before him. I feel for my gun, still slung in its holster—more than enough firepower to protect me from a frail old man. To hell with warrants.

I turn onto the road where I pulled over just half an hour ago, where I buried my fists in the boy's ribs. I pass that spot, no problem. There's no regret. Can't be. Regret will kill you if you let it.

That's what my brothers never understood. Rodrigo would always pick at me when I'd say, It is what it is, back when I was working in border protection. The facts crashed against his arrogant skull. I didn't make the policies, just followed them. It wasn't like ICE was my first choice. I'd failed to get into the police academy on four different occasions. I always got the rejection after hopeful months of waiting, the letters citing the tear in my ACL or the red ink on my juvenile record. None of that had mattered to ICE, though. They still wanted me.

I told Rodrigo someone had to protect our country against the waves of criminals pouring in, hiding behind those who actually needed help. Who better than us to tell those dirty faces apart?

You're a piece of shit, he spat.

At least I stand for something.

He would have preferred me becoming a cop. He'd said as much. But when the time came for that, he missed the ceremony.

Sonora's mismatched eyes wedge into my thoughts again, only this time she's shivering, her face bloodied like it was when I carried her in my arms, shouting for an ambulance. Even back then, I felt like I must have seen that face before.

I turn onto the road where the house waits, a mile ahead in the distance. I speed through an intersection, siren blaring, and then headlights flash from the darkness—blinding me. Tires screech; windows shatter. My car spins as a hood crashes against mine and I fight for the wheel while the world turns to streaks around me. I manage to straighten up, stop the world from spinning. A streetlamp is rushing up from the dark. My crushed hood crunches against it, and finally I'm still. The car horn screams.

You find Xolotl on a clerk's counter in the evidence garage after dashing up and down station corridors, your ears sharp at pinpointing police boots where they thunder on their hunt for you. You've already checked a million other offices and empty rooms, feeling for Xolotl's bones through the walls. Shouts echo above and below you. Alarms flood the hallways, bleaching your world into shadow and scarlet. When the shadows rip the doors away, the clerk mutters only a gasp before your ribbons coil out, snap him like a straw, and throw him aside.

Xolotl laughs when you lift him up. You FINALLY EMBRACED IT, EH? he says, pride slicking his fangs. As if it's even you in there. As if half of you isn't elsewhere, tucked away, fighting to regain mastery of your loose limbs. You clip the skull to your belt and wait behind the counter until another officer storms in. You throw him against the wall with a swipe of your hand.

The night thirsts for blood, but this time you resist it. You leave this man alive.

By the time you find your way onto the back lot, your feet are bloodied, shins splinting. Needles stab the stiff meat between your ribs. You're trying to keep yourself together, but the night is bulging out of you, wanting to join its vaster self in the sky. Out here it's stronger—it feels like it's trying to undo you. It helps you load the shotgun you swiped in haste and cock it—because you're not yet safe, they're still coming, any second now, right behind you. You dart between patrol cars as the men spill out the back doors, cracking off bullets that chase your feet.

You crouch behind a sinking van, air hissing where bullets bite the tires. The barrage of bullet dings pins you there—in your skin, your bones, one goal in your head screaming: *live—live—live!*

You stagger up, your whole body pulsing with blistering power. You brace for the kickback of the shotgun and fire two deafening blasts before taking off down the black tar road. You don't look back to check if you've hit any of them; you're halfway to the gate at the bottom of the hill, Xolotl laughing as he bounces against your hip.

The desert wants more, but you're still holding on, dodging the searchlights on precinct rooftops and ICE watchtowers.

WHY ARE YOU STILL RESISTING? Xolotl barks.

Quivers in the dirt tell you that men are loading rifles just outside the gate. You freeze. And, if only for a moment, you see hundreds of faces like yours watching you from the other side of that barbed-wire fence. You. Julian Zavala, the queer son of an immigrant mother, hardly any substance to you except the raw Teōtl power pounding in your heart and sparkling at your fingertips.

You, who want to live.

You follow the ICE fence. Up the opposite direction, vaulting over brambles and bushes and man-sized boulders, past cacti and dudleyas, all the way out into the safety of the wide-stretching desert.

EIGHT
And Become the Night

Elizabeth collapsed to her knees on the damp stones in the midnight chill. She struggled to get air back into her lungs after what Marisol had said: a gut punch to the very core of her. She could not recover her soul here. Only pieces of it remained, baked into the soil and mudbrick foundations. And Marisol had said she could not take the pieces back either.

"Then what happened to the rest of it?" Elizabeth spoke with the shattered bits of her voice, looking up at the fading shadow that was once Marisol.

The apparition's lavender scent was dissolving, its features less defined. Elizabeth was sure Marisol had expelled most of whatever it was that kept her here. Soon, she'd be alone again.

"I'm sorry," Marisol said, "but I do not know."

Elizabeth slammed a fist on the ground. "Then why am I here?" she demanded. "Where do I fit in?"

The hieroglyphs answered her this time, slithering back. Their dance showed the story of a stranger who had once, long ago, walked into town.

The man pulled a sun-bleached cart full of trinkets. He claimed he'd traveled the world far and wide before following the winds of manifest destiny right to their little town. Said his treasures came from Egypt, Rome, Greece, Mexico. Among the strange items was a full set of conquistador armor.

He spun tales of the wondrous and bizarre things he'd seen in faraway lands. He said he meant only to pass through, show off his trinkets, and maybe sell a few before going on his way. But he stayed for the winter and left in the spring. After that he returned each year with the harvest, always carrying new trinkets, always orbiting Casa Coyotl. The hieroglyphs painted the same man year after year, lean and vulture-bent around men and women who would wither as time passed. *He doesn't age*, Elizabeth thought—the traveler with the conquistador suit. Eventually his circuit grew smaller, his returns more frequent, until one year he stayed through summer. After that, he began to age—his skin growing liver-spotted, veins bloating, hair greying and thinning—and didn't leave San Ojuela until he died.

Or so the townspeople believed. But the shadows on the walls showed a different truth. One All Hallows' Eve, a four-legged beast stole a native woman and dragged her out into the desert. Elizabeth recognized the creature's feathers and batlike wings—Xolotl. Xolotl brought the woman to the man in an open field, where he split open her chest and spilt her blood for the thirsty sand. He tore out her heart and devoured its flesh. His hair darkened; his loose skin tightened.

He revealed himself to the townspeople again, claiming to be his own son.

He uses the house's power for blood magic, Elizabeth realized. *That's why he never left.*

The house was far from the other missions and tucked away from foot traffic, an intimate place just for him. The shadows flashed through decades of murder, devoured hearts, and abandoned corpses, until cars sped across the walls instead of carriages.

Until a small, frizzy-haired girl and her baby sister walked hand in hand with their father towards Casa Coyotl's gate.

"How does he do that? What does he do to use the house like that? Show me," Elizabeth demanded of the shadows.

And they did: the sun arced backwards across the stone canvas, from west to east, over and over, till night and day were passing in half-seconds and whole seasons came and went. Rain fell and rain dried. Centuries had passed by the time the sun stopped, halfway sunk beneath a long-ago horizon in an entirely different world.

The shadows no longer showed San Ojuela but somewhere far away instead, on forested hills where ruins lay scattered. Nine men stood silhouetted beneath the branches of a dead tree. Four pairs of pale feet swayed above them. The men dug four graves and buried five bodies: the shadows etched the outline of a fetus in one corpse's womb. A lone conquistador stood over the pregnant woman's grave, weeping quietly.

"Who was she?" Elizabeth asked.

"A nahualli warrior," Marisol said. It wasn't just Marisol, though. Countless other voices spoke with her. "Moctezuma had sent her and others to kill the invaders and end the foreign disease spreading viciously across the land. But when the warriors descended on the invaders in the wood at night, the invaders were ready. Not even nahualli brujería could save them from crossbows and cannon explosions. They were torn apart. All of them but her. She was alone on the battlefield of arrow-pinned corpses when the conquistador came to separate her head from her body and let her essence pour out. But instead he tended her wound and kept her with him. Fed her. Slept beside her at night. Told her she was beautiful. All while he held a sword at her throat.

"She was alone when he told her her emperor was dead, her empire sacked, the island city blasted to nothing. Alone when she learned of the disease that bubbled skin and how it had desolated her pueblo. Alone when her captor told her the colonizers would pardon anyone who agreed to leave behind their devils and accept Christ as the one true god. Alone when he said he loved her."

The shadows reached into Elizabeth to fill her with that long-dead woman's grief.

"When he offered her a home," the voices said, "what choice did she have?"

Elizabeth watched the woman give up her totems and wear European silks and practice her magic alone in a Spanish hacienda with a new husband beside her. Elizabeth watched her weep at night. Felt her harden her heart and wait out her days, looking for a moment to escape that would never come—a servant girl had seen her brujería and told the magistrate, who came with the power of God dressed in guns and swords.

Then there was the noose.

"Stop!" Elizabeth shouted.

The hieroglyphs obeyed.

"I get it," she said, tears burning her eyes. "Just—don't make me watch any more."

"It's *her* hand," Marisol said. "That he carries. All Samuel's brujería lives within it." She tapped her finger against the grave projected on the stones.

"So it doesn't even belong to him," Elizabeth said, disgusted.

"That's why its brujería is hungry and demands a price. The house heals what it can, but as the brujería must be refilled, more blood is spilt," Marisol said. She was fading quickly now. "I never figured it out when I was alive, but I could feel the house's heartbeat weaken. Only now can I see the dark spells he forces the hand to cast. The brujería is eating away at him slowly, Liz child. He's more desperate now. But the house protects you, as it did me." She took

Elizabeth by the hands, dark mist wreathing flesh, and hugged her for the last time. "This is what you're here for. If you can, mija—make him stop."

Elizabeth pulled away from the hug to find the shadows had peeled off the walls and stood in rows, countless men and women stretching endlessly through the labyrinth with Marisol at their head. Together their voices shook the earth. *Make him stop.* Elizabeth covered her ears but the words roared through.

"*Let us be the last. Kill Samuel de Hory.*"

Light beamed from their mouths—ripping apart the shadows in blinding white. Elizabeth shut her eyes, and when she opened them again, she stood alone.

The car horn screams, unending. The radio leaks static. I'm hanging off the steering wheel with the whole buckled dashboard pinching me against the seat. I fish in the dark space beside me, which I cannot turn to see, and feel edges: leather, plastic, metal. I find the seatbelt lock. I click it off, kick open the door, and wriggle in the narrow gap until I gasp and stumble into open space. Onto dirt and dry grass. I fall. Catch myself with my bad arm; burning pain shoots up my wrist to shoulder. *Goddammit!*

Okay. Damage control. There's numbness on my right side—bruised ribs, probably. I wipe the blood from my forehead and pick out specks of glass burrowed in my arm. Nothing's cut deep, nothing's broken—I'm still alive, even if the lights around me scream too bright.

For a moment, those faraway pumpjacks are the undead. Silently watching, bobbing in the distance. I spit a fat glob before turning around, and that's when I spot it. Across the intersection, beneath a swaying traffic light: a sedan with its hood smashed in, smoke leaking out. The driver's still inside. I can see his outline. He's unmoving, sitting upright as if he's made of stone, watching me.

My good hand finds the pistol hanging off my hip. Hello, I shout. Are you okay? Are you alright?

Still watching. All anyone ever does is watch.

Adjusting to the haze and smoke, I can make out the blue sheen of his eyes, the shape of his moustache. The blinking gleam of his bolo tie. It's him. He did it on purpose.

The car door swings open. Samuel de Hory bolts down the road, unnaturally fast, before I can fumble out my gun. I chase his shadow to a wall of orange trees, where I stop. I'm panting at the edge, but I don't go further. In there is darkness, and I am weak.

I holster my gun and radio for backup, hoping urgency can mask the trembling in my voice. I'm at West Vomack and La Sierra, I say into my radio.

Dispatch crackles back that all personnel are busy. Someone's escaped the precinct. I think they're saying Julian, but I know it can't be. The way I left him, I'd be shocked if he could even stand. And yet.

I wait at the wall of dark orange trees, citrus air swelling my lungs as I pant. The patrol car's horn blares, the only thing keeping the silence at bay. But I've channeled it into a wallpaper, blurred it out behind me, enough to hear the faintest creak of a metal hinge. The unmistakeable *eeeek* of a car door yawing open. The *back* door of Samuel's car.

Hand on my hip, I inch closer. I can make out the crate in the shadows, laid across the seat. It's thick and wooden and spotted with stains. It whispers my name and tells me, *Come and see.*

Elizabeth rushed towards the cabin at the other end of the lake, the reservoir her ancestors had built to keep a choke-hold on the region's water. She pushed through reeds and cypress trees and up the porch steps to the door scarred by what she'd always been told was an accidental fire. Now, Elizabeth wondered if it had been something else—the scars of brujería gone wrong.

No car waited in the gravel driveway. The windows were veiled in black. He was gone, she knew it, and before her wits could catch up to her, she pushed the door open and stepped inside. She'd come here to destroy the cabin—stop Samuel—like the dead had instructed her to do.

But they'd told her to do more than that. They'd told her to end his life. Only now, in the stillness, did she think how wrong it was to ask that much of her. *I'm just a kid*, Elizabeth thought. *Nineteen, can't drink, still new to college, just another body at the back of the dance troupe offering nothing that would make my art matter.* She still drove her mother's old hatchback, still slept with stuffies, was still afraid of the dark. And now she was standing in a killer's living room, armed only with a box of matches.

With a flick of her wrist she sparked a flame.

Burn it all.

Surely it would help stop Samuel if she let fire swallow up the artifacts whose outlines hung in the dark.

Drop the match and let it grow.

The gentle flame warmed her cheeks, her nose, her shivering fingertips. She only needed to open her hand.

But Elizabeth hesitated.

And then the back door opened, footsteps thudded, and the flame blew out.

Pain gnaws you into splinters. You stumble over gritty sand and cracked clay. The beat of the night's drums is pulling you left, tugging you right—keeping you shrouded from the officers not too far behind.

Eventually, you have to slow down. When you do, you're high on the bluffs, and the cops are just lights flickering far below. You're shivering, ragged, and starving for blood. Owls and bats have begun circling you beneath the blanket of stars, and the stink of coyotes—the night's servants—closes in. You spotted them earlier, running with you along the mountain. When you were wild, they howled with you. Your friends. Your pack.

The night's whispers are growing weaker. It's still telling you, *Let go. Stop holding on.* But you're back to being grounded firmly in your arms, your legs. *Give yourself to us*, says the night, *or the coyotes will take you.*

As you force the night's control out of your limbs, the coyotes' voices turn menacing all at once. They no longer seem to see you as one of their pack. They snarl.

You must stink of desperation and blood and *resistance*—something in need of discipline. An enemy in their territory.

I'm standing beside the car with a strip from my uniform held to my nose to shield me from the stink. It's a smell I should be familiar with by now, but I've never gotten used to decay. Rotting meat. Death—and yet I hear shifting from within the crate.

There are whispers too. *Remember when you hunted migrants? When you tracked them through a ghost town and a field of humming pumpjacks? You cornered a boy against one, and when he reached into his jacket for maybe-a-gun, you unloaded yours in his chest. Do you remember the tremors each shot sent up your arm?*

A flask of water. That was what he had in his jacket.

Sweat and oil and blood coated my hands by the time I finished burying him where no one would know. I tell the whispers that they *shouldn't* know any of this. There were no witnesses, only pumpjacks bobbing, bobbing.

ACT IV: POWER FORGED IN BLOOD

The whispers—no longer whispers—they sound like the voice of Samuel de Hory—shout, *Do you remember the lies you told Sonora after the doctors stitched her back up? When she showed you her brother's picture, telling you she'd gone out to the desert to find him? Did you notice the family resemblance?*

I see him in her face every time I visit.

I know, the voice laughs. *I know you, Sheriff Jackson!*

I know in the pit of my stomach that the crate in the back seat is not a crate. It's a coffin.

The coffin lid swings open.

"Who's in here?" Samuel shouted into the living room where Elizabeth had dropped her snuffed-out match.

By then she'd made it out through the front door and skirted around the house to hide beneath the back porch, where she peeked between wood planks. Samuel pushed open the back door above her, prowling. "Liz, niña? Is that you?"

You're running but everything hurts, everything burns, each breath is glass cutting up your lungs; you can't go on. You fall in the desert dirt, ready for coyote jaws to rip you to pieces, but then you spot shelter from this storm: a place between rocks in a ravine where you can hide.

A dead boy rises out of the coffin. Eyes sewn shut, mouth full of spiders. Bruised and raisiny, the corpse of Oliver Ruvalcaba clambers out of the car and walks towards me with a limp-hanging hand lifted high above his head. He's laughing. I barely make out the gleam of the knife he's holding. The voice chants. *Kill him. Kill him.*

Kill him. The world goes black and white: just me and him, and the knife.

I draw my gun as he brings the blade down. I fire, again, again, again.

One chance, Elizabeth thought, folding herself up tight beneath the porch amid crumbling dirt and matted cobwebs. *I blew it, Marisol. I'm sorry.*

Samuel paced the floorboards above her. Between the cracks she saw pus-green liquid dripping from his wounds. It slithered between the floorboards, dropping heavy to the soil at her feet. He shouted her name across the lake.

"Elizabeth! Come back! Elizabeth, it's just me!"

The same words her father had used the night of the accident, when Marisol had told them to wait and hide in their room while she talked him down.

Elizabeth shook away those thoughts. She focused on her freedom, which lay just a sprint away in the woods—towards home. Safety. *The house will protect me.*

As soon as Samuel stopped shouting, he stormed into the house, his steps a pounding heartbeat, out what must have been the front door to shout for her again.

He'll come back. He'll check under here next.

The footsteps were getting louder again—louder! Elizabeth bolted, as fast and as silent as she could. Out into fresh air, through reeds and mist, until the lake house shrank behind her and the shouts faded.

She didn't stop until she was back in Casa Coyotl and had locked its doors against the dark.

You crash into a ravine somewhere cold and far from everything. Here it's quiet, and the rocks seem warm. Your pulse eases down to a solid, rhythmic *tha-thump, tha-thump.* You tear away your jeans to find your ankle a mangled heap of stinking, rotting flesh. Canyons of exposed rawness glisten bright pink between blackened skin. The smell brings up sour bile in your mouth. Even the freshness of the air stings.

It's going to take you, Xolotl says, hanging off your hip. You'll join us soon. But that's not bad. You made it this far, fought off your nature for this long. Most don't. Take pride in that. It's okay. You can grieve for a while if you want; I'll understand.

You don't want to die.

You don't want to leave your mom all alone in the house she bought when there were three of you. You try to stand, but the pain yanks you down. You scream at Xolotl.

"I'll do anything. Please!"

You don't want to become the Teōtl your blood aches for you to be. You want to be the you that was alive and young, not the monster you are.

"Help me, *please.*"

Xolotl's eyes are voids. As you wish. His jaws snap open—teeth reaching to the moon—and in a single violent snap, before you can tell him to hold on—wait!—Xolotl bites off your leg.

ACT V
Mictlān

ONE
Pumpjacks

I HEAR THEM NODDING beyond the dark, up down, up down. Rusted gears grinding while engines purr and the dirt beneath them trembles. Up down, up down. Always.

I'm Lucas Jackson; I'm seventeen years old when I'm arrested for the third time in my life after slipping a bottle of vodka into the middle pouch of my backpack in some corner store with buzzing fluorescent lights. The glass clinks against the zipper teeth. The clerk tugs my arm when I try to stroll out. You aren't going anywhere, kid, he says. The cops are already on their way.

The officer who unlocks my cell is Officer Jesse Florez. Eyes brown, uniform navy blue. Skin as dark as mine. His breath is all coffee beans, and against those walls—white and chipped, with the smell of Simply Green creeping from the cracks—he looks like Night. He unlocks the handcuffs and my hands breathe. He calls me *Mijo* in a tone my own father never used—my father, who forbade Spanish in the house, hated when Mom would speak it to us, said it blocked him out. My father, who used to lash our thighs raw with the sting of his belt. He's dead now—good fucking riddance.

I itch my wrists and Jesse Florez tells me, Mijo. You're running out of time.

He points one strong finger across the hall to the other holding cells, where battered adults litter the benches, a glassy look in their eyes. An unlook, with matte pupils. The stink of stale urine and alcohol—I've been mouth-breathing the whole time here.

One day soon you'll be a man, Jesse says. Damn it, look at me! Listen. You can do something good, or something great, or be a blessedly mediocre man like most of us. But stay on this track you're on, and in a few months I'll see you back here with adult charges, and you won't ever cross this line of bars again. Do you understand? Lucas?

He sets his hand on my shoulder; I want to kick him in the teeth. Stomp on his guts, because that's what I'm good at. But I don't do anything, do I? I certainly don't want to cry. Men don't cry.

Do you hear that? Jesse Florez whispers. He pulls back and searches the room, staring through walls as if there are windows I cannot see. This room is stone blocks painted over in globby white, but he looks past the walls all the same. Sounds like pumpjacks, he says. Do you hear them, Lucas?

I do. They're right outside.

Jesse Florez's battered and calloused hand swallows my shoulder. He shouts again before plunging me deeper into the darkness, further away from those precinct walls. Do you hear them!?

I shut my eyes, because I know there are terrors in the deep, and I thrash for solid ground.

I'm standing in the desert.

I'm Officer Jackson, I'm twenty-six years old. I work for the Immigration and Customs Enforcement agency of the United States—the only place that will take me despite the ACL scarring on my left knee. I've spent months already tracking down families and dragging away parents with expired visas who were hiding behind their children. I've flushed them out in the desert or picked them up at the courthouse. But tonight I hunt.

ACT V: MICTLĀN

I've tracked a coyote and his party into the oil field. I've lost my partners, and my phone is dead. The field is alive with the chorus of pistons. Up, down. Up, down. I search between metal and shadows for a hand or maybe a foot darting past. There!

Their back glows white against the dark and they're curled up against one of the machines, their soft skin kissing metal—making themself small, as if they were another gear in the pumpjack's grind. I've visited this moment so many times, over and over again. Sometimes I freeze and watch that human ball shivering. Sometimes I try to speak to them, but my voice turns to syrup and clogs my throat. I try to stop the inevitable, but I can't. I do what I always do—what I actually did—and draw my gun, feel the holster's leather grip releasing, then the weight of it, the world sighted down the barrel. Only this time the replay cuts away to Sonora instead, crying for help in a windstorm's rage. The pumpjacks vanish. The desert gapes wide. I cradle her in my arms as I shout for help and sand pelts my back. Her face is bloodied, same as her brother's was before I shoveled dirt over his brows. As we wait for the help I fear won't ever come, she beams a smile and asks me, Do you hear the pumpjacks? They're still here.

Her face twists into a mask of agony and disdain. She wails, Sheriff Jackson, wake up—wake up! Or we'll have to go through this all again. Don't make us feel this again!

I don't think I know how.

You have to, she says. Terrible things wait in the next place. You have to wake up, Lucas, you have to!

The next memory screams in fast like a car crash, and I'm alone amongst wreckage, approaching the coffin. The dead boy is waiting for me in that coffin. I want to run but keep moving forwards. I reach for my gun—it's not there. I'd be brave if I had my gun.

The coffin swings open and my hands fly up to shield my face. The hands of the boy inside are doing the same. I know those hands—know the fear winding his muscles tight. Eventually, the hands sink down, and I meet the face that I hardly recognize except through an animal instinct deep inside me. His face is mine, from a long time ago. He's just a child, small and overweight, with soft cheeks and large round eyes hiding behind tight ringlets.

I'm not going to hurt you, I say, but his hands go back up.

I said I'm not going to hurt you—I'm safe.

I'm hunching at the coffin's edge now. I step forward, fill up the space. Get your hands down, I tell him. I said I'm not going to hurt you!

He cowers back into the corner of this dark room we're both in, tries to hide among X-Men toys and robots with chipping paint that he's yet to grow out of. He's saying, I'm sorry—shouldn't be here. But his hands are still up, and behind his fingers his eyes are wide with fear. Dad said I wasn't supposed to be here.

I'm not your father.

He'll find me here.

No, he won't, *I'm* here. Just put your hands down.

But he will! Javier and Rodrigo only save themselves!

I grab his hands, and he starts hollering. Tears are sliding down his cheeks. He's shouting that he's sorry, that he doesn't want me to hurt him, and he's batting me with his hands over and over to block his face while my own voice pounds his into submission—I'm not your father! I'm not going to hurt you—goddammit, shut the fuck up! Shut the fuck up! Shut the fuck up! Shut the fuck up! Shut the fuck up! Shut the fuck up!

I wake to pastel hospital walls.

I'm lying on a thin mattress with green sheets in a room only big enough for a single bed, where the TV softly murmurs a movie about some masked, knife-wielding killer. The room smells like hand sanitizer; my shoulder throbs. The man snoring into his magazine at the foot of my bed stirs when I sit up.

Fuck, you're up early, he says before exiting without another word. I'm left listening to the squeak of his boots quicken as his steps recede down the hall.

He brings back with him a man in a black suit who hands me a suit to match, all folded up with my sheriff's hat resting on top. He's blond and fair-skinned and has no wrinkles, which tells me he's one of those grown-up Ivy League kids. Never saw inner city streets until they popped up in lecture hall videos. His parents' parents had already bought his career with generational nepotism. He tells me to call him Franklin, says that he's in charge of this investigation now—and that my friend Nicholas Raymond is dead.

The next few hours pass by in a blur. There's a ceaseless revolving door of authority as I regurgitate the story over and over again to Franklin and Sharon and SWAT captains and investigators and city officials and the reporters who squeeze into my room. All the while, my head goes back to Raymond over and over—living, talking, asking how's my day—dead. His eyes are scooped out in the pictures. Franklin said it was better if I didn't see but I demanded to anyway. The pictures show a skeleton cling-wrapped in skin. Raymond's dead. Jesus fucking Christ, he's dead.

I want to shove them all out into the hallway. Every last one. I want to call Raymond—he should be awake right now, he should answer his phone. I want to call his wife or mine, to give or get some kind of stability here—I want to cry—but I don't. I'm a man. I have a job to do.

By the end of it all, Franklin has briefed me to the world I've woken in: four officers died last night. Julian Zavala killed them. He escaped custody, but all the security footage crackles and darkens once the boy stands up in his cell, and the murk doesn't dissipate until after sunrise. Samuel is missing too, and San Ojuela county has stretched its resources thin conducting a manhunt for the both of them. There are emergency broadcasts, officers outside Samuel's house, search parties scanning the desert, but the missing men are ghosts. They prioritized escape, and that's why I'm still here.

I was told backup found me alone on the roadside with the orange groves all around. My patrol car was totaled to shit and wrapped around a streetlamp's pole, but any other vehicles were gone.

Nothing there but you—and your empty gun, Franklin says once more before he leaves the room, hand resting on the silver door handle. What did you open fire on?

They've all asked, and I've tried to search my memories each time, but the thoughts are running ink on dissolving paper. All I find are piercing headlights, tires screeching, my stumble out into the desert air and the whispers that raked my ears. *Murderer.*

Don't worry about it, Franklin says, and I realize I've taken too long to answer. He asks a new question: Do you know much about rattlesnakes?

I don't understand the question. He adjusts his tie. He says, Never mind, it's not that important.

I check myself out an hour later. The doctors say I should count myself lucky I didn't suffer any major injuries. Some bruises; a couple of new stitches in my already inflamed shoulder. The worst: a puncture in my gun hand, where something sharp slid in and then out, leaving a thin and dribbling smile. I might never use my pinkie finger again, they say, but I can still shoot, which is all that matters.

The drive back is quiet. Most people in this town are either at work or school during the day, so the shops are sleepy and the streets empty. Tonight, Halloween night, they'll come alive. There'll be carving of jack-o'-lanterns and the rush to the stores for last-minute costumes and candy and snacks for parties. Main Street's already full of people setting up the stage and booths for the pumpkin

ACT V: MICTLĀN

festival, and I pass button-eyed scarecrows bound with lights and cotton cobwebs. I told Sharon the city needed a curfew tonight, but she didn't listen. Said they wanted to keep this as quiet as possible so everything would look like Business As Usual if you squinted.

The apartment's empty when I unlock the door and swing it open. There's only the morning's staleness inside. Not Diana, Diana's at work—she texted me that when I tried calling her on my way here, wanting to let her know I was okay. Her text promised we'd talk tonight. So, it's just me for now. Alone in the staleness.

That's okay, though. I've gotten through so much alone. Like when I broke my body pushing myself through the academy and neither of my brothers ever asked how I was doing. Like when I sat between scoffing peers at my graduation ceremony while our police chief stood at a podium and spoke about showing the rest of the country what good policing is through diversity and progressive reform. Rodrigo was not there. Javier was not there. Mom was, at least, and of course Gran and Diana. The three of them clapped when I stood with the rest of my class, and I soaked in the cheers after months of getting knocked down and climbing back up. I didn't think about the boy who died out in the desert; this was going to be a new life. Our sergeant gave the signal and we saluted as one, recited our vow: *On my honor, I will never betray my badge, my integrity, my character, or public trust. I will always have the courage to hold myself and others accountable for our actions. I will always uphold the constitution, my community, and the agency I serve.* The happiest day of my life.

I shower in frigid water and the droplets are beaks pecking my back. I wrap myself in a towel and the fabric is sandpaper chewing up my shoulder. Not just my shoulder—the soreness runs down my bicep, reaching for my gun hand. In the mirror I study my dark arms, legs, and face, tacked onto a pale body. My stomach hangs in loose and raisiny flaps that used to be plump and grabbable; I've long since killed that body. My shoulder burns bright red. I have to twist myself around till I see stars to get a look at the rash—ridged bundles of dead and flaky skin. I itch it, and the skin falls. Rawness peeps through underneath.

I lean my ass against the cold sink and I pluck and pluck until the mirror is spattered with blood and yellow pus and my shoulder is flayed. Eventually blood stops welling up. But before I can rebandage the wound and dress myself in black slacks and button-up, I notice that something else is leaking out instead. Something black. I dab it with a towel—the fibers are barbs scraping through me—and pull the towel back to see the stain is thick, iridescent like crude oil.

TWO
Set Phasers to Fun

THE BURSTS OF CHATTER in the women's locker room pecked at the nape of Elizabeth's neck. She stood corpse-still on cold tiles while the girl in the mirror looked back with dry eyes and a washed-out face. Exhaustion carved dark creases beneath the eyes, and harsh lighting scrubbed the skin splotchy and red. One cheek was raw and scabby where the glass had split her face—that mark would fade but never disappear. The girl in the reflection almost had Elizabeth's indigenous nose, her soft jaw. But—

That's not me.

That morning, she'd rewatched videos of old performances and tried to remember flexing her body tight into a single muscle that hinged and twisted and burst high above the earth with quick kicks—*that* girl was Elizabeth. Carving the stage with the focused precision captured on her mom's shaky-cam videos.

Watching the recordings had gutted her. She couldn't remember what that felt like, to embody the dance's hunger and pain and joy like that—to be someone so alive.

All she recognized now in her reflection were the eyes. Only there was something *different* about them. The weekend at Casa Coyotl had felt like years, and her reflection showed some fresh age;

the house had taken its price, rubbed some of its weariness into her. She poked the cheek that was supposed to be hers, rubbed the eyelids, opened her mouth and scanned teeth. What had changed?

When she was done, she'd figured it out. She looked like Dad.

She was a coward, like him. She'd failed to do what Marisol and centuries of murdered people had asked. She didn't kill Samuel de Hory, couldn't even burn down his home. Instead she choked, and her moment passed. Then she ran away, just like her dad had tried to do when his life exploded around him.

Now the dead, the chupacabras, the vampires, and the constant sweltering heat were miles away. Elizabeth was home. Back in Oceanside, where the air smelled like sunscreen and sea salt. Coyote House's brujería felt about as far away here as the old self she'd seen in those videos. It had stopped being real.

You should be dead, the mirror girl mouthed. *Not Marisol. The gift of being able to see the dead is wasted on you. If you were gone, you wouldn't have to try and fail again and again; you wouldn't have to take up so much space.*

She could still do it. End her life. She still knew how. Even had old plan Bs and Cs and Ds piled up, just in case. It would be an exercise in control: end her grief with finality, leave this place, become the void that soulless people went on to being.

But her stomach always threatened to jettison its contents at the thought of following through. Someone would find her body, and her mom would have to see it; that thought alone broke her heart. She'd decided a better solution was to get the hell away from Casa Coyotl, pretend it didn't exist—like so many other unpleasant things.

Of course, now that she was back, Jannah and Kylie and some of the others from her troupe wanted to know what it was like out there, if the stories were true, if Dark Liz had seen anything scary.

"I was worried about you," Jannah said, giving Liz's dead heart a flutter. "Was it all right? The funeral, that is? You didn't murder Mary?"

No, just abandoned her and Mom on a serial killer's hunting grounds.

Never mind that the house would try to protect them—she'd told Mary that morning to never ever wander beyond its walls alone—she'd left them all the same.

"I'm fine," Elizabeth said. "It was fine. Just long. I'm tired. I wanna get practice over with so I can go home and watch TV and die."

Kylie nudged her. "Oh, come on, I'm sure you got a story or two about the house. Did you end up seeing any of your ghosts?"

Elizabeth shook her head. "It was just a broken-down old house."

They left her alone after that, shuffling out with their water bottles, dressed in black leotards. Elizabeth lingered, the last to exit the locker room. Before she stepped out into the hallway, she swore the croak of some bodiless thing echoed from the dark.

"Go away, ghost," she sighed. "I'm not in the mood."

Desire—that dance of possession—the dance of eyes.

Elizabeth waited with her body tucked, her face behind her hands, while the stage lights burned into her bare neck, until *ksh!* the cymbal's chime yanked her up with the other dancers and jerked her into their rhythm of crackling pivots, bends to the floor, high kicks. But her own feet dragged. Exhaustion wouldn't let go. She hadn't slept at all the night before, waiting alone in the kitchen of Casa Coyotl clutching a knife, thinking Samuel was coming for her. Now her limbs ended in clumsy rubber blocks.

She searched for the thread of Marisol's rockera rhythm that used to guide her dances. She found the tails of the beats but when she'd reach out for them, they'd scurry further away into blackness. The arches of her feet strained under her weight like branches ready to snap. Her shoulders screamed. Her thighs burned and burned, but she didn't falter until her whole body had gone numb. Then she crashed against the wood and her stomach constricted to retch sour bile across the studio floor. The music cut.

Afterwards, Elizabeth cleaned herself up quickly, alone in the locker room, before escaping to the parking lot where the wind grabbed her hair and threw it back against her face. She unlocked the car Brian had let her borrow, got in, shut the door, and banged her head against the steering wheel. Only once she was done and just sitting there breathing did she start to cry. It leaked out slowly at first. Then the seam ripped and all of Elizabeth spewed out. Everything she'd tried to keep balled up and small inside of her: grief, pain. Anger at Julian, at her father, at her mother, and finally at Marisol who'd asked the impossible, setting her up to fail. All of it wrenched itself out and left her emptier than she had been on the dance floor with a pool of vomit before her. A wrung-out rag.

She was no longer sobbing, though her eyes still stung, when someone tapped softly on her window.

Jannah, cheeks flushed with sweat, hair flowing messily over her shoulder.

Shit!

Elizabeth wiped her eyes and rolled down the window. "I'm fine," she said.

"Of course you are." Jannah smiled warmly, and goose bumps pulsed from Elizabeth's shoulders to shins. "If you were crying or something, though—I wouldn't judge. I'd consider it very healthy, given the week you had."

ACT V: MICTLĀN

"Me? Never," Elizabeth said, forcing a smile. She wiped her eyes. "Gotta repress that shit, or we'll never be successful, tortured artists. Right?"

"*Successfully tortured*, more like." Jannah said. She leaned in and crossed her arms on the window frame, the smell of her a dozen hands reaching in, hugging Elizabeth tight. Pulling her closer to drink in whatever it was that Jannah wanted to tell her. In her soft, scratchy voice, Jannah said: "I know, I know—obedient daughters and Mexican mothers. So she said no to the Halloween party. But the Elizabeth I know wouldn't worry too much about that. Your mom's miles away, and you're an adult, and you have a car, and—besides, you're the one who's always telling me that asking for forgiveness is so much easier than permission."

"Jannah—"

"What I'm saying is, you're still invited to Kylie's. I'm going. And, well, it would be kinda cool if you came with me."

The way her lips came together and parted to make that word. *Me*. Elizabeth's newly cleansed body was a muscle clenching tight, heart thumping. *Do it, do it!*

"Only kinda?" she said to Jannah, her mind already made up.

Jannah smiled, all of her perfect crooked teeth shining. "Only kinda."

They passed through a side gate into the backyard of the sorority-sized house Kylie called home, where music and laughter waited. The sky had dimmed to eggplant purple, and out on the streets, clusters of kids wandered in search of candy. Jannah led the way, pulling Elizabeth by the hand. The floodlights made the gold scorpion on the back of Jannah's jacket gleam—her costume was from the movie *Drive*. Elizabeth wore a black dress with a white Peter Pan collar, the kind that would win you comparisons to Wednesday

Addams. But with it she had a wide-brimmed hat with a wreath of marigolds and chrysanthemums, and a camera bouncing against her chest. She wore her face in Día de los Muertos paint: bone-white, teal, and orange flower petals haloing her eyes. A calavera grin. La Muerte.

Elizabeth had never been to a neighborhood this ostentatious before. She'd known that capital-L Large houses existed behind community gates, but she'd never realized *how* large. There was Casa Coyotl, of course, but that was an outlier, a monstrous and dilapidated relic in an otherwise normal-looking town. These homes were not only brand-new and enormous but mass-produced, a whole army of giants looming down the block.

In the backyard, Nobuhiko Obayashi's 1977 cult classic *House* played, projected on a screen behind the pool deck. People were lounging in lawn chairs or wading in the water. The air was heavy with booze and sweat and bong smoke; string lights glittered. Most of the guests were strangers, but Elizabeth knew the faces from the dance company. "Dark Liz! Hey!" they'd chirp. Or, "Oh my God, Dark Liz, I didn't know you'd be here!" Or, "Whoa, sick costume. La Llorona, right?"

Eventually, though, with so many eyes perceiving her, sticking to her, Elizabeth fought against her broad shoulders and wide hips. She tried collapsing her edges into herself to take up as little room as possible as she shadowed Jannah. Soon other dancers would pull Jannah into their circles to talk, and Elizabeth would be discarded to the outside of the circle, desperate for something to anchor her. So she started looking for the one thing she knew would free her from her too-tight skin: some decent fucking weed.

She needed only to step around the corner behind the poolhouse to find a group of guests laughing around a bong. She hadn't touched the stuff for over a year now, not since an incident where the dead had crowded around her with pained eyes. But ghosts, she had learned, were nothing. They didn't matter. So she sucked in the hot dampness, let it burn down her throat and crackle in her chest. Exhaled long ghost tails into the dark.

Anxiety off her back, Elizabeth tried her best to blend in. She danced with Jannah to awful karaoke and held her hand tight as they darted from room to giggling room, both of them out of breath and sweaty. She bounced jokes into conversations and won a round of beer pong against film majors without ever taking a shot. Her troupe cheered for her when she landed the killing blow, chanting *Dark Liz! Dark Liz!* until those words lost all meaning.

The weed had left Elizabeth's mouth tacky. She tried to keep the high going, wedging into conversations, mirroring the humor and shooting off jokes, but only got eyebrow raises and awkward laughs that made her feel small. Smaller. Her smallness a pit, pulling the rest of her in.

She wore her smile firm, a dam walling back her anguish, and retreated from the crowd. She slipped away easily—they wouldn't notice—searched the house for wherever the hell it was she'd left her purse. Found it in Kylie's room, tucked away: a soft place where the music was muffled and voices stopped politely at the door. She was digging for her keys when Jannah slipped through the door and clicked it shut behind her.

"There you are. I turned around and you were gone. I wanted to—what are you doing?"

Caught, like a guilty child. "I was—going to my car to get my face paint. It's all smudged. Oh!" She spotted cheap Spirit Store paints left on the vanity. "There's some here, so no need!"

She began fumbling with the paint, reapplying outlines to the teal flower petals around her eyes, but her hand was too shaky, her breathing uneven. She poked herself in the eye and winced. "*Fuck!*"

Jannah took the brush from her hand, saying, "Oh, just let me do it," and told Elizabeth to lie on the bed.

Elizabeth did as she was told. Once she was comfortable between the pillows, Jannah tried to apply the face paint standing up but couldn't seem to get a good angle. (She might, Elizabeth thought much later, have been pretending it was harder than it actually was). Finally she hopped up onto the bed and straddled Elizabeth's waist. She painted with intense concentration. When she leaned forwards, her hair brushed Elizabeth's cheeks. Her steady breaths touched Elizabeth's lips as she delicately tapped on the last details.

It was just the two of them between the peach-painted walls of that liminal space, with muffled pop music rumbling the floor from below.

Alone.

Elizabeth's whole body was a guitar string wound up tight and wanting to be strummed. Wanting a strummer. Wanting to be wanted. Because her body was her vessel, and if she herself—her soulless, empty self—had no value, well, at least there was still the vessel. A vessel could be taken for a ride, or offered up in exchange for cheap affirmations—she'd done that so many times before with desperate boys. Those moments left her hollow in the end, but she'd told herself they were all she could afford.

Jannah was looking at her. Perceiving that she was there, their bodies pressed together. Her eyes focused, rings of umber, holding Elizabeth's. Breathing slowly as she dabbed the face paint. Blood rushed to Elizabeth's face and other places bristled with want want want.

But her muscles were stone, locked with *what-ifs* and second guesses until the moment passed. And Jannah leaned back. "There," she said.

Elizabeth sat up too, and for a second they were face to face, nose to nose, mouth to mouth. An inch apart.

Kiss her, you idiot!

ACT V: MICTLĀN

Elizabeth did. Hands on Jannah's cheeks, taking in the taste of her. When Jannah pulled back, she muttered, "Holy shit." But Elizabeth craved more. She wanted to be more: daring, brave, up for anything. So she pulled Jannah back in until the pillows muffled their soft sounds.

Jannah's hand found her chest. "Are you sober?" she asked.

"Yes."

"Do you want to do this?"

"Yes."

"Are you sure?"

"Yes!"

Jannah's lips were sweet and tasted like sunscreen. She pushed Elizabeth back against the bed, kissed her neck, unbuttoned her shirt, unclasped her bra. Elizabeth followed suit. She wanted it—hungered for it. She was ready—until she wasn't.

She found herself pushing Jannah away. "Wait," she said.

Jannah pulled back. She softly asked, "You alright? Did I fuck up?"

"No, you're fine! I'm good, I'm good," Elizabeth said. "I just...I changed my mind."

You're not going to cry, you're not going to cry, you're not going to cry.

Elizabeth began to bawl. She got up and started throwing her clothes back on, saying, "Shit—fuck—I'm so sorry! I didn't—I'm—*fuck*!"

"It's okay! Really!" Jannah scrambled to console her, but just then the door swung open from the bathroom that connected to the other bedroom, and out stumbled Kylie and her girlfriend Vanessa, their hair a mess, both fumbling with their matching bat wings.

Vanessa noticed Elizabeth and Jannah first and untangled herself from Kylie.

"We were just checking on things in here," Kylie said with a smile that showed she knew no one believed her.

"The fixtures are very sturdy," Vanessa added with a nod.

It seemed to take a moment for them to connect the dots as to what they'd walked in on, but then Vanessa pointed and a toothy smile bloomed across her face. "Dark Liz…and Jannah! Liz, I didn't know you swam upstream!"

Kylie shoved Vanessa aside and asked what was really going on. She pointed to the makeup streaking down Elizabeth's cheeks.

What could she tell them? That she was fine, even though she was a tearstained mess? That she'd abandoned her family? That she wasn't even sure she knew who she was anymore? Or maybe that she'd lost her soul, and would never get it back.

"I just—froze up," said Elizabeth. "So embarrassing."

"Our dark queen has fallen victim to Queer Cold Feet," Jannah said, kissing Elizabeth's cheek. "Nothing to be ashamed of. Same thing happened to me plenty of times."

But it wasn't just that, was it? Elizabeth thought. Shocking herself, she said, "No, it wasn't that."

For a second Jannah looked almost scared.

"No, Jannah, I really like you!" Elizabeth told her. "I've been into you for ages. But—but—"

"But what?"

"But you're so fucking *talented*! And confident and self-assured!" The floodgates were open now; there was nothing to hold back the word vomit. "You're fucking incredible on stage, and you're gorgeous, and just being able to hang out with you tonight I—I don't know. You're gonna go on to be incredible, and I don't know if I'll ever get unstuck out of where I am."

Elizabeth would have kept on going, spilling out her guts, but Jannah started laughing. She laughed until her face glowed red, a butterfly swarm of *ha*'s. Elizabeth wanted to shout at her.

Jannah caught her breath and said, "Dude. And here I thought *you* were the cool one."

Elizabeth was speechless.

"What?" said Jannah. "You think I'd text you as much as I do if I didn't *like* you?"

"Sounds like they've got a lot going on," said Vanessa, pulling Kylie toward the door.

Elizabeth gulped and wiped her eyes. "No, I—can we all just stay here? For a minute?"

Jannah nodded.

"Sure," said Kylie, gently.

Elizabeth found she couldn't speak, at least not right away. So the other girls did one of the kindest things anyone had ever done to or around her: they sat on the bed and shared insecurities of their own, taking turns. Vanessa had lived on her own since coming out when she was eighteen; her family didn't talk to her. Kylie's family accepted her but not to the point of financial support. She'd taken out huge loans to pay for school and was scared they'd ruin her life.

When it was Elizabeth's turn, she told them about all her scattered parts, and how she didn't know which one was really her. "I thought I'd find out back home, but...stuff happened and I ran. I left my family and I left things unfinished with a friend I abandoned a long time ago. And now I'm back here and this fucking awful, empty feeling is still burrowing inside me. And I don't know how to fix it."

Jannah patted her shoulder. "So go back."

Just like that. As if it was so simple.

Then, with her arms crossed, she added, "Go finish whatever it is you need to do there. Talk to them. Just try."

But the dead are out there. Chupacabras too. Maybe some previous version of Elizabeth had the courage it would take to face them; that Elizabeth wasn't her. It was the one who danced like she had a soul.

And yet it was this one that kissed Jannah.

Hadn't she fought a chupacabra too—and *won*?

She'd stared down ghosts, followed one through a cosmic maze that showed her the story of San Ojuela. She'd watched as Julian bent bones to his will as easily as the breeze pushed leaves. She still loved her Tía Marisol, and dark things, and tarot cards, and platform boots, and pressing her hands into the dry beans at Mexican grocery stores, and watching spaghetti westerns and B-level Godzilla movies.

Wasn't that enough? To do this one last thing?

Yeah. She decided it was.

"You're right. I gotta go back," she said. First to herself, then to them. "I gotta go *home*."

Elizabeth threw on her sweater, and after exchanging a few more encouraging words she'd hold in her chest, the girls came together for a final hug. When they pulled away, tears welled into Elizabeth's eyes again. She said goodbye to Kylie and Vanessa. She said goodbye to Jannah, who told her they'd talk later.

My friends, she thought. *Huh.*

She ignored the thought that this could be the last time she'd ever see them. She'd think about that later, on the drive back to San Ojuela on a dark and empty road, but for now, Elizabeth or Dark Liz or whoever the hell she was bade her friends farewell and stepped back out into the Halloween night.

THREE
The Fear

It takes all the daylight hours for your leg to grow back fully. Molten skin solidifies; the feeling of ants tip-tapping along the soles of your feet returns. The sky becomes swaths of soft pink and molten lava.

You sit up in the ravine you've taken refuge in to study your new appendage. The rock you've been resting against holds you a moment before it releases you. You leave a damp sweat stain behind; the pores of the rock's rough sediment are stamped into your back. You sit in a puddle of your own crunchy blood on copper sand cooked by a relentless sun. With your new leg stretched out in front of you, you wiggle your toes.

Last night, Xolotl ripped off your leg in a single, violent thrash to stop the venom and Teōtl power coursing through you. You passed out from the pain and woke to the stink of rotting meat with the sun high above you, buzzards orbiting its whiteness. Scorpions, spiders, millipedes, and all the other desert bugs had crept from under rocks and begun to burrow into your stump. They reconstructed white bone with a pulp of spit and slime: fibula sprouting first, then tibia, all the way down to the pebble-sized bones of your toes. Next, they spun a webbed nervous system and clothed it with muscle. Insulated it with yellow fat and stretched white cartilage over bone before smoothing over the top with copper skin. Now that they've finished, your leg looks just like it used to. It's got the same freckles your mom always said made the skin look like tortillas when it paled in the winter. The same scars you've always had tallying your shins.

Same snake bite with its venom blackening your veins.

"It's still there," you say, but you're not surprised. You'd only allowed yourself a sliver of hope that it wouldn't grow back with your leg. Not enough hope to hurt.

It's only a mark, Xolotl says. He stands above you, a man now—man-shaped thing—a shadow with the coyote skull atop his shoulders and a crown of feathers cutting the sky. Beady eyes glow red in each hollow socket. The feathered creature you met chained in Samuel's basement was a poor imitation of the whole Being you see before you now, no longer a rabid dog tied to Samuel's will. Seeing him, you understand what it means to say the Tēteoh are true essence.

After biting off your leg, he split it with shadow knives that seeped from his marrow and laid out the two matching halves. He whistled for bones, and they came to dance, and with the incense left at the bottom of your bag and the blood that fountained out of your leg, he began his spell. Both slabs of flesh bubbled out into fully formed limbs and sent up tendrils that merged with the shadows blooming from the skull. Xolotl, graced with two legs again, stood upright for the first time in eons. A god.

When he stretched, mountains trembled. When he yawned, deep desert canyons inched wider. He gasped and valleys rumbled. You felt this, the whole desert stretching with him.

All that mark does is tell you what's already inside you, Xolotl tells you. That's what you are; you can't change that. Only embrace it, boy. It's the fight against it that

ACT V: MICTLĀN

WILL KILL YOU. YOU'RE YOU. THERE'S NOTHING YOU CAN DO ABOUT THAT.

You want to drive him away—because he used you, lied to you. Tricked you into gathering the materials he needed to forge himself into a god again. But you can't blame him, not really. You can't even be mad at him. It wasn't anything personal, and at least he's done his best to help you in return.

You lock eyes with his. Those beads of red invade your thoughts, scan them inside and out, and when he's done, you're not sure if it's just you, or if there really is sadness in his sockets.

SAMUEL WAS USING YOU TOO, he says. AS HE DID ME. HE ONLY MEANT TO SUCK AWAY YOUR POWERS AND LEAVE YOUR BODY TO THE DIRT LIKE HE DOES WITH EVERYONE ELSE. YOU'RE NOT STUPID, BOY; SURELY YOU MUST HAVE KNOWN THIS.

"Shut up!" You bare your fangs, but the god of deformity merely tilts his skull.

IT'S HIS NATURE TO REAP. TO TAKE AND THEN MOVE ON ONCE HE'S USED A THING UP AND NOTHING'S LEFT.

"I know," you snap again, holding back the tears tapping cracks in your voice. Samuel once found you like this—broken, empty. You were so easy to groom. "I get it. You don't need to explain it anymore. He did it—you did it. But you're done with me, yeah? So why are you still here? Just. Go. Away!"

You wish you sounded strong when you said it. Not like the broken little boy you are.

With what strength you have left, you throw a rock at Xolotl, but he halts it—holds it still in space, inches from his teeth.

The rock thumps to the dirt.

As you wish, the dog-god says—god of twins, god of fire, god of lightning. And of deformity, sickness, and misfortune too, because Xolotl contains multitudes. He leaves you holding nothing as the shadows wrap around him and drag him down into the earth.

You regret telling him to go away as soon as you're alone again. Deep down, you always did know Samuel was using you. He said you were special and showered you with praise, and you listened because—god! it felt good—all you'd ever wanted was to be important to someone. Xolotl was right, and you're disgusted with yourself.

SAMUEL WAS USING YOU. The words echo in your head. But it's not just Xolotl and Samuel who use you—everyone does.

Elizabeth never has.

You don't know where that thought comes from. You try and shoo it away, but it's true. She asked for your help Saturday afternoon, but that wasn't why she hugged you. You think that, maybe, she'll forgive you.

You sit there among your rocks, shivering and bitter. Your kingdom of stone and bone and insect carcasses. You watch the sun sink behind ragged mountains and soon enough the shadows lengthen across the desert and it's dark once more. The sky's a deep blue-black when the night's hum returns to lull you to sleep.

You wake to a whisper behind your ear.

Get up, it says. *They're almost here.*

On your feet again. Fists raised. You scan the dark with your coyote sight. Has it been minutes or hours since you shut your eyes? You don't know, but hunger groans inside you, and by the shifts in the wind you know the night has changed.

It no longer wants to cradle you. It's bearing down heavy; the night is angry with you.

Your memory of Oliver is watching you again, this time perched high up on a boulder, looking as gaunt as you must be. "Well, hurry up, you idiot," he says. The smile across his throat jeweled red. "You just gonna stand there, or you gonna haul some ass? They're coming."

ACT V: MICTLĀN

The dead boy points toward the jagged mountains and you feel what he meant by They. Their heavy breathing, their claws pounding on desert dirt—the night's agents. Coyotes. Solitary, reclusive animals collected into an unnatural pack possessed with the desert's hot rage; hungry to rip up your body and set your true self free for the night to take.

You reach up to take Oliver's outstretched hand, then stop. Because he's not really here. Just make believe. And your hand would just pass through his. Instead, you suck in stars and moonlight and leap leopard-style from boulder to boulder until you're standing on the ravine's edge looking in.

Oliver crooks his gaze at you; he has to look up now instead of down. He's a miserable shape still crouched in the same spot he woke you from.

"Come with me," you tell him—even if it's not him. Because you wish you'd left with the real him on his journey. He shrugs. You tell him, "I'm sorry. If there was anything I could do to fix it I would, but there isn't, so I can't."

He shakes his head, and in his gentle voice he says, "Even if you could, you can't ever make up for everything else you've done. It's like Xolotl told you, the best you can do is give yourself up to the gods."

And lose myself.

There's nothing left to say to him. *Thump-thump-thump-thump* goes the night. The coyotes growl louder; there's a smell of rot on the air.

You back away slowly at first, then turn to run. You leave Oliver and head back into the world—toward home. Reduced to your base instincts, you think only of your mamá. She'll protect you. Just as she always has. You only need to make it across the miles in your haggard, dragging body, without getting caught by Samuel or those roaches of cops who must be infesting the streets by now, all wanting you dead.

You search the black warehouses on the edge of town, looking for a place to hide from the coyotes. You're just coming up with an idea when your phone begins buzzing in your back pocket. Hoping it's Mom, you answer, but it's not, it's—Elizabeth?

She shouts through the phone. "Julian, we need to talk." Wind whips behind her voice. She's driving—speeding. "Look, I'm sorry about the other night. I'm sorry about your serape, and for the shit I caused, and I'm sorry for how I treated you when we were young."

You want her words to bounce off you, to mean nothing, because she *should* be nothing to you. But she isn't. She says she needs you, and you're terrified. She is your raft in the storm, what can save you from the night that wants to tear you apart.

You reach out for that salvation.

Your side is cramping like there's knives digging in. Through desperate, mangled breaths you tell Elizabeth she's gotta help you. That the coyotes are coming. That she has to *hurry.*

She doesn't question it. "I'm ten minutes out from San Ojuela. Where are you?"

You're between death and dirt, so you tell her instead where you're going to be. She says she's on her way and tells you to hold on, stay on the line, but you stumble—drop your phone and don't stop to pick it up. Coyote howls rip across the sky, so close you swear you can feel the hot breath of the pack. You just keep going, hoping Elizabeth finds where you told her to go.

You change course, head down now-vacant streets to the last safe place you have, the place you've always gone to when there's nowhere else: the ruins of the San Ojuela Mall.

The mall sits across an empty parking lot, fenced off from the rest of the town, with caution signs and sun-faded *No Trespassing* warnings zip-tied to the rusted chain-links. You used to come here a lot when you needed space and loud music and walls to bounce back your screams, a place where you knew no one else dared venture except for those too unfortunate to have another home. You try climbing the fence, but your feet are cinder blocks pulling back to earth. You can't get up in time. The coyotes are rushing in. You let go and keep running, scanning for Elizabeth or an open gash in the fence.

The coyotes howl. Snap at you from the dark. You hear their hungry breathing.

Even with the wind pushing you, you're not fast enough. You're stumbling, and the desert night is cold. Each breath of air you suck in is ice stabbing your ribs. The wind chill bites your ears, but you keep running, running. Until the moment when, dried out and wrist-thin, you collapse against a lonely tree, sides heaving.

She's not here. You came as fast as you could, but she's gone. It's just you and the coyotes. They emerge two by two from the dark, scraggly but massive enough to swallow a human head whole, their fur thick and black as if they're formed from the night itself.

You can't ever make up for everything else you've done, Oliver's voice taunts in your head. As if your grief and hurt are just pocket change, and you'll die here regardless.

You get up. There's nothing left for you to do but raise your fists to the pack of them, because if there's anything left of you, it's the boy this town taught how to fight. And you will not go down easy.

The coyotes are tensing to pounce when a screech rips through the night. There's a *pop*—hissing air—headlight beams that split the pack as a hatchback roars in. The coyotes scatter, but they're not fast enough. The car's grille bites into the largest one and the wheels chew up its hind legs. It claws at the hood until the car bashes it against the fence and both are stilled. Metal crumpled, windshield spiderwebbed, the coyote's blood soaking into cracks and gears. And the night reaches down to take the last of its child's breath.

The door flies open and out drops a black wraith with a flare in her hand. She thrusts its crimson glow high above her head. Her hat blocks out the stars; her face is smudged with blood and calavera paint. It really is her. Elizabeth rushes towards you.

She's shouting swears for every stride it takes to reach you. She tries to hoist you up but doesn't have the strength on her own, and your new leg is burning. It only takes a few quick, heart-pounding seconds for the shadows to arrest their flight and stalk closer again.

Elizabeth waves her flare at them, but they no longer flinch from the light. You can smell the fear on her skin, feel her trembling hands.

"They're not supposed to get that big—Julian, what the fuck are those!?" she shouts.

One coyote leaps onto the roof of the car and the metal buckles under the weight—Elizabeth shouts. Her eyes are terrified moons in sea of black eye paint.

"Julian, do something! Now would be a good fuckin' time for some brujería!"

"I can't," you tell her. "I got nothing." And they'll chew her up same as you.

Elizabeth mutters something you can't hear.

"What?"

"The magic. It's sentimental power, right? It comes from blood? That's what fuels the brujería?"

You nod.

Under her breath she says, "Fuck me, I hope this works."

The coyotes howl.

Elizabeth bites into the faded scars that crisscross her wrist and pulls away after her teeth split the skin. "Drink it."

"What?"

"That's all the times I hated myself to the point of breaking. This is the hand my dad held when I was scared of the dark at night. This is the hand I used to clean up spilt beer, and the one I've used to dry my eyes. It's the hand I lead with in dance, the finger gun I used to use when we played cops and robbers. I was the villain and you wanted to be the hero, remember? This is the hand I use to brush Mary's hair. The one my tía held when I needed it the most. So if grief isn't enough…how about love?"

You watch her blood run. A coyote growls and snaps nearby. She drops the flare. The light rolls away.

"Shit! Julian, just take it!"

You shut your eyes and grab her wrist. You plunge your fangs in.

Warm iron fills your mouth and pulses through you. You hold out your hand to the coyotes and flex. They yelp and squeal and by the time you open your eyes again, they're nothing but a stain glistening red beneath the moonlight.

FOUR
Wanted

GUTS LAY SPLATTERED across the dirt and drenched Elizabeth's dress. Steam and stink rose off what was left of the coyotes.

Elizabeth had watched Julian do it, strong with her blood humming through him. She'd seen the shadows lash out from his fingertips, plunge into the coyotes, and rip until they were pulp. The animals, if they were animals, had howled and yelped as it happened, but he didn't stop. Now he—Julian, or the monster he truly was—swayed drunkenly in the night's chill. His eyes burned red. Elizabeth was horrified.

When he reached to help her up off the ground, she shrank back. She was pressing her sweater down to stop the bleeding on her wrist. It stung. She could feel the exact place where his needle teeth had punctured her. The intimate sensation of her blood rushing out; feeding him. She wanted to scream—like the dying coyotes—to run away somewhere and hide and wait for all this horror to end. She'd escaped. Why hadn't she stayed gone?

It took her a moment to realize Julian was speaking to her. She eased back up onto her feet. "What?"

"I said we have to go," Julian said. He was looking at the gore as if *he* couldn't fathom that he'd done it either. "This is a goddamn grindhouse set. We can't be here when the cops find it. And the coyotes—more will come."

"Where is there to go?" Elizabeth asked with a hint of hysteria.

Julian rolled back the fence where Elizabeth's car had torn it open and held the gap wide enough for them to scrunch through. "My place," he said. "Eventually. There's a shortcut I know."

He offered her his hand, but Elizabeth refused to take it. She was frightened of his violence, how easily he'd just pulled bodies apart. This new Julian was sullen and withdrawn, and there'd been so much bitterness in him the last time they spoke—when he'd said he wanted nothing to do with her.

He might still despise me.

She'd be easier to kill than a coyote pack.

She kept her mouth shut, afraid anything she might say would either chase him off or provoke him, and in that silence he crawled under the fence. Elizabeth lingered for a moment amid the guts and darkness outside. Then she went in after him.

They ran across the sea of asphalt up to a darkened entrance of the San Ojuela Mall, which had shut down years ago.

"You don't think there's a way around?" Elizabeth asked, peeking through the windows. "I'm going to assume it's not up to code in there anymore."

Julian didn't seem to hear that. He began removing select planks of wood from one of the windows until a person-sized opening formed. "Haven't you ever broken and entered?" he asked.

Plenty of times, but this wasn't those. Those were times of mischief at Sunday School or in football fields after dark. Those were games. Here, there was nothing but blackness in a gutted window frame.

Here, she was alone with Julian—the creature he was.

When she said nothing, Julian forced a small grin. "Doesn't matter. Now you gotta." He slid into the window's mouth. Popped back up on the other side. Called out into the dark, "Anyone home?"

The building spat his words back: *HOME—home—home.* Even from outside, Elizabeth could see eyes blinking open in the shadows. They came forward slowly, creeping out of the dark. Wrinkled and sun-dried faces. Elizabeth stepped back; Julian stepped in deeper. One of the specters had an old woman's face with leathery skin and thick shoulders, and in her hands she held a lantern that she switched on to chase off the dark.

"You brought a girl?" she said to Julian with a smile.

"Someone I used to be close with." He didn't mean it in any particular way; his tone was flat, but it stung.

Elizabeth surveyed the encampment in the lantern light. Tents and shopping carts lined the walls. Damp squares of cardboard tiled the floor, and the stink of stale urine hung in the air. For the moment she'd lost sight of Julian. The old woman told her to come inside, and this time she didn't hesitate. She climbed through the window.

A young guy lounging on a nearby bench, who must have been older than Elizabeth by only a year or two, complimented her face paint when she landed inside. She hoped that he and everyone else would assume the blood was just part of the costume, not the actual guts of half a dozen monstrous coyotes. Hoped the paint hid the redness of her blushing cheeks.

She located Julian standing nearby. An older man was inspecting his face. "You look like hell," the man concluded. He offered them food and water, but Julian refused.

"I'm sorry," he said. "We can't stay. We just need a safe place to pass through."

The man rolled his eyes. "Pigs have been crawling everywhere today. Go ahead, but be safe. If you see any trouble, give us a yell."

Julian thanked him, and Elizabeth waved goodbye.

"The two older ones are Stephanie and Adam," Julian said. "Stephanie served in the military. Adam has a master's degree in biology."

The two of them journeyed away from the lantern's gentle glow towards the belly of the mall, Julian leading, Elizabeth following a safe distance behind. He didn't seem to mind the wood splinters and glass shards crunching beneath his bare feet—another reminder of his un-humanness. When they reached the interior entrance of the department store and the darkness of the concourse yawned before them, her feet rooted to the ground. Fear gripped her, constricted her lungs. She had long been afraid of the dark and now the deepest matte blackness she'd ever known awaited her. At her side was a boy who reeked of death.

"It's safe," he said with an outstretched hand. "You can trust me."

He worked for Samuel, puppeteered the dead like Samuel. Slaughtered animals. And yet he'd saved her life.

"Here," he said. "Watch this." He took a deep breath and raised his other hand. When he released the exhale, a jade flame gasped alive in his palm, more beautiful and wilder than anything Elizabeth had ever seen.

The heat of the dancing flames kissed her cheeks as the darkness retreated. It wasn't just destruction; it was warmth and light.

To hell with fear, she thought. She took Julian's hand, the one that wasn't on fire.

Together they followed the corridor past vacant shopfronts and graffiti murals that splashed across the walls like tattoo sleeves, telling whole histories of those who'd come and gone. Elizabeth caught portraits signed with Twitter handles; bubbled emblems, flowers, and boxy robots; words of love or hate or affirmation, written in neons or pastels, with dripping lines and delicately painted lens flares. Full paragraphs filled spaces between windows—messages that Elizabeth imagined only sender and recipient could decipher. Some were signed *Zavala*. Julian's surname.

She stopped at the food court, where moonlight shone through the honeycombed ceiling, casting light along chipped marble ledges and overgrown palm trees. She remembered sitting with Mary and Marisol and Dad between these trees when they came to escape the summer heat a long time ago.

Julian tugged her hand; they had to keep moving. She tucked away the memory and they emerged beyond the food court into the cool night air, where they followed a dirt path into a neighborhood with big hedges that could hide them from passing cop cars. Julian led her toward the undeveloped side of the neighborhood, where construction vehicles waited like sleeping beasts, and from there to a flood-drain tunnel.

Inside, the air was cool and damp, and their footfalls echoed. Elizabeth's heartbeat raced until the tunnel spat them out in a creek she recognized. At the top of its banks, Julian undid the latch of his own backyard fence and showed her the place to climb through his bedroom window.

Vinyl monsters still occupied the bookshelf—the same tokusatsu toys he used to collect when they were kids. The same records he used to play for her checkered the walls, which were still that same off-white. His drawings of spacemen and aliens on large strips of construction paper, inked in marker with an artist's precision, were still tacked around his desk. Years had passed, and the only thing added was the dust.

She turned to Julian, who was looking into a dirty shoebox on his desk. Was she right that her old friend was still there, somewhere deep inside? People didn't *really* change, did they? At least

ACT V: MICTLĀN

not completely. They just grew, adding layer on top of layer—a law of human superposition.

When Julian noticed her staring, he asked her, "What?"

She gestured to the box.

He told her that it was nothing, smirked it off. "What now?"

What a question that was. Elizabeth had spent the entire drive from Oceanside brainstorming ways to kill Samuel de Hory. But she couldn't do that—could she? Certainly *couldn't* ask that of Julian.

As always, she'd arrived ill-equipped and without a plan, guided only by the knot in her guts that tugged her back here. And here she was, with Julian standing before her—her beautiful friend, corpse-thin and brittle but his collar bones sharp, face delicate. He smelled like decay, but warm sand too. And nopales and desert flowers. His irises hinted at black, even as the whites around them approached red.

Elizabeth stepped closer to him, and he stepped forwards too. Fangs peeked through the space between his lips. His fists were clenched—artist hands, hands that butchered coyotes—and his eyes looked starved and hungry. He could hurt her, yes, but he'd led her through the dark to get here. Only scared and cornered animals lashed out.

Relax, Elizabeth told herself. Tried to. Had to. *You can trust Julian.*

Unlike with Jannah, she knew exactly what it was she wanted here. Someone not tied to family or romance: a friend, who could meet her in the soft spaces between social performances, who knew who Elizabeth was even when she didn't. The friend she used to confide in, watch movies with—share tamales with, the delicious ones his mom used to make. Someone who could see her.

She hugged him. Held him tight in her arms even as she felt the low growl rumble in his chest. Because when she peeked, she saw the glint of his fangs sliding away, and his eyes fading from black and red to the brown and white she'd always known.

"So Samuel's decaying?"

It was past midnight now. Elizabeth was pacing across Julian's room, trying to absorb what he'd told her. Samuel was a kind of vampire. A thing that fed off the tōnalli of house and people alike. A dead hand powered his brujería—the same hand Mary had seen in the woods.

"He's been needing more victims," Julian said from the foot of his bed. "And more frequently. He said one used to last him years, but now it's weeks. It won't be long until he has to kill another."

Elizabeth suggested a tip-off to the police, but Julian didn't want anything to do with police. "Okay, well...but he's hurt," she said. "The other night, when I saw him, his head looked all wrong. What if you use your powers to make an army of skeletons or a giant fuck-off shadow monster or something to fight him? Instead of police?"

Julian had his arms crossed. He was looking elsewhere, as if he wasn't in the room at all and her words had to find him, lead him back. "No," he said finally. "I told you, that's not how any of this works. I don't have full control. I don't know *how* I did what I did earlier, only that I can."

Elizabeth was at a loss.

"Why'd you even come back here?" Julian demanded. "I already told you San Ojuela isn't worth it. Sell your aunt's house and forget all about this shitty town. Nothing good happens here. You can leave, and I'll do what I have to do."

"And what's that?" she asked—a bit too sharp, so that he jolted, his eyes now fixed on her.

He laughed darkly.

"You look like a ghoul when you laugh that way," said Elizabeth. "Anyway, I'm not leaving. I can't. I promised Marisol."

Julian squinted. Then his eyes widened, as if he had just remembered their conversation on the lakeside two nights ago. "You saw her, didn't you?"

Elizabeth nodded. "I lost my soul to her house years ago, and I'm still not sure why. But I know that I can see ghosts because of it, and they can speak to me, tell their stories. I saw her—and a lot of others with her. They asked for the killing to stop. So I'm at least gonna try."

"Why you?"

"Fuck if I know. It's not like I can get my soul back." Liz sighed. "But if there is a way I can, you know, *rectify* losing it, then I *want* to do it. That way, everything that's happened isn't just broken. It's useful. My suffering can mean something."

"*Your* suffering?" Julian bit. "*I* was here, *I* stayed and let the house swallow me, not you. So after you do whatever it is you mean to do, you'll get to leave—and I'll still be here. Stuck with the mess."

"But is that what you want?" Elizabeth ignored what he'd said about her leaving a mess. It wasn't a mess she was going to make, it was a mess that was already here, had been for a long time. But she who could see ghosts and the Boy who could make bones dance—together, she believed they could fix it. "I mean, would you leave if you could? You don't *want* to stay here, right? Do you want your *mom* to?"

Julian turned away. Scanned the records on the walls—his father's.

"I'll help you guys," Elizabeth said. "Afterward. I won't just leave again. I'll do whatever I can, whatever my family can. Casa Coyotl and its resources were left to me." When he turned back to her, Elizabeth touched his hand. "Julian, I *promise*."

He wasn't looking at the records; his eyes seemed fixed on something in the corner of the room. Nothing was there but the walls. Whatever he saw, it wasn't something Elizabeth's sight could show her.

"You said you see ghosts," Julian said. "Do you see anything there?"

Elizabeth shook her head. "No, I see no one here but us."

"Right. It's nothing. Just someone stuck in my own head." He shrugged, then inhaled. "Alright, let's hear it. How are you going to do this?"

"I have to burn it down," Elizabeth said, a new energy taking hold of her. "All of Samuel's junk and that whole fucking cabin for what he did. It needs to be ash."

"Yeah. What *he* did." Julian got up and went back to the box on his desk. He looked inside. "The cabin isn't the only place where he feeds, though, you know. It's the whole hacienda," he said. "You'd have to get rid of all of it."

"No," she said. "Never that. The cabin will have to be enough."

Julian was quiet. Finally he said, "Samuel's looking for me. I could keep him busy. That would give you enough time to get the gasoline we keep for the lawnmowers in the utilities shed near the stables. Soak the place, then light it up."

Elizabeth didn't speak, only stared as the weight of the plan set in.

"Then, if I don't come back," Julian said, "whatever you do, don't wait for me. You run. You get your mom and Mary and my mom and you go far away and don't ever come back. Got it?"

She shook her head. "But you will come back. Right?"

He was looking past her again, outside to nothing or everything. Then he remembered to smile. "Yeah."

Together they drew out the details of their plan of attack on a yellow legal pad. When they finished, Julian ripped a corner of the

ACT V: MICTLĀN

page away and began a note addressed to his mother. "Just something I have to do, you know? In case she worries. She worries so much."

With the note written, they were ready. But when Julian set it down on the coffee table in the living room, and Elizabeth opened her mouth to speak, he shushed her.

"What?" she whispered.

The journey to Julian's house had been quick and quiet through vacant streets. Only now did headlights slither through the curtains.

Julian said, "There's people outside."

Elizabeth could hear it now, the sound of a car grumbling to a stop, of footsteps hurrying around the house. The lights stopped moving. They were fixed on the curtains now, glowing through them in flickering red-blue, red-blue.

Then a metallic voice bellowed from the yard: "Julian Zavala. This is the police. Come out with your hands above your head."

The note fluttered to the carpet. What color was left on Julian's face vanished. "Shit," he muttered. "Shit—shit!"

He backed away from the windows, toward where the walls would shield them. Through the door, Elizabeth saw figures clustered behind the lights, the outlines of heavy guns in their hands.

"We know you're in there," the officer with the megaphone shouted. "We have a warrant for your arrest for the murder of Oliver Ruvalcaba."

"Julian, what the fuck is going on?" Elizabeth hissed. "Julian?!"

"Get down," Julian snapped. "It's going to be okay—it's got to be okay. Go hide until they're gone. Then we'll go back through the creek."

Elizabeth backed into the kitchen—bumped against the pantry door and almost slipped in something dark and sticky on the linoleum. The door creaked. She could squeeze inside, wait for Julian's signal. But even in the dim light she could trace the dried streaks running to it from the counter. As if something had been dragged. And whatever it was waited just beyond that door.

Elizabeth reached for the handle. Opened it. A hand flopped out first, pale and gaunt, then a twisted arm, a scruff of hair.

Then Elizabeth's animal screams brought the rest of the world crashing through the door.

FIVE
Penny Board Rider

THE ANOMALIES that plagued Mary's Halloween had begun early in the morning, when she found her sister pacing the inner courtyard of Coyote House, barefoot on the cold tiles, rehearsing ballet techniques. The sun had only just begun evaporating the fresh dew.

"Couldn't sleep," Liz said when Mary asked why she was up so early—and Mary believed it. All night, each time Mary had shut her eyes, the rotting hand would curl out from the dark, grab her again, and pull her someplace low and damp where light couldn't reach. A basement, maybe? A hole, six feet deep? She guessed Liz's night had been the same.

Mary noticed the packed suitcase by the door at the opposite end of the courtyard. Their stepfather had driven out to attend the funeral, but his primary function was to drive Liz back home for classes and rehearsals. In other words, Liz had an excuse to leave San Ojuela today; Mary did not.

"When are you coming back?" Mary asked.

"I'm not," Liz said casually in the middle of a stretch.

"Wait, what the hell are you talking about? You're just going to leave me here all week trapped with the hand—and Samuel—by *myself*?"

Liz came over to grab Mary's shoulders and pull her in until the world was just her eyes. "You could come with me today. Mom will be fine here on her own—the house will keep her safe. You don't have to be here."

"But—" *Come with me.* It was what she'd wanted her sister to say. To keep them together. But then that was it, there would be no coming back. No fixing what was broken. That was why they'd come, wasn't it? To make a list, then fix the broken things.

Mary shook her head, waiting for the punchline of whatever joke Liz was trying to tell. When none came, the only words she could find to say were, "Are you serious?"

"Stay then. With Mom if that's what you want. But if you stay, *do not leave this house.* Got it?"

Mary still didn't answer; Liz told her to think about it. After that, she cooked eggs con chorizos for both of them and placed warm tortillas in the folds of a cloth. They ate without a word, as if this cursed and haunted house were the most mundane place in the world.

When the time came for Brian to drive Liz home, Mary was still stuck, unsure of what to do. Mostly she felt bad about abandoning her mom, so in the end she chose not to choose. Her sister clicked the door shut behind her while Mary watched from the landing.

The second Halloween anomaly was the cops, who came knocking at the door a few hours later. Mom and Tía Araceli were in the kitchen, so it fell to Mary to end the barrage of knuckles on wood.

"I heard you the first time," she said as she opened a bar of space the officers could speak through.

The officers, noticing the hesitation in her eyes, stepped back and flashed smiles. The officer up front was dark-skinned, Latino by the look of it. Barrel-chested, and at least double her height,

ACT V: MICTLĀN

with a cowboy hat that shielded his eyes and hers from the sun. His left arm was tucked into a sling across his chest, and his hand was wrapped in stained gauze. The second cop was ghost-white except for his cheeks, which were pink from the California sun.

"Ain't ya supposed to be gunnin' down Texas Red with that big iron on your hip?" Mary stood her ground, looking up at them.

"I'm Sheriff Jackson. There's been a serious incident. Is there an adult home I could speak to?" He peeked into the foyer. Mary raised her voice to pull his gaze back.

"Hey! I don't care who you are, I know my rights. This is our house, and you ain't coming in until I get a warrant in my hands."

The sheriff chuckled. "I beg your pardon. But this is serious."

"Police violence *is* a serious issue, indeed," she added. "It's a societal one! I'm simply making sure you respect our unalienable rights to—"

The officer behind him stepped up. "Please go and get an adult right now. There's been a crime—"

"Really? Who'd ya shoot?"

"*Mary Katharine Remolina!*"

Her mother's shout yanked her off whatever pedestal she thought she stood on and banished her from the first floor of the house. But Mary went straight to the terrace on the second floor where the laundry units sat in the shade beneath a bleached pink awning and pressed herself flat against the sun-baked floor. Listened carefully for stray words from the conversation happening in the living room below her. She caught her mother's apologies, repeated over and over, and she heard one of the officers say he wanted to search the lake cabin. She caught the word *murder*, murmured in the sheriff's deep tone. Then Julian's name, and Samuel de Whatever. *Missing* came next, then *investigation*, and soon enough Mary began fitting them into shapes. Had Liz called them about Marisol? No, they would have mentioned *poison*. The boy in the poncho was involved, but how? Someone was dead. Mary was sure it would be Samuel who'd killed them.

But if you stay, don't leave this house.

Shivers crawled up her spine.

She wiped off the beads of sweat sliding down her forehead and went back to her room, where she waited for the officers' heavy footsteps to tromp out of the house.

"Don't worry, Ma'am," she heard the sheriff say. "We're leaving a couple of patrol units to monitor the grounds. Your family will be safe."

Later, while she was channel flipping in search of anything decently spooky to watch, the news flashed helicopter footage of the San Ojuela police precinct. The caption beneath read "Three Dead in Jailbreak." Mary changed the channel, unwilling to find out more.

The third and final anomaly came after dinner, once Mary's mother, Tía Araceli, and the friends who'd stayed overnight had gone out to the courtyard for wine. Mary was left to watch the twins, Will and Blake, who were Tía Araceli's kids and Mary's semiannual cousins, seen only on Christmas and the Fourth of July. They were only two years younger than she was, so of course she was left to babysit them. She was allowing them to watch whatever horror movies they could find on TV.

"I think *Halloween* would be fun to watch next," Will said as credits to *The Blob* scrolled up the screen behind him. He had a mouth full of chocolate. The last of the bar Mary had given to muzzle him was now stains on his fingertips. Disgusting.

Blake groaned. "But *Halloween* is *also* old. It's booooorringggg."

"No, idiot, I'm talking about the new one," Will said.

"Which *one*?"

They were both dressed in DIY costumes, Will a toilet-paper mummy and Blake a glow-in-the-dark fanged vampire. Mary had thrown a costume together too in a desperate attempt at normalcy, an all-black ninja suit with a mask and two plastic katanas to pull it together. But the sword sheaths had proved too bulky and the mask too hot, and the twins had beaten the swords to the point where both of them drooped pathetically like SeaWorld orca fins, so Mary had ditched the costume. All that was left was the black shirt and pants she wore now, snuggled up on the couch with Angel Eyes, about whom the twins had agreed not to snitch to her mother.

"Is the new movie scary?" Blake asked.

"It's a *Halloween* movie," Mary said. "Big ol' masked guys gonna stab a bunch of teens, and that will only make you two want to watch it more, and once you do you won't be able to sleep, which isn't an issue for me since I'll be in my room and you're in the guest room. So go ahead."

The twins were deciding between *Halloween* or *Texas Chainsaw* when the anomaly struck. Mary's phone began to buzz.

"If I have to listen to *The Blob*'s theme song one more time, I'm going to shoot myself," she said into the phone, out in the hallway.

"Hey to you too," Liz replied, but for naught—there it was again, the theme song scraping Mary's skull with its funky trumpet.

Liz said she was about twenty minutes out from San Ojuela and not to tell Mom she was coming.

Mary said, "Me? Snitch? Never."

"Good. Now, I need to ask you something. It's important. Have you seen Samuel or Julian today?"

"The cops came here!" Mary said. "They were looking for both of them." She explained that from the way it sounded, neither was home and both had gone missing the night before.

Liz swore under her breath and explained that she needed to find Julian. That he was the key to all of it.

His name was ice down Mary's spine. "Are you sure we need *him*?"

"He's not that bad, Mary. He's been the one stuck here with all this shit while we were living our lives. He'll know how to help."

"Well, do you have his number?" Mary asked. "Did you try calling him?"

"Yes, actually, twice, but he's not picking up."

"Well, keep on calling him, then—try his house. I just need a minute to give everyone the slip and then I can meet you. After you pick me up, we can—"

"No." Liz's voice shot through the phone. "Mary, I was serious when I told you to stay put."

"But I can help you, I—"

"I said *no*, Mary!" It was a tone Mary had only ever heard from their mother, protective and scared. Ready to fight tooth and nail. "This isn't a fucking game, okay? I'm doing this on my own, and I need you to sit it out. Literally, don't do anything Mary-like at all. Whatever you think you should do, don't. Stay there and keep everyone there safe, do you understand?"

"But why?" she shouted alone in the hallway, like the child she was still.

"Because you're not equipped for this. Julian can help and I have my sight—you don't. I'm sorry, Mary."

Silence.

"Mary, can I trust you to stay?"

Mary gave her word. But before Liz hung up, she asked one last thing: "Why are you the only one who can see ghosts? Why not me?"

They'd both survived life with their father. Mary couldn't remember most of it, true, but that only solidified that it must have

ACT V: MICTLĀN

been bad. If Julian was a key, what was Mary's place in all this? Or was she an afterthought again?

Liz sighed. "I don't know. I wish I had an answer for you. I love you." The phone clicked silent. Mary stood in the hallway, waiting.

Peeking back into the living room, Mary saw that the twins had chosen *The Exorcist* and foresaw her future of talking them out from behind the couch, gently explaining the magic of practical effects.

Nah, screw this.

Liz was a stubborn ass and would sooner dig herself deep in a hole than ask for Mary's help. Even if she sure as hell needed it. Mary tied on her shoes, slipped on a green flannel shirt that was two sizes too big, got her skateboard from her room upstairs, and bided her time. Finally her phone pinged on a location Liz had stopped at. According to the app she wasn't that far away, just a thirty-minute skate ride, if Mary hurried. She'd help, whether Liz liked it or not. Mary threw on her backpack. That left one final challenge: escape.

"Will. Blake," she called, sauntering back into the living room. Both of them perked up. "I'm your favorite prima, right?"

Blake spoke first. "Well, you're our only cousin close to our age."

Mary shrugged that off. "Unimportant." She pointed to Will.

"Yeah, you're fun."

"Great." She sat between them on the couch. "Listen, sweeties, bros. I wanna go get us some better snacks from down the street, but my darned mother thinks I can't leave you two alone. She said I have to *babysit* you guys."

They groaned, both complaining about how they didn't need to be babysat and were perfectly capable of watching themselves.

"I know! I know!" Mary said to them. "It's totally unfair, and uncool, so I think I got an idea where we can both win. If you guys cover for me, I can go and bring us back some actual candy—instead of this health shit your mom brought—no offense, by the way—and we'll eat like kings. And then we'll surprise our moms with a big ol' 'See, we told you we could watch ourselves, we didn't die at all!' How's that sound? We got a deal?"

Unanimously they laughed. "Deal!"

Excellent.

Soon after, Will went to the adults in the courtyard to ask for help readjusting his mummy wrappings. As they attended to the poor little child, Mary slipped out the study window and dropped into a bed of rose bushes. Thorns pricked her legs, but she waited there, hunching down as the patrol officers passed on their circuit. She noted how pathetically similar this was to all her stealth video games—as soon as the officers' chatter faded, she darted to the fence, scrambled over the bricks, crashed into a sprint on the other side, and didn't slow until the house was far behind and she was gulping in the night air. *Free at last.*

She tucked her hair into her beanie and, once on the main road, hopped on her penny board and took off into the night.

Up and down dim-lit streets, Mary searched. She checked downtown, all the main streets; found nothing and kept going. Followed the app to the last place her sister's icon had rested, the ruin of a mall at the west edge of town. There, crashed into a chain-link fence, she found Liz's hatchback. And horror: so much red. So many bones. So many animal jaws, splattered across a slaughtering ground.

What the fuck—what the actual living fuck, Liz?!

The stench of it was heavy and metallic. It threatened to pull her dinner back up out of her stomach. She needed all her will to hold herself together as she circled the mall, yelling for her sister. Her throat was torn to all hell by the time a woman in rags climbed out of an abandoned department store and shook Mary's senses back into her by the shoulders.

"Hey—hey! It's alright—they're fine! Your friends passed through not too long ago."

Mary explained that Liz was her sister, and the woman pointed in the direction Liz and Julian had gone, giving directions on the fastest route across town. Soon enough, Mary was on the move again, wind flapping her shirt. She watched her own icon blipping closer to where Liz's had finally updated, right at the edge of town. Perfect.

She skated through the empty, under-construction neighborhood the woman had told her she'd reach first. Cut across a golf course where the grass was dewy and green—avoided the sprinklers hissing all around. Crouched on her board again, she flew downhill past gated houses and community pools. Took a right and went down a few blocks to where dark houses sagged behind dead lawns, and where sun had taken so many bites out of the pavement that Mary had to pick up her board and run as fast as she could in her hand-me-down sneakers. Eventually she reached the overpass the woman had told her she'd find—the one that meant she was close. And she was close, she could see it in the pixel art. Liz was somewhere right over—there, where emergency lights were blinking.

She picked up her board and slid down the slope into the creek, praying to god that Liz was okay. Her shoes squelched in mud and the chill bit her toes. She just needed to follow the creek up a little farther, to where the houses were. She'd get there soon, she just needed to catch her breath.

Pop!—Pop!—Pop!—Pop! ripped through the air.

Her heart sank into her guts and she ducked reflexively. She knew that sound, every kid did. Those sounds scored every video of scattering crowds in every school lockdown drill.

Gunshots.

Right up at the end of the creek. Mary rushed along the incline at the creek's edge. It was too dark to see much apart from the glow of sirens beyond reeds and fences and the moonlight shining off the rippling water. *There!* She followed the ripples. Someone had to have made those, just now. Probably the same someone making the whimpers she heard up ahead.

It has to be Liz, she thought. *If she's walking, then she's okay.* Mary almost stood up to shout Liz's name but her tongue curled back in her mouth. It was *his* silhouette she saw, standing in the mouth of a flood drain.

Samuel's eyes shone dull silver, and even here she could see the rough edges of bandages across his face and skull. She could smell the rot from here. He was hunched, limping, and his voice was hoarse. Had he gotten thinner? A suited skeleton in the dark.

"Do you believe me now?" He spoke to someone in the reeds, his hand stretching a single damning finger to the house beyond Mary. "*That* is what they do. To *us*. They say they'll help and protect and accept, with platitudes and sweet songs, but every single time it's a mask. They only protect what they can own, and they're disgusted by us. They turn on us, beat us into the dirt because we want equal footing with them. You're not one of them, Julian! You will never be!"

It was the Boy sobbing. "I—I don't know what to do now," he choked. Mary tried to make out the shape of him through the reeds but couldn't. What he said didn't sound like a monster's growl, though, just the voice of another broken child. She listened to the broken voice repeat over and over: *They killed her, they killed her.*

Please, not Liz, Mary thought. *It can't be Liz.*

"Come back with me." Samuel's voice shifted from ragged stone to soft beach sand. "It's not too late. Even when Xolotl was bound to me, he refused to share his secrets with me, a mere *man*. The

Tēteoh are *pretentious*. Blinded by zeal and disdain for humans… but they shared their secrets with you, Julian, didn't they? No matter the price your body pays for it. With that power, I can still help you. That bite on your leg, I can still—"

"Just take it," Julian croaked. "Whatever happens to me, I don't *want* this anymore. Just take it and finish it."

Samuel stepped further out of the drain, crouching down with an extended hand. "If that is what you wish."

The Boy stood up with him, as did the creek's shadows all around them. The wind howled, and shapes Mary dared not look at followed them. Into the sewer's maw.

When she finally stumbled out of the creek and onto the main road, Mary saw that the cops had formed a line to hold back a crowd of onlookers. She couldn't hear a thing over the shouting.

"Liz!" she called, pushing her way through the crowd. "Liz!"

An officer grabbed her by the shoulder and shoved her. "Get back!" he barked.

Mary scrambled away before the line of them trampled her. She couldn't see clearly over the crowd, but she'd glimpsed it: the house, windows shattered, the door splintered in. Bullet holes pocking the walls.

A pair of EMTs rushed out of the house, carrying a uniformed officer on stretcher between them. Again just a glimpse, but Mary was sure: splintered bones stuck out in places they shouldn't. Nothing but her own nausea shoved her back this time. She watched the EMTs cram the officer into the ambulance with wide, horrified eyes.

A fire truck waited beside the ambulance, and there on the curb behind it Mary finally spotted Liz. Alive; trembling. Her face was pale and washed out, with smudges of black and teal and white staining her cheeks. A tinfoil blanket had been wrapped around her and she stared ahead at the street, a blank expression on her face.

Mary ran to her, caught the tail of the stream of words Elizabeth was mumbling to herself.

"It was her. She was dead, all mangled up." Liz blinked at the sound of Mary's footsteps approaching and looked up. This time, she spoke clearly. "I told you to *stay home*."

"What happened? Are you okay?" Mary hated standing while Liz sat. Having her older sister look up at her always struck her as intensely wrong.

"Samuel killed Mrs. Zavala. It's over." Liz looked back up the street. "Julian's gone."

Mary shook her head. "I saw him with Samuel. I think there's still a chance we can get him back. But—"

"Get him back?" Liz snapped. "Look around you! Julian's the one who did this. *Not Samuel.* He's k—he hurt people, Mary. I can't do this anymore. I can't."

"But—"

"But nothing!" Her voice splintered. "I was so stupid, I thought I could fix things. Marisol couldn't even fix this—she did her best and look what happened to her. I'm *tired*, Mary."

Each word was a gut punch knocking the wind out of Mary. She wanted to scream and kick, but all she could manage to do was brace for the next blow. She'd had her suspicions about Julian, but what Liz was saying didn't seem right. She felt it in her chest; the Julian she'd seen down the ravine wasn't the same angry wraith she'd met at the house. "Well, I'm not tired," she said. "I'm going to get him back, even if you won't."

"Mary, no." Liz reached for her. Mary jerked back.

"You're not coming, huh?"

Nothing.

"You're my sister. You're supposed to help me—set a good example for me."

ACT V: MICTLĀN

"*Stay here*, Mary! Stop playing and have some common fucking sense for once in your life!"

Fine. She got the hint. Enough time had been wasted, and now a cop was walking towards them. Before he could say a word, Mary dropped her board and skated away as far and fast as she could back into the night.

She stopped on an empty street corner downtown, out of breath. All the restaurants and shops had closed for the night. She dialed her mom's cell to tell her to get everyone out of Casa Coyotl. Samuel would take Julian there, she knew it. He'd have to. Liz had said the magic came from the house.

As the call rang, sirens chirped in the background.

"Where are you?" her mother answered. "The police are moving us to the station. They're saying the house isn't safe and that Liz is with them."

Good. They were already out.

"Mary? Mary, are you there? Can you hear me? Tell me where you are, Mary, right now. This isn't a game."

Mary hung up the phone. Better yet, shut it off.

A patrol car came roaring down the street, and Mary darted into a nearby alley where she crouched behind a dumpster and waited for the siren to fade. Emerging, she noticed the antique store across the street. She thought of the antiques that crowded the house: a suit of armor, weird stones, a Spanish sword. They were Samuel's—he'd said as much. Overflow from his store.

She crossed the street and peeked into the window, tried making sense of the figures inside. There were just dolls and books and rocks on shelves, nothing that looked important. Nothing she could use to gain a fighting chance; she had to go.

She went to turn, but as she shifted her weight, her feet clung to the ground.

She tried to step backward, pull her legs to move. They would not. Mary began to tremble. It was her arms next, bound by invisible wire that dug into her skin.

She tried to scream but her jaw, too, locked up and the scream died with nowhere else to go. She stood there a twisted figurine, terror welling up, stinging her eyes. Samuel swung open the door of the antique store from inside and stepped out, his eyes shining pale like moonlight. Julian shadowed him, holding something narrow and sharp in his hands.

"What a coincidence," Samuel said to Mary. "I'd have preferred the other one. But you'll do just as well."

A knife. It was a knife in Julian's hands. Mary's eyes met his—red and glowing, coal-black in the center. The skin around them was just as red, just as raw.

The Boy shook his head, making no expression at all. "Mary. Didn't I tell you not to go looking where you weren't supposed to?"

SIX
Mujeres Protegiendo a Mujeres

THE EMT peeled Elizabeth's eyelids apart to drill a light in. "What's your name and age again, hon?"

Elizabeth Remolina. Nineteen.

"And you're a dancer, hmm? How long have you been dancing?"

Six years.

"Your own idea? Or did someone inspire you?"

My Tía Marisol.

"I'm sure she must be proud."

She's dead.

Elizabeth heard herself speaking the responses, saw officers swarming like ants around the outside of Julian's house, but her thoughts were hooks—reeling her back inside, to the moment where she was shrieking as the body of Mrs. Zavala spilled from the pantry. Elizabeth had kicked her away, slapping off the residue that clung. Julian had reached Elizabeth's side before she made it to her feet. She scrambled back from him too—deeper into the kitchen between the counters and sink, putting as much space between her and the dead woman as possible. Julian was the one wailing now, his voice shattered into broken dregs that told Elizabeth he wasn't the one who'd hurt his mom. Regardless of what the officers were saying now. The realization of who'd actually done it—that was a twist of icy hands inside her. It was nauseating.

Julian was calling his mom, telling her to get up, get up, *please get up!* as the front door was bashed open. At the same instant, the kitchen's sliding doors burst into shards. From all sides black shapes poured in, clotting the exits. Elizabeth watched them tear Julian from his mother's corpse—throw him down. Swarm him. She didn't notice the officers that had grabbed onto her until they were pulling her out, away from Julian, through the door.

She watched, helpless, as the bodies crowding her friend all snapped back with wet crunches. Photos jumped off the walls. Shadows spilled in the shattered windows and blackness invaded the house. The darkness picked Julian up and set him on his feet, and Elizabeth met his burning eyes for a split second before they vanished into the night. Then guns blasted.

"They're going to take you down to the station to give a statement," the EMT was saying. "You're looking okay, just some minor cuts and bruises. You're safe now."

Safe. Safe. Safe.

But what about Mary?

Elizabeth had watched her run away, just as she had watched the officers swarm Julian and get thrown back. Just as she'd watched when Julian set fire to his serape and used it to torch Xolotl. She'd just watched.

And now Mary was gone.

She's going to get herself killed.

It's my fault.

Elizabeth had tried telling Mary that it was all over, that there was no use, that only death waited for them if they continued. But Mary had disobeyed, like she always did. And Elizabeth had let her.

I'm useless.

ACT V: MICTLĀN

"Is she ready to go?" an officer asked the EMT. He wore a cowboy hat and his right arm rested in a sling. The red and blue lights carved up his face.

"Yeah, just give her a minute. She's been through a lot."

"Well, hurry it up—she might know where that asshole went so we can get him before he hurts anyone else."

"Sheriff, please."

Elizabeth stopped listening. She dug her phone out of her pocket and held it in her hands. The black screen reflected a small and smudgy face with her father's eyes.

The memory of him washed her with needles. How long had she held onto that rage? Left it sticking out of her, the wounds festering and sore? He'd promised to fix everything—the girls just needed to pack their things. What would have happened if Marisol hadn't intercepted them? She'd given Elizabeth the bedroom key and told them to lock themselves in, then talked him down until the morning came.

I'm not him.

George Remolina was also the man who showed her Kurosawa movies, who'd bought her first camcorder when she said she wanted to make her own films, who'd supported her aspirations for theater, who'd trusted her with stories and hugged her when loneliness made her small, even when his own darkness ate him up from inside out.

It doesn't matter. I'm not him!

Elizabeth yanked out the thorn of him. The words that came to her were in a language she thought she'd lost: "No te perdono, Papá," she said to his eyes in her reflection. "Pero ya no quiero seguir enojada."

Then Elizabeth dialed her mother's number. Because she knew where Mary was going, and this time she would not sit back and watch.

"Elizabeth?" Kat answered. "We're at the police station. Are you okay? Are you on your way here? Is your sister with you?"

A gentle shadow stood on the porch of Julian's house. Officers passed through it but didn't seem to notice. The ghost of Mrs. Zavala. She pointed out towards the night—no, towards Casa Coyotl. Towards her son.

"No, she's not here. But Mom, I'm okay. I'll be there soon," Elizabeth said. "I'm just calling to tell you thank you. For everything. And I'm sorry. And...I love you. I need you to know that." She hung up the phone before her mother could say anything to change her mind, not knowing she was the second daughter to do so that awful night.

The sheriff and the EMT were still arguing. An officer with bandages around his head sat on a gurney between them. None of them noticed when Elizabeth stood up and shrank away, down the street, towards the orange groves and Casa Coyotl. To descend into the underworld and bring her sister back.

SEVEN
Did He Who Made the Lamb Make Thee?

Casa coyotl exhales, weak and empty, after you've kicked its doors in.

She's gone. It was all that filled your head along the quiet drive here, as every pothole jolt solidified your reasons for coming. When you first saw what they'd done to her, you didn't believe the corpse was her—it couldn't be. Your mother had seemed as solid and enduring as the desert mountains. You'd never imagined a world where you existed, and she did not. If there was ever a single truth you held in the marrow of your bones, it was that she of all people would always be there. She'd never leave you.

She's gone. She's gone, she's dead, and you're alone. Liz saw you for what you are. Horror filled her eyes and she didn't fight it when the officers carried her away, so when Samuel found you with nothing left but your will to survive, your choice was easy. You'd give him that too, along with your power.

Inside la Casa, the lights are still on, and deeper within the house a TV echoes. They must have fled with haste. Leaving the house vacant for you.

The house's breath grabs at the baby hairs on the nape of your neck when you gently step inside—a reminder that this is not your home, that you are a trespasser. A couple more steps and the wood beams above you groan *OUT—OUT!* That always happens when you pass these walls. It's a futile taunt that quickens your pulse, shivers your spine. You're more alive here than anywhere else you've ever known.

"We don't have time for this," Samuel says, limping in behind you, navigating around the two policemen you left twisted and gurgling on the steps. You smelled them hiding in their patrol car as soon as you reached the property. You savored each scream when your shadows dragged them out. You liked it—you're the kind of monster that likes to hurt people. To think you ever tried convincing yourself otherwise.

Samuel stinks of the fluids that soak the bandages wrapped around his skull. He's dragging Mary, bound and gagged, stiff but breathing. "More police are on their way. We have to hurry."

Your power is more elusive between the walls of this house, even if every moth-dusted inhale of its air fuels the fire in your lungs. Samuel's brujería always slips a little too. Power costs more here—but can be so much greater once the price is paid.

You help him carry the girl up the grand staircase. By the time you reach the top of the steps, Mary is gagging, thrashing within the ropes that bind her arms. You make the mistake of looking back and glimpse her manic, terrified eyes.

Go deep inside, you remind yourself. Find someplace nice, like the space beneath the bleachers where Riley Torres first kissed you, where he said *I love you* a week before he died. Or go further inside to the afternoons you spent with Dad, watching cartoons beside his hospital bed and eating dry, starch-flavored sandwiches. Or go to a few weeks ago, when you still had Mom, and for once you ate at the table together, joking about where you'd go if you could go anywhere, once you'd graduated continuation school. Mexico City, maybe. Or the Yucatán—the world was giant and you were a speck, and the vastness of it all terrified you.

ACT V: MICTLĀN

Pick any memory and stay there, relish it one last time. Soon enough this too will be over.

You share this advice with Mary when you reach the back room and bind her to a wooden chair that groans as you finish the knots around her wrists. "It won't hurt. It's just an unraveling. I'll be right here. I'll be doing it with you." You hope it helps. You ignore the pleading caught in the damp rag across her mouth. You turn away; it's all you can ever do.

"The ashtray isn't here," you tell Samuel, but he shrugs you off.

"We don't need it now. This is enough." He's right: you feel it here, where the walls are bare and the floor is scored, kinetic energy swelling all around.

When Samuel unties Mary's gag, she spits in his face.

"Let me the fuck out of here!" she demands.

He shushes her like a baby. "It's going to be okay," he says, gently. "It will hardly hurt at all. Your blood is what we need. Its potency is strong enough to start the ceremony. To fix me, bring my self back, and rid Julian of his growing burden. I'm sorry it has to be this way, but I'm left with no choice. I promise, like all the others, I will not forget you."

"I don't want my name in your fucking head!" She tugs at her restraints, abrading skin. She's searching her brain for something else to say when her eyes bug out. You see it too—the Hand, creeping out from beneath the white of Samuel's shirt. The hand that raked her arm when she went snooping where she wasn't supposed to. It knows her, leaps to her. Catches itself on her chest.

You've touched that hand before, felt its rage and hunger. That's all it has left of itself. It hates you. And Samuel. And everyone else. And why shouldn't it?

As the hand climbs up her chest and throat to her chin and cheeks, Mary opens her mouth to scream, but that's what the hand wants—to shove its fingers down her mouth, pry her jaws wide despite her teeth digging into its rotting flesh.

Mary gags but can't spit it out—the fingers have clamped around her tongue. This is it. You hand Samuel his obsidian dagger.

Samuel drags the tip of his blade down her tongue, and your whole body cringes wire-tight listening to her wails and watching the blood bud. He slices his own palm next, then yours. The dead hand lets go of Mary and crawls back to Samuel, jerky with its need to survive, survive, survive. It interlaces its fingers with his and black veins slither from the gash in its wrist up to the raw and angry spot on the inside of Samuel's elbow. Where he's fed his life to it so many times before. The veins cram into Samuel and he jolts—gasps with ecstasy before whispering a small prayer. The words are in a language you don't know; you've always hated that he knows those words—the culture of *your* ancestors, not his—better than you. All his lectures have been gloats reminding you of your total separation from your people. Your isolation. When he utters the last clicking syllable, the dagger takes flame.

The ceremony begins.

He lights the candles with the dagger. They reek like burnt hair as he places them at the corners of the room, where shadow figures begin rising from the floorboards. Next is aloe leaves for health, then the jaw wrapped in snakeskin. He lays down a cat's skull with feathers bound in red thread, owl feet, clay figures, cards, and other things that you can't make out in the candlelight but feel instantly, their power fishhook-tugging at your veins. In Nahuatl—the tongue you do not understand, but that is ingrained inside your bones— Samuel recites his incantations, and the words wash over you.

Now it's time to sink inside yourself. To the place where your body feels far away and the world detaches behind it even farther, receding more and more into the distance. You're going somewhere better, somewhere safe. Soon you'll see your mother again.

ACT V: MICTLĀN

Your body begins to shiver. You can see it at a distance from this place you've sunk to. The marks on your legs stretching and wriggling upward until your torso is wrapped in blocky markings. Beaming with so many neon colors that the far-off rest of the world fades to grays, blacks, and whites.

Let go, the night's whispers tell you, and you watch your own eyes shut. They open again but are red no longer—instead, galaxies shine through. Then a crown of burning feathers blooms above your head, the flames crackling the color of jade.

From this distance, you can see so much more. You see canyons and desert mountains, valleys with sprinting coyotes, owls soaring amid clouds. You see busy highways and gentle coastlines. And you can feel the life buzzing within them. You are the cacti, the dirt, the oil and water caverns beneath the earth, all breathing with the night. You're in all those places, spread out everywhere, leaking up and out into the stars.

You have become the night itself.

You stretch yourself across cities and borders. You are with brothers and sisters driving through the dark or camping under clouds. Lovers sleeping in apartment buildings, or people awake and alone working graveyard shifts.

You are no longer alone. You feel them all.

You're with the hundreds of thousands of families forced to flee their homes for safety, only to be bound and caged and left on cold concrete under sterile warehouse lights. And that breaks your heart. All of it does. Rebuilds and shatters it, over and over, until you're adrift in all this life and joy and sorrow and pain. It's too much to bear; the weight of it all forces a crack down the middle of your skull.

But before it fully splits you open, something grabs you and pins you in place: Mary's damning eyes.

Cutting though the world to see you, Julian.

Samuel will slit her throat—crack open her chest and scoop out her beating heart. It's sad, but it's what must be done. The gods themselves had to burn alive to create this world. And yet there's foolish desperation in her eyes. The kid thinks you of all people can save her.

Wouldn't Julian want to?

A voice calls to you across space:

JULIAN? Xolotl's gravelly voice. HIJO DE TU MADRE, YOU DID IT. WHERE ARE YOU?

Nowhere. Everywhere. I'm right here.

He finds the real you in the calm of that deep-down place, appearing suddenly beside you. Here, where the world is a far-away breeze, Xolotl is the god all the stories have said he is: charcoal-skinned, with a dog's head. Sculpted armor, geometric and jeweled, with feathers in red and gold and green and black. Ears of corn sprout from his shoulders two by two, and between his armor plates blooms the double maguey flower.

DO YOU REMEMBER HOW MY STORY ENDED? he asks. WHEN I'D FLED FROM THE GODS OUT OF FEAR OF SACRIFICE?

You do. Xolotl's twin brother—Quetzalcōātl, the feathered serpent, the morning sun, the Teōtl of wisdom and wind and life—found him trapped in his wet axolotl form after the other Tēteoh had burned his upright legs. Xolotl hid among the magueys and maíz fields, but his twin kept finding him. Chasing close behind until Xolotl was cornered, and Quetzalcōātl could slit his brother's throat.

BUT DO YOU KNOW WHAT HAPPENED TO HIM BECAUSE OF IT? Xolotl asks. You don't, so Xolotl tells you: MY PRECIOUS TWIN QUETZALCŌĀTL DIED WITH ME. HE KILLED HIMSELF. BECAUSE, YOU SEE, I AM HE. AND HE IS I. WE ARE THE TWO SIDES OF A SINGLE SOUL, QUETZALCŌĀTL AND I, ONE AND THE SAME. WHEN HE KILLED ME—TO USE OUR ESSENCE TO ALLOW YOUR SUN TO MOVE

AND BRING LIFE TO THE WORLD WE CREATED—IT WAS HIS OWN THROAT HE SLIT. IT WAS I WHO ALLOWED THE SERPENT TO BITE YOU, AFTER CENTURIES OF WAITING FOR YOU TO COME ALONG. TO MAKE YOUR POWERS WHOLE AND FREE YOU FROM THIS HORRIBLE MISTAKE OF A WORLD.

You hear Samuel's voice, faint and far away in the colorless background. He's telling you that it's time, *they're* coming. He holds the burning dagger against your throat. The hand's tendrils have slithered through him into you, waiting at your neck to steal this power. *They* are at the front doors of Casa Coyotl, and the back doors too, guns drawn. You see them, the cops storming in.

WHAT ARE YOU WAITING FOR? KILL THEM AND CLAIM THEIR SOULS. DON'T YOU KNOW WHAT YOU ARE?

You think of Xolotl's story and remember his other tale, of Huītzilōpōchtli birthed fully formed and armed with the feathered serpent as his weapon.

The desert tells you quick-blink stories of other gods you've almost forgotten, but whose memories you've kept safe down in your marrow—Huītzilōpōchtli's journey through earthly kingdoms, his stoning at the Fall of Tenochtitlán; Tlāloc's execution along with the rebels who battled industrialists in some forest in Michoacán; Tēzcatlipōca's self-inflicted flaying, where he cast the bits of his soul to the night to light the paths of migrants trekking northwards beyond manmade walls. There are so few of these Tēteoh left, and they're all so scattered, their stories dwindling. That's how you know the answer to Xolotl's question. It's bringing brightness within you.

You tell Xolotl, Samuel, and anyone else who hears: "I am all of them returned. And together, we are something new."

Because, like Xolotl, you are vast multitudes.

Xolotl laughs. YES! EXCELLENT! YOU GET IT NOW, BOY!

You don't celebrate yet; the men with their guns are almost in the courtyard, trigger fingers itching. Violence is all they know, but you know it too and mean to teach them your version.

Mary stares with awe at your shadow-tattooed body crowned with flame. She's terrified, and she's looking to you for help. You realize you don't want her here for this. You do not want her to die. With a thought, you burn away her restraints and Samuel doesn't even notice. She runs for the door. The cops are almost here—their boots pound up the steps—but no matter. You've already summoned your weapon.

It comes barreling from the desert—roaring. You commanded it to life a night ago, and the night saved it for you, fed it bones and bugs to make it strong—that's why it wasn't on your desk when you went home with Elizabeth. The little snake left and it grew. You've felt her slithering toward the property since you spread yourself across the night. You first saw her through a bat's eyes, from high up in the air: your own feathered serpent. You see what the resurrected snake sees, feel what she feels—right now, the rough earth beneath her belly scales, the zigzag of serpentine locomotion. She's an extension of you, and you puppeteer her long, muscular body as easily as you do your animal bones. You drive your monster down from the hills, making sure she crushes the patrol cars littering the road and whips the debris aside. You bare her fangs as you crash through the doors, pouring your snake-self in, ready to tear all these men apart. Your throat is hot with the wind and desert fire swelling up inside, impatient to be unleashed, to finally burn this world that's hated you to ash.

EIGHT
Just a Man

Bleeding. I'm bleeding. I'm stumbling over my own feet, but I don't stop running. Where am I? I don't know—somewhere in the house, I never left—but the hallways have twisted and grown, then pulled away to an open space too big to be anywhere indoors. It's dark, and there are stars above me, and the desert's breath kisses my cheeks. The horror is behind me.

Echoes of crackling gunfire reach me from far away.

Don't look back.

If I turn around, there will be a monster ripping my men to pieces. Agony erupts from my radio, their screams chopping through the chaos: We need backup right fucking now! Officers down! Officers—

I yank the radio off my left hip and throw it far enough into the darkness to kill the screams. I start running again, further into the vastness, putting distance between me and the horror. I'm still bleeding. I reach for my phone to call Diana but don't feel anything; it's only when I stumble and try to catch myself that I remember my right arm is gone. My shoulder feels light, my whole body off balance from the weight that's missing. There is only space where there should be mass.

It had come out of nowhere. The serpent roared through Coyote House, crashing down hallways, belching flames. I thought it was a bomb at first—that the boy had been crazed enough to rig some explosives. I should have ordered everyone to surround the house and sit textbook-style with their thumbs in their asses waiting for Julian Zavala to step out, bloody palms reaching for sky. It would have been the sensible thing. No one would have been *eaten alive*.

When we heard the shouting of the Remolina girl inside the Zavala house, it was then that I first decided, *To hell with procedure*. The sick fuck was killing her. We rammed in the door, stormed the house, and fed ourselves straight into the mouth of something evil. The way the darkness seemed to turn hot and solid—how quickly he dug fingers into chests—ripped out spraying hearts—I saw Julian Zavala wasn't a boy at all. That thing was a demon. Sent to devour all that was precious.

That was why I rushed us in when we reached Coyote House. This wasn't about justice, not anymore. Not about bringing in just another bad guy. No, it was bigger. This was the sum total of all the evil buried in all those individual bad guys "just making mistakes"—the exact disease I was born to battle against. The Boy was *that*.

I sent us into Coyote House to blast Evil away, but Evil tricked us and caught us from behind with a monster of feathers and scales and fangs. It rushed past the other officers, up the grand staircase and down the hall, ignoring the gunfire until it found me. Our eyes met, and I swear it knew me.

I reached for my gun, like we're all taught to do when danger is barreling toward us, when it's our life against theirs. I took aim, despite the pain in my bad shoulder—fired—and felt a dull tug in return as the serpent's jaws engulfed the gun, along with my hand and the rest of my arm, and ripped it all away. Then: weightlessness. I didn't even have time to yelp.

ACT V: MICTLĀN

The world burst into red and ringing silence. My men opened fire and the beast tore them apart. Franklin ran, but the serpent pinned him against the wall with the fat tube of its body, clamped its jaws around kicking legs, hoisted him high, and rag-dolled him till the parts of Franklin flew here and there.

Bullets didn't stop it—the chunks they blew off sprouted scorpion legs and crawled along the walls before fusing back into the creature's mane. The serpent vomited fire and flattened Officer Mason, scorched Sergeant Doyle's scalp. I snapped back to reality when Lieutenant Jordan fell at my feet, his intestines spilling out like smaller, slicker snakes.

I ran.

As fast as I could. Deeper into the house over charred bodies and twitching limbs to this nowhere place.

I'm running still.

I have to keep going. Diana and Gran are waiting for me back home. They'll tell me that I helped save those Remolina girls, that I'm brave and did something good. But right now the job's not done.

A few steps further, the darkness pulls away to reveal a field of massive pumpjacks outlined in moonlight. They loom above me, black and shivering skeletons. I trip; the ground shoots up to kick my cheek.

Get up, I tell myself.

Survive. It will come for me, I know it, with shadows and chupacabras and other night terrors. I think of Sonora: her bloodshot eye, her kind face, same as it was years ago when the monsters tried to rip her apart. If I can get to her, she'll understand. She'll help me. I just need to get up and get to her.

I don't move. It's dark, and I'm shivering. My eyes adjust to the skeleton shapes surrounding me, watching from all sides, bobbing up and down. The soft sounds of churning gears hiss just like they did when I buried Sonora's brother on a hot night.

Just lie here then, I tell myself. Rest for a minute or two.

Yes. I decide to do that. I'm exhausted, and the warm dirt feels like cushions. I just need to rest. I shut my eyes and listen to the pumpjacks humming. They tell me they're proud of my work, unlike Mom, Javier, Rodrigo. When I wake, they'll know too, they'll finally say they're proud of me. The pumpjacks ease me to sleep, their metal shifting, digging down, up. Down, up.

Down, up.

Down.

Up.

Down.

NINE
The Serpent

From the wood's edge, Elizabeth watched Casa Coyotl burn. Horror tightened her chest. She was exhausted, her clothes heavy with sweat—discomforts that were unimportant in comparison to the monster strangling the walls of the place she'd once called home. Its scales were arcs of teal breaching the roof's terracotta tiles. Its rigid feathers fanned into a spiny mane. It weaved in and out through busted windows, gaping doorways, its body everywhere—an endless nightmare.

The serpent stank of meat and brimstone. Even from across the yard, she could feel its heat.

Elizabeth had come in through the south gate to avoid the cop cars at the front of the property after her last long haul through back lots and orange groves. She heard the shouts, the gunfire cracking off beyond the trees. She rushed through thick brush hoping to get there in time, get Mary, and get the fuck out, fast; to hell with everything else. But then she saw it—and froze to the spot where she stood now, blinking. Listening to the noise, the howling flames. Was this a dream, something only her eyes could see? The serpent's bellow shook the trees, and reality grabbed her by the throat—it was real.

It was alive.

What the hell am I supposed do?

It was a plea to Marisol or any god that could reach out to grant her bravery, tell her how to survive.

The serpent constricted tighter around the house, shattering glass and cracking walls. Its flat head arched from the courtyard high into the night, the snout large enough to swallow her whole. Its jaw unhinged and thick muscles flexed to vomit jade flames as wild and ragged as its feathery mane. Elizabeth staggered back into the woods and away from the terror. No answer would come from the darkness. What could she possibly do? It was a giant, and she was so, so small.

Something gold gleamed in the corner of her eye. It swayed from a dead tree branch, delicate and undamaged, exactly where Elizabeth had chucked it into the trees several days ago: Marisol's pocket watch?

She grabbed it. Felt its weight—all the tōnalli of her family burning within. She clicked it open to see what had been: the picture of her father, Mary, and herself back when she believed better things were possible. Elizabeth squeezed it shut, absorbed whatever power might still be inside. Then she turned to face the burning house—her house.

If I go, I'll probably die. Elizabeth reminded herself that she'd lost her soul, and there could be nothing after this life for someone like that. *But Mary's still inside.* Elizabeth headed towards the flames.

Though the oak door that led to the kitchen where Marisol had once cut mangos for her, Elizabeth entered the fire. She stepped carefully around debris, trying not to draw the serpent's attention, using her sleeves to shield her from the smoke. Above her, the wooden beams of the ceiling groaned, and beside her, flames clawed the walls. "Mary!" she shouted. "Mary!" But the smoke seared her lungs, and the blaze swallowed her shouts.

She moved into a hallway the flames had yet to claim—it seemed the chaos hadn't yet spread to the west wing of the house—and entered an abandoned, haunted world. She ran through the library to the living room. She looped all the way around to the foyer and grand staircase, where the fire was just beginning to reach. If Mary wasn't down here, she had to be upstairs. Coughs tore Elizabeth's throat; further up, the smoke was even thicker. But just as she was about to head up the stairs anyway, she caught the sound of her name.

"Liz? LIZ!"

It came from the living room. Elizabeth raced back, searched frantically, and at last found Mary huddled behind the couch. In the library beyond, two police officers were reloading their weapons without so much as a glance toward the young women.

Five strides and Elizabeth was at the couch. "Come out of there!" she shouted. "We have to go!"

Mary shook her head and pressed herself deeper against the couch's spine.

"Mary, we have to go *now*. I know you're scared, I'm fucking terrified, but—"

"You didn't see it! The snake—it's Julian—he's killing everyone! I'm *not* going!"

"Mary, there's no time—"

Gunfire exploded in the library, louder than any monster's roar. For a heartbeat, Elizabeth thought her eardrums had been blown away. She turned in time to see the serpent rear back cobra-like, its feathers blanketing the ceiling as the bullets tore into its body. In a flash, it struck: head shooting across the room, jaws stretching to devour the body of one of the officers. Legs crumpled to the ground.

The other officer ran into the living room and out into the foyer. There were crunching noises in the library. Then the serpent lunged into the living room, seeking the man who'd fled.

Elizabeth flattened herself against the wall as pieces of the serpent, torn away by the bullets, skittered along the walls, feeling their way back to the tube of its body. It wasn't moving with the agility she had seen earlier. It seemed sluggish now, shuddering as it paused to absorb the wriggling bits back into its mass.

It has to heal, Elizabeth thought. Quickly, she turned to Mary. "Are you sure the snake is Julian?"

Mary looked up, baffled. "No shit it's him! I saw him change."

Elizabeth grabbed her shoulders. "Then I'm going to ask you to trust me. Run when I tell you to, get out fast through the front door and don't look back. Don't wait for me to follow. Just keep going and I'll hold it off, alright? Do you trust me?"

Mary was shaking. Her eyes were huge, focused on Elizabeth. Was that how she'd looked, the night Marisol found them after the crash?

"What about you?" Mary asked.

Elizabeth smiled. "I'll be right behind you."

Mary nodded. Elizabeth was already looking past her for the thing she hoped was still there. And there it was, its pommel jutting from the top of a shipping crate against the bookshelf.

Her mother had been dumping Samuel's treasures into boxes all weekend, wanting to get rid of them as fast as possible. This had been one of the last things she'd tossed in, along with the chainmail and plates that matched it.

Elizabeth grabbed the sword's handle with both hands. *Be bold, be bold.* And pulled it loose with all her strength. She adjusted her stance to carry its weight. Its blade gleamed in the pale green flames and reverberated with brujería and the centuries of violent history tempered into its metal. *You can do this,* she told herself. *It's just like using a knife. Let gravity do the work.*

She grabbed Mary's hand and squeezed as the serpent began to flex and writhe again, flicking its tongue to taste the air.

"You ready?"

"Yes."

Elizabeth kissed her sister's forehead. "Now run!" She shoved Mary out into the foyer and stood blocking the doorway to give her time. She muttered to herself, *Be brave.* The monster wasn't quite moving yet. She took a few trembling steps forward, lifted the sword high, brought its blade down on the snake's spine with all her weight.

The monster's hollow wail shook the house. The body arched to the ceiling, then crashed back against the floor. The blade had lodged itself a foot deep into the flesh, exposing vertebrae and muscle and sludge. Elizabeth scrambled for the grip and tried to yank the blade free. The serpent was retracting back into the library, then further; the doorjamb knocked the sword loose and it clattered to the ground. Elizabeth grabbed it and turned to follow Mary—stopped at the sight of so much snake now coiled in the foyer.

Elizabeth hoped Mary had gotten out before the endless coils flowed in. She couldn't tell which way the snake was moving anymore. She couldn't get to the door, she scrambled behind the blazing staircase instead—rushed into the courtyard, throwing distance behind her with the balls of her feet, until she had plastered herself behind one of the pillars near the outdoor fireplace. Clenched her whole body tight when the serpent erupted into the courtyard, spewing angry flames.

Another way out, she thought. She needed another way. But the serpent's bulk was spooling in the courtyard, and the only way past it would have been through the kitchen—which was a wall of fire. That ancient oven had finally exploded. Elizabeth was trapped in a cage along with the handful of police officers who were also hiding behind pillars. Her breath ragged from the smoke. She scanned the courtyard, looking for something, *anything*. What if, not out—but *up*?

The clay stairs: sculpted along the courtyard's edge, brittle but intact. Only a short distance to cross in order to reach them—but that was a path leading right beneath the serpent's head, which had risen up toward the sky and was now staring down into the courtyard entire. The neon of flame glowed in its throat. The slices in its spine were already fusing together.

Now or never—her last chance to pick herself back up again, like she had to in dance every time she fell and the floorboards kicked the breath out of her. It was just one last dash. One final moment for muscle memory to push her past exhuastion.

She reached into the back of her head, found her rockera beat. She grabbed it. Focused on it, let it rise and fill her ears until the music sounded real. Then, with the noise and terror held at bay, she sprinted out into the courtyard.

She kept the sword raised as she passed the serpent, her shoulders flaring, her side stabbing with pain; she twisted on her toes the way Marisol had taught her and used the momentum to swing— split open the serpent's belly. It reared back. Elizabeth snapped down, darted forwards, and leapt back up on the other side, where she vaulted over a section of sliding tail. She kept going, her body flowing to the beat of Los Crudos, and Vulpes, and Los Caifanes, and Café Tacuba, and Hombres G, Sana Sabina, El Tri, Mano Negra, Tijuana Now!

Elizabeth's bass guitar strummed her up the stairs and she bolted down the hall, jade fire swallowing the steps behind her. The snake's hiss came close at her heels. Hot breath reaching closer,

ACT V: MICTLĀN

closer. She reached the drawing room door and swung it open, then threw herself inside and slammed it behind her.

The Boy stood at the center of the smokeless drawing room. His arms were outstretched with shadows flowing from them, and burning feathers crowned his head. His toes dangled inches above the ground. A dead cop in a sheriff's hat lay face down on the floor before him. At his side was the man—the monster—who'd killed Marisol and so many before her, who'd made her think he was a friend when she was young, who'd corrupted this house with his desire to possess: Samuel de Hory. He had one hand spread across Julian's chest and looked to be deep in concentration. It appeared he was struggling to drag the shadow streams into himself.

Elizabeth charged—raised the sword up high and swung it down hard onto Samuel's hand. Onto both the hands: his own and the severed, rotten one entwined with it, the undead creature he had been feeding for so long.

Elizabeth's stroke wasn't perfect, but the sword was sharp and heavy enough to send several black fingers rolling to the corners of the room. What was left of that rotten hand seemed to go into shock. It dropped to the floor and contracted as if in pain, struggling to cling to a life that Samuel had extended long past its course. Elizabeth raised the sword again and skewered it all the way through, pinning flesh and bone to the wood of the floor, watching black sludge ooze out until it was empty. She gasped with relief when it stopped moving. As if, finally, a soul was free.

Samuel, waking from his trance, must have cried out, but Elizabeth didn't hear it. She only felt him shove her away to get to the hand. He shoved the sword too; it wobbled and clanked to the floor. He collapsed around the hand and cradled it to his chest. But it was too late. The blood that the brujería needed to keep it on life-support had been carved out. Already its flesh began to wilt and flake away. Soon it was just ash falling through Samuel's hands.

Elizabeth turned to Julian, unsure if he was even conscious. Outside the room, the serpent thrashed and slammed against the door.

"Julian? Are you there?" She stepped around the dead sheriff, fighting off nausea, and approached. His eyes were a sea of stars. The shadows flowing around him seemed to stretch through the windows and join with the night sky.

He blinked and echoed his name, questioning. "Julian?"

She stepped a little closer and inhaled his scent of fresh rain on clay, hoping that her own smell, her touch, her face would remind him he still had someone living and breathing on earth who cared.

"Julian, come back. You have to stop."

The twin galaxies in his eyes looked to the dead sheriff. "But I don't want to stop." He pointed. "He wanted to hurt people, so I hurt him. I made him see his sins before he died, and it felt incredible." Dimples punctuated his soft smile. "*I* feel incredible—whatever I am now. I'm everywhere and I feel everything. Everyone's grief and joy and hope. And I can help them. I can get rid of everyone else who's hurting us, like the little men trying to escape downstairs, and then we'll be free."

"Killing everyone won't stop the hurting," Elizabeth said, her own grief rising up and filling the space inside her. "We *all* hurt each other."

"I can end that too. I'll rid us of our bodies and replace everything unpleasant with ecstasy and joy. I can end it all."

The door was splintering. Bowing in. The snake's roars were more desperate on the other side. Twin fangs pierced the wood, huge and glistening, ripping out chunks as they withdrew.

"Is this really what you are now?" she pleaded, trying her best to ignore the fear welling up in her. This had to work. "Or is there

ACT V: MICTLĀN

something else left in there? You can take all these forms and feel all these feelings—it doesn't mean you have to give up your soul for it. You can hold on and still be you. You just have to stop this."

The stars in his eyes welled up like tears. "Mom," he said. His voice cracked. "She's gone."

Elizabeth reach up to grab his hands. When he flinched, she held on tighter. "I know."

"I'm searching and searching across deserts. I can't find her, Liz."

"I know, I know. I'm so sorry. So sorry." She pulled him down, closer to her level.

"Why are you helping Julian?" he asked. "He hurt so many people. We—*I* hurt so many people."

The door bowed, blazed, then burst into splinters as a fanged snout pushed through, fire leaking from its cheeks, its eyes—Julian's eyes—raging with his grief and desire to kill.

Elizabeth searched her heart. "Because a long time ago I was scared of everything, and you taught me how to swear to keep me safe."

The serpent's jaws snapped opened to swallow her in purifying hellfire. She shut her eyes and braced for the pain. Tried to trust Julian in spite of everything. Pulled him in, hugged him tight, and waited for as long as it took for his feet to come back down to solid ground.

The strike from the serpent never came. When she opened her eyes, she was staring down the gullet of a massive throat. The snake was frozen in midair, its eyes fixed on hers. Recognizing her.

The shadows began to slide off it, slowly at first and then in waves. Teal scales, fading and dissipating. Until all that was left was an ordinary dead rattlesnake at Elizabeth's feet, hardly a foot long.

The color of the room returned. The black tendrils receded into Julian's skin, and his crown puffed to smoke. He went limp in her arms, lighter than she'd thought he was. It was her Julian, just a bit different. New.

Without the force of his shadows to push it back, the smoke poured in. It choked the room; flames licked at the walls.

Time to go.

Elizabeth was steadying Julian, wiping tears from her eyes and his, and getting ready to rush back through the house when a groan cut the air. A streak of white-hot, blinding pain shot through Elizabeth's spine.

"No!" Julian screamed, fully awake again.

Something cold was lodged in Elizabeth's back. It slid out. A bloody stump spun her around and Elizabeth watched Samuel plunge his black dagger into her chest. She gasped, felt warmth flood her mouth. Saw thick red spatter on Samuel's face.

"You ruined it," he shouted. Ripped the blade out, dug it in again, this time into her stomach. Again. Again. Until the fire reached his heels, and then his heart.

As it consumed him, Elizabeth fell back, coughing, wetness soaking her clothes. A dull burn throbbed in her skin, but that pain was so far away. Someone was holding her, telling her to hold on. Hold on. It was alright, though. She'd never expected to get this far, to get this old. Everything else was bonus.

She'd done it.

For once she'd done everything right.

TEN
The Fearful Cemetery

A GIRL WALKED ACROSS THE DESERT at sunrise, dragging her sister on a penny board behind her, holding her by the cold, stiff hands. A tight grip. Sweat pooled between their palms, but Mary would not let her sister go. She kept on walking, dragging her board through dirt and prickling weeds, following the dot of a cat rippling in the distance.

Mary had waited just outside the gates of Casa Coyotl, keeping close enough to watch for Liz emerging from the flames, though she knew her sister would kill her for it later. There was gunfire inside and a roaring monster too; she wouldn't leave without knowing Liz was safe. Bit by bit, however, the flames wrapped around, embracing it whole, and still there was no sign of her. A few last gunshots echoed from the courtyard. In the distance Mary heard the blare of fire engines—too far away to arrive in time. She was about to wade into the blaze and dig until her skin charred, if she had to, when she spotted a small figure struggling down the porch.

It was Julian. Holding a body, limp in his arms.

Mary ran to him, denying everything that came into view. This—this *trick*. Only it wasn't a trick. When she reached him on the gravel path, she was sure that the body was Liz and that Liz was no longer breathing. She was pale, with dark blood seeping through her clothes. Mary shouted at Julain to do something, but he kept muttering to himself.

"I have to go with them. I don't have time. Mary, you have to find me. They're taking me to the graveyard."

She punched him out of frustration, because what else could she do? But her fist passed through air as the shadows pulled him into the night itself and left Mary alone, clutching her sister's body. Mary tried to lift Liz, but her sister was too heavy, too limp. She searched for a way to help her move Liz and found it in the shape of her penny board resting where Julian had vanished. She fumbled the body onto the board and began to tug her sister away from the house—but to where? Julian had said the graveyard, but she didn't know any graveyards nearby. She didn't even have battery in her phone anymore. It was just her, alone with Liz…and was that Angel Eyes, watching from the road? His tail flicked from side to side. He seemed only mildly annoyed by the chaos before him.

Mary called out to the cat. "You know where he went, don't you?"

Angel Eyes blinked and scampered away from the gate. Mary followed.

She followed for hours, as dawn blazed into day and the sun beat down from high over the desert. The column of smoke from the ruined house was no longer visible in the sky behind her and the sounds of fire trucks had long since faded. There was nothing around but the mountains to the north and west—and a graveyard, a few hundred yards ahead.

The graveyard was old, with no paved roads leading in or out. Half of its headstones had been swallowed up by dirt and time; what graves remained spiraled out from a circular plaza at its heart.

There Angel Eyes stopped in front of three dark figures whose ragged clothes swayed in the breeze.

The closer she got to them, the more fear dug into Mary's chest. The middle figure was Julian-shaped. He had the Boy's hair, his build, and his black-painted nails. But in the daylight he looked different. Taller, maybe? A halo of feathers burned softly above his head. A serape that looked as if it were cut from the night sky hung off his shoulder.

He spoke no louder than a whisper, but the desert carried his sorrowful voice across the graveyard to Mary. "I didn't mean to leave you behind," he said. "They wanted me here fast."

He gestured to the figures at either side of him. The one on his left had a masculine shape, with a doglike head atop his shoulders. A coyote head, maybe? He had charcoal skin, and his armor and facial features were blocky and asymmetrical as if etched from hard stone, and they were trimmed with shining gold and feathers. Even from a distance, this figure smelled of maguey flowers, and he watched Mary with sunken eyes. He was the one Liz had called Xolotl.

The pale god standing to the right of Julian, whose crown was horrible, Mary would not look in the eyes.

THIS IS NO PLACE FOR YOU, Xolotl said. GO BACK HOME AND LIVE YOUR LIFE BEFORE THIS DESERT CLAIMS YOU TOO.

She ignored him and kept her sight on Julian. Once she was right up on all three of the gods, she placed Liz's body at Julian's feet. "Fix her," she demanded. Panting. Pleading. "Please."

Julian looked at her with those sad, sleep-deprived eyes.

Xolotl barked. DON'T LOOK TO HIM FOR HELP. IT WAS WRONG OF HIM TO POINT YOU HERE. EVEN WITH ALL THE POWER VESTED IN HIM, THE BOY CAN'T DO WHAT YOU WANT. DON'T WASTE YOUR TIME CHASING THINGS NO ONE ON EARTH GETS TO HAVE.

"Like what, *a second chance*? Not even—I'm asking that you guys pay up for doing nothing while she fixed everything."

Xolotl growled. You're all just humans, he said. All your lives have the same little value, all of them equal, none of them infinite. Your sister spent hers.

"Fix her!" she shouted at Julian. "You conjured a fucking kaiju! You folded shadows like paper! You burned down our home and left us there to die, so you owe me this at least. This—this one miracle and that's it. Please, Julian. If that's still you in there at all. She's—"

Mary's voice broke at the utterance. "—dead. But she was your friend."

The third god laughed, and his laughter scratched fault lines deep within the earth.

He smelled like meat and maggots and stood tall like a pillar of stone. Liz had pointed out a bust to Mary in the living room at Casa Coyotl just a day ago, with a skeletal face and jade stones shining from the eye sockets—that was what she saw in the third god's face. The plaque had read, *Lord of Mictlān*. His feather crown eclipsed the sun.

Elizabeth Remolina has been on her way to me for some time, the Lord of Mictlān said. My wife foresaw it when she catalogued these. From his shroud he drew two laminated photographs: one of Mary as a child, sleeping; one of curtains draping an outline where Liz should have been. Your sister will be crossing to the underworld with all the other souls who died last night.

But Liz doesn't have a soul. Mary recalled all the times Liz had tried to tell her she'd lost it. *What will happen to her?* At the time, she'd thought it was all pretend.

The Lord's eyes beamed blinding jade. You can ask me or Xolotl or Julian, it doesn't matter. No Teōtl can bring back the dead.

ACT V: MICTLĀN

There were things they didn't tell you before you died, Elizabeth realized. Not that anyone could tell you anything from experience, in most cases—but she'd spoken to the dead on an occasion or two, and there were things they'd all neglected to tell her.

That you'd be weightless. And cold. And damp. And everything would smell vaguely of TV static—that old-office smell.

Elizabeth stood in the courtyard of Casa Coyotl, flanked by its white clay walls, uncrumbled and unburned. The sofa had been freshly dusted, and the tiles shone the way they always did when Marisol had just mopped. None of it should have been there.

The house had burned; she'd seen it happen. Jade flames devouring the wood as a raging serpent smashed down the walls. For a moment the pain of stab wounds echoed in her chest and she panicked. Elizabeth hiked up her sweater and traced her fingers across scarless skin where the wounds should have been.

"Mom?" she called. Then *Marisol*, *Mary*, even *Papá*. No one answered.

She followed the courtyard walls, peeking through windows to the house's interior. She had to get right up on them to look past her own reflection. The first window showed her two girls exploring what they made believe was a castle:

"If I'm the queen of this place, then you'll be the princess," the older girl said to her sister, running up the grand staircase before stopping to catch her breath at the top. "Or we can both be princesses. And Tía will be the queen."

I remember this, Elizabeth thought. She and Mary would race down the halls when they tired of being princesses, out the doors and through the woods to cannonball into the lake's murky water.

The next window showed an older memory: the girls sat on the living room rug, playing with stuffed animals while their aunt and father chatted at the coffee table behind them. The window after that showed the elder sister and a Boy watching old spaghetti westerns, and the one after that, a memory of Marisol brushing her hair. Each window had a different warmth, some like sun rays and some like heavy fleece blankets, all of them candied nostalgia that Elizabeth could not look away from. She soaked up each memory, unsure how many times she was watching them loop, until she began noticing the smaller details in the backgrounds—like the sharp whispers between father and aunt while the girls played with their stuffed animals. He was telling Marisol that he was willing to be some kind of martyr in the divorce. How pathetically self-centered.

"And look how that turned out." Elizabeth said it out loud. The younger Liz looked up and caught her eyes. Elizabeth's guts wound tight.

"Did you hear that?" Little Liz nudged her sister.

Elizabeth pulled her hands away from the window and they made a skittering noise along the glass—the same noise she'd heard through the walls as a girl.

"There's something in the walls."

No.

She ran to the next memory over, to a Mary with tears in her eyes while she wandered her castle. "I don't want to be a princess," she sobbed. "I want to go home. I want my mom."

"This is our new away home," Liz said to her. "We'll see Mom soon. It's going to be fun; you'll see."

Elizabeth pressed herself closer to the window and her breath fogged up the glass.

"There it is again," Liz said. "There's something breathing in the walls."

No, no, no.

Panic constricted her chest. She ran to the next window, hoping it wasn't true, couldn't be true. Looked down at the two sisters in their bed telling their father that they'd heard footsteps just a few seconds ago. They pointed to the window—their ceiling—to

Elizabeth looking in, and her father told the girls that nothing was there.

Elizabeth felt like screaming. "*Oh my god.*"

Her father pointed to the curtains. "If there is a ghost, those curtains are ghost catchers. They'll protect you, even if I'm too far away."

Elizabeth staggered away from that window too and quickly—desperately—checked each memory that lined the courtyard. The visions in the windows no longer false or idealized. She confirmed all the other times she'd haunted her own life.

In the last window, she saw her childhood self with a bowl of fresh-cut mangos. When little Liz inspected the window, Elizabeth banged on it so the girl jumped.

"Stay away!"

She kept banging on the window, even after the girl had run off and nobody else was there to hear her, and she emptied out all her screams until she crumpled to the floor, her insides a vacant bag.

"Mija, ¿por qué estás llorando?"

Elizabeth choked down her whimpers and wiped away her tears. Blinked into focus the woman who was standing near the hearth, warming her hands.

"Marisol?"

"There's nothing to cry about, Liz child. It's over now, you can rest."

She looked as young and alive as she had been when Elizabeth's father first jerked to a stop in front of the house years ago. Elizabeth ran to hug her. Held her in her arms for as long as she could, inhaling that comforting lavender smell.

"I thought you were gone," Elizabeth said when she pulled away.

"I am, or will be again. But They said it was the time of year when we were allowed to return for a bit. I heard you, so I found you here." She looked all around her, her eyes soaking up the house. "You recreated it so well."

Elizabeth shook her head. "I don't understand. I don't have a soul. I'm not supposed to be here. I'm supposed to be—"

"Nothing?" Marisol chuckled. "I guess you're realizing now that you shouldn't always listen to your mom about the nature of the supernatural. She's Catholic, after all. Not equipped for this in particular."

Elizabeth considered this. "You're not a ghost like me. Eventually, you'll have to return. But I'm stuck here, aren't I?"

Marisol shook her head. "The well-adjusted dead have no reason to stay behind. Something is keeping you here in this place you've built for yourself, like all other ghosts. I wish I could take you with me."

Elizabeth wiped her nose with her sleeve. "There's a lot I'd like to do. Or should have done. But I never could. Always something in the way, you know?" She wanted to ask Marisol what was over there, on that unspeakable other side. Her chest ached for it. She wanted to know what it felt like to move on.

"I clung to the living world as long as I could to protect you," Marisol said. Elizabeth had always crooked her head up to look at Marisol—now Marisol was the shorter woman—and as Marisol reached for her shoulder, Elizabeth brushed her hand away.

"But what you did was *wrong*, Tía." Tears started again. "You held onto this house then *forced* it onto me and told me to kill Samuel because I was the only one that could. As if you had any right to make me do that. As if I even had a right to own the house— how could any of us?! It was *delusional—I* was delusional for thinking I could find something here to fix me."

She turned back to the walls and old wood and delicately painted tiles forged by countless indigenous peoples at the behest of the Spanish who'd ravaged that land. She looked at all those pristine windows and all the glimpses of *had-beens* shining inside, embedded with the fragments of who she was.

"Oh," Elizabeth said in a sad, small voice. "I get it now."

She'd never lost her soul; it had always been with her. It was just broken. A surviving sliver of the younger one she'd scattered so heedlessly into her room, her house, her dad, her mom, Mary, Marisol, toys, movies, the comal she heated tortillas with, her ballet shoes, her friends. It just needed more time to keep on growing back.

They've both forgotten you as they argue. Sun baking your skin, you watch the gods' backs: Xolotl and Mictlāntēcuhtli. Your kin. But Mary is Elizabeth's sister, and you've decided she is your kin too.

"I'm not leaving my sister out here like this!" she weeps.

Xolotl tells her he'll help carry Elizabeth back.

Mary's nose is runny and she's stomping her foot on the cobblestones, kicking up dust like a child, but what else can she do? You want to tell her that you understand. That you too have a gaping cavern in your chest where your mom was ripped out. Where one moment you were speaking to her and she was smiling, breathing. And the next: nothing. A fresh emptiness beside all the other losses: of your father; of Riley, the first and only boy you ever loved; and now, of Elizabeth Remolina.

But you're also wondering about your serpent, made from the juvenile rattlesnake you once tried to will back to life.

Didn't try. *Did.*

When Mictlāntēcuhtli has had enough of Mary, he silences her with a single bony finger. He cranes his neck to stare down at her terrified eyes. I TRIED BEING PATIENT WITH YOU, BUT TEST ME AGAIN AND YOU WILL SEE, CHILD, WHY I AM THE GOD OF CANNIBALS. GO

AHEAD. IT'S BEEN CENTURIES SINCE LAST I CHEWED HUMAN FLESH.

You want to say something; you feel it down in your bones. A reverberating confidence surges through you. You open your mouth and tell them, "Wait a second." Very suddenly all eyes are on you. Small you. Young god of Compassion, and Grief, and Trauma, and—Hope? Yes! Hope too—and empathy. Because those are what you choose to rule. You ask Mary and the two gods what day it is and you see an understanding glint in the gods' eyes.

Mary tilts her head. "November first?" Her eyes widen too. "Oh, shit, *Dia de los Muertos*."

Following the instincts now unlocked deep within you that whisper through your blood, you speak a name as familiar to you as a dry breeze. "Mictēcacihuātl."

She forms out of the heat ripples reflecting on the horizon.

Smoke rises off her; her wide-brimmed hat unfolds. She grows larger until you realize that she's no longer far away but standing right before you, and it was the earth that contracted and pulled her forwards. Gaunt and smelling of sugar and marigold flowers. She towers over all of you, casting you in her shade. The queen of Mictlān.

She steps between the other gods and Mary, points a finger to Xolotl, and says, YOU HAVE BEEN AWAY FOR TOO LONG. To Mictlāntēcuhtli, whose shadow is so much smaller than the one she casts, she says, AND YOU, DEAREST HUSBAND, SHOULD KNOW BETTER THAN TO TORMENT A LITTLE GIRL. A polaroid camera hangs across her bare chest. A red veil masks her face.

The Lord of Mictlān speaks through his skeleton smile. MY LOVE, I—AM SIMPLY TEACHING RESPECT.

STOP IT, MENTIROSO, she bellows, whipping the sand up into twisters. YOU'RE CRUEL. YOU OVERSTEP YOUR PLACE.

WE NEVER USED TO OVERSTEP, WHEN THIS WHOLE WORLD WAS

ACT V: MICTLĀN

ours to step on, he protests.

And before this world, we had little. The cosmos saw fit to rid it of us. Now go back to your land of souls, my love. These are my most sacred of days, and you should know your place.

As you wish, my love, the Lord of Mictlān says.

The dead woman lifts her veil just to her lips—or the place where lips once were. With flayed, wet gums and pink-stained teeth she kisses his cheekbone and then he's gone, swept up in a murder of crows that scatters out in all directions.

Xolotl tells her that he will not leave you, that he is here to teach their ways. As he says this, the Queen of Mictlān shrugs him off. I always preferred your other half. Quetzal never would have blamed the mortals for his own capture. Be better, Xolotl…I know you are capable of it. Xolotl grumbles but she ignores him, turns towards you instead. Why is it that you've summoned me here, mijo?

You nod to your friend, Elizabeth, dead under the sun. "Because her soul has not yet passed on. She's still here, with the returning spirits. You can put her back, right? She doesn't have to go." When she looks at Elizabeth, you tell her, "She saved my life. And Xolotl's. She killed Samuel de Hory."

Queen of Mictlān scoffs. Too long had Samuel de Hory abused our power. You feel her smile stretch behind her veil. You're a clever one. True, I have not yet claimed Elizabeth's bones. Today, when my world overlaps with yours and with a soul freshly dead, then yes. Just this once, a soul can return to life.

The Queen of the Underworld holds Elizabeth, her fingers cradling the blood-clotted hair. She digs fingernails into flesh—cracks open Elizabeth's chest. Mary winces as the dead woman removes her sister's heart.

You tell Mary that it will be okay.

Mictēcacihuātl whispers now in a language as familiar to you as air in your lungs: SHE NEEDS A NEW HEART. THIS ONE WILL NO LONGER BEAT. AND A TŌNALLI PRICE MUST ALWAYS BE PAID. She's looking at you, not Mary, because both of you know what needs to be done, and you won't allow Mary to trade her life for Elizabeth's.

There is the feral, rageful part of you that still wants to fight and flee and preserve above all else. But you've already thought this through. You spent the night thinking of Xolotl's story, of Quetzalcōātl's sacrifice when he slit his and Xolotl's shared throats. Gods don't die the same way humans do. Once you are undead, you'll still exist, just without fear or pain or breath. You're willing to pay that price. That's why you let Mictecacíhuatl split open your own chest, spilling your life over Elizabeth. It doesn't hurt, even if you want it to.

The Queen of the Underworld bites out your beating heart gently. With shadows, she sutures it into the cavity where Elizabeth's was, and then the heart begins to *thump-thump, thump-thump.*

Elizabeth doesn't move. Mictēcacihuātl watches with nothing in her eyes.

MY LORD HUSBAND WAS RIGHT ABOUT ONE THING, THOUGH, she says, flowing away from the body. WE CANNOT FORCE LIFE UPON SOMEONE. WE MUST WAIT, INSTEAD. ELIZABETH MUST CHOOSE TO LIVE.

The voices were just out of sight, somewhere beyond the courtyard walls.

"Do you hear that?" Elizabeth asked Marisol.

Did they come from the porch? The flower garden, maybe?

ACT V: MICTLĀN

They were all around her, the worlds muddled, but the voices clear: Julian's, Mary's; others she did not recognize.

We just have to wait, a woman said. *It's up to her.*

"They're calling you to go back," Marisol mused. "And here I thought there'd be no more surprises."

Warm air brushed Elizabeth's arms, but the sky above was cloudy. Her toes and fingertips tingled as if all her limbs had fallen asleep and were only now waking up. Her heartbeat, which she hadn't even noticed was gone, was thrumming again in her chest.

Elizabeth rushed back to the windows, hoping to get a peek at whatever was happening. She pressed her nose up against the glass and found herself looking down at her own bloody corpse. Three gods stood around it with Mary watching.

"They're...waiting for me?"

"A second chance," Marisol smiled. "I think you've earned it. You just have to open your eyes."

Elizabeth pulled away from the window. "You won't be there." The words heavy with grief. "I've doubted for so long if there's anything left out there for me." The words escaped from somewhere deeper than her heart, and like pollen on the air, there was no gathering them back once let free. She meant them.

Elizabeth spun around and drank in the walls, the tiles, the sun beaming down. Here, with all these memories, she could be happy, right? She wouldn't have to suffer the way her father and Marisol before her had.

"But these memories won't hold," Marisol said. "You'll see them again and again until the details fade. Then you'll be—"

"A ghost without a face."

The windows of the courtyard shifted into a flipbook of all the nights when Elizabeth felt helpless. Crying alone in bed, in her car, in the school bathroom, the locker room, the back room at whatever summer job hired her. Elizabeth had never pictured herself surviving into college. The future was a black hole sucking in everything. And yet the future kept coming too fast for her to stop it.

Whatever laid beyond the event horizon terrified her. A world where she might not continue dancing professionally; a life that led nowhere. It was terror like she'd felt in the darkness of the San Ojuela mall, holding Julian's hand, walking through vacant corridors, and watching flames bloom from Julian's palm to illuminate the murals.

Or when fear was a knot in her chest as she leaned in to taste Jannah's lips.

The courtyard walls began to crack, their corners chipping and crumbling.

The windows settled on showing her the rubble, the burnt scars in the earth that were the remains of Casa Coyotl. There would be no more murders there. No more ghosts. The bones buried deep beneath the foundations had all finally been shown the door and had left without shutting it behind them.

Because of her.

Marisol laughed the faintest laugh. "It wasn't so bad for me, mija," she said. "I stuck around because for a while there I got to be a part of something great. I got to see you grow."

The walls blew away to dust.

The memories too.

Whiteness beamed through the space and Elizabeth woke with air filling her lungs and a dry sun beaming above her. Mary squeezed her tight, and Julian smiled. Julian—her boy who could make bones dance—he would tell her, before he walked off to become a ripple on the horizon, that he felt people's prayers, that their hopes and pains filled him now that his own were gone, and that he'd go to them, because bringing her back was not enough to pay for what he'd done. He would tell her about her new heart

ACT V: MICTLĀN

and would promise Elizabeth she'd see him again, even if she knew with an ache deep inside of her that it wasn't true. But she would remember him—his eyes, his dimples, and his crooked teeth as she saw them in the moment when she woke, when he and the old gods stood back to watch Elizabeth cough and suck in air—fully, wholly, finally, alive.

ACKNOWLEDGMENTS

In the years it took to bring this novel from its initial, primordial, putty self, sculpt it, slice its edges, and trim its fat into the novel-shaped thing you have before you, I spent a lot of time thinking about this acknowledgments page. The absence of any one of the people mentioned here would have changed the trajectory of my life, of my writing career—of the story you have just read. All of my being has been delicately puzzled together by the people I've met along the way, just as this book came about thanks to the help and kindness of those same people. A list of names feels inadequate to capture their vast multiplicities, yet here is my attempt at an inventory of those to whom I owe the world.

First, I'd like to thank my Mamá and mi familia for supporting my writing and my identity, and for allowing me to feel comfortable in pursuing my passions, especially my ride-or-dies William, Adonis, and Keilani for putting up with my bullshit. I'd like to thank my editor Christine Neulieb, who believed in my novel and help shape it into the creature it is now, as well as Feliza Casano and the rest of the Lanternfish team. I'd like to thank Dr. Nalo Hopkinson, who was my first writing mentor and saw the potential in my little ideas; and Sam J. Miller, Ted Chiang, Gwenda Bond, and Sheree

Renée Thomas for pushing me beyond what I thought were my limits. I thank my teachers Ashley Sheaff and Rebecca Briggs for kindling my passion to write in the first place, and I'd also like to thank mi otro familia, my Clarion cohort, the 2022 Ghost Class, whom I can depend on—and have depended on—for anything whenever the world gets too large. This includes but is not limited to: L. P. Kindred, Shingai Kagunda, T. K. Rex, Gwendolyn Hicks, Niv Sekar, Sam Asher, Chelsea Sutton, Mary Thaler, Sam Lasman, Theodora Ward, Anna-Claire McGrath, Alyssa Greene, Stefen Holtrey, and Jenny D. Williams. Y'all are the best.

Lastly, of course, thank you for everything, Kendell. You know who you are.

ABOUT THE AUTHOR

M. M. OLIVAS is an alumna of the 2022 Clarion Science Fiction and Fantasy Writers' Workshop and the 2023 Under the Volcano Writers Residency. Her short fiction has appeared in several publications, including *Uncanny Magazine*, *Weird Horror Magazine*, *Apex*, and *Bourbon Penn*. As a trans, first-generation Chicana, she explores the intersection of queer and diasporic experiences in her fiction. She currently resides in the San Francisco Bay Area, earning her MFA in creative writing at San Jose State University and collecting transforming robots. More information about Olivas and her fiction can be found at olivasthewriter.wtf.

YOU MIGHT ALSO ENJOY...

These Bones by Kayla Chenault

Pour One for the Devil by Theodore C. Van Alst, Jr.

The Salt Fields by Stacy D. Flood

The Quelling by Barbara Barrow

(14 Day)

-- JAN 2025

**EMMA S. CLARK MEMORIAL LIBRARY
SETAUKET, NEW YORK 11733**

To view your account,
renew or request an item,
visit www.emmaclark.org